Impenitent Ties

Splintered Empire Book Three

Erin Robinson

This novel is entirely a work of fiction. The names, characters and incidents portrayed in it are the work of the author's imagination. Any resemblance to actual persons, living or dead, events or localities is entirely coincidental.

Editing by Yvette Rebello at yreditor.com

Proofreading by KMorton Editing Services

Cover by Maria at Steamy Designs

For the girls who like their red flags decorated with tattoos and unhealthy coping mechanisms. Konstantin's here for you.

Contents

Author's Note

This is an adult dark mafia romance. It contains on-page violence, murder, graphic depictions of torture, as well as birth control manipulation. For the full list of content warnings, please visit the author's website at authorerinrobinson.com/content-warnings.

Additionally, it contains spoilers for the 1940 film Brother Orchid. If you haven't seen it yet and you enjoy old gangster films, I highly recommend it.

Chapter 1

Nadya

I've never looked into it, but there's no way a private jet is a sound investment. Beyond the upfront costs of buying a freaking plane, the ongoing expenses have to be eye watering.

Jet fuel probably isn't cheap. A place to store the plane when it isn't in use is probably even worse—especially in the Bay Area, where real estate is almost as much of a racket as the criminal syndicate my fiancé runs. Then there's the cost of maintenance and insurance. And on top of that, you have to factor in the salaries for the pilot and crew.

If Konstantin has a decent bone in his body—which I'm admittedly not holding out much hope of—then that alone has to cost a small fortune.

There's no way this metal tube hurtling me and everything I care about across the country can be justified financially. Any accountant worth their salt would have told Konstantin that, but I doubt he's ever had someone tell him *no* when he wants something.

Cost isn't a factor to a man like him. Once he sets his mind to something, he gets it, damn anyone who stands in his way.

Shaking my head, I turn away from the window.

The sooner I get my mind to stop clawing at quicksand, the sooner my heart will get the memo.

By this time tomorrow, I'm going to be married to a man I hardly know, and there's not a damn thing I can do about it. Because no matter how much I hate to admit it, Konstantin is capable of giving me the only thing I actually care about.

Not money, not power, not all the luxuries in the world.

But he can keep my little brother safe.

I've looked after Alexei since we were teenagers. Our dad was thrown behind bars, and within days, Mom took the opportunity to grab what was left of his money and leave us in the dust.

No matter how old we are, taking care of him will always be my responsibility.

I'll do whatever Konstantin wants if it means Alexei can sleep at night without having to worry about someone coming after him. I'll put my life in hands covered in so much blood I have to wonder if they were ever clean to begin with.

An arranged marriage is a small price to pay for my brother's safety.

"Have you found a new accountant yet?" I ask, keeping my voice low.

The roar of the jets will probably prevent Alexei's girlfriend, Emiliya, from waking up, but I want to let her rest. Alexei looks like he hasn't slept in days, and something tells me she's been working her ass off to keep him from blowing this deal to smithereens.

She deserves a break.

"I was hoping you'd still do it," Alexei says, tearing his eyes away from Emiliya's sleeping form. "I'll give you remote access to all the system files, and I can email you everything else."

There's a pleading note to his tone that makes the weight on my chest that much heavier.

"Oh, a digital paper trail?" I raise a brow, leveling him with a look that makes him cringe. "The feds will love that."

Even if he wouldn't be setting us both up for embezzlement and money laundering charges, there's no way in hell he's organized enough to get everything I need from Chicago to California on a consistent, timely basis.

If I'm not in his face to demand the paperwork I need, I'm not going to get it. He needs someone who can call him on his shim while I'm across the country and further away from him than I've ever been in my life.

Someone who can make the numbers look good on paper and keep him out of prison.

"I'm serious, Alexei. You need to find someone."

"I will," he groans, leaning his head back until it hits the luxuriously soft leather seat. Every surface in this overpriced hunk of metal screams indulgence and extravagance, making my heart ache for the cozy apartment I've left behind.

It was all soft fabrics, fluffy pillows, and comfort. Now, I'll never see it again.

"I'm vetting a couple of candidates. I'll interview them when we get home." Alexei sighs, rubbing the bags under his eyes. "What're you going to do if you're unemployed?"

"I'm thinking of it as an early retirement." He sighs again, rolling his eyes while I chuckle despite the dread pressing me into my seat. "I don't know. Maybe I'll find another pottery studio. Or maybe I'll spend all my time at the beach."

"The beach?" he scoffs. "In San Francisco?"

He can tell me it isn't warm there as much as he likes, but it has to be warmer than Chicago.

"I didn't say I had to get in the water. I'll bundle up in sweaters and take up metal detecting." I lift a shoulder dismissively, refusing to voice the plethora of questions that kept me awake last night.

How much of my life will still be mine once I'm in Konstantin's home? Will he let me continue doing pottery? Will I be allowed to leave the house without him? Or is he going to keep me like a doll, only to be taken out when he wants to show me off?

As much as I enjoy teasing Alexei about my upcoming marriage, there's a pit in my stomach every time I consider the harsh reality I'm facing. Not only because of the unknowns, but because the more word spread about our upcoming nuptials, the more strangers in our circle were eager to let me know Konstantin's reputation.

Bloodthirsty. Vicious. Cruel.

I've never had the opportunity to get to know him. On the two occasions we've met, I don't think we even exchanged a dozen words. The only thing my imagination has to work with are the worried looks and whispered warnings that have plagued me for months.

"I'll find something to do." Nudging Alexei with my elbow, I smirk. "And if I can't find anything else, there will always be my new husband."

Alexei groans, and I grin. His disgust is easy to play off. While he's busy being interested in anything other than what I'm saying, I don't have to pretend I haven't lain awake every night for months, waking up in a cold sweat whenever I do manage to fall asleep.

"Listen, I'm not blind. I don't know why you expect me not to notice how hot Konstantin is."

Alexei squeezes his eyes shut like my words physically pain him. "Can we *not* talk about whether or not you find Lavrov attractive?"

"Fine." I sigh, shaking my head. "If you're going to be a prude, I'll wait until Emilya wakes up so I can talk to her about it."

His nostrils flare with a deep breath.

I wish I could laugh at him, but if I tried, I'm not sure it wouldn't let loose the choked sob I've been keeping locked behind thick steel and iron bars.

I want to go back to how things were before Konstantin waltzed into our lives.

Back to before private jets and extravagant shows of wealth that don't matter. Before wedding plans and packing to move to a city—hell, a *state*—I've never been to before.

I want to go back to the days where I spent my time crunching numbers and pretending my brother was nothing but a normal businessman. I'd kill to go back to spending my nights gossiping with my best friend and dragging her to pottery classes she only tolerates because she enjoys my company.

It wasn't an exciting life, but it was mine, and I was happy with it.

At least Alexei will still have Emiliya. He has his work. He won't be alone, brooding in his condo all the time.

And maybe if there's some distance between us, he'll learn to appreciate it when I reach out and actually answer his goddamn phone. Or, if he doesn't, I'll have to become twice as annoying until he finally learns his lesson.

"I don't know what your issue with Konstantin is," I say with an irreverent air I don't actually feel as I turn to look out the window. The land miles below us is obscured by fluffy clouds. They look like the perfect place to lie down and sleep until this nightmare finally passes me by. "You've talked to him while we've been planning the wedding, haven't you?"

He must have, since Alexei's the one who grimly let me know Konstantin had already handled our travel arrangements when I asked him about it. And from how often he scowls at his phone, I assume they've been in steady contact since Alexei stepped into his new role as the leader of the Chicago Bratva.

"Yeah," he grunts, rolling his neck. "We've talked, but that doesn't mean he isn't an asshole."

"Good thing I'm used to dealing with men like that."

Alexei glares, but when I raise a brow, he doesn't try to argue.

He sounds almost hesitant as he says, "You know, if you've changed your mind, all you have to do is say the word. I'll take you home. I don't care if I have to hijack this plane or steal a car and drive us all back. I'll do it."

"I know you would."

That's the problem.

Konstantin is powerful enough that he was able to compel the dangerous men my brother was facing to fall in line and back his rise to power. I don't want to know what he'd do if Alexei decides to make him an enemy instead of an ally.

"But what happens when the consequences come knocking?" I ask. "Do we steal another plane and run forever?"

"I don't fucking care, Nadya. Whatever Konstantin does, I'll deal with it." There's so much tenderness in his voice it makes my chest ache when he says, "I want you to be happy."

Alexei might not care what happens, but I do.

No matter how old he gets, I'll always remember how dejected and scared he was when he realized it was the two of us against the world. If I can do something to let him hold onto the sliver of happiness he's found, then I'll do anything in my power to make it happen.

"You know I love you, right?" I ask.

My throat is tight, my words almost lost over the roar of the engines, but Alexei hears them anyway.

He nods, one corner of his mouth curling upward in a smile that doesn't reach his eyes.

"I love you too."

Do you? I almost ask. Is he grateful Konstantin's taking me off his hands? Is he glad he won't have to worry about me anymore? Will he miss me at all?

Neither of us say anything for the rest of the flight, too caught up in our own disappointments to bother with words.

Chapter 2
Nadya

Despite the harsh sunlight baking the grass as much as it is the weathered stone of the wedding venue, everything is even prettier than it looked in the photos the wedding planner emailed me.

Ivy crawls up the walls, the trees flutter in the breeze, and even the blue sky seems like something ripped straight out of a painting. While everything else on the drive from the hotel seemed dry and crispy, the vineyard around the building is thriving. Luxury seems to be entrenched in every leaf and blade of grass, making them impervious to the drought and heat threatening to fry everything else to a crisp.

I pick at the hem of my dress as it flutters around my knees, wondering how difficult it would be to snatch the keys from Alexei's hand, jump into his rental, and leave him behind to deal with the fallout of running away.

Who really needs a wedding rehearsal, anyway?

The whole thing should be straight forward. Everyone goes down the aisle. I follow. I pretend the ceremony is something I have a vested interest in. And then it's over. Cue the drinking and dancing.

Why waste everyone's time practicing?

"Are you melting, or are you having some sort of silent panic attack?" Alexei asks, checking his watch for the fifth time since we got out of the car. "Because I'm not sure you know this, but we're late."

I hate being late. It's inconsiderate to everyone who's expecting us, it's rude, and it definitely isn't making a good impression on the people I'm going to be stuck with for the foreseeable future.

But expecting me to show up for this farce isn't making a great impression, either.

I shift in the heels Konstantin had sent to the hotel, ready for me as soon as we landed. They match the white dress I found hanging in the bathroom like an unspoken command.

Couldn't he at least let me be comfortable? Because right now, my feet hurt, and I'm terrified I'm going to brush against even a speck of dirt, or get caught on something and ruin the dress before anyone gets to see it.

I'd rather be in shorts and sneakers. At least then standing on gravel wouldn't be an exercise in torture.

"I'm admiring the venue," I say without a hint of a smile. "It's beautiful, isn't it?"

If Emiliya was here, she'd distract him so I can have a moment, but Alexei wanted to keep her as far away from Konstantin as he could.

I can't blame him. I just wish I'd been given the same opportunity.

"Fuck this," he grumbles, turning around. "Get in the car. We're going home."

"We're already here." I shake my head. "Let's go inside. The sooner we're done with this, the sooner we can have dinner." He gives me a look. "What? I skipped breakfast and I'm starving."

Not giving him a chance to call me on my bullshit, I walk toward the door with a confidence I only hope conceals the pressure threatening to have my knees buckling.

Throwing open the stained glass doors, I step into a room that's almost as beautiful as the outside.

The wood floors gleam, the same stone from outside lines the exterior walls, and the rest are painted a cream color that makes the space feel inviting and cozy. The vases are empty, but I can already picture what they'll look like tomorrow once they're filled with flowers.

It looks like something ripped straight from the dream wedding Pinterest board I put together when I was in college.

My heart lurches at the reminder of all the useless dreams I whispered into the dark, begging them to become reality. I don't think I realized how hard I was still clinging to all those hopes until this moment.

Whatever. I'm twenty-eight. I'll get over it.

My pity party can wait until I'm alone at the hotel and have access to the minibar.

"There you are!" calls a shrill, almost panicked voice that I've only had the pleasure of dealing with over the phone. Somehow, Winnie Blackburn sounded far more soothing with distance. She looks flustered, her hair wild from the heat, and her cheeks flushed with frustration.

"You're late," she snaps, glaring at me before she goes back to stabbing at her phone like it's personally offended her.

"Sorry," I say as sincerely as I can. "Our flight was delayed."

Alexei just manages to hold back a snort, but from the look of her, you'd think I was late for the actual wedding, not a game of dress-up for grownups.

She doesn't need to know how long I stood outside psyching myself up.

With an irritated sigh, she checks the time, a line forming between her brows. I don't bother hiding the way I roll my eyes. Even though I've stalled my ass off, I can't be *that* late.

It's not like anything could've started without me anyway.

What's the worst that could happen? Dinner gets delayed by a few minutes?

I know for a fact the caterers are being paid handsomely to be here because I'm the one who confirmed their contract. If we run more than a half hour over what we planned for, they get paid double.

Something tells me they'll be fine if we run a little late.

Apparently, my wedding planner disagrees.

"We'll have to make up for it somehow," she grouses under her breath. "Now, hurry up. If we want to stay on track, you can't keep dillydallying and wasting everyone's time."

"I suggest you watch your tone around my fiancée, Miss Blackburn," says a low voice that's haunted my dreams and nightmares alike for months. It lights up every nerve in my body, the sensation dancing under my skin until it finally settles low in my stomach. It feels suspiciously close to butterflies, and I fist my hands at my sides, threatening to squash them before they become impossible to ignore.

As he emerges from the shadows, Konstantin Lavrov is just as devastatingly attractive as he was the first time I saw him. He towers over everyone, his muscular physique just as eye-catching as it is intimidating.

Black ink decorates nearly every visible inch of his skin. Everything below his jaw, from the sliver of skin exposed near his open collar, all the way down to where his shirtsleeves are rolled up, down to his fingers.

And like the last time I saw him in person, I have to force myself not to stare.

It isn't in my best interest for him to know how he affects me. In fact, I'd go so far as to say it's dangerous for him to know that if circumstances were different, I'd be tripping over myself for an introduction.

Especially since it's impossible to miss the gun holstered at his side.

No matter how good-looking he is, he's still a violent criminal with no regard for anyone but himself.

"Mr. Lavrov!" Winnie exclaims, pressing a hand to her chest. With my fiancé in the room, her cheeks turn even redder, drinking in his appearance much in the same way I was.

I bite the inside of my cheek before I say anything I'll regret.

"I was just—"

"Berating my fiancée," he interrupts, folding his arms over his chest until the dark fabric of his shirt pulls taut over his biceps. "I heard. And I'm certain I'm paying you more than enough to understand your place here, Miss Blackburn."

"I'm so sorry," she gushes, not deterred in the slightest as she puts her hand on his forearm, her skin pale against the dark ink. He remains unmoved, but his glare is so ice-cold it steals the lingering heat I felt from standing outside.

She backs away like the looks burns.

"If you're going to apologize to anyone, don't waste your breath on me." He nods in my direction. "Nadya is the one you insulted."

I barely manage to keep myself from shivering as the weight of my name on his tongue coats my skin like warm honey.

Winnie's eyes flit to mine as if she managed to forget I was even here.

"It's fine," I say with a wave of my hand. "I'm sorry we're late. Now, would you please show me where we need to be so I'm not the cause of even more delays?"

When Winnie looks at Konstantin, he lifts his chin.

"Make no mistake," he intones lowly. "No matter how generous my fiancée is being, you're not nearly as important to this wedding as you seem to think you are. And if you so much as look at her the way you did when she first arrived, you'll find out exactly how easy it would be for me to replace you."

With every word, Winnie's shoulders climb higher and higher, until they're boxed around her ears, and I'm one step from getting between the two of them so he finally backs off.

This is why I have to ignore how hot Konstantin is. He's being relatively tame, and he's still managed to cow our wedding planner to the point that she's blinking back tears.

If this is how he behaves around strangers, what's he like without an audience?

I'm not sure I want to know, but I'm certain I'm going to find out sooner rather than later.

Winnie's heels click as she scurries to retreat, but when I go to follow, Konstantin moves to block my path.

"Alexei," he says, not taking his eyes off me. The sun through the windows shines a whole spectrum of colors, painting him like it was made for this exact purpose. "Would you be so kind as to follow Miss Blackburn outside? I'd like a moment with Nadya."

The earlier venom in his tone is nowhere to be found. Instead it's replaced by a gloating note that has Alexei snarling, his posture defensive as he shifts even closer to me.

"Go," I tell him. "I'll be there in a few minutes."

Alexei searches my face, but if I'm going to make it out of this marriage alive, I'm going to have to learn to deal with Konstantin at some point. As little as I want to be alone with him, I want to deal with Alexei getting shot because he's a stubborn hooligan even less.

After a long moment, my brother nods, still looking at us over his shoulder as he heads in the same direction Winnie left in.

I'm watching him go when Konstantin's hand brushes against mine, the simple touch burning under my skin like a coal mine struck by lightning.

It's the same as it was when he kissed the backs of my fingers the day we met.

He put on such a show of being a gentleman that day that I'd been confused. Alexei had shouted down the hall like he was terrified, but the only threat I found was a man with a wicked grin who wore his confidence like it was the most natural thing in the world. And when my eyes met his, everything else faded to black, his gaze making me feel like I was caught up in a dream.

I've spent months hoping I'd imagined that feeling. But hope is a fickle bitch, and I don't think she likes me very much.

"You can't let people talk to you like that anymore," Konstantin says, breaking whatever spell he cast on me.

"Excuse me?"

"The way Miss Blackburn spoke to you," he says with a shrug. "It was dismissive, crude, and short. That may have been something you were willing to tolerate before, but tomorrow you'll become my wife. How others speak to you is how they speak to me. You'll need to stand tall and know your own worth."

"Being tied to you doesn't mean I have an excuse to talk down to someone." I lift my chin a little higher, until I'm faced with the silent promises glinting in his eyes, darkness swimming in the blue of his irises. "No matter how important you think you are, you're still just a man."

One corner of his lip quirks up, demanding my attention even as he leans closer, giving me full freedom to take in the lines of his face, the flecks of darker blue in his iris. Goose bumps spread over my arms when I can't bring myself to look away.

"But I'm not *just* a man, am I? If I were, you wouldn't have looked ready to run the moment you saw me. You wouldn't be looking at me like I'm a beast, wound tight like you're anticipating the moment I strike."

He lifts his hand, and I flinch a moment before his thumb strokes over the base of my throat.

"You might be used to going through life like you're anyone else, but we both know I'm far from being another face in a crowd. And as my wife, you'll have to get used to demanding the respect you deserve."

I tear my eyes from his, glancing around for anyone who might be able to pull me free of his orbit, but we're alone, and I can't bring myself to pull away.

"I expect the world to treat you like a queen. It's time you get used to the idea."

"I'm not going to treat someone like crap because you expect me to," I say, my voice shakier than I want it to be, and Konstantin moves so close I can feel the heat radiating off him. My cheeks burn.

"If you think I treated her like shit, then you've lived a cushy life, *solnyshka*."

The nickname snaps me back to reality as much as the implied threat does.

My life has been far from cushy, but he doesn't know that. He doesn't know me at all.

I pull away from his grasp, refusing to think about how easily he lets me go, and storm toward the direction Winnie led Alexei, needing space until the ground can resolidify underneath my feet.

Konstantin's laugh follows me, a booming sound that could stop me in my tracks if I let it.

"You can run for now, but don't think we're done here, Nadya," he calls.

If I were running, I'd already be on my way back to the hotel, putting him so far in the rearview mirror I could pretend I never met him at all.

***

I've never wanted to smack someone in the face as much as I do Konstantin as he pulls my seat closer to his, his hand lying heavily over the back of my chair as if it belongs there.

Even when Alexei is being his most obnoxious, I've never been this mad.

I look at the small audience, contemplating saying something, but I don't know the men Konstantin brought with him. I don't know how they'll react if I say something they consider rude, or what Konstantin will do, or how much leeway I have here.

Even the presence of my best friend, Blair, does nothing to soothe my simmering temper and fragile nerves.

While everyone else is talking, she shoots me worried glances, searching my face like she's waiting for a signal to grab my hand and run.

Between her husband and my brother, Konstantin would probably struggle to catch us, but there would no doubt be bloodshed. And even then, I don't know how far she'd be able to run when she's entering her third trimester.

It's a hopeless pipedream anyway.

I said I'd marry Konstantin, and I've never been the kind of woman to back down from my word.

I just wish I could hold her hand and tell her I'm okay without anyone else listening in.

In the few months since Alexei and Konstantin came to this arrangement, she's spent every minute she can spare with me. Packing up my apartment, offering to let me hide in her house, asking what she can do to help. She's been so damn worried, and the guilt of adding anything to her busy schedule has been eating me alive.

But asking her to be my matron of honor felt like one of the few things I could control. I need her support.

I push around the food on my plate, doing my best to ignore everything around me.

Blair's nervous glances. The way Alexei's practically counting the minutes until we can leave. The way Konstantin's presence scorches against my side as he acknowledges a man sitting across the table.

I cringe when I accidentally make eye contact with him, his decidedly unfriendly expression forcing me to confront exactly the kind of people who are present at this dinner.

Other than me and Blair, is there anyone here who doesn't have blood on their hands?

I've been happy to ignore everything Alexei's done, but even the officiant looks far too comfortable with the company around him to be innocent in this life.

What could be more romantic than being surrounded by criminals who are being as subtle as a brick to the face while they discuss business the night before your wedding? Who needs flowers and love when you can have blood money and arms deals?

For what feels like hours, I try to retreat into myself so I don't start screaming, until Blair and her husband, Andrei, excuse themselves.

I rush around the table to give her a hug before they can leave, silently begging her to lend me some of her strength. When I try to tell her how much I appreciate her being here, my throat squeezes shut, but from the way she smiles, she hears me anyway.

Not sparing Konstantin a glance, I excuse myself from dinner and escort them to the entrance, smiling when I hear Alexei making vague excuses so we can get out of here. But even his agitated voice does nothing to mute the click of expensive leather shoes. The looming presence behind me gives away who the steps belong to before I can even think of turning around.

"You okay?" Blair whispers, her arm linked through mine as we reach the front doors.

Beyond the stained glass, the sunset offers little light, obscured by clouds so thick they might as well be as black as the night itself.

"I will be," I answer, hoping I'm telling the truth. "I'll see you first thing in the morning?"

She nods, even as Andrei wraps an arm around her waist, urging her to follow him. She shoots him a pleading look, but the truth is he has no more power in stopping this train crash than I do.

No one except the man behind me does, and even though I know it's useless, Blair's concern sparks a flicker of warmth in my chest.

I ignore Konstantin until their car is gone, tearing down the gravel road like they can't get away from here fast enough.

"May I have a word?" Konstantin asks, his voice washing over me like a wave, snuffing out the tender embers of calm Blair loaned me.

"Do I have a choice?" I can't help but ask.

He lets me hold my stubborn silence for a long moment, only moving to the other side of the doorway to stand beside me, as if he has all the time in the world.

When I do look at him, he looks relaxed, his hands in his pockets, and a curious look on his face.

How did he manage to get through the whole rehearsal dinner without so much as a single hair falling out of place? Even his shirt is still crisp, like he's just stepped off a runway.

Meanwhile, I feel gross from standing in the heat, and my hair's probably doing an excellent impression of a bird's nest.

"Always. You always have a choice with me."

"Not when it comes to getting married," I point out.

"No," Konstantin concedes with a tip of his chin, his cheeks covered with scruff. "In every other aspect of our lives, you'll have a choice. But this marriage is happening whether you want it to or not."

I figured as much, but the words still feel like chains dragging me to the floor.

"Then say whatever you like," I say, hating the despondency in my voice. I hate the way his brows crease even more.

Slowly, Konstantin slips a velvet box out of his pocket.

"I thought it was about time I gave you this."

He opens the box to reveal a white gold ring with a perfect diamond in the center, gleaming as it captures the last few rays of the dying sun. He takes it out, twisting it around with steady hands to show off the tiny diamonds that line the entire band.

My stomach drops.

Objectively, it's beautiful. It's stunning, clearly expensive, and everything a girl on the cusp of her wedding should want.

But it's not what I ever would have picked out for myself.

The longer I look at it, the more I hate it.

I hate what it stands for. I hate that I didn't have a choice in what he picked out. I hate the hours I'm going to have to spend scraping clay out of all the nooks and crannies around each stone.

Because my gut tells me Konstantin's going to make a fuss if I ever try to take it off, even if it's only to protect the stupid thing.

"We wouldn't want you to show up to our wedding without an engagement ring, would we?" He smiles, but it lacks any of the easygoing charm he had during dinner. Without warning, he grabs my hand, pulling me against his chest and slipping the ring on my finger faster than I can protest. "It might send the wrong message."

"And what message is that?" I ask, snatching my hand back. "That we don't even know each other? Or that this is all a business transaction between you and my brother? Because from where I'm standing, both of those things are true."

"Perhaps you need to change your perspective, *solnyshka*."

I shiver at the way his eyes glint.

He brushes the back of his knuckles over my cheek, trailing them down my jaw and throat until he's tapping his thumb over my pulse where it pounds wildly under my skin.

Just like that, I'm frozen, my fight fleeing like I wish I could.

Every inch of my face burns as he scans my expression until I start to squirm.

The sound of a growl registers only a moment before Alexei shoves himself between the two of us, like it's his job to protect me instead of the other way around.

My eyes remain glued to Konstantin's face, bracing for his anger, but instead he looks amused, smirking like he's holding back a laugh.

"I look forward to seeing you tomorrow, Nadya," he says with a wink that makes my stomach swoop.

Chapter 3

Konstantin

The shot burns the whole way down, making me hiss as I turn back to Viktor, glaring at his shit-eating grin.

"That's the only one," I tell him seriously, grimacing at the spark in his eyes. He knows I typically avoid drinking, but he has his own visions of how tonight is going to unfold.

I'll indulge him for a while, but the last thing I want is to show up to my own wedding with a hangover. In fact, I didn't want a bachelor party to begin with, but Viktor wouldn't be a Lavrov if he wasn't stubborn as a mule.

"We'll see about that. Do you like your present?" He smirks, amused, happy, and likely drunker than he'll admit as he gestures across the room.

The man tied to the chair makes a noise that sounds like a protest at being called a present, despite the position he's in.

Bound, gagged, and entirely at my mercy.

His eyes are wide with terror, his cheeks stained with tears, and if I look close enough, I'm sure I'll find him sweating like a pig despite how cold this room always is.

I almost want to ask why he seems so surprised to be in this position.

Ronan Dowd has owed me money for months, far longer than most get. He's had ample opportunity to scrounge up the cash and pay me back, but instead, he's avoided me time and time again in favor of maintaining his gambling habit.

As it turns out, the consequence is being served up as entertainment for my bachelor party.

I wonder, was the high he got out of losing my money worth it?

For once, the awful clawing under my skin isn't threating to bleed me dry. After spending only a few hours in Nadya's company, I already feel settled in a way I haven't in the months since I last saw her.

I take in a deep breath, savoring the fear and frost in the air.

There are times where I really don't give Viktor enough credit, and one of those times was definitely when he pitched the idea of expanding his restaurant to include a butcher's freezer in the basement.

It's proved to be worth every cent, and then some.

"You know me so well," I tell him.

"Of course I do." Viktor grimaces as he downs another shot from the bottle I haven't looked at too closely. "You said no drinking to excess, no strippers, and no getting arrested, which means I had to get you the only other thing you actually enjoy."

He nods his head in the direction of a baseball bat leaning against the wall. As I wrap my hand around it, Ronan flinches, trying in vain to scoot his chair further away from me.

But no matter how far he gets, there's nowhere for him to go. I give the bat a few practice swings, already knowing exactly how this is going to play out.

He'll try to get away. He'll scream and cry, and when I undo his gag so we can have an overdue conversation, he'll beg me to let him go.

I'm so sorry, I'll do anything, I'll get you the money, he'll promise.

I roll my eyes. Every time we get someone down here, it's always the same song and dance.

Honestly, it's a little disappointing. We do all the work to get them into the freezer alive. It's the least our guests could do to keep things interesting.

On my next swing I pivot, putting my weight behind it as I aim for Ronan. Over his muffled screams, there's a satisfying crunch as the aluminum bat connects, crushing his kneecaps.

He may be a prick, but Viktor's right about one thing.

I do like violence.

Especially when it's offering me a welcome reprieve from the anticipation that's had me checking the time every five minutes for the past three weeks.

But who can blame a man for being excited for his wedding day?

For months, I've been haunted by Nadya Trenina. The first time I saw her, curled up on her brother's couch while she tried to look as small as humanly possible, the angry, incessant itch that's always bubbling right below the surface went silent, even while my heart clenched so hard I thought I must have been dying.

With one flash of Nadya's doe eyes, I felt calm in a way I can't remember feeling before. I didn't want to leave behind Alexei's joke of an alliance or abandon him to die a painful death while I profited from his corpse. Instead I was determined to capture the stillness she inspired, no matter what it cost.

But the moment she was out of my sight, so was my first taste of peace.

If keeping her close is the only way I can have it, then so be it.

I'll make Nadya my wife tomorrow, and in time, she'll learn to stop being so afraid of me.

I can give her anything she'd ever want. She may never be happy about it, but she'll learn to be content.

Ronan sobs even harder when I move away from him, angling for his shins with my next swing. He tries to twist away, but Viktor took the liberty of making sure his legs were secured to the chair before I even got here. No matter how much he wants to get away, he isn't going anywhere unless I want him to.

Sometimes, I'm forced to remember how much I love my brother.

The bat connects with a snap, and while it has nothing on the sweet melody of Nadya's voice, the sound helps quiet the throbbing in my skull.

"Oh, come on, Ronan. Don't ruin my fun." I sigh, resting the bat over my shoulders while he cowers, his face a mess soaked in snot and tears. "Weren't you listening? It's my bachelor party. And no one likes a spoilsport."

Viktor snorts while Ronan grows impossibly paler. With a disappointed shake of my head, I drop the bat to the ground.

I grin to myself when he cries out before I turn to the table of instruments Viktor has laid out for me to play with.

All my favorite tools are prepared, gleaming under the lights, but my eyes linger over a knife I've never seen before. The wood grain of the handle gleams, standing out against the Damascus steel blade. I hover over it, not quite sure whether I want to dirty up such a pretty piece on a waste of space like Ronan Dowd.

Giving in, I let out a low whistle as I brush my thumb over the handle.

"You like that one, huh?"

"I do. Who left it behind?" Whoever it was, they aren't getting it back. I pick it up, running my thumb against the edge of the blade with just enough pressure to slice the skin, and I practically groan.

"Me," Viktor says with a shrug. "Well, technically, it was Vasily. But I'm the one who gave him the idea. Consider it a wedding gift from the two of us."

I chuckle.

When I flash him a look, Viktor's grinning like the little shithead he's always been.

I can't tell if I'm touched by the gesture, or annoyed that he's trying to take credit for what I'm sure was entirely Vasily's idea.

"You'll have to thank him for me."

He dips his chin, the only acknowledgment he bothers with before I turn and swipe the knife through the gag wrapped around Ronan's head.

It cuts through the fabric like butter.

A lesser man would weep at the sheer beauty.

Ronan's gasping sobs are loud in the small room, crashing through my euphoria. It puts me on edge.

As excited as I am to put my new gift to good use, tonight isn't the night. It deserves more. With a sigh, I slip it into a leather holster on the table and tuck it into my pocket for safekeeping.

"P-please," he begs, beseeching me with his eyes. "I have a cousin who can get you the money. I just need to talk to him."

"I might be inclined to believe you, but you've had so long, Ronan." I click my tongue, shaking my head. "If you're so sure your family is going to help you, why haven't you reached out to them yet?"

He shifts, moaning pitifully when the movement disturbs his shattered legs.

I know for a fact his cousin could cover the half a million dollars he owes me without issue, but between the sports gambling and his delightful coke habit, Ronan Dowd is a walking neon sign that proudly proclaims *liability* for the world to see.

No doubt his family is well aware of his problems. Even if he did reach out to them, the fact that he's managed to rack up such a large debt is a testament to the likelihood they've washed their hands of him.

Either way, it works for me. I don't have to worry about anyone gunning for my head when the night's over, and I get to have some fun in the process.

"They threatened to cut me off," he admits, his cheeks burning bright red as he turns his face away. "But I *swear*, Konstantin, I can get you the money. Just let me go."

Viktor lets out a harsh laugh before he downs another shot. "You're not making a great case, my friend." He coughs, squinting at the bottle like he's just realized it tastes like shit. "If you want him to let you walk away…"

Slowly, his eyes drop to Ronan's legs. He hisses sympathetically.

"Well, not walk, but maybe *drag* yourself out of this room alive, then you want to make him think you have a shot of paying him back. Right, *bratan*?"

I shrug nonchalantly in answer.

Tears slip past Ronan's jaw, his eyes cutting back and forth for anything that will free him.

"Please, Konstantin, I swear—"

"No. You *swore* last time we spoke. That was four months ago, and what happened, Ronan?" He shakes his head, a dozen half-formed protests on his lips. "Oh, that's right. You dropped off the face of the earth, and I never got my money. But can I be honest with you?"

His lower lip wobbles as I pick my gun up, making a show of checking the chamber to make sure it's loaded.

"It's not about the money. My brother went through all the trouble of tracking you down and bringing you here to celebrate my wedding. I'd look like a real dick if I let you go."

I try to look sympathetic, but it's apparently more than Ronan's dignity can stand. He barges past denial and bargaining and sweeps right into the depression and anger that I suspect will last him the rest of his night.

He screams, spitting vitriol and regret like the walls will grant him mercy.

Unfortunately for Ronan, no one in this building will give him what he's so desperate for. Neither Viktor nor I have ever been inclined toward such an act, and Viktor rented out his own restaurant for our private party tonight.

Vlast is full of men on my payroll who will do nothing without my say so. If they somehow manage to stumble upon Ronan, they'll turn a blind eye and go back to their revelry, taking full advantage of the opportunity to get drunk on my brother's dime.

Even the chefs and waitstaff cleared out hours ago. Viktor has a crew coming through in the morning to get everything cleaned and prepped for opening tomorrow night, but until then?

Ronan has a better chance of getting a sympathetic ear from the chair he's sitting in.

I fold my arms in front of me, waiting for him to wear himself out.

His clothes are ragged and dirty, and his hair is a mess. What sort of state was he in when Viktor found him? Getting home from another night out? Caught in the throes of yet another bender?

I've been happy enough to lend him money because his failure to pay me back would at least entertain me. But no one else around here would dare take on that amount of risk. And the banks wouldn't touch him with a ten-foot pole.

How has he been funding his lifestyle while he's been hiding?

"Are you done?" I ask when he curls forward, testing the strength of his bindings in an attempt to become a smaller target. It's a pathetic sight, and his tears are limiting how much I'm able to enjoy this.

While I'm busy here, how much damage is Alexei doing to poison Nadya against me?

She doesn't even know me, but she acted like I was nothing short of a monster during the rehearsal, and she was somehow even worse during dinner. Her overly bright smiles did nothing to mask the fear in her eyes, nor did the way she watched me like she was waiting for me to lash out.

I won't pretend I'm a saint, but I'm not entirely evil.

I'll have to take my time with her. Once she's in my home, I'll turn on the charm and pretend to be something I'm not if that's what it takes.

As long as I can breathe freely, I'll do whatever I have to.

I tap the bottom of Ronan's chin with the barrel of my gun, forcing him to meet my eyes as he wails uselessly. I search his face, unable to contain my grin when I don't find any signs of his earlier fight.

His terrible will to live is gone, resignation making him despondent. He doesn't look like he's reached acceptance—not quite—but he's no longer striving to win me over.

Perfect.

"Just think, Ronan. This all could have been avoided." His eyes slip closed as he swallows thickly. "Actions have consequences, and none of us are immune."

I press the gun against his forehead and pull the trigger.

The bang echoes through the room so loudly Viktor chokes on his next drink. He coughs, beating a fist against his chest while Ronan's brains drip down the wall in a bloody mess that's going to be a pain in the ass to clean.

At least it won't be my job.

"If you show up with a hangover tomorrow, I'm going to kill you. You know that, right?"

"Nah," Viktor protests, his voice rough as he stretches his arms above his head. "You love me too much to kill me."

"That's debatable."

His grin is obnoxious, and if he were anyone else, I'd let him know exactly what I think of him. Unfortunately, he's right.

Not that I have any intention of inflating his ego by letting him know.

I holster my gun, biting back a groan when I spot a splatter of blood on the cuff of my sleeve.

Damn it. I liked this shirt.

"Well, did you have fun?"

When I don't answer right away, he laughs, loud and joyous. He grins, showing off sharp teeth and even sharper eyes despite how much he's had to drink.

"Fine, old man. We'll get you home. The sooner you go to bed, the sooner you can become Mr. Nadya Trenin."

I'd snap at him, but he has no clue how much I'm looking forward to it.

In a few agonizing hours, I'll be able to take the woman who struck me with an arrow and brought the dead organ in my chest back to life as my wife.

Chapter 4
Nadya

I t's taking so long to do up the miles of delicate lace and pretty pearl buttons that I'm tired from just standing here.

They go so far up my dress that I have no chance of doing them by myself. Blair had to wave a white flag five minutes ago when her baby started tap dancing against her ribs, and Emiliya seems as sick of the whole thing as I am.

"If I tear your dress with my manicure, you're not allowed to get mad at me," she huffs, blowing a lock of hair off her forehead.

"At this point, you could rip it off entirely and I'd thank you."

Between the weight of the dress, the makeup, and the way my hair is styled within an inch of its life, I can't tell if I feel like a princess or a glamorous mannequin.

But when I look in the mirror, I look like everything I secretly dreamed of when I was a little girl.

"There," Emiliya eventually sighs, stepping away so she and Blair can both inspect my appearance. "You're all done."

Perfect curls twirl around my shoulders every time I turn my head.

My makeup is flawless, this dress is the most beautiful thing I've ever worn, and the venue is absolutely stunning. Yet I still can't help but wish Konstantin had let us have a simple court-house wedding with only our families as witnesses.

"You look perfect," Blair says with a smile.

"I know," I lament, gesturing around at the room we're in. "Everything's perfect. Even the bouquet is perfect." I point accusingly at the bundle of stargazer lilies and delicate white flowers.

"And that's a problem?" Emiliya prompts, folding her arms over her chest.

The bright pink is a stunning contrast against the soft cream and sage green that decorates every inch of the building.

Sometime between last night and this morning, Winnie managed to transform the space into a work of art. It feels like the walls themselves are trying to celebrate a love story that isn't real.

The only thing that's put a damper on the fairy tale is the way Winnie looked at me while I took in all the flowers, like she was worried I was going to say something.

Wedding planning means making a million tiny choices that don't mean anything to anyone except yourself, and the flowers were the only thing Konstantin and I argued about throughout the whole process.

Because in all my visions of a perfect wedding, there were lilacs.

It was fine for a fantasy, but the reality is that I'm getting married in June, not on some pleasant spring day. No matter how much I want them, lilacs are so far out of season that even if Winnie had been able to find a source for them, the cost would have been astronomical.

I was willing to accept that, but Konstantin tried to insist she figure out a way to get enough to cover the vineyard in the purple, fragrant blooms until they rivaled the grapes.

Only after three days of tense emails that were all filtered through Winnie did he finally back off.

Since the moment I agreed to marry Konstantin, I've been putting on a brave face. I've pretended to be alright with this whole thing. I packed up my whole life not knowing if I'd ever see the city I called home again. I bit my lip and held my tongue so my brother can be safe.

But for as much money as Konstantin's paid to make everything a dream come true on the surface, he can't buy the things that really matter.

A partner who wants to marry me because they love me.

Someone who can't wait to spend the rest of their life with me. Who can't imagine a life without me when we aren't together. Someone who would do anything for me and I'd do the same.

The Bratva has already taken so much from me, including things I didn't know it was possible to miss.

Everything from my parents, to the goofy smile Alexei used to wear so naturally, to the hope I'd find someone who'd love me despite all my failures and shortcomings.

But how the hell am I supposed to explain all that without sounding like a whiny child?

Instead of answering Emiliya, I ask, "Which do you think is more likely, Konstantin having an ex show up to make a scene, or Alexei dragging me out of the building before I even make it down the aisle?"

"The second one," Emiliya answers without hesitation.

Somehow, her utter certainty makes my lip wobble. Neither of them misses it, rushing to comfort me before a knock on the door freezes the air around us, anticipation leaving no room for my tears.

"Who is it?" Blair calls while Emiliya moves toward the door, hovering her hand over the lock, unsure if she should try to stop whoever it is or not.

"The groom," replies the same voice that echoed in my ears every time I closed my eyes last night.

Konstantin.

My heart starts working double-time as Emiliya looks at me with a silent question.

"No," I hiss. "Absolutely not."

I need time before I can face him again. A chance to catch my breath. Talk to Alexei. Have a stiff drink.

I don't know what I need, but I know I'm not ready to deal with him yet.

I make desperate eye contact with Blair as she wraps her hands protectively around her belly, making me feel even worse.

Her doctor told her she's too far along to travel such a long distance, but she didn't let that stop her. She's still here, against her doctor's orders, and Konstantin's only going to stress her out.

She might be flying back with her family tonight, but she's still here to support me, and that's more than I could ever ask for.

"Tell him we can talk after the ceremony," I blurt, ducking behind a curtain, silently begging Blair to move further away from the door.

If he kicks it in, she's a sitting duck.

"Now isn't a great time," Emiliya relays, sounding surer of herself than I feel.

For a long, tense moment, Konstantin doesn't answer.

I'm not foolish enough to find hope in his silence.

He isn't going to take no for an answer. He'll do whatever he wants, and the rest of us are going have to deal with it whether we want to or not.

I clutch the curtain tightly when Blair positions herself between me and the door.

Across the room, the lock flicks open without Emiliya's help. She throws herself against the door, but her weight is nothing in the face of Konstantin's strength.

He opens the door like she's nothing but a feather, forcing her backward. Just as quickly, she finds her balance again, squaring her shoulders and glaring.

As much as I admire how badass she looks, she's only five foot five, and Konstantin's at least six and a half feet of pure muscle, tattoos, and determination to see me. He might be buttoned up in a tuxedo, but nothing could make him unimposing.

I only wait long enough to catch a glimpse of the fire in those cold eyes as he slips a key into his pocket before I duck behind the curtain, guilt pressing down on me when I realize I'm abandoning Emiliya and Blair to face him alone.

But at least I know that if either of them screams, Alexei and Andrei will come in here with guns blazing.

I want to tell myself they would if I yelled, but I'm not ready to face what would happen if I'm wrong.

"While I appreciate the way you two are trying to keep me away from my bride, I'd appreciate it even more if you'd allow me a moment with her. Alone."

There's no room for argument in his voice, despite phrasing it as a request.

Something about that causes heat to stir low in my gut, waking up parts of me that I really don't want to deal with right now. Or ever, really.

I fiddle with the beading along my waist, doing anything I can to distract myself from the overwhelming presence separated by only a few layers of fabric and a couple of determined women.

The edge of the curtain pulls away, giving me enough space to take in Blair's worried expression as she searches my face, taking in every ounce of the dread I'm sure is plainly written there.

"Do you want me to kick him in the balls?" she asks, the corners of her lips twitching up despite herself. It startles a chuckle out of me, lifting some of the pressure on my chest.

Her faint smile lends me enough strength to shake my head.

If I want to survive a lifetime at his side, I'm going to have to start somewhere. What better opportunity than a quick conversation in a building full of armed witnesses?

Besides, if he tries anything, I have my favorite knife strapped to my thigh. It'll be a struggle to reach it under the mountain of fabric disguised as a skirt, but knowing it's there is still comforting.

I smile back at her, shaking my head as I take the edge of the curtain from her. "But I appreciate the effort."

"For the record, I do *not*."

Konstantin looks perfectly at ease when I poke my head out. He's not at all fazed that all of us are glaring at him like the intruder he is. Emiliya is still standing in front of him with her hands on her hips, refusing to be intimidated.

Before she steps away, Blair squeezes my hand in hers.

"If you need us, we'll be right outside the door."

With concerned glances, they both leave me alone with the hulking beast who's staring at me like he's been starved for a glimpse of me his entire life.

The sunlight streaming through the old, warped windows softens his appearance but does nothing to make his presence any less consuming. Even with his hands in his pockets, his posture screams *power* so loudly I wonder how he's able to navigate the world without everyone around him immediately scrambling for cover.

"It's bad luck for the groom to see the dress before the actual wedding," I protest when he takes a single step toward me. He freezes on the spot, tilting his head to the side as if he's considering it.

Honestly, the last thing I care about is something as temperamental as luck. I just don't want to risk getting caught up in the gravitational pull Konstantin seems to have over me.

Whenever we're in a room together, as soon as I meet his eyes, I'm unable to look away, and it's terrifying.

It's like he'll consume me whole if I give him so much as half a chance.

If I have to let him to keep Alexei safe, then so be it. But I'm not such a martyr that I'll throw myself on that sword before I absolutely have to.

"You'll have to forgive me." He grins, looking like a predator ready to strike. "I didn't realize you were so traditional. I just wanted to make sure everything has lived up to your expectations so far."

"It's great," I deadpan.

He looks around the room, his eyes narrowing when he catches sight of my bouquet, waiting inconspicuously in a vase by the door.

"I wish it all could have been exactly what you wanted," he mutters mostly to himself. "But none of this is what you wanted, is it?"

I don't bother with an answer.

Without invitation, he moves closer until he's able to reach out and stroke his fingers over a lock of my curled hair, smiling faintly.

This close, it's impossible to ignore his cologne, a clean and spicy scent that does nothing to dissuade the way I find myself leaning into his touch, helplessly caught up in him despite how much I want to shove him away.

Of course this isn't what I wanted, but I'm in no position to fight it.

"I need to finish getting ready," I point out.

"I know, but there's something I wanted to do before the ceremony."

"What's that?"

Slowly, so I have no choice but to feel every moment, his hand shifts from my hair to the back of my neck, pulling me closer and slotting his lips over mine. All the emotions I've been trying to keep under control erupt like wildfire, blazing out of control as he dominates me with a slow, deliberate kiss.

Each brush of his lips against mine turns me inside out, exposing everything I've been desperately working to conceal to before putting me back to rights.

Oh, this is *bad*.

His tongue urges me to open for him, and the first stroke against mine undoes me.

I'm trapped under his spell, his to do whatever he wants with.

The curtain falls away as I press my hands against his chest. I'm already unbalanced in these heels, and my knees feel weak, ready to collapse.

The moment is frozen in time, and all I want to do is collapse in his wake and let him burn me alive, regardless of how many people are waiting outside for us to put on a show.

They can wait forever as long as he doesn't take this feeling and leave me alone in the cold.

When he pulls away, I can't help but whimper.

"I didn't want our first kiss to be in front of a bunch of people I don't give a solitary fuck about," he whispers, his lips still brushing against mine with every word. There's something almost mystified in his expression, so unexpected that I'm at a loss. "But now I don't want to let anyone else see you at all."

Without blinking, Konstantin drops his hand to mine, lifting it and pressing a kiss to my ring. The butterflies I thought I had under control burst free in a riot that tickles my ribs, threatening the air in my lungs with a breathy sigh.

With a slow smirk, he drops my hand and steps away, looking me up and down.

Awareness filters back in, urging me to hide, but for the life of me I can't figure out why.

"You look beautiful, *solnyska*."

Sunshine.

He's called me that before, but this time it doesn't grate on my nerves. It settles over me, warm and comforting.

Shaking my head, I snap out of it, pushing him away so I can breathe again.

"You're an asshole, Konstantin," I mutter.

"I never claimed to be anything else," he agrees with a shrug. "But in less than an hour, I'll still be yours."

He backs away without another word, staying close enough that the fluttering sensation in my stomach is trapped there, torn between making a home and fleeing for safety.

CHAPTER 5
Nadya

"Alright, big guy, time to get a move on," Emiliya announces as she bursts through the door with Alexei in tow. Konstantin's smirk only grows when Alexei spots how close we're standing, stopping dead in his tracks to glower.

If my cheeks weren't bright pink and I wasn't ready to melt into a puddle at his feet, I'd snap at Konstantin for antagonizing my brother.

But anything I say will probably come out as a whimpered plea instead of a demand, and I'm not ready to deal with that sort of embarrassment today.

Emiliya purses her lips in barely contained amusement. "Unless you've changed your mind, we need to finish getting ready," she says, checking me over for anything out of place.

"By all means," Konstantin says as he dips his chin. He winks at me, and I want nothing more than to smack the cocky look off his face.

With more gentleness than I would have thought a man like him was capable of, he says, "I'll meet you at the end of the aisle, Nadya."

He walks away with the unearned confidence that comes naturally to a man who knows he's going to get whatever he wants.

Even the sound of Alexei slamming the doors shut behind him can't drown out his infuriating chuckle.

As long as I can hold onto this feeling, resenting Konstantin with every breath will be easier than I thought.

Or maybe I'll end up strangling him in his sleep tonight and run away before the consequences can find me.

Either option is fine in my books.

"If that man lays a hand on you, I'm going to fucking kill him," Alexei mutters as he stalks toward me, his eyes skirting over my arms like he's expecting to find bruises. When he doesn't find anything except a dress that costs more money than anything I've ever owned, he lets out a sigh.

"You look beautiful."

I smile, grateful for an excuse to shove my emotions to the side.

"Thank you. I dressed myself and everything."

Blair snorts, but I can't drum up the will to glare at her for it.

Besides, if I had tried to put this dress on myself, I probably would've ended up tangled in the skirt with half of my makeup wiped off. I needed help at every stage of putting it on.

If I can't free myself at the end of the night, I'm using my knife to shred it to ribbons. No matter how pretty or expensive this dress is, there's nothing on earth that can make me ask Konstantin for help.

"There's still time to change your mind if—"

"No," I snap, cutting him off before Alexei can try to talk me out of this.

He flinches, and I close my eyes, taking a deep breath.

Softening my tone, I say, "I'm doing this. I know it isn't what either of us want, but you're not going to talk me out of it. And it would mean a lot to me if you'd at least try to be supportive."

After a long, tense pause, Alexei's shoulders slump like the wind has left his sails, leaving him stranded and alone. I want hug him, but if I do, I'll only end up crying, and there isn't time to fix my makeup again.

"Fine. But if you ever want out..."

"You're only a phone call away."

Alexei nods, choosing to look out the window rather than at me.

I wish I could ignore the problem that way, but no matter where I look, there aren't any distractions.

Emiliya's touching up her lipstick in the mirror, Blair's standing next to the door with my bouquet in her hands, and Alexei looks like he's going to puke. I swallow as I look at the clock.

In a few minutes, I'm expected to walk down the aisle and smile like someone who's so in love they're dizzy with it.

Emiliya presses a kiss to Alexei's cheek before she whispers that she's going to find their seats, flashing me a smile that's so clearly forced I almost want to call her out. Instead, I take her cue and mimic the expression, take the flowers from Blair, and wait for Alexei to snap himself out of his fugue.

I clutch the flowers so tight there's no way they're going to hold up long enough to look good in photos, but I can't bring myself to care. Even if I wanted to, I doubt I'll ever look back at today with the fondness required to reminisce over wedding pictures.

Blair squeezes my hand and slips into the hall, giving the two of us a moment alone.

"I'm sorry," Alexei whispers as soon as she's gone. "I'm sorry you have to do this."

"I don't," I say, lifting a single shoulder. "You've made it clear that I don't."

"Then let's leave. Let's turn our backs on this deal and never mention it again."

I close my eyes against an unexpected wave of tears. He sounds like this wedding is tearing him apart at the seams, like he wants a time machine so he can go back in time and forget Konstantin even exists.

"You know I can't do that to you."

"Be selfish," he pleads. "For once in your life, forget about me. Pretend I'm not part of this arrangement."

When he looks at me, all I can see is my baby brother. The kid who needed help with his math homework. The man who takes charge of so much but is so miserable it pains me to watch. The only reason I didn't fall apart as soon as we were on our own.

"Do you really want to go through with this?"

No.

No, I don't.

I'm fucking terrified. Of Konstantin. Of losing Alexei. Of not knowing what's going to happen.

But I'm not going to be yet another member of our family who abandons him.

Biting my cheek so hard I taste blood, I nod and leave the room, following Blair and hoping Alexei doesn't force me to do this alone.

The closer we get to the doors leading to the ceremony, the clearer the gentle music of the string quartet is as it filters through the glass.

It's such a dissonance from the cacophony of fear and dread threatening to crush me, an endless refrain I desperately wish I knew how to quiet.

A man loops his arm through Blair's and leads her outside at the same time Alexei steps beside me. I nearly sob with relief.

"You know, I don't think your maid of honor is a *maid* at all," Alexei whispers, wrenching me out of my panic. It's as if he knows exactly how close I am to losing the war in my chest.

Beyond the glass doors, a crowd of faces look back at us, waiting for the spectacle to unfold like it's their personal entertainment instead of my life crashing down around me.

"Yeah? What gave it away? Was it the kid waiting in the front row, or that she's pregnant?"

He hums, making a face. "I don't want to gossip, but I heard she's on her second marriage."

"What a scandal," I whisper back, managing a small smile. Something in him seems to settle with it. "But I think it's a little late for me to find someone else for the role." I gesture outside, looking at everything except the man at the end of the aisle standing with his hands folded in front of him.

Alexei groans dramatically. "Guess you're stuck with a matron of honor."

"Good thing I like her."

"At least someone does," he mutters.

I jam my elbow into his ribs as the music changes, the dulcet tones scratching against my nerves like a funeral march.

A terrible buzzing fills my ears, muffling everything. The music. The crowd. The pounding of my miserable heart.

Alexei's arm links with mine before we're hit by a wave of humidity as the doors open, the heat slamming into me like a wall.

There's no way I can do this.

Konstantin's guests are dressed in their finest clothes, and the heavy weight of their stares presses down on me until I'm ready to collapse.

I cling to Alexei like a lifeline, my other hand crushing my bouquet so hard, the stems threaten to snap in half.

If the flowers fall apart, will Konstantin be angry? Will he put on a front while we're around people but say something as soon as we're alone? Is his anger loud and violent, or quiet, building to a boil that consumes everything in its path?

By the time Alexei's prying my hand off his arm, my breaths are shallow and it feels like my heart is trying to tear a hole through my chest. Somehow, he manages to look calm despite the storm brewing behind his eyes, but I'm about to lurch into the depths of a full-blown panic attack.

Before I can, warm hands that definitely don't belong to my brother frame either side of my face. Rough thumbs stroke over my cheeks until I look up, meeting a steady shade of blue that feels like a life vest in an endless sea.

"You're alright, *solnyshka*. Just breathe," Konstantin says just loud enough to break through the fear screaming in my head. I clutch to the way his eyes soften, letting him anchor me until I'm able to gasp in a full breath and everything slows down enough to let me think.

He doesn't rush me.

For what feels like minutes, Konstantin holds my face, slowing his own breathing until I'm mirroring it. Even after I feel Alexei step away and the officiant start to shift restlessly, he doesn't move. When I'm able to swallow around my cotton-filled mouth, I nod.

"Thank you," I murmur hoarsely, glancing around.

Fuck.

"You can do this," he says so softly I have to strain to hear him over the plants swaying in the breeze. "You're more than strong enough."

"I know I am," I find myself saying, like I'm trying to convince myself as much as I am him.

But he's right. I *can* do this.

Because I love my brother, and he'd never ask me to do this for him.

Because I managed to keep our lives from falling apart when everything else did.

Because I have no choice.

One corner of Konstantin's mouth twitches upward, and it relights the spark of anger I've been trying to nurse. Blair gives me a worried look when I hand her my ruined bouquet, and even my weak smile doesn't soothe her.

But when Konstantin squeezes my hand, he makes it difficult to focus on how she's feeling. He nods at the officiant, urging him to speak.

I fall into the charade, focusing on the soft music, the fluttering flowers on the archway over Konstantin's shoulder, and the sweat dripping down the back of my neck.

Maybe if I ignore what's going on around me, I'll be able to wrap myself in a blanket of numbness.

It would be so much easier than the way the officiant's words hit like clubs, bruising me even as I parrot them back. Out of the corner of my eye, I glance at Alexei.

He's staring at his shoes, his knuckles white as he clings to Emiliya's hand.

Swallowing back my protests and complaints, I say, "I do."

Konstantin's face lights up in triumph while my stomach turns.

***

Blair's son, Niko, laughs as he darts through the crowd, playing with a little girl one of Konstantin's guests brought. Blair watches from her seat while Andrei lurks around the perimeter of the room, alternating between watching Niko like a hawk and stealing glances at Blair.

"My brother is avoiding me," I lament, keeping half an eye out for my new husband.

After how emotionally draining today's been, the last thing I need is for him to catch me unaware. I'm not sure I can deal with him before I drink an entire bottle of champagne and vent to my best friend.

I have to take advantage of her proximity for as long as I can. When she goes home tonight, I have no clue when I'm going to get another chance to see her.

Losing her is going to be almost as hard as losing Alexei.

They'll both be fine without me. I know that.

Blair has her family. She'll be busy looking after Niko and the new baby before I know it, and Andrei has her back no matter what happens. She doesn't need me to be happy.

And Alexei's a full-grown man. Despite my best efforts, he's fully capable of defending himself through whatever means he deems necessary. He's not the kid who needs me to hold his hand or comfort him after a nightmare.

But I still need them.

"He just wants to see you happy," Blair says, shaking her head. "And I don't know if you've noticed, but your brother has the emotional maturity of a walnut."

"Hey," I protest weakly. "That's an insult to walnuts."

"You're right." She laughs, but the sound is frail. "He's more like a rock. An angry rock who doesn't know how to cope with seeing his sister so miserable."

"That's not a very good metaphor," I mutter as I twist the stupid ring around my finger. She gives me a look I wish I couldn't feel. "I thought I was doing a decent job of hiding it."

"To most people, probably." Blair shrugs. "But Alexei knows you better than most, and he's going to need some time before he stops feeling like he's let you down." She pushes my champagne glass closer to me. "At least, that's the impression I've gotten from how often he's called Andrei to complain about this whole thing."

That almost startles a laugh out of me.

I don't know how Emiliya's been able to keep Alexei as calm as she has today, and frankly, I'm not sure I want to. All I know is that if it weren't for her, he probably would've left as soon as the ceremony ended.

"I've *been* giving him time," I say, trying unsuccessfully to keep the whine out of my voice. "He hasn't wanted to talk to me, he's been ignoring my texts, and if I'm not around, who's going to nag him until he answers my calls?"

I don't want to leave things unsettled like this. I need to know he'll make peace with this arrangement before he leaves. I need him to know that I still love him as much as the day he was born. I want him to forgive me for twisting his arm and demanding he let me do this.

"Emiliya can..."

Blair's words trailing off is the only warning I get before a hand covered in tattoos brushes against my shoulder, making my stomach flip.

"Mind if I steal the bride for a dance?" Konstantin asks. Without turning around, I know he's not even looking at Blair. His gaze burns over my shoulders, raising the hair on the back of my neck.

"Nope. I'm busy," I answer, while Blair's eyes dart back and forth between us. I pick up my glass and down my drink, scrunching my nose at the way the bubbles tickle my throat. "We're in the middle of a conversation. Come back in twenty minutes, ask me instead of her, and maybe we can *talk* about dancing."

Only then do I turn, smiling venomously.

Instead of wiping away the smug satisfaction he's carried all day, he seems even more pleased by my attitude.

"You're right, *solnyshka*. I handled that poorly."

Unease wipes away my grin.

"I apologize for the interruption, Blair, but I'm stealing my bride." His hand captures mine, effortlessly pulling me up to stand beside him. "I'll be sure to bring her back so you can say your goodbyes before your family leaves for the night."

I reach for Blair as he pulls me away, but before she's even able to stand, Andrei appears at her side with Niko on his hip, keeping her in place. He glares at Konstantin, who's entirely unaffected as he spins me around and leads me to the dance floor, dragging me away from two of the only people here who would actually try to protect me from him.

"Try to smile, wife. It's your wedding day."

When enough time has passed and the rest of the world forgets I don't actually like my new husband, I vow to smother him in his sleep and pass it off as a heart attack.

"I have an actual name, you know."

"And it's nearly as beautiful as you are," Konstantin says as he twirls me into the center of the dance floor. The music shifts to something slower as he pulls me back into his arms, and I can't help but roll my eyes.

"How much did you have to pay the DJ to get him to do that?"

"Nothing," he answers, looking more amused than he should. I give him a flat look as he pulls me into his chest with a firm hand on my waist.

We're close enough that I have to tilt my head back to meet his eyes. I'm not used to feeling short, especially not when I'm in heels, but next to him, I feel almost dainty.

"Besides, I'm already paying him for his work. Why shouldn't he help set the mood?"

"Because it isn't part of his job description," I answer bluntly, hating how flimsy the argument is. Technically, sure, it might be part of the job description, but it defiantly wasn't written into the contract.

It isn't fair how good it feels to be pressed against Konstantin. His body is as firm as he is big, hard and hot through his tuxedo, primed to burn me if I forget myself for a moment too long.

"Has anyone ever told you how lovely you look when you blush, Nadya?" he asks. My face burns at the way he looks at me as he says my name, his eyes full of a promise I'm not ready to cash in on.

Konstantin looks at me like he knows everything he needs in order to absolutely ruin me.

I'm in so far over my head that it would be funny if it wasn't treacherous.

"Tell me, are you going to blush that pretty when I spread your thighs and bury my face between them tonight? Or will you hold onto that fire and pretend you hate it while I touch you?"

To my dismay, the heat in my face creeps lower, burning even hotter when his eyes dip to my lips.

Unable to bear the weight of his gaze, I look away.

"Don't get shy on me now." He chuckles. "Would you feel better if I told you how badly I want to devour your pussy? How I can't wait to hear you cry my name when you come on my cock? Do you want me to tell you how I couldn't sleep last night because I was consumed by the way your mouth popped open when I gave you this ring?"

He brushes his thumb over my ring, leaning close with every word until his lips brush over the shell of my ear with every word.

"Would you prefer if I told you how hard I was as I pictured painting your lips with my cum?"

I glare at him, but as soon as I meet his eyes, the rest of the world fades away. His hooded gaze transports me somewhere else entirely, until it's just the two of us.

Pull away, I tell myself.

If I had any self-respect, I'd drive the heel of these stupid stilettos into his foot and let him know how little I appreciate his crudity, but—*fuck me*—I don't want to. The stubborn side of me is melting for him, ready to fall into his depths and let him do whatever he wants.

With every word, the paper-thin shields I've been using to hold myself together are at risk of falling apart and leaving me utterly defenseless.

Get it together.

If I fall for his charms now, I'll lose what little leverage I have in this relationship. If I want any chance of keeping my head, I can't give Konstantin an inch.

I push a hand against his chest until I feel like I can breathe again.

"We have guests," I hiss between my teeth. "Can't you at least pretend to be decent until we're alone?"

My voice betrays me, making it clear how eager I am about the idea, and I curse internally.

Konstantin takes a slow, considering glance around us.

The rest of the reception is oblivious to my inner turmoil, ignoring us, like we're trapped in a bubble. The only exception is Blair, who's watching us like she's waiting for an excuse to come to my defense.

"I don't know about you," he says lowly, "but there are very few people in this room whose opinions I care about." When I don't reply right away, Konstantin sighs and loosens his grip. "But I do care about yours. So, if you insist, I'll behave."

"Don't lie to my face," I mutter under my breath.

He only winks, moving us through the crowd, like dancing comes to him as naturally as murder and violence likely do.

"I wouldn't lie to you. I've heard that a good relationship is built on a foundation of trust and mutual respect."

"Relationships born of attraction and affection, maybe. I'm not sure relationships that come from an agreement with a third party and only benefit half of the people involved really count."

Konstantin hums, rocking his head from side to side.

"By your definition, we're already halfway to a relationship, then. Because try as you might, you can't hide your attraction to me, and I've never denied what you do to me."

"Being horny isn't the same thing as attraction," I point out flatly.

Konstantin laughs, the sound loud and unrefined. It sticks out like a sore thumb among all the evening gowns and tuxes.

People look our way, but when they see who it is, they smile to themselves, content to pretend we're nothing but a happy couple celebrating.

Whatever Konstantin says, I'm not stupid enough to fall for his tricks.

"We'll see about that," he whispers against the shell of my ear while goose bumps break out over my arms. "You might be surprised with what you find when you let your guard down."

CHAPTER 6

Nadya

The longer the reception drags on, the more frustrated I get. When I try to get a drink, Konstantin's at my side. If I sit for a moment, he sits beside me. I go back to Blair, and he hovers over my shoulder like a menacing shadow.

Apparently he's no longer content to wait for me to come to him.

Now, he's all too happy to step in and watch as I lose everything I had. My independence, my life, even time with the people I love. All of it has been traded for the massive diamond on my finger. I consider ripping it off and chucking it across the room, but the odds are too high it would hit someone and crack open their skull.

I'd rather avoid unnecessary bloodshed at my wedding if I can help it.

Heat scorches along my spine as Konstantin wraps his arms around me, granting me the distraction I need but will never admit I want, as I watch my brother walk away with nothing but a hug and a kiss against my temple as a goodbye.

Despite myself, I lean into Konstantin, letting him support me so I don't end up chasing after Alexei.

I've never been away from him for more than a week or two. Since the day he was born, he's been by my side, but if I don't let him leave right now, Alexei will drag me away with him before Konstantin even knows what to do.

"I don't like seeing you upset, *solnyska*."

He drops his chin to the top of my head, and the rumble in his chest comforts me as the door closes behind Alexei and Emiliya. I feel more alone than I ever thought I could in a room full of people.

"I'll get over it."

If I'm anything at all, I'm adaptable. Nothing has managed to break me so far, and I refuse to let it happen now. Especially not when it would likely further Konstantin's goals.

He hums, holding me tighter.

"We've spent enough time here. Our guests can entertain themselves for the rest of the evening, don't you think?"

I want to argue out of instinct, but as I look around, I can't drum up the willpower.

Blair and her family left an hour ago to catch their flight, and Alexei and Emiliya were the only other people here that I actually knew.

"Forget everyone else. They can get drunk and dance to their heart's content," he murmurs into my shoulder. I shift my head to the side, and Konstantin takes it as an invitation. His lips brush against the spot where my neck and shoulder meet, sending shivers down my spine. "Let me distract you for a while, Mrs. Lavrovna."

It'd be so damn easy to give into him.

It might be the worst thing I can do, but I'm so tired. In the past twenty-four hours I've left my home, moved across the country, said goodbye to my best friend, and gotten married to a man I've never had a real conversation with.

I don't have what it takes to fight him right now.

My throat bobs on a swallow as I twist in his embrace and wrap my arms around his shoulders. When I stand on my toes and press my lips against his, it might be the dumbest thing I've ever done, but I can't find it in me to care.

Especially not when he winds his fingers into my hair, keeping me in place as he takes whatever he wants from me, leaving me no room for my grief. There's only Konstantin and the all-consuming way his lips move against mine.

When he pulls away, I bury my face in his chest, wrapping myself in the smell of his cologne and the smooth fabric of his tuxedo.

I'm only distantly aware of him lifting me off my feet and scooping me into his arms. He carries me away from the music and laughter of the strangers in the ballroom and toward the front of the building, all the way to the car waiting for us.

Before he lowers me to my feet, I pull my head back for one more look at the beautiful building. Lights spill out the windows, and around us there's nothing but signs of life: laughter, music, and conversation. But it's all so far removed from how I feel that it might as well be miles away.

The only thing that can touch me is the way Konstantin looks at me like I'm everything he's ever wanted.

It's probably nothing but smoke and mirrors, the imaginings of my bruised heart, but I'll gladly fall for it for a few hours. I'll let him hold me until it no longer feels like the world is spinning out of control.

I'll take the reins again in the morning.

For now, I'm content to drift and watch Konstantin drive toward the hotel. The trip doesn't take nearly as long as it did this morning, but it's still long enough for the numbness to burn away with every passing moment, fading more and more until it's gone entirely.

The distance I've been trying to keep is nowhere to be found. Instead, it's replaced by a bubbling anticipation that has my pulse pounding as we step into the elevator.

I'm hyperaware of how tight the space is, and when it stops to let someone else on, Konstantin's honey-dipped growl hits me almost as hard at the evidence of his arousal when he presses himself against my back.

The man on the other side of the doors stumbles backward, raising his hands with wide eyes while Konstantin stabs the button to close the doors. The air around us grows thicker with every floor we climb.

"Hey!" I protest as he lifts me bridal style once we reach our floor, carrying me like I weigh nothing. Before I can fight free, Konstantin's lips are on mine.

His lips are intoxicating as he lets us into his room.

The fluttering in my stomach explodes as he nips at my lip sharp enough to leave me gasping.

Without even touching me, Konstantin has me wetter than I've ever been before, giving me some small spark of hope. This might be a loveless marriage, but it doesn't need to be completely miserable.

I pull back, feeling lightheaded.

The way Konstantin looks at me makes me feel like prey caught in a trap, but for once, I want to be caught. I want him to sink his teeth so deep into me that I don't remember what it's like to ever be afraid of him.

I bite my lip as he sets me down the bed, staring at me with dark eyes.

"You have no idea what I'd do to have a taste of you," he says, ripping off his bowtie and dropping it to the ground at his feet. Following his lead, I hurry to kick off my heels. As soon as they clatter to the floor, Konstantin has his hand wrapped around my ankle.

He's already shed his jacket, his hand disappearing under my dress as he runs it up my calf, crawling over me until my legs fall apart to make room for him. He grunts in approval before he dips his head, running his lips up my throat while I whine breathlessly.

His touch winds me tighter, exploring every new inch of skin as he pushes up my dress. His rough touch and claiming kisses are devastating in how they capture all my focus. I can't think of anything else except him until he freezes, pulling back enough that I blink at him.

He's smirking, and I don't even care why.

"What's this?"

"What's what?" I sound breathless, like I've been drugged by just a few kisses.

His hand flexes against my thigh, his fingers prodding at the knife holster strapped to it.

Oh, shit.

"What were you planning to do with this, wife?" he asks against my throat. "Were you hoping to use it against me?" Before I can reply, he groans, grinding his hips against the mattress. "Were you planning to put that knife to my throat while I fucked you with my tongue?"

I shake my head, but he only chuckles.

"You can try, Nadya," he says, slowly slipping the knife free of the holster. "But be careful. If you decide to attack me with it, it will only turn me on."

"Oh?" I ask, my heart in my throat.

"A woman who knows how to defend herself is the sexiest thing," Konstantin says as he sits back on his knees, the knife glinting in his hand as he inspects the blade. It isn't anything impressive at first glance, but it's sharp as hell, and it's devastating if you know how to use it.

"Does that mean you're going to give it back?"

If he does, I'll show him exactly how I wield a blade.

He hums, using the tip of the knife to trace along the neckline of my dress, not pressing hard enough to cut. I hold my breath, not wanting to risk his hand slipping.

"I will. But first…"

So quickly I can barely track the movement, he slices down the front of the dress, the lace falling free to expose me breast to navel. I gasp, but he pays me no mind, adjusting his grip before his arm rears back and he throws the knife to the side.

I gape at him, speechless when I find it embedded in the wall, pinning the edge of the curtain in place. Fixing him with the fiercest glare I can muster, I snarl, "If you've damaged my knife, I'm going to gut you with the broken blade."

Not flinching, he pulls up his pant leg, revealing the knife holstered at his ankle. He pulls it free to show off the beauty he's been hiding. My hands itch to reach for it, but I'm wary of setting him off with any sudden moves.

"If it's damaged, you can have mine."

I can't tear my eyes away from the blade, covered in striations that look almost like wood grain, mimicking the handle. I don't even realize I'm staring until he sets it down on the nightstand, tapping my cheek until I turn my head to look at him.

Fuck me.

Konstantin shrugs his shirt off his shoulders, answering the question I was too scared to ask. Every inch of his chest, shoulders, and arms is covered in gorgeous designs that undulate as he moves. Every bit of skin, from his throat to his waistband is a living, breathing work of art.

Unbidden, I whimper.

In what universe is it fair that someone like him gets to look like *that*? I'm no stranger to good-looking men, but Konstantin is on a whole other level. The muscles, the scruff on his jaw, the way his dark hair looks incredible even though he's been running his hands through it.

Everywhere I look, there's another piece of him to admire.

I'm busy watching the way his shoulders move when he says, "As much as I enjoy you looking at me like that, I'd love to return the favor." He grins, standing so he can pull off his belt. I'm frozen as I watch him.

My stomach clenches when he clears his throat, leveling me with a look that compels me faster than anything ever before, sending me scrambling to shove off the ruined remains of my dress, leaving me in only the skimpy thong Emiliya managed to talk me into wearing.

The dress was low-cut enough that she couldn't talk me into the matching bra, but Konstantin doesn't seem to care. His hungry gaze catalogs every new inch of skin.

I toss aside the useless fabric, and when I look up, Konstantin's naked. He's naked, and he looks like someone rooted around in my subconscious and plucked every dirty fantasy from my head, put them all together, and placed them in front of me.

He slowly strokes his thick cock as he watches me.

Konstantin's tattoos don't stop at his waist. They trail all the way down his legs. Geometric patterns and shapes I can't make out. There isn't an inch of him that's unmarked.

He smirks, the new ring on his finger glinting as he moves his hand up and down, squeezing when he gets to the base of his cock.

"Keep looking at me like that, and I'll have to wait to find out what you taste like." Konstantin licks his lips slowly while my flush burns from my cheeks all the way down to my breasts. "And I've been dying to taste you, Nadya."

He laughs when I glare at him, desperately fighting for composure. Without pretense or presentation, I take off the underwear. If he doesn't like it, he can shove it. But from the way his cock twitches in his hand, my rushed, efficient movements do nothing to cool his desire.

He's looking at me like he's memorizing every line of my body. My breasts, the curve of my hips, the shape of my spread legs. His eyes linger there, and a silly, self-conscious part of me worries whether he like the curls there, or if he's disappointed I'm not bare.

But he doesn't say anything derisive.

If anything, he looks even more eager, his hands flexing as if he's holding himself back.

When Konstantin crawls over me, I'm torn between fleeing and begging him to touch me. He kisses his way up my body until his weight presses me into the mattress. It feels like a revelation from the devil.

"If you're hoping I'm going to beg you to go down on me, you're out of luck."

I gasp while his tongue flicks against my nipple.

"I'd never ask you to beg," he answers roughly, pressing a kiss to my breastbone before he slips lower. "It's below you, *solnyshka*. The only thing I want to hear from you is my name on your lips while I learn what your body needs with my tongue. Tonight is about your pleasure."

He props his chin against my hipbone, waiting for my permission before venturing further.

Despite the nagging voice in the back of my head warning me I'm making a mistake, I nod. His grin is both triumphant and dangerous, and I wonder if I should tell him he's wasting his time.

Only a couple of guys have ever gone down on me before, but it was never something I loved. I was never sure if it was because they were only doing it out of a sense of obligation, or because I was too caught up in my head to relax, but it always seemed like more effort than it was worth.

Before I can say anything, Konstantin parts me with his tongue, groaning low in his throat as he dips his head, licking up my slit with one long swipe of his tongue.

And I immediately realize my husband is *very* different from every other man I've been with. He works my pussy with a single-minded focus that steals the air from my lungs, leaving me panting. I gasp, my back arching as his tongue lashes against my clit.

Nothing about his enthusiasm makes me think he's doing this out of obligation, and the way he hooks my legs over his shoulders gives me no room to retreat into my head.

All I can do is *feel*.

His tongue. His fingers. The way he moans against my clit until I feel like I'm going to explode.

"Oh, fuck. Konstantin!" I gasp. Every breath is an effort, pleasure crashing down so hard I feel like I'm dying.

No matter how hard I grab at his shoulders or grind myself against his face, Konstantin is unfazed, taking his time like he isn't shattering my entire perception of sex without a single word.

I throw my arms over my face, biting my forearm so I don't scream so loud the rest of the hotel thinks I'm being murdered.

My orgasm tears through me faster than ever, leaving me breathless and trembling. My eyes are squeezed shut, and I'm not sure if I really am dying or if I'm the most alive I've ever been.

I don't realize how tightly my muscles are still clenched until Konstantin pulls my arm away from my face, kissing the mark my teeth left behind and smoothing back the hair matted against my sweaty forehead.

He kisses me, giving me no choice but to taste my own arousal on his lips. It shouldn't be hot, but somehow, it is.

His cock is hard against my stomach, leaking precum and he lets me come down from the glimpse of heaven he gave me with his mouth as his tongue slides against mine.

"I need you to fuck me," I pant with a boldness I didn't know I was capable of. Because even though he just gave me an earth-shattering orgasm, I need to know what it's like to be surrounded by my husband. For at least the span of a night, I want to know what it's like to let him consume me.

Konstantin's smirk is downright pornographic.

"Is that so?"

His breath is warm against my jaw, his hands demanding as he runs them over me like he owns my body. If he were anyone else, I'd smack his hands away, but he feels too good. I'm almost hypnotized by the way his tattoos stand out as he splays his hands over my hip, keeping me from arching into him.

"Don't you dare tease me," I snap with an edge to my tone. "I already told you I won't beg."

"And I already said I don't want you to."

He sits back, sliding the head of his cock through my wetness before he nudges against my entrance.

"Tell me, Nadya, are you on birth control?"

I nod, wrapping my legs around his waist. I'm not going to ask him for what I want again—at least not with words. But I'm so desperate to know what he feels like inside me that I could cry.

"That's a shame." The way he clicks his tongue is the only warning he gives me before he sinks into me, stretching me around him and hitting me so deep I forget how to breathe.

"Fuck," he grunts. "You feel even better than I imagined you would."

Slowly, he withdraws until only his tip is resting inside me before he shoves his way back in, even deeper.

He doesn't waste a single second, driving into me while his hands clutch my ass. I move with him, needing this as much as he does. There isn't an inch of space between us, and if there were, I suspect he'd do whatever it took to eliminate it.

This man is going to destroy me, I realize in a rush.

I thought his mouth was magical, but I don't know how I've been able to go through life without knowing what it's like to be properly *fucked*. He surrounds me, consuming me with every stroke.

Choking on the way he hits every sensitive spot inside me, I freeze when his hand shifts from my hip to cradling the back of my neck, holding me so close it's a wonder I can breathe at all.

"It's like you were made for my cock. Made for *me*," he rasps.

Even if I were physically capable of arguing, I wouldn't. It's like he's turning me inside out, rearranging every fiber of my being and putting it all back exactly how he wants it. He's exploring me like a new instrument, finding everything that makes my body sing for him.

I want to find a way to bottle this feeling and keep it. I want to cling to the hope that we'll find a way to make the rest of our marriage feel like this all the time, instead of this pleasure being something that will be contained to his bedroom.

"Come for me, wife," he groans, his lips brushing against my throat. "I want to feel you fall apart around me while I fill you with my cum."

As much as I don't want to obey him, his pubic bone grinds against my clit while he thrusts so deep I can practically taste him in the back of my throat. Whatever I want doesn't matter.

Without conscious choice, I shatter into a million pieces, making desperate whines while I dig my nails into the firm muscles of his back.

"Nadya," Konstantin groans. "You're perfect. So fucking perfect." He sinks his teeth into the meat of my shoulder and moans a sound so hot it should be illegal, stilling as his cock throbs inside me.

My muscles are jelly as my ears ring.

What the hell was that?

I don't realize I've asked the question out loud until Konstantin chuckles, tracing the marks his teeth left with his lips. He pulls away slowly, and I have to hold myself still so I don't reach for him as he pulls out.

Without his touch, I feel both empty and cold.

Instinctively, I try to close my legs, but his bulk stops me, holding me open with a firm hand on my thigh.

"Let me look at you," he says, his voice rough with satisfaction. I'm too fucked up to snap at him or pull away, loose-limbed while he takes me in. Konstantin licks his lips before he hovers over me, kissing me with a tenderness that feels out of place for an arrangement.

CHAPTER 7
Nadya

Konstantin's expression is placid as he drives toward his home in San Francisco. The landscape shifts from vineyards to traffic, the sprawling buildings getting closer together mile by mile until they're practically on top of each other.

He's apparently content to let each mile pass without a word, not bothering to point out a single thing that flies by the window. But that's fine. I'll cling to my silence like a shield so I don't have to look at the pleased way his lips curl whenever he catches me looking around, taking in the scenery with rapt fascination.

Despite the circumstances, I am looking forward to exploring a new city.

I've only left Illinois a couple times before, and when I did, I never went far. As he winds the car through the streets, I catch glimpses of water between the hills. I press my face against the window to get a better view, but he chuckles under his breath, sucking away the excitement that briefly lifted my mood.

I slump in my seat, refusing to look at my new husband as he turns off a private road into a long driveway, passing through a gate and ignoring the half dozen armed guards standing watch.

I glance around the front of the property, and no matter where I look, there are even more men studiously avoiding looking in our direction as they patrol.

Damn it.

Of course Konstantin would be the type to keep security all over his house.

Is it always like this, or is it a special occasion? Because if this is the typical amount of security Konstantin employs, I'm going to lose my mind in a matter of days.

Ever since Alexei moved out of the house we grew up in when he was nineteen, I've lived alone. And the few times he tried to push me to accept a bodyguard, I nearly ripped his head off.

I like being able to do what I want, when I want.

Privacy is important to me, and when we pull up to the house, all I can think about is the guards looking inside the massive windows, observing my entire life like I'm stuck in a fishbowl.

There's a huge wall surrounding the property, lined by sparse bushes that offer no room for anyone to hide. Beyond it, mature trees loom far enough away that they don't even offer shade. There's a bitter taste in my mouth as I realize that even though the landscape while we drove here was beautiful, it'll be next to impossible to see it from indoors.

The house itself is stunning, yet I can't help but resent it. Three stories with walls made up of glimmering windows and perfectly cut stone. I squint, turning my head when the reflection off the windows becomes more than I can bear.

"They're all coated with one-way film," Konstantin says like he can read my mind. "You might see someone looking in occasionally, but the only thing they're able to see is their reflection. No one can see what happens inside."

I nod to myself, not quite believing him as he parks in the garage. I take in several sports cars lined up in neat rows, occasionally broken up by something more practical.

When I spot a camera in the center of the ceiling, I freeze.

"How many cameras are there?"

"Many." He shrugs. "If you want you know the exact number, you'll have to ask my brother. He's in charge of my security team."

"And are they all as easy to spot as that one?"

Rather than answer, Konstantin twists in his seat, looking at me with an intensity that makes me squirm.

"Follow me. I want to show you around your new home." A chill runs down my spine at his clipped tone as he gets out of the car. I hurry to follow, unwilling to risk getting lost in this massive house with no one to guide me.

As soon as I step inside, I'm struck by how bright the space is.

How bright, and how lifeless.

Everywhere I look, there's nothing but white. White walls, white furniture, even a white rug lining the hallway.

My lip curls.

Who the hell has the patience to deal with all this? It has to be a pain in the ass to keep clean.

Konstantin clears his throat, and I make eye contact with him as I slip off my sneakers. If he wants to have the most boring house of all time, I can't stop him. But I won't drag my dirty sneakers over the clean floor for someone else to deal with.

With long strides, he guides me through most of the ground floor, only leaving a few doors shut and continuing on when I ask about them. But everything is the same.

No color. No personality.

There are no real indications anyone lives here at all. The only signs of life are the men patrolling outside across a flat yard and the occasional camera capturing every move we make.

Each new room is so similar to the last that this whole house might as well be a hotel.

When he leads me to his bedroom, I shake my head, refusing to follow him inside.

"I'll take one of the guest rooms," I insist.

The look Konstantin gives me is so severe, it's no wonder everyone has tripped over themselves to cater to him. Everyone, from the person who delivered room service this morning, to the valet fetching his car, has dropped everything to give Konstantin whatever he wants, both said and implied.

It's nauseating.

"You're my wife. We're going to share a room."

"I'm your wife in name," I agree. "But this isn't that kind of arrangement."

"Isn't it?" Konstantin asks with a raised brow. "It seemed like that kind of arrangement when your pussy was squeezing my cock like it was afraid to let go last night. It seemed like that kind of arrangement when I woke up to find you plastered to my side. And it definitely seems like that kind of arrangement when your cheeks light up when I haven't even touched you. Like you're remembering everything I did to make you moan my name while you fell apart for me."

I slam my eyes shut while I take a deep breath, doing everything I can to ignore him.

"This is business," I mutter. "There's no reason why we should have to live on top of each other."

I don't know how I'll survive if we do. I need to find my own footing before I can broach the topic of being with him again. Because if I learned anything last night, it's that he's right.

The attraction between us is undeniable, and if I'm not careful, feelings are bound to show up sooner or later. And if they do, I'm at real risk of losing myself to a man that will never care for me.

A man like Konstantin doesn't do love. He doesn't do softness. He'll never look forward to seeing me at the end of the day unless he's looking to get off.

He only knows brutality and manipulation.

A man like him requires wits and awareness and walls so high I'm not sure how I'll maintain them.

But I have to try.

Konstantin frowns, and whatever he's going to say is cut off by his phone ringing.

"Blayd," he swears under his breath, tearing his eyes away from me. I breathe a little easier at he makes a face at whatever he sees on the screen.

"I have to take this, but this isn't the end of the conversation," he says, his voice sharp.

I shrug, already turning to explore on my own.

Whoever is on the other line, I don't want to know what's so urgent that they need him the day after our wedding. I have enough ideas about what sort of man my husband is. I don't need to hear all the nitty-gritty details of what he does for a living.

I didn't want to know when it was Alexei, and I don't want to know now.

"It is," I call after him without turning back.

He grumbles, but I pay no mind as I look through the remaining rooms, determined to find the least lifeless one to claim as my own. The only thing any of them have going for them is the view.

From the upper floors, there's a clear view of everything beyond the yard. Between the trees outside the fence and the glittering water and boats below, I could spend hours watching everything outside.

If only my attention wasn't constantly being pulled away by the men patrolling along the fence line, visible even when I'm standing on the highest floor.

This amount of security is ridiculous.

You can see for miles in nearly all directions, there was only one road leading up to the house, and if the building's too big to be monitored by a few cameras and maybe a *couple* of guards, then it sounds like Konstantin needs to downsize.

Huffing, I flip the guards off, even though they can't see me.

A low whistle has me whirling around, pressing myself against the window. In the doorway is a man giving me a slow look up and down, his lip trapped between his teeth.

"You've been here less than an hour, and Konstantin's already managed to piss you off?" Despite his playful tone, he's looking at me like I'm his next meal.

Fuck that.

"Who the hell are you?"

"He didn't tell you about me?" he asks, pressing a hand to his chest. If it weren't for the smile in his eyes, he'd be the very picture of offended. "I'm hurt. But I guess Konstantin was a little distracted yesterday, huh?"

He gives me an expectant look, and only then does the smirk click.

He's the same man who stood next to Konstantin during the ceremony.

"I'm Viktor," he says with a grin. "Your new brother-in-law. I would've introduced myself at the wedding, but my brother can be a real brute when he wants to be. Though when it comes to a woman as beautiful as you, I can understand why."

Oh, *great.* He's a flirt.

Though now that he mentions it, I can see the family resemblance. The same dark hair, the same blue eyes. Viktor's shorter than his brother, but that doesn't take much since Konstantin looks like he's half giant.

And from the way Viktor's looking at me, they share the same condescending *I'm better than you and I know it* attitude that makes my skin crawl.

My fingers itch to grab my knife and warn him off, but something tells me Konstantin wouldn't take too kindly to me maiming his family.

But there's only one way to find out, isn't there?

Fortunately for Viktor, I left my knife in my luggage. Which, as far as I know, is still in the trunk of Konstantin's car.

"Nadya." I introduce myself with a sickly-sweet smile to cover up how uncomfortable his gaze makes me. "I'm sorry Konstantin failed to introduce us yesterday."

"As am I." He leans against the doorway, blocking the only exit as he tilts his head. "Now, I have to ask. What're you doing in my room?"

"Your room?" I ask, glancing around for any indication the room belongs to anyone and finding nothing. "Is that why it's so bland? To reflect your dazzling personality?"

There's a long beat where I wonder if Alexei was right when he told me I needed to learn to bite my tongue around strangers before Viktor breaks into a loud laugh. I let out a relieved sigh.

"Oh, I like you, Nadya." He grins. "Something tells me Konstantin has his work cut out for him."

Before I can tell him how right he is, a flash of color sprints through the door and under the bed like a giant rat. I shriek, jumping on the nearest piece of furniture to get away from it.

Please don't be a rat.

Viktor laughs so hard he doubles over.

"What the hell is that?"

"I take it Konstantin also failed to tell you about Spaghetti?"

"Spaghetti?" I repeat incredulously while he opens one of the drawers on the dresser to pull out a plastic bag, shaking it until the mass under the bed crawls out.

And, to my great relief, it isn't a giant rat. It's just a fat, orange cat, who immediately starts screeching as it scratches at Viktor's shoes, staring at the bag in his hand like it's the holy grail.

Wordlessly, I climb off the furniture and pray Viktor never shares word of this with anyone else. "Konstantin failed to mention a cat."

Viktor tosses me the bag, grinning when Spaghetti chases after it until he's blinking his green eyes at me, showing off a spot of white above his nose and tapping a paw against my foot. I crouch down so he can sniff my hand, but he rears back, seeming to unhinge his jaws like a snake before he goes straight for the bag in my hand.

I pull it back before he's able to tear it apart.

"In that case, Nadya, meet Spaghetti. Spaghetti, this is your new mom."

I pour out a couple treats, dumping them on the floor when he ravenously tries to eat them from my hand.

"He has excellent taste in people. Which means he hates my brother almost as much as you probably do."

I jolt at the accusation, but don't deny it.

The way Viktor's smirk grows makes my stomach clench uncomfortably.

Spaghetti, apparently content with his snack, rubs himself against my legs before he rolls over, showing his fluffy belly and blinking at me with a desperate expression.

"Something tells me this is a trap," I say, even though I'd love to see if the fur on his stomach is as soft as it looks.

"Nah, it's not a trap," Viktor says with a shrug. "Look at him. He's too fat to hurt anyone."

I narrow my eyes at Viktor as he laughs.

"Okay, fine. It's a trap. My brother makes me feel like a moron when I fall for it. I didn't want to be the only one," he says as the cat starts purring, batting at my hand until I reluctantly scratch his chin. "I told you he has excellent taste."

"What kind of name is Spaghetti, anyway?" I can't help but ask.

"He likes sleeping in a colander." As if in agreement, Spaghetti yowls, his tail lashing back and forth until I run my hand over his side.

"Right," I sigh. "Makes perfect sense."

Chapter 8

Nadya

When Konstantin insisted I follow him when he finished his call so he could show me something, I wasn't sure what to expect. But after seeing how plain the rooms I poked through were, I half hoped it was something like a sex dungeon so he could say there's *something* in this house that wasn't ripped straight from the world's most boring interior decorating magazine.

I definitely wasn't expecting to be led down the hallway he breezed past earlier and being struck dumb when I found a vase filled to the brim with lilacs.

The same flower we argued about having at the wedding. The one I asked him to stop pushing for when I learned how much it would cost to have them. Konstantin doesn't acknowledge them, only giving me an undecipherable look while he hands me a key and nods toward a closed door.

"What's this?" I ask.

"Open the door and find out."

Keeping one eye on him, I unlock the door, cautiously opening it to reveal a bright, open room lined with mostly empty racks. There are a few packages wrapped in paper and plastic, and a table along one wall that's empty except for a small scale, but none of that's what gets my attention.

Because in the corner, tucked next to the floor-to-ceiling windows and bathed in sunlight, is a pottery wheel. One that looks like the fancy wheels I spent way too many nights looking at online but couldn't bring myself to buy. Partially because they're expensive as hell, but mostly because I had no room in my apartment for a dedicated pottery space.

It was fine, especially since I'm still starting out. But there's space for me to practice here.

I turn slowly, dumbfounded when I find another shelf full of carving and trimming tools waiting to be broken in. I won't have to hurry to be the first one to the studio so I can get the tools that aren't so worn they're impossible to use. And with all these open racks, I can try so many different projects and let them dry out as much or as little as I want.

"I didn't know what sort of kiln you'd want," Konstantin says with a shrug. "But once you pick one, I'll have it delivered and installed wherever you like."

This is quite possibly the kindest thing anyone has ever done for me, but I can only gape at him.

I know for a fact I never mentioned pottery during our wedding planning. In fact, before this exact moment, I didn't realize Konstantin was capable of the emotional depth required to see me as a person with interests outside of him.

"How'd you know?" I ask, clearing my throat, hoping it'll erase how choked up I am.

"Despite what you think of me, I do want you to be happy here."

"You asked my brother, didn't you?"

One corner of his lip twitches upward, too big to be a smirk, but not big enough to be a smile. It looks unfairly good on him.

"I did. He told me to eat my own gun."

Yeah, that sounds like something Alexei would say.

"After a spirited debate over how effective my death would be to make you happy, he mentioned you enjoy pottery." He nods at the room. "I figured a studio would be a more effective way to make you smile than a funeral."

He brushes his fingers against the hem of my shirt.

"Besides, you look nice in bright colors. I don't want to see you in mourning black."

All the sudden, I'm not so sure I want to see him dead at all. Instead, I kind of want to kiss him.

Before I get a chance to say anything, Konstantin leans close enough I can see the moisture on his lower lip after his tongue darts over it.

"If I kiss you, will you hit me?" he asks, his voice husky.

I can't do this.

We're not even a full day into this marriage, and I'm already eager to do whatever he asks just so I can feel his lips against mine again. I want him in a way I've never wanted anyone, and in this moment, I can't bring myself to care.

He gave me a studio.

"There's only one way to find out, isn't there?"

"Can't wait," he whispers only a moment before his lips crash against mine. He shifts his hands and pulls me against him as I return his kiss. Unwittingly, I wrap my arms around his neck, letting out a startled sound when he picks me up, moving so my back is pressed against the windows.

Like a light switch flipped in my brain, all the reasons I shouldn't do this go dark. All I can think about is Konstantin, and the fact that he's mine. He's mine, and he wants me so much that he built a damn studio for me.

Didn't he think about how disruptive this could be? Did he consider the mess? How expensive it'll be to have a kiln and power it whenever I want? Or did he decide that it doesn't matter? That he only wanted to do something to make this transition easier on me?

Do I really even care about the *why* at this point?

Konstantin's teeth dig into my bottom lip, and I decide that, no. I don't care at all.

Not only because the way his fingers dig into my thighs is delicious, but because I'm so grateful he'd do something like this for me, I'm at a loss for words.

"I shouldn't do this," I mutter to myself as he rolls his hips, pinning me against the window while he rips my T-shirt over my head.

The cold glass is a shock to my heated flesh, making me suck in a sharp breath as I arch into him.

"I don't care what you *should* do. What do you *want*?"

Instead of answering, I wind my fingers through his hair, dragging him away from my throat, and I kiss him in a flurry of lips, teeth, and tongue that has him chuckling.

"Let me down," I gasp, still clinging to his hair.

"And why should I do that?"

With a stubborn tilt of my chin, I force Konstantin to meet my eyes. He's far too amused to be as annoyed as he sounds, leaning his head back as I pull harder.

"Because if I'm going to be stupid, then I want to ride you."

"Yeah?" he asks, raising a single brow.

"Yeah." I swallow thickly, my grip faltering slightly. Facing him like this, with his intense gaze taking in every shift in my expression like he's hungry for it, forces me to remember why I'm not typically the take-charge type in bed.

I've always been more of the type of person to follow where my partner leads me, content to go with the flow, even if it wasn't what I truly wanted.

"And what else do you want, wife?"

He stares at my lips as he says it, and a force far more compelling than embarrassment licks at my face, flaming all the way down my chest.

"I don't want you to take off your clothes," I admit through clenched teeth. "I only want you to pull your dick out while I ride you completely bare."

"Fuck," he groans, sliding me down his body. "I can make that happen." His long legs eat up the distance to turn on the lights, bathing the room with even more light. He whirls toward me with a smirk. "But I'm going to see every inch of you while we do it. And I'm going to love every second."

Spurred on by the way he adjusts the bulge in his slacks, I reach back and slip my bra from my shoulders, making quick work of my shorts and panties. In under a minute, I've stripped every piece of clothing and dropped them at my feet.

Unlike last night, this is intentional.

I could lie to myself and pretend I was fulfilling another obligation last night, that it was all about sealing the deal he made. But this? I can't pretend I don't have any interest in it while I'm telling him what I want. Not when the tension between us finally loosens my muscles, spurring me on as I cross the room, lay a hand to Konstantin's shoulder, and push him down like I have the right to.

He goes easily, falling to his knees while his hands caressing my ribs.

It's a heady rush when he looks at me like this. His eyes are hooded and so full of want, it would stop anyone in their tracks. Even more so when he reaches for his belt, gazing at me with something akin to wonder.

Despite him being the one on his knees, despite the fact that I'm standing before him without anything to hide behind, I feel powerful.

My arousal is heavy, and I'm so wet I'd be embarrassed under any other circumstance, but Konstantin's my husband. He might not have been that for very long, but he is. For better or worse. And wanting him doesn't have to be a bad thing.

Especially not when he clearly wants me, too.

"Good boy," I say softly, testing the weight of the words.

I like it a lot more than I thought I would.

From the way his eyes flutter shut, his head falling back as his whole body shudders, so does Konstantin.

He whimpers. Fucking *whimpers.*

Slowly, he blinks up at me, eyes hooded. "Say that again," he urges, freeing his cock and sitting back until he's lying on the floor, propping himself up with his elbows.

"You're such a good boy for me," I breathe as I climb into his lap, the shift of his clothing against my sensitive skin making me shiver. I've always wanted to try this, but I've never been able to drum up the courage to ask for it.

Something about a man seeking his pleasure, not even willing to take the time to strip off his clothes, while I'm totally naked does it for me. I line his cock up with my slit, slicking him up with my own arousal as I grind against him. He sighs shakily, and it echoes through me with a shock of pleasure.

"Climb on my dick, *solnyshka*. I want to see your face twist up in ecstasy as you take me from this angle." His hands flex on my thighs, encouraging me to slip him inside. "I want you in so many ways, but let's start with this. Ride my cock. Show me how much you want your husband."

I gasp when the head of his cock nudges against my clit while I grind against him.

"No," I pant as I brace my hand on his chest. The fabric crumples as I fist my hands, my planted knees on either side of his hips. "Not until I'm ready. Not until you show me you've earned it."

"*Fuck,*" Konstantin hisses. "Are you always this much of a tease?" His muscles are tense underneath me, his abs flexing with the effort it takes to not thrust upward as I grind against him. His hands shift to my hips, guiding my pace as much as I'll let him.

"Wouldn't you like to know?"

His eyes trace my skin, taking in everything. He doesn't seem to care if my hair's a mess, or that my breasts are probably smaller than the women he's undoubtedly used to being with. He shudders when he watches me sliding over his length, using him to stimulate my clit.

"If you want to be a tease, then you better make sure you come. Because as soon as you do, it's my turn. And I'm not going to be gentle."

Sparks dance up my spine, the friction just as good as his words.

"I'm not the type of man to beg, either," he continues, reaching up to pinch one of my nipples hard enough that my back arches. "But you look so pretty when you're using me. Grinding your clit against my cock. You're incredible."

His words make me gasp, my pace stuttering until the head of his cock notches against my soaked entrance.

Konstantin's hips jerk under me as he holds himself still despite the way his cock twitches.

"Do it, *solnyshka*. Take what you need from me."

I find myself nodding, unable to remember why I shouldn't do exactly that when movement in the corner of my eye steals my attention.

My blood turns to ice, every muscle in my body locking up as the thread of pleasure I'd been pulling unravels in a single movement outside the window.

"What's wrong?" Konstantin asks, his brows furrowed.

Because the man standing outside isn't looking at the glass like it's mirrored. Somehow, he's looking right *at* me. And the way his jaw drops makes it so fucking hard to pretend he's looking at his own reflection.

Konstantin looks to see what I'm staring at, his expression murderous when he glances up at the lights and back at the shocked face of the man outside. All the blood drains from the guy's face when they make eye contact, and between one breath and the next, he turns, storming away like it'll undo the damage that's already been done.

Instinctively, I scramble away from Konstantin and toward my clothes, pulling up my shorts with shaking hands.

Either Konstantin lied to me about no one being able to see in, or he set me up, and I'm not sure which option is worse. He's the one who turned on the lights. He's the one who ambushed me with a studio. But I'm the idiot who stripped for him.

I knew this was a bad idea.

I *knew* it. But did I let that stop me?

"I'm not into exhibitionism." I bite my lip to keep it from wobbling, willing anger to cloud the shame churning in my gut. "Or humiliation. So I hope you got whatever you wanted."

"Nadya."

There's a rustle of him adjusting his clothes, and it only makes me feel even more vulnerable as I yank my shirt over my head.

"Nadya," Konstantin says again, reaching out to touch my hip.

Anger is a gift right now. I forgot it earlier, but I won't forget it again.

"This is why I want my own room," I hiss, forcing my spine straight before I stomp across the room, flicking off the lights.

Sunlight still streams through the windows, but it's still a balm over my raw nerves knowing it's darker inside than it is outside.

"Look at me," he orders, devoid of any gentleness. I let out a humorless laugh.

"And I'm not good enough to have my own studio, anyway. I need somewhere I can take classes. Not be played with like a pawn in your fucked-up mind games."

Konstantin makes a frustrated sound, but I pay him no mind, slamming the door shut as I leave the room. I'll put this whole disaster behind me, but I'm never going to forget myself around Konstantin Lavrov again.

I've heard a hundred stories about the kind of man he is. Someone who can charm as easily as he can pull a gun, flipping between the two in the blink of an eye.

I should have known he'd be no different with me.

Chapter 9

Konstantin

I don't remember the last time I wanted to maim someone as much as I have Yuri over the past twenty-four hours. Because as much as I love watching Nadya's stubbornness in action, my bed was empty last night.

I stayed in the security room for hours, tracking her movements as she hauled her suitcase to the spare room furthest away from my bedroom. I watched her on the cameras when she thought she was alone, wiping her cheeks with an angry frown.

She didn't let me show her all the lilacs I had prepared for her in our room.

She never even gave me the chance to apologize.

No. She hid away, moved the furniture to bar any access to her room, and spent our second night as a married couple hating me.

She didn't answer the door when I knocked this morning. She hasn't so much as looked at me since I made the foolish mistake of turning on the lights, accidentally giving one of Viktor's idiots the opportunity to watch her being so utterly perfect.

It should have been a dream come true.

Instead, I've felt every passing minute in the way my heart races. My hands ache from being clenched into fists so no one can see the way they're shaking.

It's even worse than it was before the wedding.

At least then, I thought there was an end in sight. Now, Nadya feels even further away than she did when I had no clue she existed at all. I feel like I'm going to puke, even when I know she's just down the hall. After she slipped outside at sunrise, circling the house and looking at every window, she retreated to her studio, wielding Spaghetti like a weapon when I tried to approach her.

After all the scars that little hell beast has given me over the years, he's probably more effective at keeping me away from her than anything else in this house. He's more vicious than the shipments of guns waiting for distribution in the home gym.

I don't know what sort of treats Viktor's been slipping him to give him claws sharper than knives, but as much as my fucking anxiety makes my head spin, I don't want to face off against a goddamn cat.

I can't risk him getting confused and going after Nadya when he sees me.

And I'm not sure I trust myself around her when there's still this level of anger simmering under my skin, joining the normal creeping sensation that has me primed to lash out.

"Konstantin? Were you listening to anything I said?" Ivan snaps, his sharp tone telling me it's far from the first time he's tried to get my attention.

"Can't say I was," I answer flippantly. Despite how shitty I feel, I can't help but smirk when he blows out a long breath, his aggravation palpable even through the phone.

He wants me to be the same sort of man my father was when he ran things, but any chance of that happening died years ago. I'll be intimidating and stern when it benefits me, but Ivan doesn't realize there's nothing to be gained from replacing your entire personality with tyranny.

A well-placed threat is as effective when it comes with a friendly smile and a little eye contact as it is with a scowl and a fist to the face. I can crack a joke and laugh with my men, but it changes nothing about the power I command.

Besides, if anyone has an issue with how I carry myself in public, then they likely won't be perceiving me for very long, anyway.

While Ivan's spent years lecturing me, I've spent my time building a reputation. My name alone is enough to make most men turn away and play dumb. No matter how ruffled my lawyer's feathers get, that's not going to change any time soon.

"For fuck's sake, Konstantin," he grouses. I can picture the way he's pinching his temples, like I'm nothing but a headache.

I may not be my father, but I haven't had to flee the country to avoid federal prosecution, either.

Dad was sloppy. I'm not.

Ivan needs to get over himself.

"If it was so important, say it again. And if it makes you feel better, we can pretend it's the first time."

"Why don't you act your age and pay attention to the things around you for once?" he snaps. "I swear, if your father were here, he'd—"

"But he isn't. That motherfucker should have gotten himself killed, but he ran like a coward. He asked me to keep you on as a personal favor, but if I'm too much work, I can find someone else to fill your position." There's a long beat of silence as I glare out the window, keeping an eye on the guards as they change shifts, maneuvering around the truck getting ready to pull away.

"And if you miss Dad so much, you can go back to Moscow and join him. I'm sure my parents would be thrilled to have you."

Instead of only being a legal advisor, Ivan seems to think he's my right-hand man, and I've been allowing his grandiose delusions for longer than I should.

He's nothing to this organization. He's barely anything to *me*. Certainly not important enough to let him talk down to me.

And even though we rarely speak anymore, something tells me my father wouldn't take kindly to Ivan's bullshit, either.

"As I was saying," Ivan eventually continues, suitably chastised for the moment. "There's been noise coming out of Boston. The Irish aren't happy about you getting involved in Chicago."

I roll my eyes.

"I only ended the Russian infighting. I'm sure Trenin and The Outfit will have plenty more to fight over before they're finished."

"The Irish are arms dealers, Konstantin."

"As am I. Your point?"

He huffs out an aggrieved sigh.

"Conflict is good for business. As soon as your connection to Trenin became common knowledge, the other side refused to work with you. Both Bratva and The Outfit. The Irish were hoping the money would funnel straight into their pockets."

I don't bother pointing out that if I hadn't tipped the scales in my new brother-in-law's power struggle, then there wouldn't have been an alliance for them to leverage in the first place.

"And with the Chicago Bratva reunited, I'm sure they'll redouble their efforts against The Outfit as soon as the feds stop sniffing around," I say. "Give it a month, and both the Irish and I will be swimming in money from their little war. I wouldn't be surprised if they already are and simply failed to mention it."

It's not like I've bothered to tell Ivan about most of my business ventures. Why would the Irish? And my spies report to me. Not him.

Whoever is giving him information is likely so low on the food chain that they have no clue what's really happening.

"And how long will it take before that fight upsets your wife and you step in again?"

This is why I don't like Ivan. He's impatient, stubborn, and ambitious. He always wants to jump the gun rather than wait for opportunities to ripen.

Yes, I'm sure the war in Chicago will eventually bring danger back to Alexei's doorstep, but when word trickles back to Nadya, I'll be there, waiting with an ace up my sleeve to keep her right where I need her.

If Liam Dowd is smart, which I suspect he is, he'll expect me to have as many contingency plans in place as I need, and he'll push to get as much money as he can from The Outfit as quickly as possible.

I can always find more money, but a golden opportunity to make Nadya feel indebted to me?

Those don't come along every day.

"If you have something to say regarding my marriage, a word of warning first: you're only going to get one chance, so you better make it count."

For as much as he likes to complain, deep down, Ivan knows there's a reason no one else says a word against me. Dad may have taught me how to wield a threat like a weapon, but he never needed to teach me how to follow through.

And Ivan's going to learn that my wife is off-limits as much as everyone else will. Even to idle gossip and passive criticism.

It's his choice as to how painful the lesson will be.

There's a long beat of silence as he contemplates how far to push, to test the leeway he's been given.

"Fine," he eventually sighs, sounding more concerned than he does annoyed for once. "In that case, you should know Dowd has been trying to shove his foot in the door to get a meeting with you."

"And why on earth does he want that? He sticks to his side of the country, and I'll stick to mine."

Minus Chicago, of course. I'll happily stomp on his toes there. But everywhere else?

"He mentioned something about a missing cousin."

My head falls back against my chair, a wave of tension pounding behind my eyes. "Which cousin?" I ask, already knowing the answer. Because last I heard, Liam Dowd only had one cousin, and he'd happily written him off.

It's the whole reason Viktor gifted him to me.

"Ronan. Why? You know something about him?"

Yeah. I'm the one who blew his brains out.

Fuck. If Viktor didn't do his job and made sure Ronan's body is never found, this is going to be a massive pain in the ass.

"Tell him I'll keep an ear out and let him know if I hear anything," I say, squeezing my eyes shut like it'll keep everything else away. "But while we're on the topic of conversations neither of us want to have, do you still have the number for that pharmaceutical manufacturer?"

"Yes," he answers slowly, the single syllable dripping with hesitation. "But I thought you had no interest in getting back in the drug trade."

I don't.

I have my fingers in more than enough pies, and with the way the feds have been cracking down against drug smuggling, the risk far outweighs any benefit. I'll happily leave the drugs to the cartels and the organizations out east so I can concentrate my focus on where I know how to control the outcome.

They can draw the heat, and I'll lurk in the shadows, scooping up the money left behind when they crash and burn.

"Do me a favor and send over his number, will you?"

"Why the change of heart?"

I shrug to myself. "Don't worry your shiny head about it. As my lawyer, it probably isn't in your best interest to know, anyway." I don't need to see him to know the vein in his forehead is pulsing. "Besides, it's not really any of your business why I do anything."

I keep my inner circle small for a reason, and I'm not interested in including him in it, no matter how much he might wish otherwise.

"Of course, Pakhan," he mutters, bitter resentment dripping from every syllable.

***

"That *motherfucker*!" Nadya all but screams as soon as I open the door to my office.

I can't hold back a smile, taking my time as I follow her voice. Whenever she stops for more than a couple moments, Spaghetti's meows fill the gaps, just as outraged as she is.

His grumbling is far more justified, in my opinion, but he'll get over it.

So will she.

"Is there a problem, wife?" I ask, taking a look around the now-empty bedroom where she slept last night. Well, not entirely empty. Most of the furniture is exactly as she left it.

But the bed's gone.

While she was busy hiding in her studio and exploring the yard, I had movers come and take away every single one. The only room they didn't touch was mine.

If she wants to sleep tonight, her only options are either my bed or the couch.

She shoves past me, rushing down the hall and throwing opening every door.

Spaghetti sits in the middle of the floor, his tail flicking back and forth while his eyes narrow.

"I left your beds," I tell him while Nadya snarls out a sound so visceral my instincts scream to keep my eyes glued on her. "And your cat trees are exactly where you left them. You'll get the big beds back once Nadya gets used to things."

He turns his back to me with the dismissive air only he's able to get away with.

"What the hell did you do?" Nadya asks, her thin frame working hard to take up more space than it actually does as she bears down on me, stabbing her finger in my chest when I turn toward her. "What's your fucking problem?"

Her chest heaves, her nostrils flaring with every breath. Her rage has turned her cheeks a splotchy red that's so endearing I wonder how I've managed to go my whole life without it.

If I thought Nadya in a wedding dress was the best thing I've ever seen, then I was wrong.

It's seeing her angry. I like watching her hands flex, like she's contemplating grabbing a weapon and giving me a taste of my own medicine.

I like seeing her fearless.

Anyone else would back down, bite back their temper, and try to approach me after they'd calmed down. But not Nadya.

It's so much better than the tears she tried to hide last night.

If she's this glorious when she's wrapped up in her anger, I can't wait for the day she forgets herself and falls for me.

"Is there something wrong?" I ask, unable to keep my amusement out of my voice.

"Where did my bed go, Konstantin?"

"Your bed is the same place it was when we got home yesterday. In our bedroom."

"No." She points at the empty space in the middle of the room. "Where is *my* bed?"

I make an exaggerated show of poking my head inside the room and looking around. "Do you mean the bed in the guest room?"

"Yes, you fucking dick," she says, shoving against my chest. I don't move, and somehow, that seems to piss her off even more. "Where's the bed?"

"I did some thinking, and I decided there were too many guest rooms. We'll never have that many people over at once. So, I got rid of them."

"Where the hell am I supposed to sleep?"

Raising a brow, I give her a serious look. "You already know the answer to that, *solnyshka*. You have a perfectly fine bed waiting for you whenever you want it."

"If I have to share it with you, it's far from *fine*."

"If you would set a single foot inside the room, you might change your mind."

"Trust me," she says with a humorless laugh, teeth bared. "I won't."

Carefully, I brush away the hair that's fallen in her face while she's been busy yelling at me, tucking it behind her ear. Even though she looks ready to claw out my eyes with her blunt nails, this is the best part of my day.

If all it takes is removing some furniture to be the sole object of her focus, this house will be empty in a matter of days.

It would be worth it.

"I guess we'll find out, won't we?"

"I'm going to fucking kill you."

"I'd love to see you try," I whisper, leaning close enough my lips brush over her forehead before I press a kiss there, part of me settling for the first time since she fled last night.

Before Yuri showed up, it felt like we were finally getting somewhere. For a few moments, she forgot to hate me.

Nadya lets out a furious sound from the back of her throat and storms away, stomping down the hall and dashing down the stairs so quickly I worry she's going to fall. No sooner does the echo of her studio door slamming shut ring through the house than Viktor comes out of his room, looking around like he's expecting a threat.

"So, what happened to *my* room?" he asks as Spaghetti starts clawing at my shoes. I nudge him away, ignoring the way he glares and stretches up to scratch my calf instead.

"You have your own place," I reply with a shrug. "It's about time you start staying there."

"Come on," he groans. "It's a forty-five-minute drive from here."

"Then sleep at Vasily's."

He grumbles under his breath as I head toward the security room, cracking my neck.

Nadya can hide, but she'll never truly be out of my sight.

I have my work cut out for me, but like hell am I going to back down now. I'll capture my wife's heart one way or another.

CHAPTER 10

Nadya

Despite what Viktor told me, I didn't actually believe Spaghetti slept in a colander until this moment. Curled up on the counter, sleeping without a care in the world, is the same orange cat I've been trying to drag to bed for the past two nights.

The little traitor refuses to act as a buffer between me and Konstantin, and I'm so resentful I'm tempted to make as much noise as possible while I brew my coffee. Why should he get to sleep when I couldn't?

The first night after Konstantin got rid of every bed except his, I camped my happy ass on the couch, fully intent on keeping as much distance between us as I could. Then I woke up next to him anyway, using his shoulder like the world's worst pillow.

Last night I didn't even bother fighting. If he was going to be a *mudak*, the least I could do was make sure I was awake when he touched me.

His pleased grin when he found me already there pissed me off so much I wasn't able to calm down for hours, tossing and turning until the first rays of sunrise filled the room.

But my sleep-deprived brain is stuck staring at Spaghetti, his fat little body curled up like nothing is out of the ordinary. He's so still that I can't resist the urge to reach out and poke his side.

His head shoots up as he makes an annoyed sound, but as soon as he looks around and sees it's just me, he tucks his face under his paw and goes right back to sleep.

"Jerk," I mutter as I turn on the coffee maker, before rummaging through the cabinets in search of a mug. As soon as I pull one out, someone rounds the corner so quickly I nearly drop it to the floor.

I turn slowly, wide awake as I take in the older woman I've never seen before. And despite her salt-and-pepper hair and short stature, she looks as imposing as any of the men I've seen around the property. Her hands are braced on her hips, and her eyes are so sharp it's like she's skinning me down to the marrow of my bones.

Between one blink and the next, her expression shifts from the kind of thunderous that makes me want to hide, to smiling at me like I'm a dream come true.

I can't decide which option makes me more uncomfortable before she rushes toward me, using a strength I wouldn't have expected to pry the coffee mug from my hand.

"What are you doing?" she demands, shoving the mug back in the cabinet without so much as a glance.

"Making coffee?" It comes out more as a question than a statement.

"What about breakfast?" she asks, rushing around the kitchen to rip open cabinets and pull pots and pans out, setting them on the stove. "You're going to give yourself ulcers if you don't eat first. I won't have it."

Without hesitating, she pours the coffee down the sink, ignoring my protests.

This feels worse than anything else that's happened this week. Maybe it's the sleep deprivation, or maybe it's the accumulation of everything, but I'm close to tears as I whisper, "I really needed that." My shoulders slump while she flows through the kitchen like water, passing me with effortless determination as she pulls out everything she needs to make a full breakfast.

"No. You need to *eat*," she says, looking me up and down. I have to resist the urge to pull down the hem of the tank top I changed into before I escaped Konstantin's bedroom. "If something happens to you, Konstantin's going to die alone, and I can't have that."

"I actually think that would be more than acceptable," I mumble, more to myself than anything else.

"And if I want to see any babies running around this house before I die, it's my duty to make sure you're healthy enough to bear them. Coffee won't help."

My cheeks flame. "Who said anything about babies?" I squeak. Definitely not me. And as far as I'm aware, neither has Konstantin.

Would I like to have a child? Sure. Eventually. In some distant future so far away I can't picture it clearly. But Konstantin and I don't even know each other. Hell, I can barely stand being in a room with him.

"I did," she answers without shame, leveling me with a serious look as she cracks an egg over a pan. "He's forty-one. If Konstantin's going to have the energy to chase after his children, you two need to get a move on."

I jolt, both at her words and at the realization that I had no clue how old Konstantin is.

Forty-one. Thirteen years older than me.

No wonder he was so good the other night. He probably has more experience in bed than I ever will. I grab the lip of the counter behind me, the heat in my cheeks drifting lower as I shake my head, banishing the image of him using all that experience with me again.

"As much as I appreciate the thought," I say with a strained smile, gesturing toward the spot where Spaghetti's still sleeping in his makeshift bed, "Konstantin seems to have his hands full with the cat. I think we're a long way off from having any babies."

There's a long beat of silence before she pulls the food off the stove and looks at me gravely.

"Spaghetti is a little idiot who once tried to drink from a pot of boiling water. If Konstantin has managed to keep him alive this long, then you'll only ease his burden, and a baby will be no problem."

Before I can point out that a child would try to do the same thing, Viktor strolls in with another man behind him, yawning.

Jesus, are all men on this side of the country giants made of pure muscle, or is there something in the water? Because this guy is even taller than Viktor, but he lacks the easygoing charm that forces you to lower your defenses. No one else seems surprised to see him, but I find myself standing a little straighter, ready to put distance between us if I have to.

"Don't badger her, Tatiana," Viktor scolds, the effect of his sharp words softened as he smiles affectionately. It drops the moment he reaches for the coffee maker. "Don't tell me there's no coffee," he whines. "Konstantin already got rid of my bed. Are you *trying* to kill me?"

Tatiana looks back at me, her face showing signs of exhaustion that weren't there when she first appeared.

"I've already given up hope for this one. If I want to see any Lavrov babies, you're my last hope."

The other man chuckles under his breath as Viktor grins.

"Aw, come on. I'm a delight."

"You're something, Viktor, but *delight* isn't the right word."

Viktor rolls his eyes. "Nadya, ignore her. She's worked for the family longer than I've been alive. She's so old she doesn't know what she's saying anymore."

Tatiana shoves a plate of eggs at me, somehow prepared exactly the way I like them. I take it from her more because I don't know what else to do. Despite my hunger, the presence of the stranger and all the talk about babies have taken away my desire to actually eat.

As much as I want to run away from all of them, I don't. I shut up and force myself to eat my eggs while Viktor brews a new pot of coffee, alternating between batting off Tatiana and glaring at the man he walked in with.

At least the food is delicious.

"It's your fault she doesn't like me anymore," Viktor bemoans.

The other man shrugs, seeming amused. Well, as amused as someone who carries an air of menace like a club draped over his shoulders can be.

"If lying to yourself helps you get through the day, then think whatever you want," he says, his deadpan voice telling me they've likely had this conversation more than once. Which is the kind of thing I might know if I had any clue who the hell he is, or even who Tatiana is, but their banter carries a level of familiarity I don't feel comfortable interrupting, so I keep quiet.

If I grabbed Spaghetti and slipped away, would they even notice? Could I use this as a chance to wander outside and take one of the cars so I can start exploring the city?

I put my mostly empty plate next to the sink, hoping Tatiana isn't offended when she notices, and slowly start shifting away.

"Vasily, I'm glad you're here."

Konstantin struts into the room, freezing me in place. He looks like sin as he adjusts his cufflinks. The tattoos on the back of his hands flex with the motion, stealing my focus until I force myself to look away.

He might be pretty, but he's still an asshole.

Who the hell gets rid of every bed in the house? If he hadn't let his guard see me naked, then he could have had me in his bed willingly. Hell, if he'd apologized, maybe I'd consider it. But not giving me a choice?

Risking a quick glance in his direction, I scowl when I find Konstantin smirking back at me.

"Nadya, I was thinking about what you said the other day. So, meet your new bodyguard." In an instant, both Viktor and the other man, Vasily, are staring at him with as much frustration as I'm feeling. Konstantin's narrowed gaze cuts off any protests before they can be heard.

"I don't need a bodyguard." My protest is promptly ignored when Konstantin pins Viktor with a look, snagging the cup of coffee he'd just finished making for himself and dumping it down the sink.

"This way, we're both miserable if anything happens."

Ignoring Viktor's venomous look as well as Tatiana's pleased smile, Konstantin strides over to me.

I don't want to deal with him. I'd much rather ask Vasily what he thinks of this arrangement, but before I can find out, Konstantin's hands frame my face and pull me into a kiss, taking away all the anger fermenting in my gut with a simple brush of his lips against mine.

When I try to pull away, his hand slides to the back my neck to stroke his fingers against my hairline, ignoring the way I bare my teeth.

"Take him and find a pottery class, Nadya. If you'll excuse me, I have to get my handsome ass back to work."

"Who called you handsome?" I can't stop myself from asking. "Because it wasn't me."

His answering smirk makes my insides squirm.

"Not in words, but your thoughts are loud, *solnyshka*."

I want to smack the satisfied look off his face, but he turns before I can so much as lift a finger.

"Viktor, a word?"

Viktor stomps after him, shooting Vasily an aggrieved look before he leaves. With a small smile, Tatiana starts cleaning the dishes, leaving me with Vasily, who's still glaring at the spot where Konstantin was standing.

"Hi," I say, hoping it'll defuse the tension pouring off him in waves. "It's nice to meet you."

Vasily blinks at me before he sighs, turning toward the front door.

"C'mon," he grunts, leaving me behind to chase after him, rushing to grab a pair of shoes and my purse before he makes it to the door. "If the boss says we're going out, then we're going out."

"Have a good day!" Tatiana calls after us.

I close my eyes, silently wishing I'd been able to steal a sip of coffee before he stormed away.

Chapter 11

Konstantin

Viktor isn't just my brother, he's the only person I trust with my life. He'll always have my back, and I'll always have his. He's been with me through thick and thin, and he's the closest thing I have to a friend, even on the days we can't stand each other.

He's also a pain in my ass when he doesn't get his way.

"Why Vasily?" he whines, lying down on my couch and kicking his feet up against the back, no doubt dirtying up the leather with his disgusting boots. "He has a daughter, man."

"One he no doubt wants to go home to," I tell him, refusing to take the bait. "Nadya wants to take pottery classes, and I want her to come home to me. As long as that happens, we all win. I don't know what you're complaining about."

He gives me a look that bears no weight after a lifetime of putting up with his shit.

"Is this because I won't hand you Yuri?"

I don't bother to answer, tapping a pen on my desk until he sighs.

"Come on, Konstantin. He's been my friend since we were in kindergarten. It isn't his fault you left the lights on."

"But he didn't turn around. That *is* his fault."

This isn't all about Yuri ruining the other night, but I'm not about to tell Viktor that.

I want Vasily as Nadya's guard because he's loyal. And as much as he doesn't want to disappoint me, he wants to disappoint Viktor even less. He'll keep Nadya safe because he refuses to let either of us down.

He has too much to lose to accept failure, and I can't say the same about most other men.

Also, I enjoy pissing off my brother. It's one of the few joys I'm free to partake in.

Viktor curses under his breath, turning his head away. "You're a dick, you know that?"

So I've been told.

"If you're done whining, I had an interesting conversation with Ivan the other day."

That perks him up significantly.

As little as I like dealing with Ivan, Viktor likes him even less. Not that I can blame him. The only reason I tolerate him as much as I do is because I don't want to deal with Dad's lecture if I fire him. But he's even more judgmental of Viktor than he is of me, and my brother would like nothing more than to give him a taste of his own medicine.

"Yeah? What did the old coot have to say for himself this time? Is the weather making his joints ache? Did he get too deep in his cups and have a vision of the horrors to come?" He snorts at his own joke while I roll my eyes.

"Rumor has it Liam Dowd isn't happy that I refused to let Nikita and Alexei kill each other."

Viktor blinks, raising a brow while I scour his expression, searching for any sign he knew how bad capturing Ronan could be for my entire operation. He was drunk when we were celebrating, but did he get so caught up in his excitement that he failed to take proper precautions before he kidnapped a rival arms dealer's family off the streets?

But he gives me nothing. Nothing to make me think he fucked up, and nothing to make me think he did his job properly.

"Yeah, I don't see how that's supposed to be our problem."

"Me either. But apparently he wants to meet with me over a missing cousin of his." I want to trust my brother. I want to tell myself he wouldn't take my faith and run with it. But trust without evidence is a risk I don't want to take.

Viktor goes stock-still, his nostrils flaring as he takes a deep breath. "Who's his cousin?"

My silence is the only answer I'm willing to give, even when he sits up, burying his face in his hands with a groan.

The only reason I was willing to accept Viktor's gift was because he assured me he'd been disowned. But if Liam's looking into his disappearance, then he didn't have the information he claimed to.

This is the basic background work Viktor's known how to do since before he could do long division. Even if Ronan had been some low-level thug that was no different from anyone else, Viktor should have made sure no one would miss him.

"Tell me you did a thorough job of disposing of the body," I practically beg. "Tell me this isn't going to come crashing back on us."

"I know how to do my job," he snaps, his eyes sharp. "If, and I fucking mean *if*, they manage to find enough of him to identify, they won't be able to trace it back to us. Liam will spend his time chasing his own tail. We'll be fine."

If he were anyone else, I might believe him. The problem is, the same man that trained Viktor how to conceal his true thoughts taught me. It's a vulnerability that was systematically beaten out of us almost as soon as we were able to walk.

Even if I'm positive he's bolstering for my own benefit as much as anything else, I have no way of proving it.

But I know my brother.

He runs a hand through his hair, revealing his worry as his heel bounces on the floor.

He needs to clean up this mess on his own. The risk of it blowing up is too high, and I'm not in a good place to be caught up in it. Not when I'm trying to win Nadya over and get her settled in.

But I don't particularly want to leave him feeling like shit until everything is handled, either.

Was my bachelor party Viktor's idea? Yes. Could I have put my foot down and asked questions before we got to this point? Also yes.

But I didn't.

And if it all goes to hell, I'll step in to protect him. The only thing that makes this different from every other time things have gone south is that, for the first time, I have someone else to look after, too.

I promised Alexei I'd protect Nadya, but that isn't why I want to protect her. It's because the thought of anyone hurting her has me seeing red.

"Why did you bring Vasily over, anyway?" I eventually ask.

The corner of his mouth twitches upward for the first time all morning, popping the tension around us with the small movement.

"You're the one who told me to stay at his place." He shrugs. "Besides, I was gonna steal your wife and drive her around town. I figured showing her another friendly face might cheer her up."

I frown. Viktor isn't the type of man who would lift a finger to help anyone, not even his new sister-in-law, and Vasily is the last person anyone would describe as a *friendly face*.

"Also, we have dinner plans tonight, and I figured she wouldn't ask me to stay if she knew she was holding up our date."

Ah. There's the obnoxious ass I know.

"And who's watching Kira?" I ask.

Vasily's daughter, Kira, is as sweet as a five-year-old can get, and when he isn't working, he's glued to her side. Then again, so is Viktor. Somehow, he forgets how to be a selfish prick when he's around her, tripping over himself to cater to her every giggling whim.

"With his ex. It's her week." He spreads his arms out over the back of the couch, and grins like he's already settled on a plan and ready to go back to being himself.

Good. I don't like dealing with his emotions any more than I like dealing with my own.

Things are easier when he's happy and relaxed.

"Which means," he says, drawing out the word, "as soon as Vasily gets back here with your wife, I'm taking him back to his place so we can fuck like rabbits."

Sighing, I pinch my temples while I try to think of anything other than my brother having sex. The next shipment of firearms I'm supposed to deliver to Vegas. The trouble the cartels have been causing with the police. The odds of Viktor learning anything about boundaries.

"Didn't need to know, but thanks."

***

I'm not particularly skilled at wooing women, and until recently, I was never interested in learning. Power, good looks, and money will get you a long way as far as most women are concerned.

But I'm rapidly learning that Nadya isn't most women. She knows what she wants, and no matter who I am or how much money I have, I don't have it.

I have a gorgeous home, and all she has to say about it is that my decor is boring. I bought her a whole wardrobe before our wedding, but she's still living out of the two suitcases she brought with her, picking through cut-off shorts and T-shirts like they're designer. I built a studio for her, but the only thing she's said to me in two days is that she needs to find somewhere to take classes before she makes any use of any of it.

And even though she wants nothing to do with me, she slept in my bed willingly last night.

Sure, she ignored the flowers. And, sure, she used the throw pillows to erect a wall between us and tossed and turned restlessly all night. But it was the best night I've ever had, regardless of how little I slept.

Nadya is both a marvel and a mystery. And if she likes me, keeping her close will be so much easier than it will be if she's ready to take a knife to my balls whenever we're in the same room.

When I manage to track down Tatiana, she's in the security room, one eye glued to the monitors, and the other focused on her knitting. It isn't unusual to find her flitting from one task to the next, scurrying through the house like a bird.

If everyone I employ had her work ethic, I'd be unstoppable.

Tatiana worked as a maid for my father before he was even married, and as much as my mother attempted to make up for Dad's coldness, Tatiana was always the one we'd actually turn to for comfort.

When he left the country, she insisted on staying with Viktor and me.

She's the glue that holds this household together.

If Tatiana would let me, I'd make sure she never has to lift a finger, but she's the type of stubborn that refuses to sit idly and enjoy anything without working for it.

She doesn't bother glancing in my direction before she shakes her head with a sigh.

"I don't think your wife is too impressed with you," she says. "It hasn't even been a week, and I'd go so far as to say she already hates you." I take the empty seat next to her, scanning the monitors, flicking from one camera to the next.

Her knitting needles click together, a rhythm that's been a constant soundtrack throughout my life, softening her disappointment. Despite telling anyone who will listen that she's nothing more than my maid and cook, Tatiana has been more of a parent to Viktor and me than either of our actual parents ever were.

She was always the one we'd run to after waking from a nightmare inspired by violent scenes we were exposed to far too young. She's the one who held me after I walked in on Dad scrubbing blood from the floor when I was seven.

He squeezed my chin so hard it bruised and told me to keep my fucking mouth shut.

Tatiana held my hand until I fell asleep every night for a month.

"She should join the club, then. I'll let her know you're in charge of collecting dues," I reply.

She shoots me a weary look, the lines at the corner of her eyes looking deeper than usual.

"What are you doing with her, Kostya? That girl is too sweet for you."

"You only say that because you haven't seen the knife she hides under her pillow." I shrug. "She has a spine of steel. It'd be a mistake to underestimate her because she's polite."

"And don't think I missed the way she looked at you at the wedding." Tatiana's eyes bore into the side of my head, but I refuse to look at her. Instead, I keep searching the monitors, squinting at every face, but not finding the one I want. "Nadya didn't choose you, did she?"

From the way her shoulders slump, I can tell my smile doesn't ring true. Tatiana knows me almost as well as Viktor does. Try as I might, I've never been able to keep a secret from her. And no matter what I've done to become the man I am, she still views me with the same rose-tinted glasses she always has.

Seeing her look like I've failed for forcing Nadya to marry me is a heavy burden, and I'm not sure I'm ready to add it to everything else I need to carry.

"No," I confess. "She didn't. But I'm hoping that in time, she will."

I need her to if I want to keep the restless lashing of my soul at bay.

I've done monstrous things to the rest of the world, but I don't want Nadya to see me that way. I want her to relax when I walk into the room. I want her to run to me instead of away. I want her to give me the tender looks I've seen her give Spaghetti.

I flinch when Tatiana pats my cheek, an affectionate gesture I haven't been on the receiving end of since I was an out-of-control teen.

"You're a sweet boy. Too good for this life of yours, you know."

She couldn't be more wrong, but I won't be the one to point it out to her. If Tatiana wants to think I'm something more than I am, I'll never stop her.

Her delusions are a kindness I don't deserve, but I'm too selfish to deny myself.

Besides, she's borne witness to enough of my life to have a sense of the full picture if she wants it.

It doesn't matter how hard I fought against becoming who I am now, at the end of the day, I'm still no better than the violent brute my father wanted me to be. If anything, I'm worse.

At some point, the child who shook and cried whenever he was forced to watch another bloody execution or interrogation was killed and left where no one will ever find him. I buried him under drugs and alcohol in my twenties, tried to erase him with numbness in my thirties, and now I'm distracting myself from his memory by forcing a woman into a marriage she doesn't want.

"Spend time with your wife. Try to show her who you are underneath everything else. Get to know her, and let her do the same." She turns back to her knitting, a small smile on her face. "If you give her time, she'll learn to love you."

"You think so?"

Tatiana snorts. "If she doesn't, she's as stupid as your cat. He's the only one that doesn't."

I laugh, even though I shouldn't. "Don't let Nadya hear you calling him stupid. I think she's becoming attached to the little idiot." I smile, recalling the panicked look on her face when he sprinted out of the bedroom last night, scrambling to catch him before he could escape.

She seemed to think he'd stick around to separate us.

Spaghetti would rather puke on my pillow than sleep in my room.

"Oh, you poor boy," Tatiana croons. "I take it back. If Nadya likes that monster, then she's a lost cause. Send her home and tell her to take Spaghetti with her. We'll all be better off."

I lean closer to the wall of screens, squinting to make sure I'm really seeing who I think I am.

"Oh, and speaking of the cat," she continues, "when I took him to the vet last week, they said we needed to put him on a diet, so I bought him some different food." Her eyes narrow into a sharp glare. "That means you need to stop giving him treats."

"Sure, Tatiana," I say with a wave of my hand. "You should take the night off. I think I'll make dinner and spend a romantic evening with my wife."

Not waiting for a reply, I storm toward the front door, my fists clenched as I throw it open.

"Yuri!" I shout.

All noise in the yard ceases immediately, the men standing at attention like they've been trained to. They won't interfere. Most of them don't even glance in Yuri's direction, careful not to draw my ire.

He freezes by the front gate, looking around like he can't make up his mind whether to escape or not. But as I draw closer, he only lifts his chin, standing with his spine straight.

Good. We both know he wouldn't make it far, anyway.

Chapter 12
Nadya

It's my first time exploring the city, and somehow, I'm already sick of San Francisco. In fact, if I wasn't so exhausted and defeated, I'd ask Vasily to turn the car around and take me back to the house so I could try to sleep this terrible day off.

But as it stands, he'll probably keep up his silent stoic-and-miserable routine, and I'll only end up feeling even worse when he ignores me entirely.

So far, our conversation has consisted of Vasily grumbling and making hand gestures, until I finally took the hint and put the address of where I wanted to go in the GPS. But I didn't know I would be setting out on this grand adventure, so the only pottery studios we've stopped at have been the few I managed to find in the midst of panicked Google searches.

The small amount of optimism I was clinging to that finding a new studio would be easy was dashed at the first place we went to. The unhelpful woman who greeted me was happy to let me know about their classes, but she was just as eager to let me know how long their waitlist is.

I'd have to wait five months before I could even sign up.

The second studio was even worse.

Apparently everyone in the state is trying to take pottery classes, and they're all determined to find somewhere within an hour of Konstantin's house to do it.

Vasily's been driving for ages, and between the anxiety from being in a new city, the traffic, and the stress of two disappointments in a row, I'm almost ready to hop out of the car and walk around until I find something to do to that doesn't make me feel like I'm going to lose my mind.

But Vasily would probably chase after me, and then Konstantin would be an overbearing prick as soon as we got back to the house, and we'd end up having an argument that I, frankly, don't have the energy for right now.

So I sit in the car, stuck in yet another wave of bumper-to-bumper traffic that makes me want to scream.

In retrospect, it was probably only sheer luck that I was able to find a studio straight away in Chicago. It was even luckier that I managed to click with the instructor on my first lesson.

Though, now I wonder how much my last name had to do with it.

I never tried to leverage either Alexei or his connections for anything, but how many people in Chicago are named Trenin? And how many more people are willing to bend a few rules or make a spot in a class available if it means keeping Alexei off their back?

Probably more than I want to think about.

But across the country, my name means nothing. Hell, it means less than nothing, because my name isn't even Trenina anymore. I'm supposed to be Nadya Lavrovna, and I have no clue who the hell that's supposed to be.

All I want to do is waltz my happy ass into Alexei's condo and bother him, or hunt him down at one of his clubs and assure myself that he's staying out of trouble, but that's thoroughly off the table.

If Konstantin won't let me sleep in a different room or even leave the house without one of his thugs, something tells me a trip home is out of the question.

Unable to tolerate any more silence, I look at Vasily while he glares at the road in front of us like it's personally offended him.

"Konstantin said your name is Vasily?"

"Yep," he answers shortly. I wait for him to say more, but he seems as thrilled as I am to be stuck here.

"Have you worked for him long?"

"A while."

If we were to get in a crash, I wonder what would be more likely to break: the window, or his thick skull. Part of me thinks the poor window wouldn't stand a chance.

Another agonizing mile passes, only broken up by the GPS proudly announcing our next turn, and if I had any clue where we were, I'd get out and walk back on my own.

Screw what Konstantin would have to say about it. That sounds like a problem for him to deal with, not me.

"Do you have any idea why Konstantin's forcing you to deal with me?"

"Presumably because Viktor delights in pissing him off, and since I'm fucking his brother, I tend to be at the boss's house more often than he'd like," Vasily says with as much gusto as someone announcing they've discovered the sky is blue. My brain skips like a record, and it takes me longer than it should to comprehend what he said.

"I'm sorry, I thought we were still at the awkward-silence stage of this relationship. Not blurting out that you're fucking my brother-in-law."

"Listen, it's not my fault Konstantin didn't tell you. And it's not like I told you how big his dick is." He shakes his head, amused with himself. "Besides, I'm going to go out on a limb and say you're fucking my boyfriend's brother, so"—he lifts a single shoulder—"it's only fair."

I blink at him, torn between shock that he's said so much, and amusement because I think he might actually be joking. And that clashes with the serious, grumpy persona he's been showing off all morning.

"That said, if you could refrain from telling me anything about my boss's dick, I'd take it as a personal favor." His face scrunches up as he thinks. "Actually, you know what? Let's forget this whole conversation. I don't even know why I said anything."

More than anything else today, his palpable disgust allows me to relax, laughing until my stomach hurts.

"Oh, man. I think we're going to get along just fine, Vasya."

He narrows his eyes, glancing between me and the road in equal measure.

"Vasya?"

"Yeah. I need a friend here. And since you decided we're close enough to talk about our sex lives—"

"I just said we shouldn't, actually."

I give him a look that has him sitting straighter in his seat. "If we can talk about our sex lives, then we're close enough for nicknames."

He shakes his head, clearly not agreeing with me, but he doesn't try to argue, either and I'll take that tiny victory for what it is.

"So," he says, taking a turn. "Why're we going to so many pottery places, anyway? Were the first two not good enough, or what?"

My smile falters, the tiny boost to my mood fading as quickly as it came on.

"I'd take lessons from a guy in a back alley if I had to, but he'd probably have a months-long waitlist, too." I sigh. "The least they could have done was mention it on their websites so I didn't waste your time," I mutter.

If this last place doesn't have any openings, I don't have it in me to go to a fourth. And if they have an even longer waitlist than the last two places—which, as I look around at the high-scale businesses and shops around us as the distance on the GPS ticks down, seems pretty damn likely—I'll have to ask Vasya to drive all the way back to one of the other studios before we finally go back to the house.

And even then, neither of them offered extended courses. I'd only take a single class before I have to do this song and dance all over again.

My shoulder slump.

Maybe if I look up tutorials online I can scrape by until I find my footing and build my confidence. I was just hoping for more guidance before I got to that point.

By the time Vasily stops the car, idling in the middle of the road despite the angry driver honking behind him, I'm resigned to my fate of leading myself through the dark and hoping nothing explodes when it goes in the kiln.

I'm about to open my door so he can safely circle the block when he puts a hand on my shoulder, holding me in place.

"Hold on a second," he says, pulling out his phone.

He taps the screen a few times, then looks through the studio windows. It isn't until the guy in the car behind us sticks his head out his window, using more colorful language than the situation demands, that Vasily finally nods for me to go ahead.

I hurry to get out before the guy decides to escalate things, peeking through the window before I head inside.

Sunlight streams through the windows at the front of the shop, making the dark green walls and wicker furniture seem cozy instead of suffocating. It's a welcome balance between the all-white everything of Konstantin's house and the busy, cluttered vibe of the other studios.

As soon as I walk through the door, the woman at the front desk hangs up the phone and greets me with a bright smile.

"Hi, can I help you?"

"I was wondering if you have any spots open in any of your classes?" I ask, plastering a smile over my brittle confidence. "I just moved to town, and I didn't see anything that said you guys were booked out on your website."

The corners of her eyes tighten slightly, and my shoulders slump as I brace for yet another failure. I'm about to apologize and back out before she can dismiss me when her eyes dart around the desk, glancing between the computer and the phone repeatedly before she finally looks back at me.

"Give me a second, and I'll check. What's your name?"

"Nadya." I force a grin, feeling like a fraud when I say, "Nadya Lavrovna."

The woman stills, losing all interest in her perusal of their calendar. "You know what?" she asks, "We just had a cancellation. If you'd like, I can get you signed up for one class, or we can do a six-week trial and then go right into a three-month course."

Her overly bright smile makes me glance over my shoulder suspiciously. Vasya's still waiting in the car out front, stone-faced as he ignores the man now pounding on his window, his face red as he shouts obscenities and empty threats at someone twice his size.

"Or we can do a year," she rushes to add. "Whatever's best for you."

"On your website it said you guys only offered three-month reservations."

"We're trying something new," she replies a beat later than she should. "In fact, you can join us for our class this afternoon if you'd like."

"Right." I sigh. "And I'm sure the phone call you took before I walked in had nothing to do with it."

Her eyes are so wide it's a wonder they aren't popping out of her skull. If her palpable fear didn't make me uncomfortable, it might even be funny. Instead, I'm torn between relief that I've finally found a place I can keep learning, and anger that Vasily went behind my back to pull strings.

"Absolutely not." Her voice is reed thin, trembling almost as much as she is.

I don't know who Vasily texted before he let me out of the car, but I have a sinking suspicion my husband has something to do with this. Whether I'm going to strangle or kiss him for it remains to be seen, but either way, I won't make it this poor woman's problem.

I sign up for the three-month course.

And even though I'm frustrated, I'm still smiling when I walk outside, hurrying to the car before someone calls the cops on Vasily.

Chapter 13

Konstantin

My phone pings with a text as soon as Vasily's car pulls through the gate. I run a hand through my hair, tossing the towel I've been using to keep things clean over my shoulder while I give everything one last check.

Dinner's ready, the candles in the den are lit, and I'm wearing the same pants I was wearing when I caught Nadya staring at my ass yesterday.

She was ready to spit fire when she realized I caught her, but I can't wait for another chance to rile her up. I'm just hoping I'll be able to ease her in and have her tell me about her day before she brings out the claws.

I pull a bottle out of the wine cellar just as the front door closes.

Vasily texted me updates every time they stopped, but it did nothing to ease my nerves. According to him, Nadya seemed upset. Not just frustrated, or overwhelmed, but near tears.

Nadya is many things, but easily defeated is not one of them. Even before our wedding she seemed more angry than she did sad.

Though, from what he told me when they stopped to explore town for a while, she cheered up considerably after I made a quick phone call.

Hopefully she hasn't managed to totally lose track of that happiness.

As I near the entryway, Nadya's lilting, melodic laugh nearly cuts me to my knees. I watch as she grins at Vasily as he helps her carry her bags inside.

Seeing her happy does something I can't explain to my insides, drawing them tight and cutting them loose at the same time. I've never seen her laugh like this, not even when she was with her friend at our reception.

But seeing it directed at another man—knowing that if she ever realized how much I enjoy her quiet brand of joy, she'd go out of her way to hide it from me—sours the feeling before I get a chance to enjoy it.

Like the little hellcat she is, Nadya turns, her smiles dropping the moment she sees me. A throb of pain overwhelms me before I'm able to suppress it.

Nadya can cling to her anger for a little while longer, but after tonight, I'm putting an end to it. She's going to learn to like being here. She's going to learn to like *me*.

Maybe, eventually, she'll learn to love me.

Huh. I like the thought of that.

"Did you have a good day, wife?"

She looks back at Vasily, but he's busy being exactly what he is—a good soldier. Ready to be used at a moment's notice, seen and not heard when he isn't needed.

His back is straight, feet planted firmly, and one hand clasps the opposite wrist as he waits to be dismissed. His eyes are on me, and for the life of me, I can't figure out how someone like him managed to make Nadya laugh as freely as she was when they walked inside.

Her shoulders slump as she looks at him.

"Yeah," she mutters dryly. "It was great."

"Good." I nod at Vasily. "Take off for the night. I'll see you tomorrow," I tell him, shifting my full attention to Nadya. I didn't get a chance to fully appreciate her this morning. Between antagonizing Viktor and trying to make her happy for once, I was distracted.

It was a mistake.

One I don't intend to make again.

Her shorts only highlight her long legs, and even when she's wearing a bright yellow tank top and flip-flops, she makes being beautiful more effortless than a model ever could.

"Have dinner with me," I say, tearing my eyes away from all that soft skin as I remember the way her thighs squeezed me tight while I drove myself inside her. With a hand against the small of her back, I urge her forward, ignoring the way she grumbles and tries to twist away from me.

All her fighting ceases the moment we make it to the living room.

Dinner is plated up and waiting on the coffee table, there's a movie queued up on the television, and candles are set up strategically to cast the room in a romantic light that I'm hoping will put her at ease.

"Is that *Brother Orchid*?" she asks when she tears her eyes away from the television, eyeing me with a skepticism that feels undeserved. When I nod, she rushes forward, throwing herself on the couch as she grabs the remote.

"I take it you're a fan?"

The way she looks at me almost makes me squirm, a feat no one else has been able to achieve in decades. She's both skeptical and cautiously happy, like she isn't sure if she's allowed to be or not.

"It's my favorite," she admits reluctantly.

"That so?" I ask, as if I didn't spend longer than any sane man should scouring everything on every social media profile she has. I want to find the keys to her heart, and Alexei refused to answer my texts.

With a nonchalant shrug, I say, "I thought you might enjoy dinner and a movie. Though, I have to warn you, I gave Tatiana the night off, so if the food isn't up to par, the blame lies solely with me."

Nadya snorts, folding her legs over each other and pulling a plate into her lap.

"I also wanted to apologize for the other night."

She freezes with a fork halfway to her mouth. The only sign of life is the way her eyes turn deadly at the reminder of what happened. My hand aches when I flex it at my side, the skin split from giving Yuri a black eye and a broken nose.

If I'd had my way, I would have plucked his eyes from his head, but as much as I like annoying Viktor, I don't want to deliberately push him into walking away from me. I had no choice but to settle for wounding the prick for now.

But if I ever see him on my property again, that could very well change.

With a fixed jaw, Nadya turns away from me.

"Did you do it on purpose?" she asks, tone harder than I've ever heard it before. "Did you set me up?"

"Did I do it on *purpose*?" Anger brews in my gut, harsh and untampered. All I wanted was to see her. I wanted to see how far down her chest her blush went. I wanted to learn every reaction Nadya has so I could wield her pleasure the way she deserves.

And when I saw Yuri, all I wanted was to see him dead.

"You're my wife," I hiss. "No one should ever see you that way except me. I had a lapse in judgment in turning on the lights, and I'm sorry for it. I really am, but *solnyshka*, I would never share you like that. Especially not with some twerp my brother demands I keep around in the name of his own nostalgia."

I run a hand through my hair, grinding my teeth as I say, "No, Nadya. I didn't do it on purpose. It was a mistake. One I have no intention of repeating, and if you ever see that man again, all you need to do is mention it. I've already made it clear to him that he's no longer welcome here, and if he forgets, he won't get to make that mistake again."

With a heavy sigh, I sit next to her, barely noticing when she doesn't flinch away. She keeps our staring contest up while I wonder how I've already managed to lose control of this evening.

Nadya frowns down at her plate, poking at it with her fork.

"You shouldn't talk about your employees that way," she eventually huffs before inhaling a bite like she's starved. Her eyes slip closed, her head falling back as she chews.

My jaw flexes as she sinks into the couch, digging into her dinner like I'm not even here. But even though I want her attention to be on me, watching her is nearly as enjoyable. I find myself staring as she presses play on the remote, ignoring me in favor of the movie.

"Yuri is Viktor's employee," I say, more to myself than anything else. "Not mine."

She hushes me, waving her hand in my direction with her attention rapt on the television. Smiling to myself, I take the second plate, but it might as well be flavorless compared to the wide array of emotions playing across Nadya's face. From private smiles, to a captivating sadness for the characters on the screen.

Every emotion is written plain as day, making my heart lurch in my chest when she frowns as the credits roll.

"I've always hated the ending," Nadya says with a sigh. At some point, she relaxed and ended up curled into a ball, laying her head on a pillow and resting her feet in my lap.

I work my thumbs up and down her claves in a slow massage, taking full advantage of her distraction.

"But he was happy at the monastery."

"Yeah," she sighs. "But I liked the romance. Even though I've seen it a dozen times, I always want Sarto to fight for Flo. I want to see him give up his whole life for *her*, not his own fulfillment. I want them to move past the toxicity and choose each other."

"But what if they were happier without each other?"

"What if they weren't?"

Nadya doesn't look at me, but she relaxes marginally, stretching her arms above her head, her shirt riding up to expose a sliver of her stomach. When she doesn't immediately tug it back down, it feels like a small victory.

"Thank you for all this," she says so softly I wonder if I'm hallucinating.

"Any time."

When she sits up, I brace for her to pull away and leave the room. I expect her to be so caught up in her own stubbornness that she'd rather leave me alone than accept a small act of kindness. Instead, she pulls her feet out of my lap and scootches closer, until her shoulder brushes mine.

"Did you call any of the pottery studios I went to?" she asks quietly.

For a moment, I consider lying. I don't want to lose the little progress we've made by confirming every miserable thought she has about me. But I dismiss the thought as soon as it's there.

I won't insult her intelligence by pretending she doesn't know what kind of man I am. The least I can do is use some of my weight to make her life a little more bearable.

"If I'd known you were going to have problems, I would have called the one closest to home first," I admit, unable to focus on anything but the heat of her arm scorching through my shirt.

"I would've been mad if you did," she says with a shrug that makes my skin buzz in a way that's so different from what I'm used to. Instead of wanting to crawl away from it, I want to lean into the sensation.

"Why's that?"

"The studio you called was the coolest of all the ones I went to. The instructors at the other two?" She scoffs, shaking her head. "They were assholes. Even though the girl at the last studio was scared shitless, she was polite. She didn't treat me like I didn't matter. Even before she knew my last name."

The thought of her using my last name sends a shot of pleasure through my chest, effusing my whole body with a lightness that feel foreign. It's the kind of feeling one could become addicted to if they aren't careful.

I'm not sure I want to be careful.

By bits and measures, Nadya relaxes until she once again has her legs sprawled over my lap, leaning into me while I run my fingers through her hair while she tells me about going shopping with Vasily. She complains about the traffic, the fact that Vasily didn't let her pay, the impatient *mudak* they encountered on the street.

She talks until her words are nothing more than a low whisper and her glares and bitterness are packed away for the night. Until her muscles are lax, and her head rests against my chest as we lie together like lovers.

She relays every minute detail of her day until she forgets all the reasons she resents me, smiling as she says, "I think I could learn to like it here eventually."

"I like it when you do that," I find myself unable to resist telling her.

"Do what?"

"Smile. Tell me about your day." I tuck her hair behind her ear, nearly shivering when she leans into my touch. "I like getting to know you."

Nadya looks at me like she isn't sure what to say, but I'm not looking for a reply. For once, I really do just want to spend time with someone. I want to bask in everything she's been withholding.

Then she sits up, and in a moment I never would have imagined happening again so soon, Nadya leans forward and presses her lips to mine in a tentative kiss that tests the limits of my control.

She's soft and pliant against me, and I kiss her like I've wanted to for days. It's like the taste of her alone is enough to loosen the weights around my neck. For these few moments, I'm not treading water, waiting for the next cross I have to bear.

It's just the two of us. Two people with no other worries except for each other.

When Nadya's tongue brushes tentatively against mine, she lets out a breathy sigh that goes straight to my dick. It's a shot of pure lust that echoes everything I've craved since she stormed away from me in her studio, everything I've refused to push for.

Nadya gave me a taste of what it's like to be wanted by her, and even when I've lain beside her at night, wanting nothing more than to pull her against me and pick up where we left off, I told myself the next time I had my wife, it was going to be because she craved me so much she couldn't stay away.

I should let her control the pace.

Not just because I enjoyed her being in control far more than I thought I would, but because I don't want to risk doing anything to send her running again.

I *should*.

But then she shifts her legs so she's straddling my lap, and all my attention is drawn to the scorching heat of her pussy through our clothes.

All my good intentions are shot the moment Nadya rolls her hips, grinding against me.

"Konstantin!" She laughs as I flip us over, pinning her against the sofa, pressing against her so she can feel every inch of how much I'm enjoying our little make-out session.

The way her lips pop open while she stares at me, like she can't figure out what just happened, sends a thrill down my spine.

With gentle hands, I trace along the strap of her top, slowly sliding it down her shoulder to expose the red flush that trails down her chest.

"Look at you. Blushing, breathing heavy..." Her plush lip is trapped between her teeth, and I've never wanted to have someone's teeth sink into my flesh more. I want her nails, her teeth, her sharp eyes, and even sharper words.

I want her to tear me apart and take out all the ugliness so she never has to see it again.

I want to hold onto this feeling for the rest of my life.

"Tell me," I whisper, brushing my lips over her jaw, "if I reach into your shorts, would you soak my fingers with your arousal?" She wrenches her head away from me, pulling back to glare.

Even though she's clearly trying to look annoyed, there's too much lust in her eyes for it to have any weight. She can hate me with every fiber of her being, but it's impossible for her to hide the way her eyes trace the line of my shoulders

Nadya wants me, and she fucking hates it. It'll take more than a single evening to undo it, but that's fine.

She's worth it.

"You'll never know," she says, her voice breathy despite how cutting her tone is.

I hum, sitting up just enough to pop the button on her shorts. I chuckle darkly when she shivers.

What a beautiful, stubborn woman.

I can't wait to watch her break for me.

"Take off your clothes, wife. I want to look at you." When she opens her mouth, I cut her off with a squeeze to one of her thighs. "You can pretend you don't want this, but I'm not a fool, Nadya. If you insist, you can even leave your panties on." I smirk, dipping my fingers under the waistband of her shorts to trace the lace edge of her panties. "I'll enjoy taking them off you later."

With a frustrated huff, Nadya sits up and takes off her top, tossing it over the back of the couch and drawing all my attention to her exposed breasts. Immediately, I'm filled with a rush of heat, watching her dusky nipples pebble in the air.

"You weren't wearing a bra?" I grind out.

She's been running around town all day, and her body was separated from any man who wanted to look by just one thin piece of fabric?

"I don't need one most of the time." She shrugs, motioning at her small breasts. "And I don't like wearing them."

My muscles bunch tight, prepared to argue the point, but when she lays a hand on my forearm to scoot back so she can strip off her shorts, all my anger fizzles out. Her fingers dig into my tattoos, bracing herself as she stands.

That simple sight, Nadya using me for balance, nearly knocks the wind out of my lungs.

Seeing her standing in front of me, her eyes wide and trusting, is enough to bring me to my knees.

"Now you," she urges, sinking onto my lap like a temptress, completely oblivious to the effect she has on me. Nadya is sin and temptation personified, and it's all I can do to resist locking her away where no one else can ever see her again, where I can neglect my responsibilities and trace every inch of her skin until I know her more intimately than air knows the inside of my lungs.

"Let's keep it like this," I tease. "I want to watch you play with your nipples while I fuck you with my fingers. I want to see you dripping for my cock."

Before she can protest, I grip her thigh with one hand and pull her panties to the side with the other. I thrust one finger inside her.

Fuck. She's so tight it's a wonder I fit in her at all.

Nadya is going to strangle my cock when I take her again. I hadn't been with another woman since before the first time I laid eyes on her, and now, I can't imagine how I ever thought I'd want anyone else.

She whimpers a sound that makes my cock twitch, her soaked pussy stretching when I add a second finger. The wet slide of my hand between her thighs is music to my ears, and if I didn't think she'd castrate me for it, I'd pull out my phone to capture this moment so I could look back on it for the rest of time.

"Tug on these pretty nipples," I prompt, flashing her a grin that's all teeth. "Or I'll gladly lavish them with the attention they deserve."

It's such a shame my wife's smart enough to take the threat for exactly what it is, rushing to take her breasts into her hands. My cock practically weeps with how much I want her, but I'm determined to make her come before we leave this room. And if I give in now, it'll be so much harder to wear her out tonight.

The faster I work my fingers, the harder she fights to hold back her moans, until her legs are clenched so tight around me I wonder how she isn't falling apart.

But her quiet, stubborn resistance feels like a challenge, and I've yet to find a challenge I wasn't ready to face head-on.

When it comes to Nadya, I doubt I ever will.

"Let go for me," I say, surprised at how rough my own voice is as I scrape my teeth against the delicate column of her throat. "Let me feel this cunt around my fingers as you come. Soak my hand, *solnyshka*." I crook my fingers, rubbing against her G-spot until she's gasping.

I sink my teeth into her collarbone hard enough to leave a warning for anyone who tries to look at her in the days to come.

"Doesn't it get tiring? Fighting me?" I ask as she whimpers, her back arching while her muscles tremble with the effort of holding back. "It'll be so good when you let go, Nadya. All you have to do is give in."

Her hips buck, every movement urging me to go faster, to work her that much deeper.

"Please, Konstantin," she whines. "More. I need more."

I click my tongue, trailing my mouth lower and lower. In her ecstasy, Nadya has left her poor breasts unattended, and I'm nothing if not a man of my word.

"Don't beg. You never need to beg. You just have to come. If you come on my fingers, I'll give you everything you want as soon as I get you to the bedroom."

She huffs, her fingers digging into my biceps as I run slow circles on against her clit and tease her nipples with my teeth, soothing them with my tongue when she hisses.

"Or I can fuck you now. But if I do, you're not going to come for hours. You're going to be so full of my cock you'll forget what it's like to be without me. You'll feel me for days, *solnyshka*. I'll drip down your legs so everyone knows who you belong to."

"Damn you, Konstantin."

"Oh, I'm already damned." I press a kiss against her throat. "But you have to choose. Are you going to keep being stubborn?" Her whole body is practically vibrating against me, screaming to be pushed over the edge. "Or do you want to surrender and let me take care of you?"

Nadya throws her head back with a long moan as her muscles clamp down on my fingers so hard my dick weeps sympathetically, begging me to ignore my plans and sink inside her like I'm nothing but a mindless beast.

But I can't. As much as I want to lose myself in her right here and now, I need to fuck her to the point of exhaustion even more.

She pants against my hair as she comes down, looking dazed as I smile.

"Good girl, *solnyshka*," I murmur, pressing featherlight kisses against her shoulder. "You did so good. You're so perfect."

"I hate you." She sighs, but there's no venom in her words, especially not when she leans into me like she knows I'll never let her fall.

"I know." I smile, adjusting my hands to hold her as I stand. Nadya moves with me, wrapping her arms around my shoulders. "Let me take you to bed, and I'll make it up to you."

***

Nadya is sound asleep. For the past hour, her breaths have been soft and rhythmic, but I'm still careful as I slip away from her, tucking the blankets around her worn-out body so she doesn't stir and notice my absence.

I'm only planning to be gone for a few minutes, but the lower the chances of her interrupting me, the better.

I kiss her forehead before I fish out the hidden package I received from Ivan's pharmaceutical contact and slip into the bathroom.

When I flick the lock behind me, it feels obscenely loud. I pause, but there's no noise from the bedroom. Nadya is still out like a light.

Perfect.

My heart pounds in my chest, excitement making my hands shake.

Because my wife is so headstrong she could wear down a mule, and until she has reason to stop, she's going to keep fighting me with everything she has. And as much as I want her to give into me on her own, I don't want to wait until I'm on my deathbed to see it.

I want her to want me. I *need* her to stop seeing me as the monster who upended her life for my own gain.

Even if that's exactly what I am.

I slide open the drawer she hesitantly claimed as her own. Her small makeup collection is neatly organized, bottles and brushes lined up side by side. Behind them lies the little packet of pills that she dutifully takes every morning.

Pulling it out, I compare it to the sugar pills in my hand, popping out the right amount until they're identical.

I'll have to give Ivan's man that much. If I wanted to get into the trade of counterfeit drugs, it seems he knows his stuff.

Too bad my interests are far more personal.

By the time she finds out what I've done, I can only hope that I'll have burrowed myself so deep inside her with my cock, with my cum, with the meager affection my battered heart is able to give, that she'll never have a hope of getting me out. I may never be able to win her love, but I can keep her by my side.

I dispose of the evidence and slip back into bed, taking Nadya into my arms. Wrapped in the sheets that smell like her, with her weight pressed against my chest, I fall into the easiest sleep I've had in years.

CHAPTER 14

Nadya

Vasya nods his head as I get into the car, silently picking clay out of my ring. He seems to read my mind, turning up the radio to fill the quiet between us as we drive toward the house.

Halfway through my second class at my new studio, it hit me that everything feels comfortable. Not quite normal, but somehow a little bit better than things were when I was on my own. Easier. Not quite as quiet. Definitely less lonely.

Even when Konstantin isn't at the house, someone else always is.

Sometimes it's Tatiana pushing me to eat more and telling me I'm too skinny. Sometimes it's the guards around the house, always present, but never approachable. Occasionally it's Viktor, whining about one thing or another. A lot of the time though, it's Spaghetti, hanging out with me in my studio while I try to replicate what I learned in class.

And I'm not sure how to feel about it.

Because I still feel like everything in Konstantin's house is a puzzle, and every time I'm close to figuring out how I fit into it, the pieces all change and I'm right back where I started.

It's hard to really relax when it feels like the ground is constantly shuffling beneath my feet.

Or maybe it's just that every time I look outside, there's bound to be more than one man patrolling the yard and armed to the teeth. I keep my knife with me wherever I go, but there's a reason you don't bring a knife to a gun fight.

As welcome as the people inside are, the men outside remind me that I'll never be able to walk away without approval from someone else. Even Tatiana's loyalty lies with Konstantin.

And even though he's been something akin to sweet with me, I'm not ready to test the lengths he'll go to in order to make sure I don't leave the house without his permission. And I definitely don't want to know what he's told his men to do to keep me there in his absence.

I'd much rather pretend Konstantin is no different from any other man so I can keep enjoying the way he kisses me softly before he leaves in the morning and fucks me so hard I can't remember my own name at night.

Just thinking about Konstantin makes my cheeks burn so bright I have no choice but to turn my head away from Vasily so he doesn't figure out what I'm thinking.

Because as much as I enjoy his company, he's the last person I want to talk to about my relationship. Not just because I'm worried he'll retaliate by telling me things about him and Viktor that I can't unhear, but because I'm not sure I'm ready to tell *anyone* about the tender sparks in my chest that feel an awful lot like affection.

No one else needs to know about the way my stomach flips pleasantly when Konstantin brushes his hand against mine right before he leaves. Especially not when I'm still busy wondering how the hell he's been so successful at breaking down every wall I've tried to erect between us.

Thank god Konstantin's supposed to be out late tonight, because I need time to myself. His presence, while more than welcome lately, is bordering on suffocating, and I need to process everything without him clouding up my judgment.

I just want to curl up in bed and watch a movie.

And if Konstantin's out late enough, maybe I can convince Spaghetti to cuddle with me until I fall asleep.

Honestly, I'm not sure which one of them hates sharing a space more. Spaghetti is on edge whenever Konstantin walks into a room, but Konstantin isn't much better. He looks like he's bracing for an attack until there's at least one closed door between them.

I wave goodbye to Vasya as he drops me off, noting the way he keeps his eyes glued to me until I close the door. The guards around him keep their eyes averted, doing their normal routes around the house.

I take comfort in the fact that when I checked for myself, all the windows are mirrored, exactly like Konstantin said. The guards can't see in unless it's night and all the lights inside are on. And it means no one has been able to see me when I look outside, watching them patrol. They're always hyper-vigilant, prepared for whatever threats may try to get onto the property.

Of course Konstantin wouldn't settle for guards that only pretend to care. His people would always act like they're expecting an ambush at every moment, and if they so much as close their eyes for even a moment, the cameras are just waiting to watch them slip up.

At least the bedroom is on the second floor. As long as I don't look down, I can pretend they aren't there, and I'm all alone.

But at the end of the day, I'm unable to deny the truth. I'm surrounded by strangers in a house I'm still not quite comfortable in, and I'm so unfamiliar with the city that even if I did manage to go out, I'd be stuck staring at my phone for the most basic directions.

Just thinking about it makes me antsy.

What if something happens and Konstantin isn't here? What if I'm out and get separated from Vasily?

The more I try to think about anything else, the more my mind spirals, caught in an endless loop that gets worse the longer it goes on.

Typically, my favorite way to break out if it is by bothering Alexei until everything feels settled again, but that's not exactly an option when I'm across the freaking country.

Then again...

I spin my phone between my hands, watching as Spaghetti sniffs Konstantin's half of the bed, his face frozen in a look of disgust as he blinks at me. I check the time.

It's a little after seven, which means it isn't *that* late in Chicago. Besides, it's not like Alexei is the type of person who goes to bed early. And I haven't spoken to him in the two weeks since the wedding.

He might be an annoying little shit, but he's *my* little shit, and I miss him.

I shoo Spaghetti off my pillow and settle in to have a little chat, making myself comfortable as the phone rings. When it drops off and the robotic voicemail message takes over, my shoulders fall with familiar disappointment. I call again and again, but every time the stupid voice repeats Alexei's number and tells me he's not available, I feel even worse.

By the fifth time I listen to his voicemail, I'm so frustrated I could start throwing things, grinding my teeth together to keep from screaming.

"If you're planning to live long enough to marry your girl-friend, you'll call me back in the next ten minutes," I grit out, wishing I could stalk into his condo and give him a piece of my mind the way I used to.

Because I can't stand the thought of telling Alexei over the phone that it feels like he cut me out of his life the moment my last name changed. It's not just that he hasn't called me since the wedding, he hasn't even returned any of my texts beyond a short *I'm busy, call you later* that never manifest. It's been way too long, and for the first time, I feel like the life I had before Konstantin is nothing but a distant memory.

Like Alexei locked me in the same cabinet as Mom and Dad. Something to be thought about on special occasions, but ignored the rest of the time.

Before I can sink any deeper into my dread, I FaceTime Blair, knowing she'll find a way to cheer me up. Because I need to cling to the good.

And despite how I'm feeling, today *was* good.

The little trinket box I made in class turned out well, I was able to sort through some of my feelings while I worked, and Spaghetti managed to be in the same room as Konstantin for five whole minutes this morning without hissing.

I should be happy. And instead, I'm throwing a pity party.

"Nadya!" Blair says with a grin, the happiness on her face evident as soon as her face fills the screen. "I was just thinking about you."

Something in my chest settles with her smile. Alexei might be pushing me out the door with all his might, but at least Blair still cares.

"God, you're glowing," I say with a small chuckle. "Has anyone told you that?"

Her cheeks turn pink. That's part of what I love about Blair. Whatever she's thinking is always written plainly on her face for anyone to see.

All her frustration, her joy, her love. She couldn't hide it if she tried.

And right now? She's happy to see me. She also looks like she doesn't know how to handle the compliment, and, underneath everything, her brows are still furrowed, squinting at the screen while she looks at me. She's worried, and I love her for it.

"Don't say that," she groans. "Niko heard Andrei say it the other day, and now he keeps turning off lights to prove him wrong."

I throw my head back as I laugh so loud Spaghetti jumps. In an instant, all my worries are pushed away to be dealt with later. I feel like I can breathe, and it hits me all over again how much I miss her.

"Is Andrei backing down?"

"Never. But if Niko doesn't stop sneaking into our room in the middle of the night and turning on the light so he can keep arguing, I'm going to make him." She sighs. "I'm so tired."

"Little Bean not letting you sleep?"

"No," she groans. "Even when he does settle long enough for me to lie down, I can't fall asleep. And when I finally did last night, Niko woke me up less than an hour later." She runs a hand down her face. "I almost cried."

I wince sympathetically.

"And you haven't knocked Andrei over the head and told him to put an end to it yet?"

"I want them to work it out on their own."

"You know, if you're interested in leaving them behind for a while, there's plenty of room here. I bet I could even get Konstantin to put one of the beds back in the spare room for you."

Blair's eyes narrow in that too-knowing way of hers that makes me want to squirm.

"And... is everything going okay? Between you and Konstantin?" Blair asks softly, her concern hitting me straight in the chest even as the corners of my mouth twitch upward. "What was that?"

"What was what?"

"You smiled." She chuckles. "Oh my god. You like your husband, don't you?"

"Nope. Absolutely not. He's awful," I say, shaking my head so she can't comment on my grin. "He has a tiny dick. I hate him, actually."

Her laughter is the balm I need.

"What I got out of that is that Konstantin has a massive dick, and you love it."

No sooner do the words leave her mouth than Andrei's face appears over her shoulder, glaring at the screen.

"Blair doesn't need to hear about your husband's dick," he grouses while she smiles up at him. "And I need to get her to bed."

We say our goodbyes, but I'm still smiling after we hang up.

I load up a movie on my laptop to keep me company until my own husband gets home.

***

"How did you manage to steal my cat, *solnyshka*?" Konstantin's soft words wake me as he closes my laptop and puts it away, his voice wrapping around my sleep-addled brain like a gentle hug. "I need you to wake up and get him to move so I can go to bed without fearing for my life."

Still half-asleep, I tap my hand against the leg Spaghetti's using as a pillow. When he stirs, I press against his side, silently asking him to move. He doesn't wait, hopping to the floor and leaving the room without noticing the man closing the door behind him.

"Thank you," he whispers, pressing a kiss against my forehead as he lifts the blankets and tugs me close enough that I don't have to worry about him seeing the smile I bury against his neck.

No matter how high I build my walls, or how much I tell myself trusting Konstantin will only bring me trouble, I can't help it.

I *like* him.

He's everything I should hate, but I still like him. If I couldn't hide it from Blair, then it's only a matter of time before Konstantin sees it for himself. And when he has his arms wrapped around me, holding me close without any expectation of more, I'm not sure I care if he does.

He's warm, the lingering smell of his cologne cocooning us like a weighted blanket, and despite how dangerous he can be, I feel safe.

With bleary eyes, I trace over the tattoos on the back of his hands.

If he figures out how I feel on his own, he's going to gloat. He doesn't deserve the satisfaction.

Though it's probably a mistake, I brush my lips against his throat and whisper, "I like you, Konstantin."

Under my head, the muscles of his shoulder and chest tense for a split second before he melts, keeping his lips pressed against the top of my head.

"I like you too."

"You're going to hurt me, aren't you?"

"I'll try not to," he promises, but his words melt into my dreams, fuzzy and not quite real as I fall back asleep.

Chapter 15

Nadya

It's a tough pill to swallow, but I think I'm ready to admit that I was hallucinating every moment I thought I enjoyed pottery. In fact, every second I ever spent with clay under my nails, every minute wasted getting friction burns from the wheel because I still can't figure out how to add enough water when I work it, has been nothing but a waste.

If I have any self-respect, I'll walk out of here now and burn the lovely studio Konstantin made for me to the ground.

I glower at the collapsed mound of clay that was supposed to be my latest piece, wondering if it would look better if I scraped it all up and dumped it on the floor, but that'd just make a mess.

The piece I finished last week cracked in the kiln, I have no way to salvage this disaster, and I'm so frustrated I'm prepared to throw in the towel and give up the whole hobby for good.

But that would be a waste of both my time and Konstantin's money.

I settle for punching the ruined clay back until it's a mound that has some hope of being recycled. I just can't let it know how much I hate it.

I wipe my hands on my apron and grit my teeth, so I don't start muttering obscenities under my breath, and get back to work.

I might not be able to make a lamp that would've looked great in the living room, but I can probably manage to whip up a vase before it's time to go home. Even if it's sloppy and I have to wait until next week to really work on it, I can still get started on making a piece with more personality than Konstantin's entire house.

And if I make a vase, I can start replacing the boring glass ones that seem to be filled with fresh lilacs every time the old flowers start to wilt. If I make enough of them, maybe it'll eventually look more like a home than a showroom.

The man at the wheel next to me gives me the same sympathetic smile he's been shooting me since the lamp started to wobble. The bitter part of me wants to snap and tell him exactly where he can shove his pity, but it's not like it's his fault I've bit off more than I can chew, even if something about him rubs me the wrong way.

I just need to suck it up and focus on what I can control. Like avoiding eye contact so I don't end up like the poor soul he sat next to last week. That woman ended up leaving early so he'd stop talking her ear off.

All I have to do is ignore his too-interested gaze and smiles that make my skin crawl. And then I have to bite my tongue and wipe away my unease before I join Vasya in the car.

If he finds out about my discomfort, so will Konstantin. Then I'll never see the guy again. But neither will anyone else.

I don't want to talk to him, but I don't want his death on my conscience, either.

So, no matter how often I feel his eyes on me, I'm determined to ignore him.

Shaking off the sensation of being watched, I transfer my vase to the drying board. It's too wet for me to trim or really even shape, but I'm not planning on coming back here until next week, so I have no choice but to wrap it in plastic and hope it doesn't get so dry that it cracks like my trinket box did.

I glance out the front windows, making sure Vasya is still parked out front. As expected, he's sitting in the car, looking bored out of his mind while he scrolls on his phone, poor guy. After a moment's hesitation, I leave my purse where it is instead of getting clay all over it and move my vase so it can dry.

I make a mental note to talk to Konstantin later and see if he can find someone else to take me to class. If he insists I need to have a bodyguard, fine, but there's no reason it has to be Vasily.

Anyone is capable of sitting on their ass while I go inside and fail to make art out of mud.

As I step into the back, I wonder if I should offer to skip next week's class. That way, Vasya can spend some well-earned time with his daughter instead of shadowing me for an afternoon.

Maybe I can even convince Konstantin to take a few hours off and accompany me himself.

I pull out a sheet of plastic, shaking it out and smiling to myself as I picture Konstantin folding himself into one of the stools with a dirty apron stretched across his chest. As soon as my vase is wrapped, I try to move it to the drying racks, but it wobbles as someone grabs my arm.

"Hey!" I protest, trying to yank free of their hold.

They only dig their fingers in harder, dragging me further behind the wall separating the main room and the drying racks, and I have no choice but to watch the vase fall to the floor, the board clattering as it crushes the wet clay. I barely even register the disappointment over the pounding of my own heart.

My sandals slide uselessly on the dusty floor as I'm dragged further away from the windows—away from Vasily's watchful eye. It's like I'm weightless. No matter how hard I struggle to pull away, to resist their hold, they pull me along unimpeded. The hand on my arm is a vise, clamping down so hard I know they're leaving marks.

Konstantin is going to be *pissed*.

I twist around, ready to rip someone a new asshole, but my words stop dead when I see the same creepy guy that spent more time watching me during class than he did working on his project.

He isn't grinning anymore. Now he's looking at me like I'm a puzzle he can figure out just from watching my reaction.

He's looking at me like I'm his *prey*.

"What's your problem?" I snap, subtly glancing around while my heart drops.

In the time I wasted trying to salvage a vase, everyone else must have wrapped up their work and left for the day. No one is lingering by the racks. There isn't a single soul around to see what's happening. There's no one to raise the alarm.

I don't know where the instructors are, but something tells me that if I scream, no one's going to come running.

I let my guard down. I felt safe knowing Vasily was out front, so I left my purse in the front room. And even if I manage break free, I'll have to sprint to be able to get my knife.

"Let go, you fucking *mudak*!"

How long will it take for Vasily to realize something's wrong? He isn't like the guards at the house. He's always alert, and no doubt just as deadly, but he's also stretched thin between me, Viktor, and his daughter. He's tired and distracted.

Fuck.

Fuck. Fuck. *Fuck!*

My breaths are short pants, and all I can think about is every self-defense class Alexei signed me up for that I promptly skipped in favor of pretending he never told me about it.

This guy is about my height—around five-ten—but he easily has fifty pounds of muscle on me.

I can't fight him without a weapon. I can't get away.

And I don't know when, or even *if* help is coming.

I'm so fucked.

"Relax," he says with an infuriating sense of calm.

Relax. Like he didn't grab me and drag me into an isolated corner. I bare my teeth, fully prepared to use them as a weapon if he pulls me any closer. I might not have his physical strength, but I can sure as hell make him bleed if he tries anything.

I'd like to see him tell me to relax when I tear open his throat and let his blood mix with the dust on the floor.

"I just want to talk to you about your brother."

Ice fills my veins, stealing the warmth my panic tried to bury me under.

"What?"

Nothing could prepare me for the way I freeze when he pulls a badge out of his pocket which proudly declares him to be Special Agent Chance Jacobs with the FBI.

Oh, I'm not just fucked. I'm fucking dead. No matter how hard I've worked to avoid getting entangled in Bratva bullshit throughout my life, you don't have a family like mine without learning the cardinal rule of *don't talk to cops*.

Not when your father is already in jail for the Bratva. Not when your brother is a pakhan at war. And *definitely* not when you're married to a pakhan.

Talking to this *ublyudok* would be nothing short of suicidal.

Anything I tell him, no matter how innocuous, would cause problems. For Konstantin, for Alexei, shit, even for Blair.

I refuse to make the lives of the people I care about even harder than they already are.

Lifting my chin, I look down my nose at this guy.

Chance Jacobs.

What an asshole.

At least now I know why he was watching me during class. He was hoping I'd slip up and make his life easier.

I don't say a word despite the churning in my gut.

Rather than taking my silence for the full and complete answer it is, Jacobs prods even further. "We already know all about the war with the Italians, we just want to clear up a few details. And with your help, I can probably keep your brother out of even more trouble." He shakes his head. His smile aims for sympathetic but misses by a long shot. "I'm trying to help you out here, Nadya."

Hearing him say my name only pisses me off even further.

Liar.

The only one he's trying to help is himself, and the fact that he thinks I'm stupid enough to fall for it makes me want to spit in his arrogant face.

"I don't know what you're talking about, *Agent*," I hiss. "And even if I did, it wouldn't give you the right to accost me." Pointedly, I look down at where his hand is still squeezing my arm, the flesh around his fingers turning white. "And it certainly wouldn't give you the right to manhandle me. But maybe I should check with my lawyer."

Jacobs lets me go like I said the magic word, his faux kindness replaced by a snarl that no doubt mirrors my own.

"If you don't want Alexei to end up in prison with your father, I suggest you tell me what you know," he insists, his tone firm and authoritative.

"If you really want to speak to me, you can set up a meeting the right way. Through my husband's attorney. You have his number, right?"

I sure as hell hope he does, because I don't. I only have empty threats propped up by a pissed-off attitude. Because even I know this isn't how an official should approach an active investigation.

Which means Special Agent Jacobs is acting outside of his official capacity.

And I'm betting he'll back off. At least long enough for me to get to Konstantin. Long enough for me to talk to Alexei.

Blayd.

What if he was ordered to do this? Is Jacobs going to retaliate? What if he tries to arrest Alexei because I won't say anything?

When he doesn't answer, I fix my jaw, determined to make him think I don't give a shit what he has to say.

Still, my hands shake when I walk away, scoop up my ruined vase, and dump it in the reclaim pile before I make my way back to the front.

With every step, the creep's eyes burn the back of my neck. My hands are still dirty when I pick up my purse, but I can't find the energy to care. I walk outside and slip into Vasily's car as casually as I can while I pull out my phone to call Alexei.

"Is Konstantin working from home?" I ask, listening to the ringing that's going to haunt my nightmares.

"Yeah? What's—"

"Take me to him," I snap, my voice raw. "Now."

I've never made any demands before, and for a moment, Vasily doesn't seem to know what to do. But a moment later, he starts the car and starts driving without complaint.

I'll apologize to him later.

Blinking back tears, I listen to Alexei's voicemail message. Then I listen to it again. And again. I don't stop calling him until we're home. I launch myself out of the car as soon as it's parked, sprinting to Konstantin's office as the tears slide down my cheeks.

Chapter 16

Konstantin

Viktor shifts in his seat, his unease more and more apparent the longer I watch him. I wish I knew what has him tied in knots this time.

Is he pissed about Yuri? Or does he still want to yell at me for keeping Vasily at Nadya's side? There are a litany of reasons he could have invited himself into my office unannounced. But instead of explaining himself, he continues to sit, looking more uncomfortable with every passing breath.

And the more time he decides to waste, the less inclined I am to dig him out of whatever hole he's managed to fall in.

"So," he eventually begins, pausing to clear his throat. "Dowd managed to find part of Ronan."

I wait for more, but instead I'm treated to my brother looking at his feet like a child instead of meeting my eyes.

A core tenet of our business relies on being able to hide a body, and Viktor knows it. He looks younger than he has in years, twisting his hands the same way he did when he was scared of upsetting Dad when we were growing up.

I stay silent even though my anger boils in the back of my throat, urging me to lash out.

"How *much* of his cousin?"

"Enough to identify some of his tattoos," he mutters under his breath.

"It's been weeks," I snarl. "How the fuck were any of his tattoos still intact?"

"It's been windy lately," Viktor says with a shrug, looking smaller than I've ever seen him. "And I left him in the valley. There's a drought. With the shittiest luck in the world, his skin might have dried out instead of rotting like it should have."

I tap a pen on my desk, needing something to keep my hands busy so I don't reach across and punch him in the face.

"Why did you leave tattoos intact in the first place?" I ask, already knowing the answer.

He was drunk.

He should have kept his head, or brought along someone who was sober, but my brother thinks he knows everything. There's not a universe where he'd let someone else help him, because in his mind, he's the most capable man for the job.

He's never shown what a massive idiot he's capable of being quite like this before.

For fuck's sake, this is basic shit.

But with every new piece of information Viktor reveals about what happened with Ronan, the worse this whole mess becomes. He didn't do a basic background check. He was sloppy enough to let someone find a part of the body. He left the body *recognizable.*

If he were anyone else, I'd kill him for being this fucking stupid.

At this point, it would be easier if the cops had found Ronan. At least I'd be able to pay them off before they could do anything about it.

"Is there anything that's going to tie this back to us?"

Viktor shakes his head, dragging a hand over his face. "Not directly."

"And what, *exactly*, does that mean?"

"It means the Italians, Albanians, and Greeks have no real presence in this part of the state, and the cartels have already loudly denied any involvement in Ronan's death. It means that even if they managed to find part of him, he was still taken apart too methodically for it to have been some gang."

I roll my shoulders, dropping my head backward.

"Is there any chance we can play this off as a random killing?" I ask, already knowing how small the odds of pulling that off are. If it was random, they wouldn't have dismembered and dumped the body in multiple places over different cities.

Cities that, if I had to guess, are all within a few short miles of the venue where I got married.

It's not a secret that Ronan owed me money. And if he'd already reached out to Liam, then there's no way he doesn't have a damn good guess of who did this.

The way Viktor refuses to meet my eyes is all the answer I need.

Fuck me.

Liam's suspicion is one thing, but having actual evidence is a problem I really don't want to deal with right now.

My thoughts are cut off by the front door slamming open, and I can't help but smile. In an instant, my blood pressure drops and my jaw relaxes. I drop the pen, almost smiling to myself.

Because as soon as Viktor and I are done, I'm going to track down Nadya and let her relay every detail of her pottery class before I drag her upstairs to bask in the way she smiles whenever she realizes I've been looking forward to seeing her all day.

She still puts up a front of being grumpy about it, but as soon as I wrap my arms around her waist and pull her against me, she melts. Her ice is thawing faster than I could have ever hoped for, and once she's pregnant, she won't want to leave my side.

My wife.

Soon, I'll own every piece of her heart.

The door to my office is shoved open before I can fall into the daydream, revealing a frazzled and teary-eyed Nadya.

I'm on my feet and rushing toward her as soon as her eyes lock on me. "What's wrong?"

She looks furious, but the closer I get, the clearer I can see the terror swimming in her hazel eyes.

Whatever happened, I'm going to find it, and I'm going to fix it.

Now. Before she has to spend the rest of the night worrying about it.

I reach out and pull her against my chest.

"There was a federal agent in my pottery class," she blurts, her voice wavering.

My worry burns to ash as fury races through me. "What?"

Behind her, Vasily stands frozen in the doorway, his pale expression telling me he didn't know what was wrong until now. Even though it's his job to make sure she's safe whenever she's outside these walls.

I run my hands down Nadya's bare arms, chest heaving with furious breaths when I find the beginnings of bruises forming.

Viktor must notice them the same time I do, because he's up like a shot, pushing Vasily out of the room.

They'll both get what's coming for their failures in due time. But first, I need to focus on my wife.

"Are you alright?" I ask, deliberately softening my tone.

"He wanted to know about Alexei," she exclaims instead of answering me. A tear tracks down her cheek, carving a knife right through my chest. I hold her even tighter, pressing my lips against her hair while she clings to my shirt. "He asked me about the bullshit with The Outfit. He made it sound like he wanted to arrest him, and now Alexei isn't answering his phone. What if he's already in jail, Konstantin?"

She's practically sobbing, and I hate how useless I feel as I hold her tight, letting her hide her tears while my eyes cut to where Viktor's still standing. He's looking away, giving her the illusion of privacy, but he's still here, waiting for me to tell him what to do.

Has he fucked up?

Yes.

But Vasily fucked up worse, and at least my brother is prepared to help me fix it.

"I can't protect him from here." Nadya's voice is heart-wrenching, full of a pain so deep and helpless that I want to destroy everything until I get my hands on the man who made her this way and force him to feel the same way.

"Find everything you can," I order, keeping my tone soft as I stroke a hand down the back of Nadya's head. "I want to know everything there is to know about this fed by this time tomorrow."

He nods, already turning away.

"And Viktor?" I call. He eyes me warily, and I can't find it in me to feel an ounce of guilt as I say, "If you want to keep Vasily safe, keep him away from this house until this is resolved."

I rub Nadya's back until her sobs turn into whimpers, keeping her close while I watch out the window, waiting until Vasily and Viktor pile into the car and tear out of the driveway, far away from me.

Once the front gate closes behind them, I pick her up and set her down on the couch, snagging the throw blanket so I can wrap it around her shoulders.

"I'll fix this, *solnyshka*."

"How?" she asks, her lip wobbling all over again.

"Trust me," I whisper as I kiss her forehead. "I know it's hard, and I know you don't want to, but I need you to trust me. Okay?"

She pulls her knees to her chest, looking heartbroken as she blinks at me with red-rimmed eyes. After a breathless moment, Nadya nods, looking ready to fall apart all over again. The sense of calm in my chest is eerie, quieting the anger and worry I feel.

But it isn't like the feeling I have when Nadya smiles. It's colder. More calculating. Familiar in a way comfort isn't.

I stand, pulling out my phone and calling the contact I've been hoarding for years.

As much as I love having an ace up my sleeve and being able to hold dirt over The Outfit's underboss, I'd rather never see my wife cry because she's worried about her brother again.

"What?" Carlo Di Veroli barks after only a moment. For once, his surly attitude isn't amusing. I have no patience for his attitude today.

"End the war, Carlo. Now."

He sighs, his eye roll clear even through the phone.

"That's not my call, and you know it."

"Perhaps not." I hum. "But you asked me for a favor once. If you don't let me cash it in, I'll stop protecting the little flower you left behind."

There's a long pause that has me grinding my teeth.

Carlo wasn't even old enough to drink when he begged me to watch over the woman he had to leave behind when The Outfit's boss dragged him back to Chicago. I told him then that my protection isn't free, and if managed to forget, then it's his problem.

"She built a happy life for herself," I offer when the silence drags. "She's dating the man I have guarding her. But he knows how to handle his business. All it would take is one call, and he'll let her fend for herself."

I don't bother telling him that, for the most part, his ex-girlfriend doesn't need me to protect her. In all the years since he begged me to watch over her, I've barely had to lift a finger.

But if Carlo is anything like me, he'll never be able to let go of the nagging doubt. He'll worry about who she's with and what I'm doing to her until he sets off like a bomb.

As long as he detonates in the right spot, I don't fucking care.

"Don't you dare, Lavrov," Carlo hisses.

It's impossible to miss the thread of fear in his voice. But that's his problem. Not mine.

My responsibilities begin and end with making sure Nadya is safe and happy. And if the feds are sticking their noses into Alexei's war, then it needs to come to an end.

"From what I've been told, Gia's happy. She doesn't talk about you anymore. And if you don't want her to know what you've been up to, then you know what you have to do."

There's a long beat of silence, one that carries weight. I wouldn't even have to lift a finger to hurt that girl. All it would take would be a throwaway comment from Felix, a picture left somewhere for her to find, and her whole world will crash down around her.

Carlo knows it just as well as I do.

"Oh, and one more thing."

"What?" he asks through gritted teeth, both furious and desperate in a single breath.

I turn, looking at my wife. A year ago, I wouldn't have thought twice about threatening Carlo. But now, I think I understand why he was so terrified when I first met him.

Because if anyone threatens Nadya like this, there will be no ends to the lengths I'd go in order to keep her safe. I'd move the stars in the sky, erase every last hint of light in this world if I had to.

I'd keep her safe no matter what it took.

"If anyone touches a single hair on Trenin's head, I'll make sure your boss knows exactly where to find her. End the war and keep Alexei out of it, or I'll throw her to the wolves and leave her mangled bones on your doorstep. Do you understand?"

Nadya's eyes have lost the shine they had when she saw me this morning. Where there was a level of happiness that made my chest ache, she's now looking at me like a riddle, unraveling me with every word.

As much as I hate it, at least she's stopped shaking like a leaf.

Carlo shouts threats, cursing me while I wait in silence.

"You have one day, Carlo. Make it happen."

I hang up, making another call before Nadya can ask for answers. She's already going to demand my head on a silver platter as soon as she figures me out. The least I can do is try to salvage some of the warmth in her heart before she ices me out again.

Alexei answers on the first ring.

Wordlessly, I hand her the phone so she can assure herself he's alright. A piece of shit for avoiding her, but physically intact.

As she talks to him, her tears cease. The line between her brows relaxes, the corners of her eyes soften, and the pressure that had been building in my chest recedes. Her shoulders relax as I lean against my desk.

I've never tried to pretend I was anything less than a monster, but perhaps I should have.

Because when Nadya hangs up, she doesn't look at me like someone she could learn to love. She looks at me like she thinks even less of me than she did at our wedding.

My wife looks at me like she hates me and everything I've ever stood for.

She's far from the first person to look at me this way, but with her, it cuts deeper. Maybe because I should have known she'd never really learn to care about me.

If Nadya fell for any part of me, it was only ever going to be for the illusion I projected for her. The man who can give her what she wants. The one who goes out of his way to make her smile. The one who holds her at night and makes dinner and watches her favorite movie with her.

But at the end of the day, I'll always be the piece of shit I was raised to be. Cutting. Brutal. Prepared to do whatever it takes to get what I want.

"What was that?" she finally asks, curling her hands into fists.

"That was the war between your brother and The Outfit coming to an end," I answer honestly. "That was me guaranteeing Alexei's safety."

"And why didn't you do it sooner?" Her voice is deadly calm, only the flush in her cheeks and the fire in her eyes revealing how close she is to snapping.

For the first time, there's no rush of relief when I look at her. The anxiety that's always bubbling below the surface, ready to drown me if I forget myself for too long, is out in full force. After having a break from it, it's enough to wind me, and I have to dig my fingers into the edge of my desk so I don't collapse.

I've spent so much of my life learning to cope with it, learning to push it deep and ignore it. But under Nadya's gaze, it's so far out of my control it's laughable that I ever thought I could.

"I needed something I could use when you inevitably tried to leave me," I say with an honesty that can only come from being torn apart at the seams. "I needed to have leverage when your brother changes his mind and demands I send you back to him."

"And what now?" Her lip curls with disgust. "If I tried to leave now, what would you do?"

My heart is a useless lump in my throat, starving me of oxygen.

"I can call Carlo again. It hasn't been long. I doubt he's had a chance to talk his boss into calling off the war yet." I shrug, swallowing hard at the shift behind her eyes. "I can tell him I changed my mind, and Alexei's still fair game."

Nadya doesn't say a word as she stands, leaving the room with more dignity in her little finger than I've ever possessed.

It feels like the sun itself leaves with her.

Chapter 17

Nadya

My wrists ache, but I ignore the pain in favor of throwing yet another lump of clay on the wheel, cursing under my breath when it's as far from centered as it can possibly be. Every part of my body is begging for a break, but my mind refuses to grant one.

Because my studio is the only room where I can successfully avoid Konstantin.

Even if I have to put up with fatigue in every part of my arms, my eyes are burning from how hard I've been holding back tears, and every new pot I throw is a dozen times shittier than the one I threw at the studio. But I'll take whatever reprieve I can get.

If had a choice between dealing with Konstantin and dancing barefoot across a field of broken glass, he still wouldn't win.

Any decent man would leave the house so I can have some space, but Konstantin doesn't know the definition of the word.

If he did, I wouldn't be here. I'd be back in Chicago, and Alexei would be safe and sound without having to rely on the jackass who decided he wanted me so much, he'd sacrifice any shot I had at happiness.

I swipe my clay-streaked cheek against my shoulder, ignoring the tears cooling my skin.

I'm an idiot. I let myself forget what Konstantin is and pretended he was something else.

In his eyes, I'm nothing but a tool. No better than one of his guns. A decoration. Hell, even a fucking *pen* has more purpose in his life than I do.

I knew it before we got married, but apparently I'm a glutton for punishment, because I didn't just forget my place, I let myself fall into the delusional belief that if I learned to like him, everything would work out.

As pissed as I am, it's no one's fault but my own.

"No wonder you don't like him," I tell Spaghetti as I scrape up the clay for what feels like the hundredth time. He stretches in the dying sunbeam he's been basking in, his tail slowly flicking back and forth. "I should have let you shit on his pillow."

He blinks at me slowly, a polite agreement and forgiveness in a single movement.

Just one more vase.

I'll stop after I make something presentable. The rest of the day might have been a waste of time, but when I go to bed, I'm going to have something to show for it. I'll have something to look back on other than anger and heartbreak.

Even if it takes me hours.

By the time I make something halfway decent, the sun has long since set. My eyes are finally dry, and Spaghetti is pacing the room restlessly, waiting for me to open the door so he can explore the house before bed.

Somewhere outside, there's a dozen men still scouring every inch of the grounds, making sure no one gets in.

Or out.

I swallow the knot in my throat.

My pile of failed pottery is so large that even thinking about tossing it all together to recycle makes me tired, and the single lopsided vase I have in front of me isn't much better than the rest of the garbage.

But it's something. And if I make anything else, I don't know if I'll have the strength to crawl into bed.

As I grab a wire to lift it and prep it for drying, Spaghetti jumps into my lap and bats against the clay until the side collapses in on itself.

"No!"

He looks at me, holding his dirty paw out like it's somehow my fault. I'm not sure if it makes me want to laugh or cry, so I do the only thing I can.

I pull Spaghetti closer and bury my face in his fur, ignoring the way he swipes his paw against my apron and struggles to get free.

The rest of this gilded cage might be miserable, but at least I have him. I have somewhere I can pretend to escape as long as I ignore the men patrolling outside. I'm trapped at Konstantin's side, but I can build a pocket of space that's still mine.

Even if I know I'll never be able to escape.

Konstantin's right. If he wanted to, he could pull back any illusion of safety Alexei has. He has more power than I could ever dream of, and he's using it to keep me right where he wants me.

I help Spaghetti clean off his paw, wiping away the clay with a damp cloth while he struggles. All the pots I scrapped can be dealt with tomorrow.

But I take my time moving Spaghetti's vase over to the drying rack. It won't be able to hold much, but it still has more personality than anything else in this house. Tomorrow, I'll trim and refine it. And once I work up the nerve to go back to the studio, I'll ask about using their kiln to fire it.

At least it'll give me something to look forward to.

The house is quiet when I finally poke my head into the hallway. Spaghetti takes off into the darkness while I make my way to the bedroom. The only thing I'm interested in is a long soak in a hot bath to soothe my aching muscles and tender heart.

It's not like my feelings for Konstantin were real, I remind myself as I wait for the bath to fill. At worst, I had a crush on him. A pathetic little flame of want that could be destroyed by a bad haircut.

I'd have grown fond of anyone that was around as much as he was, right? If anyone else had been there every day, kissing me as soon as I woke up and smiling whenever they saw me, I'd have thought I was falling for them, too.

And like with any crush, I'll be fine as soon as I find something else to consume my time.

In a month, the only thing I'll miss will be the sex.

Everything else about our relationship might have been imagined, but there's no denying how good the sex was. Konstantin could fake everything else, but not the way he fucked me.

Like he was just as desperate for my pleasure as I was his. Like it was his life goal to see me come.

The water is so hot that I hiss as I sink into the tub.

A lonely ping of betrayal has me sinking even deeper, wishing it could wash away the memories with bleach as steam floats around me.

If I stay trapped in this rut, I'll end up stuck on all the ways Konstantin's capable of hurting me with until the end of time.

I need to focus on the positives.

Like the way Konstantin's wicked tongue drove me to the point of madness last night. Or how he woke me up in the middle of the night saying he had to have me. How, even though I was half asleep, he managed to tease me until I was panting and begging him to fuck me. Or the way he held me like he never wanted to let me go afterward.

I don't even realize I have one hand between my thighs until the other finds the place where Konstantin's teeth clamped down on my shoulder as he came. I gasp as I press against the bruise he left behind.

My fingers work my clit in tight circles under the water. I bite my lip when I remember the way his moans made every muscle in my body clench, how he managed to wipe away every thought in my head when he drove himself so deep I saw stars.

My head drops back as I groan, frustration pushing my release just out of reach.

No matter how quick or slow I work my clit, or what pressure I use, I'm getting no closer to what I need. In less than a month,

Konstantin's made himself the master of my body, and nothing I do is remotely close to the pleasure he's able to invoke with a few words or a simple touch.

Fucker.

Good thing I don't have to rely on myself. I'll never let Konstantin touch me again, but until my body gets on board with that plan, I definitely have a couple of toys hidden away that can get the job done.

I make quick work of wrapping a towel around my heated body, not caring if I leave wet footprints, and dart into the bedroom. I stop in my tracks when I open the door and am forced to confront the sight of my husband. His tie is loose around his shoulders and the collar of his shirt hangs open to expose the tattoos on his neck and top of his chest.

I shiver.

The arousal that was cooling reignites as I watch his strong hands work the buttons of his shirt, exposing more skin with each movement.

God, why now?

The last thing I want is to see Konstantin. Especially when he looks like the physical embodiment of sex who's just decided to strip for me.

When Konstantin looks up, his eyes pin me in place. He smirks, and I feel an echo of it all the way down my spine. My thighs squeeze together, and Konstantin—the absolute motherfucker that he is—only smirks harder.

"Nope. Get the fuck out," I snap, balling my fist on the towel so hard my hand hurts.

After the crap he pulled, he's insane if he thinks I'm going to share a bed with him. It's not happening. Not tonight, and not ever again.

Konstantin raises a brow, slowly looking around the room. "And where should I go, *solnyshka*? This is my room."

"I'd tell you to sleep in the guest room"—I shrug—"but you had the beds removed to stroke your own ego. So you can sleep in your office. Or on the edge of a windy cliff. I really don't care."

Slowly, Konstantin dips his chin, all amusement fading from his expression in a blink of an eye. He stalks across the room with calculated movements that are at odds with the storm behind his eyes.

My instincts scream at me to run, but a thrill runs up my spine at the way he's looking at me.

In my gut, I know that if I run, he'll pursue. And if he catches me, I'll be at his mercy.

Every single one of his movements is controlled and deliberate as he reaches for me. He uses a single finger to tuck a wet strand of hair behind my ear, never touching my skin, but I refuse to break eye contact. Despite all my good intentions, I find myself leaning into him until my head is cradled in his warm hand.

That single point of contact—a simple touch that manages to make me feel more settled than else anything has since I left his office—is all I can focus on until he leans close enough that I can feel his minty breath fanning over my face.

"Do you want to know what I think, Nadya?"

"No."

Any attempt to hide my arousal is lost on that single, breathless word. His pupils dilate, swallowing the blue of his irises while he traces his hand over my jaw until he's able to tug at my lip with his thumb.

Why can't his appearance match the rot and ruin that's hiding beneath the surface? Why does even the way he raises a brow, his eyes rapt as he watches my tongue trace the path he left on my lip, have to be so tempting?

Why does everything he does make me melt for him?

"I think you're mad because you care about me." His words are soft, but it does nothing to ease how hard they hit me as they cut through my arousal like a knife. But his firm hand on the back of my neck doesn't allow me to rear back the way I want to.

Before I can try to refute it, Konstantin continues, "You're scared. You want to run, and even if you hadn't listened to that phone call, you still would have been looking for a reason to hate me again."

There's a quiet hunger in his expression as his eyes search mine, but what he's hungry for, I couldn't even begin to guess.

I don't know if he's right, and frankly, I'm not sure it matters.

Konstantin hurt me. The only family I have left was at risk, and he didn't stop it because he wanted to control me.

I shove his chest, but he's a brick wall.

"If you want to hate me, that's fine," he whispers, pressing his forehead against mine while I freeze.

He's not going to give in. If he's already gone this far to get his way, then I have to expect him to have even more tricks hidden up his sleeve.

His nostrils flare before he puts both his hands on my shoulders, pressing down until I have no choice but to fall to my knees. Before I can even comprehend what's happening, I'm face-to-face with the bulge of his hard cock, simultaneously making my blood boil and my mouth water.

"You can hate me tonight. We can pretend, and we'll talk about this like adults in the morning."

He winds his fingers through my hair before he fists it tight, pulling my head back and forcing me to look him in the eyes.

"But if you're going to hate me, then you can hate me on your knees. I'll even fuck your pretty mouth to make it easier on you."

All the earlier warmth in his eyes is gone, leaving a scorching anger that's rapidly edging out his desire.

He undoes his belt with one hand, shoving his pants and boxer briefs down his thighs so his length is bobbing only a few inches in my face.

I try to pull free, but his grip is too strong. My scalp burns as he leans closer, grabbing my jaw with his free hand.

"Open your mouth, Nadya."

When I clamp my lips between my teeth, Konstantin's chuckle is so derisive it crawls over my skin, sinking its claws deep in my nerves. I'm so furious I could cry, but even if he let go entirely, I wouldn't move.

Partially because I don't want to give up an opportunity to take my anger out on him, but mostly because the way he's looking at me has arousal throbbing through me, potent and powerful.

No one has ever treated me like this, but some part of me—a part I'm too scared to look at too closely—is eager in a way I've never been before. I press my hands against his thighs, shoving with all my might.

"I said, *open*," he hisses, digging his fingers into either side of my jaw so hard I have no choice but to open my mouth, gasping in both shock and outrage.

Before I can snap it shut again, he hooks his thumb over my teeth, pulling down while he spits directly in my mouth.

I freeze, caught in the pleased glint in his expression, in the way his chest rises with rapid breaths.

"Now swallow."

I'm so shocked all I can do is obey.

"Good." He nods at me with a dark smirk. "That tongue is so good at spitting venom, isn't it? You're so good at lashing out and hiding from me. If you had behaved, you'd get it sweet. You'd get me holding you while you cried and lashed out. But you didn't. Instead, I'm going to fuck your face while you cry for me."

I'm weak. Weaker than I ever though I was. Because even though I hate him, I *want* to please him. I want it even more than I want him to soothe the ache in my core.

Knowing I'll hate myself for it in the morning, I open my mouth and lean forward to take him in my mouth.

He doesn't push, letting me get comfortable with the weight of him on my tongue as he slowly builds his pace.

This morning, I would have taken this as an opportunity to tease him. I would have tortured him with my tongue and played with his balls until he lost control and demanded I take him as deep as I can.

But things have changed.

He hurt me. And he's acting like *he* has the right to be angry.

Konstantin tests his hands on the back of my head, locking me in place with harsh hands. I take a deep breath, meeting his glare head-on.

"Tap my thigh if it's too much," he grunts before he thrusts himself so far down my throat, I gag around him.

Tears stream down my face, but it's so much better than earlier. Konstantin has the ability to take me out of my head without giving me room to second-guess a damn thing. All I can do is breathe.

He fucks my face with little regard for how I feel, and I should hate it. I should be furious that he's using me like I'm nothing but a tool for his pleasure, but I don't.

Everything is working for me in all the worst ways. The way he's holding my head in place. Every snap of his hips. His rough grunts and pants.

The fluffy towel is rough against my skin. My nipples are hard, and my pussy is practically begging me to let him do whatever he wants as long as he lets me spread my thighs and use my fingers to find relief.

But the way Konstantin's jaw is flexing tells me he doesn't want me getting off on this.

"Look at you," he moans, not breaking his relentless pace. "You're perfect with your lips stretched around me. You take me so fucking well." He grunts with a hard thrust, holding still while I gag around him. "That's it, Nadya. Let me hear you fucking choke."

He throbs on my tongue until I'm lightheaded. My eyes drift shut as I wonder if he's going to keep going until I pass out. But, fuck, it would be a welcome reprieve from the ache in my chest threatening to crack open.

He releases my head and pulls back so fast I lurch forward, watching helplessly as he strokes his cock while I gasp for breath.

"Eyes on me," Konstantin demands. He moans when my eyes cut to his, and it's the hottest thing I've ever heard. I squeeze my thighs together when the first rope of his release paints my face. His cum coats my lips, my cheeks, my lashes.

And I don't care.

All I want is for Konstantin to touch me and take away the misery threatening to make me cry all over again. I'll take pleasure from his hands a hundred times over before I choose this heartache.

"I love how messy you are for me," he says roughly, running a finger though the mess before he brings it to my lips. Obediently, I open for him, sucking his finger clean. "Dressed in only a towel. Covered in my cum. You're wrecked, and it's so fucking beautiful."

Even if it sounds like praise, the words come out like a sneer, and it makes me flinch.

But when Konstantin hauls me to my feet and presses his lips against mine, none of his cruelty is there. There's only warmth as he holds me tight, undoing the towel so I'm completely bare.

He uses the fabric to wipe my face clean in quick, efficient movements before he tosses it aside.

"Let's see how else I can make a mess of you."

He cups my pussy, thrusting two fingers inside faster than I can react. The slide is so wet it sounds obscene as he fucks me hard and fast.

Konstantin looks at me like a man possessed, like he refuses to let me go until he's gotten everything he could ever want out of me.

"You don't need me to make a mess of you here, do you, wife?" he hisses, harsh and bitter. "You're already dripping just from having my cock down your throat." With every word, he thrusts his fingers even deeper, rubbing relentlessly against my G-spot.

My legs are rubber beneath me, but a firm hand keeps me pinned against the hard planes of his chest. I cling to his partially open dress shirt, digging my fingers in so hard I'm going to shred the fabric with my nails.

His cock is still hard where it presses into my stomach.

When he shifts so the palm of his hand rubs ruthlessly against my clit, I gasp out his name.

"You're so needy, Nadya. So damn desperate for me." His teeth scrape over the sensitive spot where my neck and shoulder meet. "And you're all mine, aren't you?"

I shiver.

He's right, damn him. He's so right I could cry.

Even though my muscles are jelly, and he's making me feel so good it's like I'm going to die with every panted breath, I don't want to admit it. I don't want him to know how easy it would be for him to break me if he wanted to.

I'm his.

His to use. His to hurt. His to claim.

My thoughts are distant when he drops his free hand to my ass, easily lifting me. I sink my fingers into his shoulders, sweat dripping down my back when he pins me against the closed door.

"I'm going to make you come, *solnyshka*. And once you're fucked out and can't remember why you're angry in the first place, I'm going to come so deep inside you that you'll never question my role in your life again. You'll only be able to take it while your cunt milks my cock."

Oh, god.

My vision explodes in fireworks and every muscle in my body squeezes so tight it feels like I could snap in half as I come.

I'm dying. That's the only way to explain the way every atom of my being splits apart and pieces back together in a split second, the pleasure so intense it borders on pain.

I'm still trying to come to terms with my own oblivion when Konstantin snarls, spinning around and dropping me onto the bed. He tears off the remains of his clothes and sinks his cock into me so hard and fast I'm instantly right back on the edge of the abyss, ready to fall all over again.

"You don't get to hate me when you're this desperate for my cock," he growls, biting my breast hard enough to leave marks. "Feel me, Nadya. Feel what you do to me."

When I meet his eyes, there's something there, something sad and almost broken before he buries his face in my shoulder. A moment later, there's moisture there. *Tears,* my mind helpfully interjects.

Whether they're his tears or mine, I'm too lost in pleasure to care.

He fucks me so hard the only thing I can do is cling to him so I don't shatter into a million pieces.

"Konstantin," I pant. *"Fuck."*

Pleasure, anger, hurt. It all washes through me in waves, building with every moment until I'm burying my face in his neck and sobbing.

I'm not sure which one of us is holding the other harder when I shatter.

Konstantin groans as he throbs insides me, filling me with wave after wave of his release.

My heart is a bruised and battered thing in my chest, but I can't bring myself to let go of him while I cry. He pulls back just enough to press a kiss against my forehead, a tender act I'm not sure I deserve.

Because whatever just happened, it's clear he's hurting, too.

Chapter 18
Konstantin

When I gasp into consciousness, my heart is pounding so hard it's nearly impossible to breathe. My chest heaves as I sit up, clenching my hands against either side of my head as I greedily suck down as much air as I can.

It was just a dream.

As quietly as I can when my thoughts are a ragged mess, I slip out of bed. Nadya doesn't stir beside me, her hair a mess in the moonlight streaming through the window.

She didn't leave. She's still safe and sound in my bed, but it's impossible to let go of the images from my nightmare. It might not have been real, but the all-consuming panic I felt as I tore through the house as I looked for her was, and I still can't escape it.

No one else seemed to care. The guards hadn't seen her, Tatiana acted like she'd never even heard of Nadya, and even Viktor only gave me a bland look before turning away like I'd lost my mind.

Fuck, maybe I have.

She's safe. It wasn't real.

I brace my shaking hands on my knees, furious when I choke on a ragged breath. My cheeks are wet. I blink rapidly, willing the darkness at the edges of my vision to retreat.

Not now.

Each breath is more labored than the last.

I haven't had a panic attack in years. I've worked so hard to control them, to keep the relentless thoughts that circle my mind at a distance, but in all my plans and calculations, I never accounted for Nadya.

I never could have expected that the person who made me feel at peace would be the same one my subconscious taunts me over.

My nightmare might not have been real, but what if something *had* happened to her? What if she'd run away and gotten hurt? What if one of my many enemies who would love to use her to get to me finally got their hands on her?

It would be my fault.

Without proper protection, anything could happen. She could be tortured, maimed, or even killed.

If I was strong enough to ignore the pull I felt toward her, she would be safe and sound in Chicago.

But I wasn't.

I need her.

If I stayed on the path I'd been wandering, the collapse I've been working so hard to hide from everyone else was going to become so apparent anyone would have been able to see it a mile away.

I couldn't do that.

A cold sweat breaks out along the back of my neck.

If Nadya wants to leave, how will I convince her to stay?

I'm going to be sick.

I'm supposed to be strong. I'm supposed to be the one who holds everything together, who is unshakable no matter what happens around me. I've worked my ass off for years for this reputation, and I can't let a nightmare ruin it.

I can't lose everything now. I can't be so fucking weak that I fall apart over a single bad dream.

How will I be able to protect Nadya if I can't even protect myself?

"Konstantin?"

Nadya's tentative, tired voice freezes me to my core. My heart. My blood. The very air in my lungs.

Everything stops.

She can't see me like this. A smart man would have left the room the instant they woke, but she makes me weak. She makes me soft when I need to remain hard and unyielding. I need to be strong, or she'll leave.

And if she leaves, I won't be able to hold myself together.

She might as well kill me. At least then my life might leave an impact on her. Maybe then some small part of her might care about me.

"Go back to sleep, Nadya," I tell her, hating how pathetic I sound. Despite the weight of my many failures, despite how badly I want to collapse into her arms and let her ease my burdens for a few more hours, I gather my clothes from the floor and stand.

It takes more strength than I have to meet her eyes, and I regret it as soon as I do.

She sits up, holding the comforter like a shield as she eyes me with concern, her gaze roaming over me, taking in every inch as she makes sure I'm okay. How long was she watching me before she said my name? How much of my spinelessness was she exposed to?

"Are you alright?"

Am I *alright*? How am I supposed to be alright when my heart is still bruising against my ribs?

How the fuck can I be anything close to okay when her pity coats my skin with thick, sticky shame?

I don't know if the shame or my anxiety will be the thing that finally ends my worthless existence first.

Every instinct in my body screams to climb back into bed, to pull her against me until the weight on my chest melts away. Instead, I button my pants and grab my phone.

"I'm fine," I answer tersely.

"Konstantin—"

"I have business to deal with," I interrupt, turning my back to her before I reveal even more of the pathetic mess I usually keep hidden behind lock and key.

I need to be alone.

If I dive into work, I can start recalibrating. I can get back to the things that matter so the awful, terrified beast in my chest retreats back to its cave until I forget again.

There are so many things I need to do. So many things that will further my goals more than crying in my room in the middle of the night like a child.

As soon as I step into the hallway, I'm surrounded by the smell of the lilacs that decorate the house, their light scent something akin to a salve over my frayed nerves.

I call Viktor as I shut my office door. Despite the early hour, he answers on the first ring.

"Tell me you've found the *suka* who upset my wife," I bite out, grinding my teeth so hard I'm going to crack a tooth. If I focus on that waste of air, if I project everything onto him, I can make it to another sunrise with my mind intact.

"I have a lead," Viktor says, sounding almost as exhausted as I feel. "He signed up for the class under the name Cole Daniels, but as far as I can tell, that man doesn't exist. I scrubbed through the cameras from the studio and the surrounding streets. I have his face, but it's going to take some time to find a name. Especially if he's working undercover."

"Then send me the fucking picture."

"His photo, car, and license plate are already waiting in your inbox. Did Nadya tell you what name he gave her?"

I didn't bother to ask.

I was too busy watching the fragile bridge I'd built between us burn before I fucked her hard enough to make her cry.

I don't want her to think about that motherfucker ever again. I don't want her to remember the pain he brought her. I don't want her to think about how scared she was, and I don't want her to wonder for even a moment whether I'll allow it to happen again.

"How long until you get a name?" I ask instead of answering.

The rapid clicking of his keyboard is his only reply, and it's only familial loyalty that allows me to hold my temper.

"If you leave me alone, I can probably get you something by lunchtime. If you insist on staying on the phone with me the whole time, you'll have to give me a few days."

He hangs up on me before I can get a word in edgewise, leaving me with nothing but a silent house and the occasional flash of light from the guards patrolling outside. My mind flashes between the panic still dominating my body and the memory of Nadya's tears.

At least Viktor's *doing* something. All I've done is make her pain worse and give her even more reason to pull away, when all I need is to keep her glued to my side until I'm stable again.

I boot up my laptop and scan through my emails, doing everything I can to ignore the looming despair threatening to drown me all over again.

From the footage Viktor found, *Cole Daniels* is five foot ten, has brown hair, brown eyes, and is completely, utterly unremarkable. Everything about him is perfect for a person who wants to blend in.

In the end, it still won't give him the anonymity he needs to hide from me.

Even if I have to overturn every rock, light up every fucking shadow in the country, I'll find him.

I'll present his head as an apology if I have to. I'm going to beat his skull until he's unrecognizable, burn him to a crisp, and leave him so ruined that the feds will have to use DNA to identify the body.

For his sake, I hope he doesn't have a family. Because once I get my hands on him, I'm going to destroy every trace of his existence until he becomes nothing more than a memory. A fucking myth for his fellow agents to whisper about in the dark, praying they never meet the same fate.

It's your own fault, the despair whispers, its acid breath burning the back of my neck. *You're the one who put Nadya in this position.*

I slam my laptop shut, pacing the room. My skin is too tight; it feels like I'll burst free of it if I breathe too deep.

I want to go back to bed, pull Nadya into my arms, and hold her. *She doesn't have to love me,* I reason. Knowing the depths I'm willing to go to for her is too much for anyone to handle, much less a woman as strong and intelligent as she is.

She'll never put on blinders for me.

But wanting me? Tolerating me? She won't leave if we have that. We can build a life on that. She can have my child with that.

She won't be totally miserable because of me.

Threatening Alexei was a mistake, I can see that, but I can get her to move past it.

For hours, I pace the length of my office, alternating between staring out the window and scouring through the sparse updates Viktor sends over. It isn't much, but maybe if I spend enough time staring at it, I'll find a vital clue that will unlock the whole puzzle.

Eventually, the shadows shift with the rising sun. My head is killing me, my eyes are heavy, but at least I no longer feel like I'm one wrong move from falling apart.

I'm no closer to getting what I want, but I won't stop.

Not until I have a lead. Not until I know there's a way to make Nadya go back to ignoring all the secrets I've kept. Not until I have a plan.

When a knock sounds softly on the door, my spine straightens, my shoulders back like I'm bracing for a fight. Without waiting for an invitation, Nadya pushes the door open. There are shadows under her eyes, and she looks so... tired. Her shoulders are hunched, and she looks one step from collapsing.

"Do you want to talk about last night?" she asks after a long moment.

She must have showered at some point. Her hair is still wet, dripping onto a T-shirt that's massive on her. It takes me a few moments for my sleep-deprived mind to catch up and realize that she's wearing *my* shirt.

My heart gives a hollow pang in my chest, threatening to break through the layers of ice I've worked so hard to reconstruct while she slept.

"No."

The last thing I want is to rehash all my shame for her to pick apart. It won't make her feel safe. It won't encourage her to trust me.

I only want to fix all the damage I've already done.

Nadya closes her eyes, taking a deep breath through her nose. When she opens them again, she doesn't look at me, focusing out the window instead. She watches the guards like they're the most interesting thing she's ever seen.

"Why did you ask to marry me, Konstantin?" Her eyes flit to mine briefly before she sighs. "Why me? Why not any other woman?"

I swallow around the lump in my throat.

I've always known what to say. A clever threat to get someone to yield. A witty remark to forge a business deal. But when I'm faced with her quiet resignation, with the way her face has gone flat, I have no words. No answers. No justifications that she would ever accept.

All I have is the renewed sense of panic braying in my chest like an old dog, clawing at the paper-thin door I'm desperate to keep it locked behind.

"Fine. Don't answer me. But if you want this to be anything other than an arrangement, you have to give me something to work with, Konstantin." She shakes her head, turning to leave.

"You're still my wife," I call after her, the fist squeezing my lungs loosening only slightly when she stops. "Arrangement or not, you're still mine."

"But you aren't mine," she answers, her voice tired and sad. "You can claim me all you want, but you can't make me claim you. And until you give me a reason to, you're my husband in name. That's it."

She doesn't wait for a response before she leaves just as unceremoniously as she arrived.

It isn't until I'm staring at the empty space where she stood that I realize I *want* her to claim me. I want to be important to her. I want her thoughts to be as dominated by me as mine are of her. I want her to love me.

I don't want to fall in love on my own.

Chapter 19

Konstantin

It isn't unusual that I walk into a room only to be viewed with immediate disdain, but it is unusual for it to happen in my own home. In a matter of days, Tatiana has taken to glaring at me, the men outside have started walking on eggshells, and Nadya has turned ignoring me into an art form.

One she's managed to master.

She's worked diligently to build a wall between us, hoping it'll keep me out. Both metaphorically and physically, given the wall of pillows and blankets she puts together every night like an act of ritual worship, ensuring there's no chance we'll make contact in our sleep.

Not that it matters. As soon as she falls asleep, I reach across the wall anyway. I kiss her forehead, smooth back her hair, or just watch her until I feel some small measure of peace.

When we're awake, Nadya glares whenever I enter the room. She has her meals in her studio, and when I try to tempt her by sitting in the living room to watch one of the old movies she's so fond of, she doesn't even give me a second glance.

Do I deserve it?

Yes. Especially since I still haven't managed to track down the motherfucker that sparked this whole thing.

But there's only so much silence a man can endure before it starts to grate. The only person who doesn't look at me like I'm either a monster or a ticking bomb is Viktor, and that's likely only because he's exhausted and frustrated because he hasn't been able to get me what I need and doesn't want me to take it out on Vasily.

I know he's doing his best—there's too much riding on it for him to accept failure. If it's taking Viktor this long to find the *suka*, then the feds have gotten clever since we last had to deal with them.

But even if he had help, it's only a matter of time before we find someone who will lead back to where he's hiding.

No one vanishes without a trace. We just have to find a lead.

I watch Nadya and Vasily walk to his waiting car with clenched fists. She smiles easily, waving at one of the guards as she passes by.

It's yet another blow to my ego.

Even though Nadya can't stand having the guards around, she can still manage a smile and a kind word whenever she sees them. Meanwhile, I'd kill just to see her look at me with something other than hatred.

Even the few messages she has for me have been relayed through Tatiana. At least one of which was a demand that I let her run errands, and that I let Vasily be the one to take her. Though I'm sure Tatiana's language was much more colorful than what Nadya said, I relented.

But if Vasily so much as blinks, he's a dead man.

I stare out the window, watching until the car is gone and the gate is closed, whisking her away from me. Even after they've turned the corner and they're out of sight, I can't bring myself to look away.

The feds are sniffing around, Dowd's still lurking around somewhere, and my wife's guard has already failed once.

If I can't protect Nadya, then what can I do?

I need a lifeline to keep me sane. I pull out my phone, and like he can sense me unraveling, Viktor answers right away.

"Konstantin!"

The grim annoyance that's been present in every word he's said for days is gone, replaced by a cheeriness that only makes my mood even worse. His happiness is like sandpaper over the nerves that have already been shredded beyond recognition.

The rawness has put its roots so deep it has its own pulse, one that's even stronger than my own.

While I lie awake at night, stealing glimpses of Nadya over a wall of cotton and feathers, I've started to wonder if I'm more anxiety than I am man anymore.

"My favorite brother! I was just about to call you," he says, his grin audible even through the phone.

"I'm your only brother."

"With our father?" he scoffs. "I have a present for you."

"Is that so?"

"Yes. But you'll have to emerge from your glass tower and come to Vlast if you want to find out what it is."

I stand a little straighter, blinking at my own reflection in the window.

Viktor doesn't invite me to his restaurant often, and definitely not this early in the morning. In fact, I haven't been there since my bachelor party.

Thinking about that only adds another stone to the pile crushing my chest, so I hold back my questions and tell him I'll be there before taking off.

Whatever he has, it better be good.

Traffic winds me tighter and tighter, and by the time I make my way to Vlast's basement, I'm ready to tear off my own skin. At least none of the staff prepping for opening even look in my direction.

There's no point in pretending they don't have at least an inkling of what takes place in the freezer, but they're compensated well enough to feign ignorance. And if one of them looks at me right now, I'll have to dispose of a body *and* pay Viktor for the trouble.

Instead of being greeted by one of the men Viktor usually trusts enough to guard the basement when we have guests, I'm greeted by the man himself grinning with his arms folded over his chest and looking livelier than he has in days.

I narrow my eyes.

"I'm not in the mood the play your games, Viktor."

"Didn't think you were," he says, still grinning. "But you're going to like this. I promise."

"And what, exactly, is *this*?"

He nods over his shoulder, gesturing at the door. "Pull the stick from your ass and find out for yourself."

I roll my eyes, but curiosity overtakes my annoyance, throwing open the door and immediately stopping in my tracks.

I'll have to get Viktor something nice to pay this back. Because I'm not sure what I was expecting, but it definitely wasn't Special Agent Chance Jacobs bound, gagged, and waiting for me to work my magic.

He looks so different than he did in the official photo Viktor managed to get of him. There, he was proud and serious in his uniform. Here, he's shaken and furious.

I stand a little taller as I take him in. He didn't just scare my wife, he forced me to show my hand and lose her trust.

Torturing the man who led to the rapid collapse of the life I was building with Nadya may not fix everything, but it's better than nothing.

As I roll my shoulders back, the awful feelings that have been using my ribs as chew toys retreat. I take a deep breath, feeling like the man I'm supposed to be.

Collected. In control. Powerful.

I unholster my gun and lay it on the table of instruments.

He doesn't deserve the clean death a bullet would provide.

The agent glares from his spot on the floor, doing his best to look composed despite how he's trembling in the cold. I'm glad Viktor kept him awake. I wouldn't want him to miss a moment of what's to come.

My knees ache as I crouch in front of him, but is has nothing on the agony of every waking moment since the day this piece of shit set his sights on Nadya.

He bruised her arm.

I've missed the detached feeling that comes with power.

Control will always be better than the alternative.

"Are you scared?" I ask him, leaning close enough to take in the way his eyes are bloodshot with panic, the pulse in in his throat fluttering wildly.

"Right. You can't talk right now." I grin, shaking my head. "So we'll do this, Chance." I squeeze his jaw, forcing him to meet my eyes as my smile drops like a stone. "Blink twice if you're scared."

He keeps glaring, refusing to blink.

"Shame." I sigh as I frown. "I like it when they're scared."

"Don't count him out yet," Viktor pipes up. "Just because he didn't kill himself doesn't mean he's brave. He might just be stupid."

"True." I smirk, gratified when he finally flinches. "Maybe you think you have something to live for. Or, at least a reason to protect your life insurance. So which is it. A parent? A child?" I pause, searching his eyes. "A wife?" The color drains from his face, and I'm almost manic with glee. "There it is. You clung to your pathetic existence for her, didn't you?"

Fear is relentless. No matter how hard a man fights it, it always gets its way in the end. No matter who they were before they end up in this room, they all end up sniveling, pathetic messes, crying out to anyone they think can grant them mercy.

God. Their mothers. Even me.

But their pleas will always fall of deaf ears. I'm their judge, jury, and executioner.

It's going to be fucking satisfying watching Jacobs accept it.

"Let me explain something to you, Chance. Despite whatever intelligence you and your agency think they have, my wife is very much off-limits. And if you thought I would idly stand by and let you or any of your ilk anywhere near her, then I *sincerely* hope you did a good job hiding your wife before you decided to sign your own death warrant."

I pause to take in the state of him. Though his body is bruised, he seems largely unharmed.

Good. More fun for me.

"Now, I'm going to ask you a question, and when I take off this tape, I expect you to answer me." I keep my grip on his chin tight as his breathing changes to desperate gasps for air. "Nod if you understand."

I move my hand up and down, forcing him to nod so slowly it's almost comical.

With a hard yank, I rip off the tape slapped over his mouth, taking a chunk of skin with it. He snarls at me as soon as he can.

"I don't know who the fuck you paid off to make sure no one will even look at your operation, but I'm not here for you. I only care about Chicago," he spits.

"Then there's no reason to bother my wife."

"She has a soft spot for her brother. Everyone knows it. I'd be an idiot not to exploit it."

I sigh, pulling out the knife I was gifted last time Viktor invited me here. I twist the blade around so it catches the light. Jacobs glowers but goes silent when I press it against the spot right next to his kneecap, not yet hard enough to cut the skin, but enough to make the threat clear.

"You're right. Nadya cares deeply for her brother. Practically raised him, in fact. But if you wanted to know about Chicago, you should have come straight to me. After all, I'm the one who ended the war. At a great personal cost, might I add."

"What?" he asks, breathless with disbelief.

"Though you should also know you're lucky you caught Nadya when you did. I've been told she has a real talent with a knife." I sigh wistfully. "What I wouldn't give to watch her work you over if she was given the opportunity." I lift a shoulder in a lazy shrug. "Ah, well. Now, my question. Would you die for your wife, Jacobs?"

The agent screams his reply as I force the knife into his knee, twisting so his patella pops free of all the pesky tendons holding it in place.

"Did you know it takes seven years for someone to be declared presumed dead?" I ask over his cries. "Your wife won't get a chance to collect your life insurance before I get my hands on her."

***

Viktor tosses me a clean cloth to wipe the blood from my knife before it has a chance to dry.

For a special agent, I would have expected Jacobs to last longer. It took no time at all to reduce him to a mutilated corpse.

Viktor moves to start cleaning everything, but I wave him off.

"I've got this, but can you do me a favor?"

"Anything," he replies without hesitation. "You know that."

"Go to the house and keep Nadya company for a while. I'll clean up."

"If this is because of—"

"No," I insist before he says something stupid to snap me out of my good mood. "You did more than I asked you to, hunting him down. Go rest for a while. I can handle getting my hands dirty."

Besides, if I work my body to the point of exhaustion, maybe I can get some sleep tonight. Real sleep that isn't haunted by images of Nadya leaving me. Of her bleeding out while she curses me. Of her last breaths being used to curse my name.

"Alright. But if you need anything..."

I nod, signaling toward the door so I can start on the gore and blood.

I've got my work cut out for me.

Chapter 20

Nadya

Maintaining the level of searing rage Konstantin deserves has proven to be fucking exhausting. Especially when he's hasn't pushed back.

He hasn't demanded I talk to him. He hasn't tried to break apart the barriers I've erected. But he hasn't pretended to be sorry about what he did, either. In fact, every time I give in and look at him, he turns away.

He didn't even say anything when I begged Tatiana to ask him to let me go out with Vasya.

If he were anyone else, I'd think he's scared of what I have to say. But Konstantin?

He's either working an angle or waiting me out, and I don't know which one would be worse.

From the way Vasya huffed when I asked him to take me to a coffee shop on the other side of town, he isn't particularly happy about this turn of events either. Maybe it has something to do with the fact that this particular spot serves burnt coffee and is flooded with self-important men in suits that are cheaper than they're letting on.

But I needed an escape, and I can't bring myself to care whether he wants to be here or not.

Vasya constantly scans the room, taking in every face and tiny movement like he's expecting an ambush.

I don't bother pointing out that I doubt anyone would try to come for me in broad daylight. The only reason the creep at the studio approached me was because I was alone.

I grab my phone while I choke on another bitter, overpriced sip, grinning when I look at the full text thread from Alexei. Everything else sucks, but at least he's talking to me again.

Me

Do you want to see a picture of the worst coffee I've ever had in my life?

Alexei

Not really.

Too bad he's too far away to stop me from doing anything. Especially taking the most obnoxious photos I possibly can and badgering him with them until he gives me the reaction I want.

I might not be able to do anything about being married to an ass, but I can sure as hell annoy my brother for being one, and nothing can stop me.

"Can you take a picture for me?" I ask Vasily, handing him my phone.

"Why?" he asks, hesitantly taking my phone while I grin, shifting my coffee so it's right in front of me.

"I want to take a good photo, but I need both hands to do it."

As soon as he points the phone in my direction, I smile as obnoxiously as I can, using both hands to flip the bird. Despite how little he wants to be here, and how uneasy he clearly is about being in such a crowded place, the corners of Vasily's mouth twitch upward in a ghost of a smile.

"Is that for Konstantin?" he asks, handing me my phone. My amusement fades just as quickly as my grin.

"If it were for him, I wouldn't have smiled."

I send the photo to Alexei, adding a dozen middle finger emoji.

Me

Whoops too late!

Alexei

Where's your husband? Why isn't he entertaining you?

"You should send it to him anyway," Vasily says, lifting a shoulder in a half-hearted shrug. "I bet he'd like to know you're thinking of him."

I scoff. The last thing I want is for Konstantin to know he's on my mind. The hurt from him ignoring me the other night burns almost as hot as knowing he didn't protect my brother.

Which is stupid.

I never should have expected him to. But I *did*. Foolishly, I let myself think Konstantin might care about me enough to care about the things that matter to me.

But if he did, he wouldn't have let Alexei keep fighting. He would have squashed the war before I had to worry about the FBI spying on me and threatening my brother.

Either he's trying to give me space to make up for all the damage he's caused, or he's given up on charming me. Maybe he's decided I'm too much trouble, and he's only keeping me around because it's too much of a hassle to get a divorce. Maybe it's only a matter of time before he packs my bags and has someone drive me to the airport to take me home.

I bite my lip, ignoring the way my stomach lurches and my chest aches.

"I'm not sending him anything unless you take one where I'm not smiling. If he wants to see me smile, he has to make it happen himself."

"Fine," he sighs. "Give me your phone."

I slide it across the table, waiting for him to point it at me, but he only pokes at the screen a few times before sliding it back.

"There," he says, leaning back in his seat. "Konstantin is *Supreme Jackass*, right?"

I snatch my phone back in a panic, and right there, under my sparse text thread with Konstantin, is the same picture I just sent Alexei.

"What did you do?" I hiss, desperately searching for an unsend button.

Even if he'd taken a new photo, I wasn't actually going to *send* it.

"You said you wouldn't send him this picture. I don't want to lose my head when he finds out I'm not watching everything around you. I saved us both time."

"Great," I mutter. "Now I have to find a new name for him, because *you're* the supreme jackass." Vasily rolls his eyes as my phone vibrates with an incoming text.

Supreme Jackass

> My day just got so much better. Thank you, Nadya

I swipe the notification away without responding.

"And the boss is one wrong move from ripping off my head. You're pissed at him, so he's pissed at me. And now I'm driving you around town for shitty coffee and even worse muffins. No offense, but if this puts him in a slightly better mood, then I don't care if you're happy about it."

I sink further into my seat, turning off my phone before I'm tempted to look at it. "Konstantin doesn't deserve stupid selfies," I mutter under my breath, closing my eyes to block out the smell of mediocre coffee.

"If it makes you feel better, you can yell at me on the drive home."

"Fine." I grab my purse and stand. "This place sucks anyway."

"I told you that when you suggested it."

"Shut up, Vasya."

***

Spaghetti blinks slowly from his spot at my feet, looking between me and the kitchen with as much subtlety as he can. I know that the instant I shift from my position on the couch, he's going to take off at a full sprint, screeching his head off until I feed him.

Too bad I know for a fact he managed to con both me and Tatiana into feeding him breakfast this morning.

"Not going to happen," I tell him, meeting his stare until his eyes narrow, slowly realizing how serious I am.

If I wasn't so emotionally drained, I'd laugh. For such a friendly cat, Spaghetti's expression rivals anything his owner could dole out. But as it stands, I just meet his glare head-on, fully prepared to deal with the consequences once he decides I should join Konstantin in the pits of hell.

Our stare down is interrupted when the front door slams open. Immediately, Spaghetti turns around, hissing at whoever is making noise. His puffs up as he arches his back, but the effect is ruined by the way he takes a slow step back toward me.

I don't bother moving.

Whoever it is, there's no way they're here to hurt us. And if someone's managed to make it through the small army outside with the intent of getting to me, I won't be able to do much, anyway.

Regardless, I slip my hand between the couch cushions, tightening my hand around the knife I found stashed there last week.

Spaghetti and I both relax when Viktor strolls in, taking one look at us before he wanders right back out again. We look at each other, and a moment later Spaghetti takes off, setting his sights on a new mark.

"He's already eaten!" I call out before Spaghetti gets the chance to beg, closing my eyes. "Don't let him fool you, too."

"He already got you?" Viktor says from the end of the couch. I jump, not expecting him to be so close.

He smirks, holding a too-full glass of what looks like bourbon in either hand.

I give him a weary glance.

"Is it a special occasion, or is there a reason you're double fisting liquor at"—I glance at my phone—"three in the afternoon?"

In answer, he thrusts one of the glasses in my direction, waiting impatiently for me to take it from him. "I recognize the look on your face. I've spent a lifetime dealing with Konstantin, and you, my dear sister-in-law, have earned a fucking drink."

He isn't wrong, but if I want any chance of standing my own against Konstantin later, I need to be sober. And as much as I'd like to continue ignoring him for the rest of time, we're going to need to have a conversation eventually.

Getting drunk won't help.

"I appreciate the thought, but I'm good," I say, forcing myself to sit up.

"Suit yourself," Viktor says before he downs one of the glasses like a shot. I gape at him, but he doesn't seem to notice, putting the empty glass down on the coffee table and leaning back to watch me. "You know you have my brother tied up in knots, right?"

What? No I don't. In fact, Konstantin's probably out having the time of his life doing whatever it is he does when he isn't here.

And thinking about it doesn't stir something that feels an awful lot like jealousy in my chest.

It *doesn't*.

I have no reason to be jealous. Konstantin can do whatever the hell he wants. Murder, drugs, fucking a random woman. What does it matter to me? This marriage isn't real. I'm not someone he cares about, and eventually I'll forget about this dumb crush.

"How much have you already had to drink?" I ask.

"It's been a long day," Viktor says in lieu of answering. He takes a much slower sip from the second glass. "I'm serious, though. I haven't seen him this upset since Dad announced he was leaving the country."

"You mean the day he took over?" I ask, rolling my eyes. "I would've thought that was the happiest day of his life."

I can easily picture a younger Konstantin. Cocky, arrogant, and eager to take his father's role so he could have even more power. Viktor frowns, like the memory leaves a bad taste in his mouth.

"He hasn't told you about our dad, has he?"

His voice is so grave, I have to look away. Shrugging, I stare at the movie on the television, not really watching it.

"Not really."

"Of course not." Viktor sighs. "Konstantin and Dad never got along. They were constantly butting heads and fighting. Don't get me wrong, I hate the man, but..." He takes a deep breath, but there's something almost tortured in his expression.

"Dad was a piece of shit to my brother. Made him think that feeling anything at all, or accepting a small act of kindness, was proof he was weak. And he worked hard to make sure Konstantin internalized it."

I swallow hard.

"How'd that work out for him?"

"Awful," Viktor says with a laugh. "Konstantin still feels, he's just learned to hide it. Sometimes, he hides it so deep that I think he forgets it's there. But he's softer than he lets on."

Unbidden, I snort.

"There isn't a single part of that man that's soft."

Viktor smiles, but it doesn't meet his eyes. "He can be. When it matters."

Somehow I doubt that, but I don't want to poke at him any more than I already have. Viktor takes another sip of his drink, dropping his head back against the couch while I pull my knees against my chest.

"When I came out of the closet, Dad lost his mind. He and Konstantin had been fighting for years by that point, and Dad had decided he was going to make me pakhan and let Konstantin fend for himself." He downs the rest of his glass. All his usual mirth is gone, replaced with a quiet regret that makes him look totally different.

"I mean, you've met me. I can't pretend to be anything other than what I am. And if Dad pushed me to become pakhan, I wouldn't have had a choice. I'd have to be the one who's in control. I'd have to pretend I'm straight to appease the men. I'd have to marry a woman and act like I wasn't miserable every second of every day."

"You wouldn't."

He shakes his head. "So Konstantin buried how much he hates our dad, fixed his attitude, and transformed into the man he didn't want to be. He did everything Dad wanted so I wouldn't have to."

He doesn't meet my eyes, his foot bouncing restlessly where it's crossed over his knee.

"I know my brother can suck. He's worked so hard to become the man he is now that he forgets how to be anything else. But Konstantin is a good man under all his machismo and bolster. He's awful when it comes to people, but..." Viktor shrugs. "He's worked his ass off so no one questions him. He's become so notorious that no one would ever even think of saying shit about my life."

"He isn't a good person, but he's the best man I know." When he meets my eyes, there's something almost desperate behind his gaze.

"It's been thirteen years since he took over, and in all that time, you're the only thing my brother has ever wanted for himself. I don't know what he did you piss you off, and I don't want to know," he says. "But he's struggling."

"Viktor—"

"I'm not asking you to fall in love with him," he rushes to say. "Just talk to him. Please? Give him something to work with. He deserves that much."

He's so earnest, so desperate, that I'm at a loss for words.

His version of Konstantin is so different from the one I know that I have to wonder if we're talking about the same man at all.

The man I share a bed with can't be the same person. The Konstantin I know doesn't seem like the kind of person who would spit on someone if they were on fire, much less throw themselves into a role they didn't want to spare someone else the misery.

If that Konstantin really existed, I wouldn't be in this position in the first place. He would've introduced himself like a normal man and asked me on a date instead of arranging a marriage.

Before I can say anything, Tatiana's there, putting two bowls of soup on the coffee table. I blink, and a moment later she puts a bottle of bourbon next to them, winking before she walks away. Only then do I look around and realize how late it's gotten.

Silently, we both eat, ignoring the offering of booze as the heaviness around us starts to fade away. It allows me to breathe a little easier while I try to figure out where the picture Viktor painted fits in the life-sized puzzle I've been toying with since we first met.

Konstantin is a selfish, arrogant dick.

So how has he managed to convince the people closest to him that he's not? How did he manage to fool *me* into thinking otherwise?

I'm cut off from my spiral when I look up and see the man himself standing in the hallway, watching Viktor and I eat. As he watches us, his shoulders relax, his eyes glinting with something I don't understand. When his eyes meet mine, he doesn't say a word. Just flexes his jaw, ducks his head and turns, leaving us to our conversation.

His silence hurts.

When I say goodbye to Viktor and head to bed for the night, it's the first time I've ever seen Konstantin there before me. He's crowded on his half of the bed, leaving plenty of room for the wall I've built the past few nights. But when I slip under the comforter, I can't shake the image Viktor painted of him.

What if he really is capable of being selfless? Is it possible he's grown so used to throwing his vulnerabilities so far aside, that he's forgotten what it's like to be with someone in a real, honest way?

Has he ever even known?

I've spent every minute of the past few days so angry I can't barely think straight, but what have they been like for Konstantin? I've been so caught up in my own hurt that I haven't stopped to consider how he feels.

I grab a decorative pillow, but instead of situating it between us, I turn, tossing it to the floor before I lie down, showing Konstantin my back.

"Good night," I whisper over my shoulder so softly I doubt he even hears it as he turns off his light. He freezes for a moment, his eyes scorching against my shoulders before he lets out a ragged breath.

"Good night, *solnyshka.*"

Chapter 21
Konstantin

My breath is caught in my throat as I brush Nadya's hair from her forehead. My touch is hesitant, not quite believing she won't disappear the moment I touch her. But when I brush my knuckle over her brow, she doesn't vanish.

Somehow, this isn't a twisted dream. My subconscious has taken a night off instead of taunting me with everything I can't have. Nadya actually chose to not put up her wall last night.

She's real, and she's drooling on my shoulder.

I twist her hair around my finger, smiling faintly as her whole face scrunches in her sleep when it slips away from me like silk.

What did Viktor do to get her to let go of her anger?

There was a bottle of bourbon on the coffee table when I got home, but she doesn't smell like she's been drinking. I trace a line from her shoulder down to the curve of her hip as she sleeps peacefully, breathing easily for the first time in far too long as I take her in.

I'm not sure I've ever felt better than I do when she's this close to me.

Nadya sighs, leaning into my touch.

I don't know how Viktor made this happen, but I'm going to have to find a way to repay him.

But, much to my chagrin, his hand in delivering the special agent yesterday means I have work that needs to be done. I need to dig through every bit of information on him and tie up every loose end. I need to make it look like he ran away and disappeared, never to be seen or heard from again.

And if I can't accomplish that, then I need to plant enough of a trail to point any investigation as far away from me as I can.

Pulling free from Nadya's grasp is as painful as peeling off my own flesh, but I need to go to my office. I need to figure out what to do with the agent's IDs, ditch his badge, and figure out if his wife is the kind of woman who's going to search for him, or if we can get her to back off with a well-placed stack of cash.

Carefully, I press a kiss against the back of Nadya's hand, right over her wedding ring.

I have so much work to do, but if I want to stay calm enough to focus, I need to go to the gym and burn off some of the lingering adrenaline first. I lift weights until sweat is pouring down my face, and my body is so exhausted that my mind will have no choice but to stay on track.

My eyes linger on the empty bed when I go to shower and change, more upset than I have any right to be when I realize Nadya must have already left for the day. Without saying good-bye.

What did you expect, asshole?

One night isn't going to change how she feels. It won't take away her anger or fear.

I glance at my phone, unable to keep myself from smiling at my new lockscreen. Nadya's irreverent grin beams back at me, her ring shining on her hand as she flips off the camera.

At least I have that.

I finish up and head to my office to sort through the mountain of bullshit.

I don't even know how long I spend sorting thought things, only pausing to answer a phone call here or there, before my phone rings again. As soon as I see Vasily's name, I'm on edge.

If Nadya isn't here, he should be glued to her side. And after the other day, he knows better than to waste his time on meaningless phone calls.

Not unless it's an emergency.

The moment I answer, my heart drops like a lead weight as I hear the roar of an engine and Nadya's furious yelling as she lets out a string of curses.

"I dropped Spaghetti's food! Take me back, or I'm going to chop you into little pieces and *you* can be his next meal!" she screams with a frustration so visceral, that even through the phone, I can feel the intent behind every word.

"I have more of a chance of surviving you than your husband," Vasily snaps back, sending my blood pressure through the roof. I try to interject, but neither of them hears me as they yell, Nadya shouting more and more threats while Vasily tells her to *bring it on*.

"Enough!" I shout. Finally, they both shut up, and the only sounds on the other line is the roar of the engine and squeal of the tires as Vasily drives. "What the fuck is going on?"

"A man pulled a gun when we were leaving the pet store," Vasily says as calmly as he can, but I can hear how hard he's gritting his teeth over the thundering of my heart in my ears. The air in my lungs is heavy enough to hurt. "I got Nadya in the car before he opened fire. And now she's insisting I take her back because she seems to think—"

There's a scuffle, then Nadya's voice is much closer to the phone. After her resolute silences, even her terror is music to my ears.

She's okay, I tell myself.

She's pissed to high hell, and there's a waver in her voice that makes my chest ache, but she's okay. If she weren't, she wouldn't be making threats.

She'd be screaming in pain.

I put her on speaker, listening to both her threats and promises while I text Viktor.

"Spaghetti needs his food, Konstantin! Tell your guard dog to turn this car around, or I swear to god, I'm stealing one of your cars and going back on my own whether you like it or not," she demands.

"He has enough food, *solnyshka*," I tell her as gently as I can, my head buried in my shaking hands. Darkness fogs the edges of my vison, but I cling to her voice like an anchor. "He can live off the kibble in the cabinet, even if he doesn't like it." Self-loathing and fear have their hands around my throat, threatening to rob me of my ability to speak. "Are you alright?"

There's a short pause, then a shaky breath that dissolves into a heart-wrenching sound that tears the air from my lungs. Her choked sob has me wanting to reach through the phone and pull her into my arms. I've never felt so utterly useless in my life as I make my way outside, waiting with my heart in my throat, whispering soft assurances in a pathetic approximation of comfort.

No matter what I say, none of it touches her.

Her fear is unbearable, but I can't let it cut me down. If I know Nadya, she's going to be furious with herself for allowing anyone to see her this upset. Someday, whether it's tomorrow or a year from now, she'll look back on this and hate that she was so vulnerable around Vasily. While I can't prevent her from feeling embarrassed, I'll do whatever I have to in order to spare her from the sting of it.

If there's any occasion that should allow Nadya to feel her blind panic unfiltered, it's this.

And if any of my men so much as thinks about saying an unkind word, I'll sever their tongues so they never speak again.

She's deaf to my words, but I don't stop talking, don't stop trying to distract her until the car pulls through the front gate. As soon as it stops, I feel like my knees are going to give out beneath me.

There are bullet holes everywhere. The bulletproof glass and siding have held up, but it isn't until I see the marks that I realize someone didn't just open fire in a random place. They were shooting *at* Nadya.

Out of all the places in the city, out of all the people, someone went out of their way to hurt her.

I drop my phone and tear open the door, holding Nadya as tightly as I can. For once, she doesn't fight me, burying her face in my neck and wrapping her legs around my torso like I'm the only thing grounding her. When I stand, I meet Vasily's determined stare over the roof of the car.

"Call Viktor and tell him what happened. Every detail. Then handle it." I try to keep the anger out of my voice, conscious of the way Nadya's shaking with barely concealed tears, clinging to me like she doesn't know how to breathe.

I want to tear apart the city and burn everything to the ground until I find whoever is responsible for this. But right now, all my focus is on her.

Nadya is more important than revenge.

For now I'll have to trust my men to perform to the level I expect. I can't keep my tightly held control when it feels like someone's pulled my heart out through my throat.

I just need Nadya to feel safe again.

I carry her to the bedroom, ignoring the way her sobs pierce my chest with ice and knives that outdo anything I was able to do at Vlast. As I try to set her on the bed, she digs her nails into my shoulders, holding even tighter.

"I'm not going anywhere," I assure her. "I'm just going to take off your shoes so you can lie down, then I'm going to get you a glass of water." She pulls away, tears silently streaming down her face. "Is that okay?"

There's a panicked debate in her eyes, like she can't figure out whether to trust me or not. After everything else that's happened today, her lack of trust could be the final nail in my coffin.

I run my thumbs over her cheeks, pushing her tear-soaked hair from her face.

If Nadya wants to question me, then she's more than earned the right. I'll let her lash out and hurt me, scream in my face and call me every name under the sun. As long as she doesn't feel as awful as she does in this moment, I'll bear whatever she wants without regret.

It can't be more painful than this.

After a moment that could stretch over a lifetime, Nadya nods. I drop to my knees, slipping off her sandals, then filling a glass with water. By the time I come back to her, Nadya has wrapped herself in the comforter and tossed aside all the spare pillows.

The moment she spots me, she's reaching out, but when I hand her the water, she shakes her head. With miserable, eager hope, I set it aside and sit next to her, enclosing her in my arms, like that alone will be enough to comfort her. Carefully, I shift so we're lying down, Nadya's head pressed against my chest, twining my fingers with hers before she can retreat back into her blanket cocoon.

For what feels like ages, Nadya shivers, silently using me for whatever she needs.

Her breaths don't slow until Spaghetti cautiously wanders in. His curious eyes assess the situation before he decides to disregard his feelings for me and curl up against Nadya's side, purring until she's lulled to sleep.

CHAPTER 22
Nadya

The Bratva has always been a shadow lurking around the corner. A boogeyman I've always known to fear but never had to face. Not until Konstantin came along.

But even then, it wasn't an actual threat. It was something abstract. Knowing my brother was in danger but never knowing how. Knowing it's smart to carry a weapon, but never really knowing *why*. The Bratva taught me that the world was fraught with danger, but it was never up close and personal.

It was never a man pointing a gun at my head when all I was trying to do was pick up food for my husband's cat. It was never ducking down in my seat and silently begging the universe to let me walk away.

It was never the terrifying realization that I could die at any moment, and all I'd leave behind is a million words I haven't said and a collection of mediocre vases and mugs.

At some point in my sleep, I must have shifted and hooked my leg over Konstantin's, sprawling over him like a human-sized pillow. The longer I lie here, the more comfortable he seems to become.

I can't bring myself to pull away from his warm embrace.

Not when even sleep has done nothing to make me feel more secure. Not when his arms are the only thing keeping me from spiraling out of control. Because if I slip free, I'm liable to scream and cry, demanding answers to questions I don't even know how to phrase.

But Konstantin didn't seem to know any more than I did.

He just managed to hold himself together when I couldn't.

I shift, curling into myself, and freeze at the smooth drag of skin against skin.

I don't remember undressing, but I'm no stranger to the way the hard line of his cock feels underneath me as I shift my hips.

There's a shaky voice in the back of my head pleading with me to pull away from him, to go back to my side of the bed and pretend nothing is out of the ordinary.

But Konstantin's body feels so good against mine. I bite my lip, barely breathing as I twist around just the slightest bit, just enough to give me room to grind my clit against his rock-hard thigh.

My body is so stiff I don't think I moved at all while I slept. I was so out of it that I shouldn't be surprised Konstantin managed to get me undressed without me knowing. Hell, based on how heavy my limbs still feel, he could have done whatever he wanted with me, and I wouldn't have even known.

Despite the stiffness in my muscles and the lingering fatigue from my burnt-out adrenaline, heat stirs low in my gut at the image.

It shouldn't be nearly as hot as it is. I should retreat or cringe away, but instead my eyes fall shut with the fantasy of Konstantin's strong hands sliding up my thighs, spreading me open for him. He wouldn't think about my pleasure. He wouldn't have to wait for me to give him permission.

My body is always primed for him. He wouldn't need to do a thing before he was free to take whatever he wanted from me.

I picture the way he'd fuck me until I woke up, how I'd be on the verge of an orgasm even while he urged me to go back to sleep, whispering that it was all a dream.

Oh, fuck.

I roll my hips slowly, the slide getting easier with every moment. I'm practically soaking his thigh, shamelessly grinding against him even as I bite my lip to hold back a whimper.

Konstantin could have used me just like this. It's so easy to picture him grunting above me, moving my body like I'm nothing but a toy for his pleasure. I'm so caught up in my fantasy that I'm on the edge of an orgasm when the same strong hands I've been thinking about holding me in place fly to my hair, gripping tight.

"If you wanted to play, you should have said something." Konstantin chuckles sleepily, his lips brushing against my temple. He pulls, forcing me to meet his eyes, dark and tortured in the moonlight.

His eyes are so dark it seems like the night itself has eaten away the blue. It embraces him until he's indistinguishable from the shadow itself, like it's entitled to every part of him.

Doesn't it know that he's supposed to be mine?

I twist my head, but fighting against Konstantin's strength is even more daunting than being trapped under his too-knowing eyes.

Why am I fighting, anyway? He can give me the oblivion that will free me from the sound of bullets hitting the car still echoing in the back of my head. He can give me what I want.

I just have to let him.

He reads my resignation in my shaking breath, using the hand not twisted in my hair to urge me back to a steady rhythm against his thigh.

"Who would have guessed that under all your fire and sharp words you'd be such a slut for me that you'd reduce yourself to riding my thigh to get off?"

He *tsks*, the sound simultaneously so dismissive that it makes me want to flinch, and so panty-melting that I can't help but buck against him.

His expression remains unaffected, looking me up and down with a dismissive air that makes goose bumps erupt on my heated flesh.

I don't want to pull away.

I don't want him to stop looking at me like this, either.

When he looks at me like this, there's no room to worry about what happened earlier. I'm not concerned about how easily I'd let Konstantin use me, or how pissed I'm supposed to be.

The only thing I can focus on is the throbbing in my core, protesting how empty I am without my husband.

He drops his hand to the back of my neck, squeezing before he slams his lips down on mine in a kiss so furious it's more of a gnashing of teeth than a show of intimacy.

When Konstantin pulls away, he keeps my lip trapped between his teeth.

"Tell me you're mine," he demands. "Tell me I can have you how I need you. Tell me you won't shut me out again." He presses a hand against the small of my back, pinning me so I can't get the friction I need. "*Please*, Nadya."

I couldn't get away from him even if I tried, and at this point, I'm not sure I even want to.

Konstantin has me trapped.

Physically.

Emotionally.

He's wormed his way into every thought and breath, taking up space I didn't even know was free to take. I can't lie to myself and pretend it was just a crush when he holds me like he needs me.

"I'm not done being mad at you," I breathe, my voice tied up in all the things I'm too wrung out to admit.

"Good." He smiles, soft and pleased. "I don't want you to lose that spark. But you can still be pissed when you submit. You can still be angry when you're so full of my cum that it spills out around my cock."

I nod my consent, hating myself almost as much as I hate him.

"Say it, Nadya."

"I'm yours."

"That's my wife," he purrs, using his grip on my hip to maneuver me effortlessly until the hard line of his erection is lined up with my pussy. "Lying to my face even when you're desperate for me." I shiver when he notches his cock between my thighs, running his thumbs in slow circles over my hipbones.

Even that simple touch has goose bumps breaking out over my heated flesh.

"Do you feel that, Nadya?" Konstantin asks, rolling his hips with an agonizing slowness, thrusting just deep enough to tease. "Do you feel what you do to me? Do you feel how well we fit together?"

"If you'd actually fuck me, I might," I answer, straining against his hold so I can feel him the way I need.

With a growl I feel just as much as hear, Konstantin slams into me. I throw my head back, biting back a long moan as I dig my nails into his abs as he stretches me open. Why does he have to feel so fucking good?

If he treated me the way he does the rest of the world, I'd never want to fall into him like this. I would never trust him to take care of me.

The world collapses around me, and with each thrust, Konstantin rebuilds the foundation brick by agonizing, torturous brick. Whoever I was before him burns to ash, but even when everything lies in ruins, he's still here.

Steady, calm, and patient.

I'm not sure if I want to scream or thank him.

I bury my face in his neck as liquid pleasure replaces the blood in my veins.

In the morning, I'll probably regret this. I'll blame how late it is, or the adrenaline, or say I was half-asleep and didn't know what I was doing, but the truth is, I need him.

I need Konstantin.

He's terrible for me in more ways than I'll likely ever know, but under his gaze I feel *seen*. I can't hide, and I don't want to.

I want him to take charge and ruin me beyond recognition. I want to learn all the secrets he's hiding. I want him to trust me almost as much as I want to trust him.

"Let go, Nadya," Konstantin commands, his fingers digging in tight. "Let go and milk my cock. Let me feel you."

My legs shake on either side of his hips, my ears ringing as everything breaks.

My heart. My walls. My will to resist the pull Konstantin has over me. It all shatters as I come so hard, I'm not sure if I'm floating or dying. My eyes clamp shut as I collapse against Konstantin in a boneless heap, while he moans his pleasure, clutching my body so tightly I couldn't move if I tried.

He slams into me, hitting oversensitive nerves with every thrust until he freezes, hissing through his teeth. Konstantin comes with a strangled sound that would be enough to short-circuit my brain if I were still capable of thought. My existence has been reduced to the way Konstantin's heart races under my head, and the overwhelming too-much feeling of his cock throbbing his release.

I rest my hand over his chest, grounding myself in the way his heart pounds. It's so strong and sure, and I'm still so brittle. Konstantin's hand is soft as he trails it up and down my spine, comforting me without words.

"When you break my heart, I don't know if I'll be able to recover," I whisper against his chest, idly tracing the inked swirls covering his pec like smoke.

Silence.

Then, just as softly, he says, "I don't want to break your heart. I just want you. I want you to be the best version of yourself. I want you to let me be part of it."

I snort, but it's devoid of all humor.

"You have a strange way of showing it."

"I'm sorry," he whispers, a broken confession that's pried from the depths of his chest. He tugs on my hair until I'm forced to confront the conflict in his eyes. "I'm sorry, Nadya. I... I'm not good at being open. In my position, it's always smart to assume everyone is working an angle. Everyone wants something from me, and I have to protect the ones I care about when they try to take it."

I search his face for any signs of deception, any hint that this is another one of his games, but I come up empty. The only thing left is an unexpected vulnerability, lacquered in frustration, but devoid of guilt.

Do you care about me? I want to ask. *Is there ever a chance you'll let your guard down enough to love me?*

"I know I've fallen short at every turn." The hand on my back stills as Konstantin sighs. "I've failed you in so many ways, and I'll probably fail you a thousand times more, but what happened today won't happen again. I may not be what you want in any other way, but I will keep you safe. I promise."

When I open my mouth, my doubts and fears coalesce, binding my tongue before I can reassure him.

***

The furious thundering of Konstantin's heart under my head throws me out of my nightmare, replacing the memory of bullets hitting the car with the very real fear that has his muscles bunched tight.

"*No,*" Konstantin mutters, his voice pained.

I blink awake, my eyes snapping to his face.

His brows are furrowed, his eyes clenched shut. His chest heaves as he pants, his head thrashing back and forth.

"Konstantin?"

He groans, a sound so low and agonized that I find myself crawling closer and laying a hand on his cheek. He flinches away, fighting in his sleep like it's a matter of life and death.

In a million years, I never would have expected that a man like him, so formidable and intimidating, could look so *scared*. Sweat dots his brows, and his muscles are locked so tight it looks painful, coiled like a snake prepared to strike.

What could live in his dreams that has him this terrified?

"Konstantin!" I say again, trapping his face between my hands, holding tighter when his thrashing continues. "Wake up!"

Between one breath and the next, Konstantin flips us, pinning me to the bed with his forearm pressed against my throat. The look in his eyes is lethal, his chest heaving.

My hands fly to his arm on instinct, but I force myself to relax, sucking in shallow breaths instead of fighting him.

"*Fuck,*" he pants, scrambling away from me. "I'm sorry." Konstantin's head is in his hands as I sit up, his fingers gripping his hair, pulling so hard it's like he's trying to rip it from his skull.

"Are you okay?" I ask, reaching for him.

Konstantin jerks away, and just before he storms from the bed, I swear I see a streak of wetness on his cheek in the moonlight.

"I'm fine," he snarls, going back to pacing with his hands fisted at his sides. "Go back to sleep."

I've only seen him like this once before, and I let him push me away. I regretted it immediately.

I won't let him push me away this time.

I catch his arm before he's able to rip the door open. His shoulders tense, but I wrap my arms around his torso before he can hide in his office.

"Come back to bed," I say, pressing my face against his back. Every muscle in his body is shaking, and he's holding himself tight, like he's afraid he'll fall apart if he doesn't get away from me. "Come back to bed and talk to me."

"There's no reason to talk."

"Konstantin—"

"We're not having this conversation, Nadya. Go back to bed. I have work to do," he bites, voice clipped.

"Work can wait until morning."

"No. Let me go, and—"

"You're the one who keeps telling me that begging is beneath me, Konstantin," I snap, digging my nails into the hard muscles of his stomach. "So I'm not begging. I am *demanding*. Come back to bed. Either talk to me now or in the morning, but I'm not letting you deal with whatever this is on your own."

Slowly, he pries my hands free and turns around. I squeeze even tighter, refusing to let go.

"You're making demands of me, *solnyshka*?"

"Yes. So stop being an ass and take me back to bed."

His hands are still shaking when he brushes my hair back. I meet his eyes with a fierce glare. Eventually, he stops shaking, stroking over the planes of my face like he can't quite believe I'm still here.

"You're okay?" he breathes out, the words sounding like a question as he settles his forehead against mine. "And you want me to stay?"

How does he not get it? How can Konstantin be so smart and conniving, but so dense at the same time? How do I get him to realize I'm falling for him? That the reason his carelessness hurts so much is because I want him so much?

I want to scream in his face, but not when he's like this. Not when he's vulnerable and scared.

I want Konstantin to trust me. I want him to want me just as much when he wakes up from a nightmare as he does when we go to bed at night. I want him to let me in. Into his life, his heart, his mind. I want more than the stoic jerk who's content to pull strings in the background.

I want him to let me take care of him as much as he does of me.

"Yes," I sigh. "It was a shitty day. I want you to hold me so I can feel safe until the sun comes up."

Smiling faintly, he nods. "Then let's go back to bed."

Chapter 23

Konstantin

There are twice as many men patrolling the grounds as normal. Some circle the fence line, and others are closer, passing by the windows and doors with every sweep.

Nadya's going to kill me, but if someone was bold enough to go after her in the middle of the day, I need to be absolutely certain there's no risk of anyone attempting the same when she's home. She needs to know she's safe here.

I want her to be so comfortable in my home that she forgets there was a threat to her life to begin with. Even if that means hiring extra guards until she's able to forget how weak I was the other night.

I look back at the house. Despite being unable to see through the windows, I have no doubt Nadya's behind one of them, cursing my existence and telling Spaghetti all about her plans to slaughter me as soon as she gets a chance.

She hated the security I had in place before she moved here, she loathes having to take Vasily with her whenever she leaves the house, and even though she seems more relaxed after the other night, I'm going to keep my promises to her no matter what it costs.

Wherever she is inside the house, Vasily can't be far behind, likely offering to assist with her murder plot.

Whenever I'm not home, he's going to be glued to her side.

He might have held his tongue about how much that decision displeased him, but Viktor is not nearly as composed. He shoots daggers at me whenever he thinks I'm not looking, furious that I'm infringing on even more of his boyfriend's time.

The cops got the shooter before any of my men could get there, and despite all our attempts to bribe them or get anyone to release the man into our custody for safe keeping, it's proving more of a challenge than it should be.

Even if they were willing to share what he's told them, something tells me their interrogation techniques aren't nearly as thorough as mine.

"At least our hands are clean," Viktor mumbles with a shrug. The usual carefree persona he wears so well is locked behind a six-inch wall of steel, nowhere to be seen until this is handled and everything goes back to normal.

"I'd be more comfortable if we could get our hands on the guy and find out what his orders were."

The cops were quick to release the shooter's name after they arrested him, probably because they were thrilled to have such a slam-dunk case on their hands. Security footage from multiple businesses caught everything—from his arrival, to the moment he was tackled to the ground. Dozens of witnesses stuck around to tell the cops every sordid detail of what they saw.

But with a name like Fergus Loughlin, at least I don't have to wonder who sent him.

Dowd is a pain in my side, and I'm running out of both the time and patience to deal with him.

"Tell me you have a man in Dowd's camp," I say, running a hand down my face. "What does he have to say about this little stunt?"

Viktor shrugs as we make ourselves comfortable on the back patio, staring at the unlit firepit with a stoic look. "We have people, but as far as they can tell, Liam has gone underground. He's being a slippery motherfucker and no one seems to know what he's planning."

The pressure behind my eyes throbs as I tilt my head toward the sun.

"In that case, Vasily is going to be even more of an emotionless robot than he already is."

"He isn't a robot. You just haven't taken the time to get to know him."

"I know him well enough to know he's not going to happy when I tell him to be here until all of this is settled."

Viktor lets out a long breath, rolling his shoulders, but doesn't say anything. That, more than anything, puts me on edge.

My brother has never been the strong and silent type. He's the kind of person that always has a snappy remark on the tip of his tongue, entirely unconcerned with the consequences of whatever he's about to say because he knows I won't let anyone reach him.

But when he gets quiet, it means he's worried.

His jaw is tight as he looks over at the water, gazing at the hill below us. Each stretched-out moment of his silence presses against my chest.

"What aren't you saying?" I ask when his silence becomes more than I can bear.

"Liam didn't just go into hiding; he dropped off the fucking map. I can't find anything. No flight records, no hints of anything online. He's planning something, and if we can't figure it out before he acts, we're going to be left on our back foot again. I just... I don't like it."

"And how do you think I feel?" I practically snarl.

We got lucky the other day.

Vasily was quick on his feet and managed to get Nadya away from the danger, but what happens next time? What if he's distracted? What if Nadya is on a stubborn streak and refuses to let him do his job because she thinks she knows better?

"We'll handle it," I say, staring at my folded hands.

We don't have a choice.

***

While Vasily perks up considerably when he sees Viktor and I joining them in the living room, Nadya only sulks harder, sinking into the couch as she shoots me a vicious glare.

I know she's likely planning the delicate way she'll dab at fake tears for everyone in attendance at my funeral, but she's still the most beautiful woman I've ever seen. If we didn't have an audience, I'd push my luck and kiss the grumpy frown off her face until she melts into me like I know she wants to.

But I don't want anyone else seeing her that way.

"Can Vasily leave now? Or does he need to keep babysitting me until the end of time? Because he has plans with Kira, and those plans don't include trailing after me just because you're in a mood."

She huffs, crossing her arms over her chest. I do my best to school my expression before she sees my grin.

"Don't look at me like that."

"Like what?" I ask.

"Like you're amused. You're being a dick, and Vasya doesn't deserve it."

I freeze.

Vasya? Since when does her bodyguard get a nickname?

I made her come so hard this morning she stumbled when she tried to stand, and I can't get more than a glare.

I could kill him.

"Fine. *Vasya*"—I give him a sharp look when I say it, one that has him shifting in his seat—"can go. But he'll be back first thing in the morning so he's here before my meeting. Isn't that right?"

He meets my glare without flinching and nods.

Do I think he would so much as look in Nadya's direction? No. If he even thought about it, Viktor would kill him. And even if he managed to evade my brother, Nadya would finish the job. His survival instincts would have to be imaginary for him to stoop that low.

But do I like the reminder that everyone else is able to win her affections without so much as lifting a finger? No.

In fact, just thinking about it has me griding my teeth as he and Viktor leave, leaving me with Nadya and her prickly attitude.

I just want to see her smile. It's been days since I broke down again, and I want to hear her laugh more than I want my next breath. She's pissed, but I need her more than she could possibly know, especially since everything is so far out of my control.

"I know you hate the extra security, but it isn't going to last forever."

She's unconvinced as I sit next to her, much closer than Vasily was. A thrill runs through me when she doesn't immediately move away.

"Vasya nearly had an aneurysm when I tried to go outside earlier," she deadpans. "Whatever you told him, it was excessive."

"Why were you trying to go outside?"

"Because we have a patio. One that's on the second floor. And only accessible through our bedroom."

Our bedroom.

Ours.

A space that's just as much hers as it is mine because she's claimed it as her own.

Then everything else she said filters in.

"Absolutely not." Even if he's just passing through, there's not a universe where I'm going to let another man into our bedroom.

It's one of the few places where there are no cameras. It's the place we're free to be ourselves without having to worry about anyone else's perceptions or thoughts. Before we were married, only I was allowed in that room. The thought of her wanting anyone—much less another man—there is enough to make me nauseous.

"You can't keep me from going outside." She sighs.

I do the only thing I can, reaching out and pulling her onto my lap. She tries to squirm free, but I only hold her tighter.

"Let me go, Konstantin."

I don't. Instead, I hook my chin over her shoulder, taking her hand in mine while she tries to twist around so she can kick my shin.

"Humor me, *solnyshka*," I say, pressing a kiss to the delicate column of her throat. Slowly, she settles against my chest, tilting her head so she can look me in the eye. "This is temporary."

Nadya sighs. "I'm going outside whether you let me or not. You know that, right?"

"I couldn't stop you if I tried," I admit.

"You can't bring me to California and tell me I have to spend all my time indoors, Konstantin. I can't live on sex alone. I need warmth and sunshine, too."

I take a meaningful look outside, where the evening fog is starting to roll back in. It's been almost suffocating under the heatwave we've been stuck in, driving everyone inside before they choke on it.

"I don't want another man in our room."

"Then I'll go on the back patio. Or I can hang out in the front yard. But don't try to lock me away like a princess in a tower."

"Fine," I concede. "But Vasily will be with you the whole time. Got it?"

She rolls her eyes, tracing over the back of my hands as she relaxes. Eventually, she nods, and while it doesn't erase the boulder from my shoulders, it makes the load just a little easier to carry.

"You know, striking a deal with you is harder than with anyone else I've ever worked with," I murmur.

Nadya snorts.

"It's true. If whoever I'm dealing with gets a rise out of me, I tend to say things I don't mean, and they hold it against me. It's part of why I encourage the people I'm meeting to have a drink. But I can't do that with you. I have to consider every word before I say something stupid and make things worse."

"Say something like what?"

I hum, flipping my hand over and twisting my fingers with hers.

"Like threatening your brother, when hurting you is the last thing I want to do."

My confession lands between us with the impact of a leaf on a still lake. The slow ripples wash over us, but it's impossible to say whether Nadya notices them or not.

It feels like an eternity before she asks, "What are you trying to say, Konstantin?"

"That I'm sorry if I made you feel like you're less than the best thing that's ever happened to me."

She pulls away, and this time, I let her go. She turns so she's straddling my hips, searching my eyes like she's looking for the punchline to a shitty joke.

"I'm saying that I care about you," I offer. "That if the cost to hold your hand for only a moment was to redo my entire life—all the blood, sweat, and pain—I'd do it in a heartbeat. And if I ever made you doubt that, then it's a regret I'll carry for the rest of my life."

For a long moment, Nadya doesn't say anything, and I don't push her to. If she decides words aren't enough and she's still furious, then so be it. I'll take her anger and tears. I'll take whatever she gives me as long as she's by my side.

Eventually, she sighs, leaning forward until her face is buried in my neck.

"I'm so tired of being mad, but I don't know if I can trust you."

The memory of how betrayed she looked when she found out about Alexei flashes through me like a chill in a haunted house. Then I think about how tired she's seemed for days, how her emotions keep swinging between anger and frustration faster than I can track.

I think about it, but no regret colors the thought as I brush my thumb over her hip.

"You don't have to," I whisper against her temple. "Some people would argue that it would be smart not to. But if you give me a chance, I'll try to make it up to you."

"Okay, Kostya." The diminutive of my name hits me like a punch to the gut. Only a handful of people have ever called me anything but my name, and hearing it from her lips feels intimate in a way I'm undeserving of. "I'll give you another chance."

I hold her for as long as she lets me, hardly daring to hope she'll forgive me.

CHAPTER 24

Nadya

There's a loud yowl at the end of the hall, followed by low cursing as Konstantin does his best to keep Spaghetti from scratching at the door to my studio in a desperate bid to get inside.

I love that dumb cat, but he has been more of a nuisance than anything else in recent days. He was apparently so pleased with his contributions to his single pot that he's determined to spend as much time in there as possible, even if he's going to be alone.

Since the shooting, I haven't wanted to spend my time in my studio.

Maybe it'd be easier if I went to the studio downtown, but—and I'll never admit it to Konstantin—I'm scared.

How can I not be? What happens if the next time I go out, there's another man waiting for the moment I'm alone so he can hurt me? What if the car hadn't held up long enough to get us home?

What happens if Vasily isn't as fast?

And how did that guy manage to find me, anyway?

If I'm not safe somewhere I've never been before, how could I possibly feel safe going somewhere I've been hanging out since I moved here?

I was already worried I was going to be ambushed by another fed any time I stepped outside the house, but now? The thought of running around town makes me want to puke.

I'm sure I'll get used to the idea eventually, but maybe I need to start small. Somewhere safe.

Just not the pet store. Or the studio. Or anywhere else I'd have to be apart from Vasya or Konstantin for more than a moment.

Because I've spent days trying to psych myself up to go back to the store and get Spaghetti's food, and this morning I ended up giving up and asking Tatiana to go because I couldn't bring myself to get in the car.

Not that being home with Vasily is any better. Konstantin's doing his best to be here, but there are certain things he just isn't able to do from the house.

I turn back to the movie playing on TV, wishing there was an easy solution to all my problems.

Maybe I would feel better if I had someone I could cling to, but I can't do that with Vasily. And when Konstantin spends the whole day locked away in his office, I can't really seek him out for comfort, either.

Not that I've bothered to complain. Because I'm not at all upset that I've been bored and lonely. Because it's not like I need Konstantin, even if I am giving him another chance.

At the end of the day, he's still just a man, like anyone else. A hot man who can throw me over his shoulder whenever he wants, but also knows how to hold me so I calm down when I'm a sobbing mess, sure, but a man nonetheless.

And I definitely don't miss him when he's gone all day.

Maybe I'm just lonely.

I yawn, trying to remember the plot of this movie, but come up blank. At this point, I'm not even sure if it's one I've ever seen before, or if it's one I've seen so many times I know it forward and backward but I'm just too tired to recognize it.

Even though it's the late hours of the afternoon, I can barely keep my eyes open. It's been this way all week.

Either I'm getting sick, or stress is starting to catch up with me. Considering everything that's happened over the past couple weeks, I shouldn't be surprised I'm exhausted. I just need to relax, catch up on some much-needed rest, and I'll be fine.

I fluff the pillow under my head, willing my eyes to stay open long enough to watch this movie to the end.

***

My hair tickles my cheek, and I scowl, trying to brush it away. Somehow, I only succeed in smacking myself in the face.

The rumble of Konstantin's laughter washes over me like warm water, pulling me out of the dream I hadn't meant to fall into. One where Konstantin and I were at the beach, his arms wrapped around me protectively while I dipped my toes into the water.

"It isn't fair for you to be so beautiful, *solynshka*."

I peel open an eyelid to glare at him. "Stop calling me that," I grumble, squinting when I see how put together he looks. He must have ditched his tie hours ago, and his hair looks like he's been running his hands through it since he got out of the shower, but he manages to make it all look intentional.

As subtly as I can, I wipe my cheek against the pillow, grimacing when it's wet with drool.

Great. Just the ego boost I need.

Kostya looks like a million bucks, and I probably look like something that just rolled out of a dumpster.

"Calling you what? Beautiful?" I roll my eyes, but he's undeterred. "I've learned that you should appreciate the good things in life. And you are among the best, even if you don't want to hear it."

"That's not what I meant and you know it."

I struggle to sit up, but Kostya eases the way, pulling me until I'm standing at his side and he's able to tuck my hair behind my ear.

"And what else am I supposed to call you when you're always so happy to see me?"

He's smiling softly, and my scowl only deepens.

"Your charms don't work on me."

"Sure they don't."

Slowly, he twirls us around, one hand holding mine and the other braced against the small of my back. He must have turned off the movie when he came in and switched the TV over to play slow music, and he takes the opportunity to sway us both to the melody.

I melt into his touch as he leads us into a gentle dance, effortlessly moving us around the room. Before I know what I'm doing, I have to hide my small smile in his chest. His ego doesn't need to be stroked by seeing that, yes, his charms *do* work on me.

But when he tucks a finger under my chin, I forget to hide it. All I can focus on is the way he's looking at me, how he's always making sure I have everything I ever need or want at my fingertips without me ever needing to ask.

Konstantin didn't just comfort me after the most terrifying experience of my life, he's been looking out for me constantly since we got married. Even when he's been a colossal jerk, he's never pushed for anything I wasn't comfortable with. He hasn't even tried to cross any of the lines I've drawn.

The only thing he's ever pushed back on was when I told him I'd sleep in another room.

But sharing a space with him has been far from unpleasant. Instead of lying awake all night worrying, I've taken to falling asleep the moment I'm in his arms.

And when I came home from the studio in a panic, he didn't even question me. He believed every word I said without a hint of doubt. As soon as he saw my fear, he threw out whatever his plans were and stepped up to make sure Alexei was safe.

Because it was more important to him that I knew my brother was okay.

Konstantin smiles as he spins me away from him, his hand warm in mine. I giggle to myself as he pulls me back in, a lightness I hardly recognize filling my chest.

"Don't you have other things you should be doing?" I ask, biting my lip when I see the fond look in his eyes.

"Maybe." He shrugs, slowing the dance down until we're only swaying together. The slow movement gives me all the time in the world to take in the way he's looking at me, as if I'm the most interesting thing he's seen all day. "But I'd rather be with you than do any of it."

His sincerity nearly knocks the air from my lungs.

"You care about me," I realize out loud. He isn't pretending or putting on a show. He isn't trying to make up for something or asking for anything.

Konstantin just wants to be close to me.

"Of course I do," he says with a frown that makes the butterflies in my stomach reappear, ones that are becoming harder and harder to ignore. "Have I not made that obvious?"

Now that I think about it, Konstantin's never urged me to feel any way about him. Whether I've been angry, or wanted him to hold me, or wanted absolutely nothing to do with him, he's always welcomed whatever I give him.

I'm already halfway there, but if I'm not careful, I'm going end up flat on my ass, head over heels in love with my husband.

It's clear from the way he treats Tatiana, from the easy way he behaves with Viktor, that he cares deeply about the people he decides to let under this thick armor, and something in me warms when I realize I've become one of them.

He became someone he wanted to avoid to protect his brother, he works every way he can to protect the men who work under him, and he's done nothing but protect me relentlessly from the moment I met him.

Konstantin would be such a good dad.

There's a lump in my throat when I stand on my toes to kiss him, swallowing the emotions before they can escape me.

I'm in so much trouble.

Chapter 25

Nadya

"You'll be fine," Konstantin assures me with an easy smile I can't bring myself to believe. How can I when it looks like he's just as uncertain as I feel?

But if I spend another minute in this house, I'm going to lose my mind. I can't believe I'm actually looking forward to going downtown and walking into the studio again, but I need a break from all the guards and endless security before I snap.

For the past week, no matter where I've gone, someone's been right next to me. If Konstantin's home, it's him. But if he isn't? There are guards everywhere. Outside when I want to sit on the patio, visible from every window when I'm inside. Whenever I pass the camera room, there's always the quiet din of conversation reminding me that no matter where I go, someone's watching.

It's enough to make my skin crawl.

I close my eyes, turning my face toward the sun as if it will somehow cure me of the lingering worry that's freezing me from the inside out.

The longer we linger, the more worked up Konstantin gets, and the more the idea of leaving the house balloons into a massive feat in my mind, becoming something unachievable.

"I know," I say, desperate to reassure Konstantin as much as I am myself. "You've said it six times."

I gesture to where Vasily's leaning against the car, studiously pretending he isn't watching. His sunglasses do a lot of heavy lifting, but the subtle way his shoulders shake is impossible to ignore.

We're both being ridiculous.

Vasily knows it. I know it. I just need Konstantin to get on board, let go of my hand, and let me leave.

At this point, someone could walk up to me on the street and tell me to come with them, and I'd at least consider it if they promised I could have a full minute without anyone hovering over my shoulder.

As much as I've appreciated spending time with Konstantin, the difference between quality time and suffocation is a canyon, and Konstantin managed to break out a tight rope and cross the gaping void without breaking a sweat.

The height may have failed to take him down, but I won't be nearly as careless if I'm not given a single afternoon's reprieve.

Konstantin kisses me, and I try to let it smooth my ruffled feathers, but it doesn't quite hit the mark. Instead, I'm holding back a weary sigh when I stomp away from him, motioning to Vasily to get in the car before I slam the door shut.

No matter how much I need space, as soon as Kostya's out of sight, the worry rushes back in to takes up the mountain-sized hole he left in his wake.

The news said the shooter was arrested, and Konstantin insists I don't need to worry about getting ambushed by law enforcement again, but what if he's wrong? What if something happens? What if they do worse than harass me? What if they have a weapon that's more subtle than a gun?

I'm wearing a denim jacket even though it's hot as hell, and my knife is tucked inside it, readily accessible as soon as I need it, but what if I'm not fast enough?

I've been looking forward to listening to the calming voice of the instructor guiding me, of being given a task to focus on to distract me from the stress that's been pressing down on me from all angles. I don't even care that after I missed last week's lesson I'm probably going to be sent off to make more mugs on my own while everyone else finishes something more ambitious.

At least I'll be doing something other than sitting around and fixating on all the worst-case scenarios.

In a couple hours, I'll be fine. I'll use my time to let go of my resentment and go back to trusting Kostya to keep me safe. I'll center myself and let go of my anger.

For a couple hours, I won't feel like someone who's slowly losing their fucking mind.

It's going to be great.

I cling to that thought the entire length of the drive, but my hope is mortally wounded when Vasily gets out of the car with me. And when he follows me into the studio, it drops dead entirely. Then he takes a seat at the open wheel next to mine, and I go through all five stages of grief so quickly psychologists should study it.

With one breath, I come to terms with the situation, and with the next, I decide *fuck that* and circle back to an all-consuming rage.

"Are you fucking serious?" I hiss.

Vasily doesn't even blink.

Is it too much to ask for a single afternoon where I don't have Konstantin and his merry band of assholes breathing down my neck?

Vasya glares straight ahead as the instructor smiles brightly and goes over what we're working on today, not even pretending to listen to her.

Apparently it *is* too much.

I start working my clay, using more force than strictly necessary. If I pretend it's my husband's stupid face when I use my fists, then at least I'm doing something productive with my anger. I don't even care if all I'm doing is working so much air into the clay that whatever I make is going to end up cracking in the kiln because I'm in a bad mood.

Actually, you know what? Fuck it.

I want this project to end up so riddled with air and pockets of moisture that it explodes into a million pieces. Then, I'll put every sharp, broken shard in a box, wrap it with a bow, and give it to Konstantin with a smile so I can force him to give me that stupid, sexy smirk while I shove his face in the box.

Every time I spot Vasily out of the corner of my eye, I grind my teeth together even harder. All of a sudden, I care far less about how good of a confidant he can be, or even the fact that he protected me.

He might just be following orders, but right now, I hate him just as much as I hate Konstantin.

The longer the class drags on, the harder it is for me to pay attention to what I'm doing, my focus constantly being pulled away by the brooding statue on my right that can't even do me the favor of pretending he isn't there.

Unlike all the other women in the room—who keep staring at Vasily and giggling to each other—I'd rather he be anywhere else.

If he pretended he wanted to be here, maybe I could ignore him. Instead, he's tracking everyone like a threat, the promise of violence radiating from him like a force field that's here for the sole purpose of keeping away anyone who looks in my direction. If he'd pretend, I might not be so inclined to throw a pound of clay straight at his head to see what happens.

I sigh, glowering at Vasily when he glares at the instructor for trying to check on my work. As she approaches, he stands, grabs his stool, and puts it down much closer to mine.

If he had any sense of self-preservation, he'd take that stool and move so far in the opposite direction he'd be in a different state.

I've had more than enough time breathing in the stench of overbearing, infuriating men.

"Oh, that's…" The instructor, who's bravely risked Vasily's wrath by approaching, trails off. Her voice is far too high and squeaky to be casual, but it's a valiant attempt. She looks at the mess of clay and mud in front of me. My shoulders slump when her smile fails to reach her eyes. "That's great, Nadya. Keep going."

What did Konstantin threaten them with to get me a spot here? What did he offer? No matter how much he's paying them, I bet they'd give back every cent if it meant they didn't have to deal with me and my bodyguard ever again.

"It sucks," I mutter more to myself than to her, but she keeps smiling, her expression even more strained as her eyes dart to Vasily, before she tucks tail and retreats without a word of advice or reassurance. Even if she had tried to help me, I don't know what good it would do.

I'm so frustrated I want to cry. I thought I was being dramatic when I wanted to chew Kostantin out before we left, but now? Murder would be a mercy he doesn't deserve.

No, death is too easy for the likes of him.

When the instructor is safely across the room, relief lining every movement as she helps another student, I'm humiliated to realize I'm blinking back tears.

What the hell is wrong with me?

"It's not that bad," Vasily offers, nodding at the clay that only vaguely resembles a mug. The top has been squeezed so thin it looks more like a loose asshole than the lip of a mug.

"Yes, it is."

He doesn't argue with me, and I'm grateful for it.

For twenty minutes, I work as hard as I can to salvage my stupid project, trying to recall every bit of information I've picked up throughout my classes. But no matter how many times I try, nothing goes right.

I use too much water, my anger is making my grip too shaky to work properly the clay properly, and I can't figure out how hard to squeeze my hands to get an even wall. I glance around self-consciously, looking at the pretty birdhouses everyone else is finishing from last week without breaking a sweat.

Everyone except Vasya, who gave me his clay so I can start over and try again.

And all I have to show for it is another mess to be cleaned up.

There's a half hour left before class ends, and typically, it's my favorite part. I love when I have a base and it's time to be creative and put my own spin on a project, but why bother?

Sniffing, I wipe my hands on my apron. There's no point in staying, is there? All I'm doing is upsetting myself and wasting everyone else's time.

"Let's go home," I whisper soft enough that only Vasya can hear.

I will not cry in public.

I *won't*.

He gives me a concerned look when I toss the apron down on the stool and grab my purse.

Is it a dick move to make such a mess and not even bother to clean it up? Sure. But I'm probably never coming back after today.

Why bother? They don't want me here anyway.

I can feel the weight of the stares on my back as I walk out, waiting by the door until Vasily confirms the sidewalk is free of any immediate threats, then follow him to the car.

For once, I don't join him in the front seat, slipping into the back so I can be upset without feeling like I'm forcing him to deal with it, too. Graciously, he pretends not to notice when I turn my head away, wiping my eyes as he drives home.

The whole time, I tell myself that it's fine things didn't go according to plan. Once Konstantin drops his controlling bullshit, I'll find a new pottery studio, and I'll make it clear I don't want him to interfere. I'll only use my maiden name when I talk to people, and Vasya will stay out of sight so I don't have to worry about everyone eyeing me warily.

As soon as we're parked, I'm out of the car, running inside with the intent of hiding in my studio and making a mug I'm not embarrassed by, but instead, I'm greeted by Konstantin jumping to his feet in the living room, rushing to greet me.

"How was your class, *solnyshka*?"

When he reaches out to pull me into a hug, the fragile sense of calm I'd managed to cultivate snaps at the seams, taking all my hurt with it. The only thing left is a seething, unquenchable anger. For once, I'm prepared to let it burn until there's nothing but scorched earth.

"Fuck you, Konstantin!" I snap. "Go for a long walk in a desert and leave me alone."

I turn away before he's able to touch me, storming to my studio while he freezes behind me.

I don't bother waiting for him, slamming the door shut before he snaps out of it. A sob catches in my throat when I find Spaghetti sprawled out on his back, soaking in the sunshine next to my pottery wheel. I scoop him up, and he purrs immediately, not stopping even when I press my face against his soft belly, taking his spot on the floor before he can get any ideas of wriggling free.

Spaghetti allows it, though he does press his front paws against my cheeks so I can't force my face into his fur the way I want to.

At least there's one member of the male species in this house that doesn't make me want to tear my hair out.

I hold him until my tears finally stop and the door creaks opens.

Konstantin doesn't wait for permission, instead walking in the room and leaning against the opposite wall with a smile on his face.

And I want to hate him for it, but the longer I glare at his smile, the more ridiculous I feel.

How much of what happened was actually his fault, and how much of it was just because I'm in a terrible mood? What did Konstantin actually do to hurt me? Be a little overbearing and protective?

It's not like he was trying to be cruel.

Maybe I'm just being childish.

"I'm sorry," I mutter, studiously avoiding looking at him. Konstantin just continues smiling like he's won the lottery. "I don't know what came over me."

"There's nothing to be sorry for," he says. "You're feeling smothered. I get it." Slowly, like I'm a wounded animal, he crosses the room to sit next to me. Close, but not quite touching. "I'm the one who should apologize. I need to give you space."

I can't bring myself to do more than nod, drained from my little tantrum.

Spaghetti rolls over in my lap, rubbing his head against my hand as we sit quietly, soaking in each other's presence.

Konstantin doesn't push, and instead of rubbing against me like sandpaper, he's a gentle comfort. Eventually, I let my head fall so it's resting on his shoulder pretending that I don't still feel like crying.

When he presses a kiss against the top of my head, I close my eyes, deciding to enjoy the peace while it lasts.

CHAPTER 26

Konstantin

If it were happening to anyone else, I'd laugh at the irony. I ended a war across the country with a single phone call, but even when I'm pouring every resource into finding Dowd, I can't find hide nor hair of him.

Even though Ivan said he was trying to get in touch before everything went to hell, my attempts to reach out to him since the shooting have gone unanswered.

That's the difference between Dowd and The Chicago Outfit: I've never worked with him. There's never been an open line of communication because I've never needed one.

Why would I? For so many syndicates, I'm their main source of firearms. But another arms dealer? It's not like I'm looking to chat about marketing strategies and suppliers, and I'm not the kind of man to seek friends in my rivals.

But one of his men shot at my wife. I've spent every waking moment trying to find the fucker, and all I have to show for it is a hair-trigger temper and too many nights of lost sleep.

I'm not just furious, I'm embarrassed.

It's rare that I'm caught flat-footed, and Liam has managed to catch me so off guard that Nadya could have been forced to pay the price. I want nothing more than to burn down everything between here and Boston, leaving no stone unturned until I manage to find whatever hole he's hiding in.

When I get my hands on him, I'll destroy his life beyond recognition.

Because Nadya cried when she got home yesterday. Not because she was scared, but because she was hurt and mad. She was so furious about the measures I've taken to keep her safe that she cried into my shoulder and barely even tried to hide it. It felt like an eternity before she was able to collect herself enough to pull away, and when she did, my shirt was wet, and Spaghetti was glaring at me like everything was my fault.

I'm not sure it wasn't.

Nadya's red cheeks and puffy eyes damn near killed me, but it was still tough to tamp down the spark that felt an awful lot like joy threatening to boil over in my chest.

She's been having mood swings, her temper has gotten shorter every day, and when we're in bed, she comes almost as soon as I touch her oversensitive breasts. She might not have noticed it yet, but I have.

Which is why, even though holing up in my office all day sets me on edge and makes me want to tear out my hair, I'm doing it anyway. I've even asked Vasily to let her be alone for a while so she can have the space she needs.

Though, all I want to do is glue her to my side and shove a pregnancy test in her hands so she can confirm what I already know.

If I'm patient, Nadya will come to the realization on her own, and I won't have to worry about her finding out what I've done to give her a family. But until she does, I'm stuck between a rock and a hard place.

She wants freedom, but I can't give it to her until I deal with Dowd. And while I'm constantly worried about Nadya, I'm getting no closer to finding him.

I don't even realize how deeply I've been stewing in my thoughts until there's a swift knock at my door, and Viktor strolls in without waiting for an answer.

"Morning," he grunts as he takes a sip of coffee. Coffee that's in the mug Nadya was so proud of when she brought it home after her second pottery class. One that everyone else has automatically understood belongs to *me*.

He's wearing a linen suit, he's fresh-faced, and he's looking the sort of disheveled that I know for a fact takes him at least an hour to pull off.

While I've spent the morning prying myself from my wife's sleeping arms and doing everything I can to find Dowd, my brother's spent his morning primping and making himself *pretty*.

"Have you managed to do anything productive today?" I snap. "Or were you too busy admiring your own reflection to remember you have a job to do?"

Viktor freezes at my tone, stopping with the mug halfway to his mouth. If he damages it, I'm going to relieve his head from his shoulders. They've spent enough time supporting all that weight.

"Alright," he says slowly, moving like he's worried I'm going to launch myself at him. It's not entirely unjustified. "I'll bite. What crawled up your ass and died?"

"My patience. I need this shit handled. There isn't time to keep fucking around, and you've been no help."

Rage is liberating. I've spent so long trapped in a pit of useless feelings that I'm starting to forget who I am.

I'm the one who runs the fucking show.

As long as I remember that, we'll find Dowd, and the threat will be handled.

It's up to him how violent I have to get to make it happen.

"That isn't fair, and you know it," Viktor grunts almost to himself.

"Isn't it? You're the one I'm supposed to be able to trust. You're supposed to be the computer whiz, but you've given me jack shit. It's been almost a week."

"What do you want me to find?" Viktor finally, *finally* puts the mug down on the corner of my desk. I clench my hands so I don't jerk it away from him like a toddler. "Even if I wasn't too busy coordinating your guards and demands for more security, there's nothing to be found. I've checked every fucking corner of Dowd's operation, and no one knows where he is. His accounts are clean, and there's nothing online. Whatever he's doing, he isn't leaving fucking clues."

"Then. Look. *Harder.*"

Dowd didn't drop off the face of the earth. That would be impossible.

He's hiding somewhere, and no one manages to hide as well as he has without help. There has to be *someone* who knows where he is, and finding them could very well be the difference building the life I want with Nadya, and losing everything I've ever fought for.

When I married Nadya, I bought myself quiet, but I also painted a giant target on her back. I knew it would, but I wanted to know what it felt like to have her smile at me. I wanted to know if being with her would be enough to fix me permanently.

I wanted to build a future.

Now, my options are either I set myself as bait and hope I'm prepared, or to anticipate Dowd hunting Nadya every time she steps foot outside this property.

"Has he had any new recruits lately?" I ask. "Anyone who's been pushed out of his inner circle? Either could be the key to finding him." It might be a shitty idea, but it's more than anyone else has offered, and I'm desperate.

Viktor looks at me with his hands shoved in his pockets, eyes shining with a cloying sympathy that puts me on edge.

Fuck.

If he's noticed how close I am to losing my shit, then it's only a matter of time before everyone else does, too.

"I'll try, alright?" Viktor eventually says, his voice softer than I can stand. When he reaches for his coffee, my baser instincts win out. With a scowl, I drag the mug closer.

"Oh, come on, you don't even like coffee!"

"It's my mug."

"And it's *my* coffee."

"So? Go make more."

"Why do you care so much?" he asks, cocking a brow. "It's not even a cool mug. It was just what was there."

I lean forward, ready to rip Viktor's head off, when there's another knock at the door, one that's far more tentative than his was. After a long moment, Nadya pokes her head in, and my jaw clenches.

This is her home. Viktor only knocks to give the illusion of privacy, and even Tatiana will stroll into the room without a care. My wife shouldn't wait for anyone's permission to enter a room.

Least of all mine.

"You don't need to knock," I tell her, muzzling my temper before she thinks it's directed at her. Even though the anger is the only reason I'm not drowning, it's nearly impossible to keep hold of it when she enters the room.

Despite how deeply she slept last night, she still looks tired, and I wish she'd open up enough to tell me exactly what's bothering her. But if I ask, she'll only brush me off and dance around the question until she manages to distract me with something else entirely.

She has me wrapped around her pretty finger, and I don't think she even realizes it.

"I didn't want to interrupt."

Her eyes dart between Viktor and me, eventually settling on the mug I'm still clutching to my chest. Slowly, she smiles, warming me up more than the unbearable heat outside ever could.

I'm so in love with Nadya that it's almost pathetic, and I can't wait to see what she's like as the mother of my child.

Or children.

I haven't decided if I'll be content with just one.

"You're never interrupting," I tell her. "Viktor and I were just wrapping up, weren't we?"

He hesitates for a moment, and I freeze, fully prepared to throw the coffee in his face, before he eventually nods.

"Right."

"Don't rush off on my account. I just wanted to tell Konstantin something really quick."

Her hair drapes over her collarbone as she tilts her head, squinting like she doesn't quite believe him, but I'm caught up on the way her mouth forms my name, on the way all the light through the window seems intent on wrapping her in its embrace.

Nadya is a creature born of pure sunshine. Is it any wonder the light is trying to hold her close, doing anything it can to protect her from my darkness?

"What do you need?"

She doesn't meet my eyes as she says, "I'm going down to the water. But I'm taking Vasily, so you don't worry about it."

Even though it's phrased as a statement, she sounds like a teenager asking to borrow the car.

I hate it.

Nadya deserves better than begging for scraps. She deserves to walk into a room, demand whatever she wants, and know it'll be given to her without a moment's hesitation.

But no matter how I command Viktor, or how hard I work my men, the fact remains that I have no clue where Dowd is or what he's doing. He could be lurking in Boston, or he could be down the street.

The odds that he's off in the world minding his own business are slim to none.

If Nadya wants to go anywhere, it needs to be vetted and secured long before she gets there. And as much as I'd like to pretend otherwise, I can't make that happen on a whim.

Especially not for somewhere as public as a beach.

"No," I say, though I'm loathed to deny her anything. The small amount of hope she had allowed to bleed into her expression fades away in an instant. "Not now. We can talk about it in a few days, *solnyshka*."

Viktor sucks in a breath through his teeth, an unneeded warning that I've said the wrong thing. Nadya folds her arms over her chest as he leans away, keeping himself out of the line of fire and giving himself a clean angle of escape if he needs it.

Nadya's independence is an incredible turn on, but right now, I don't have the resources to accommodate it.

The problem is, someone who raised herself is never going to react well when given orders, nor take *later* for an answer.

As well as I'm able to manipulate a situation or think outside the box, charm and wit are no help with a woman like her.

"You might be able to dictate where I live my life, and who I live it with, *Kostya*," she hisses, all the affection I long to hear absent, "but you have no say over what I do. I was giving you a heads up, not asking permission."

I close my eyes, tension throbbing in the back of my skull like a jackhammer.

How far will I be able to push her without sabotaging the progress I've made?

"At least tell me *why* it's so important to you that I stay home like a doll instead of an actual person who has their own life, Konstantin."

"You aren't a doll." I sigh. "But you can't go galivanting around the city like a child, either."

She doesn't need all the details of what's going on. She's still worried about the feds, but they're nothing in comparison to Dowd. He's deadlier, faster, and more conniving than someone with a badge could ever hope to be.

I hate the little line she gets between her brows when she gets worried. I hate the way her shoulders tense up and she fidgets with whatever's closest to her. Every time she's ever reached for her phone like a safety blanket, I want to sweep her away to a place where nothing can ever hurt her.

"A *child*?" she scoffs, her shoulder set in a straight line. "Are you fucking kidding me?"

"I'm keeping you safe. As I promised I would," I point out, but I'm caught by the flush in her cheeks, by the way her eyes blaze with anger.

Even fuming with plots of retaliation dancing in her eyes, Nadya is the most stunning woman I've ever seen. I'm not sure if I'd rather pull her into my lap and tell her to ride me, or fall to my knees before her and tell her to use me however she wants.

As long as I get to see how far down that angry flush goes, I'm not sure I care.

But if I look at her the wrong way right now, neither of us is going to get what we want.

"You're unbelievable," she grits out, then turns around and storms away. I watch her retreat with longing, wishing I could erase the distance and give her everything she wants.

She more than deserves a beach day, and she definitely deserves better than the rocky beaches in Northern California.

As soon as Dowd is handled, I'll take her somewhere nicer. Maybe I'll rent a private island so I can enjoy the sunshine and water with her.

Viktor blinks as she slams the door. When I glare at him, he rolls his eyes.

"You want a minute to deal with that? Or are you content imagining a world where she isn't too good for you?"

"She needs space," I reply, grabbing a pen and bouncing it against my knee. "It's not like she's going to wander off without Vasily, and he's not going to take her anywhere without my permission."

"If you say so," he mutters, shaking his head. "It's your funeral."

CHAPTER 27
Nadya

The number of men patrolling may have increased, but they still follow the same patterns they always have. I watch them from the balcony outside our bedroom, waiting patiently.

Despite what my jerk of a husband seems to think, I'm fully capable of taking care of myself. I did it before him, and if he insists on treating like this, I'll still be doing it when I finally snap and slash his throat.

At this point, I have to assume Konstantin has a death wish.

I don't need him to keep me safe, and I certainly don't need permission to go out on my own.

Am I little scared about what could happen? Of course.

But a year ago, I wandered around without a guard all the time. No one called to make sure I got home safely, and no one trailed after me wherever I went. And what happened? What terrible, awful thing happened when I didn't broadcast my movements for the world to see?

Absolutely nothing.

I was fine. I was living a full, happy life.

Before Konstantin, I wasn't worried about getting ambushed or what might be lurking around the corner. I only worried about my brother and the occasional sketchy guy lingering outside the bathrooms at clubs.

But now I'm here, watching to make sure my husband's security hasn't spontaneously decided to change their patrols so I can go on a walk.

I need to be able to explore the area I moved to without making demands of anyone else's time. I don't want to keep Vasya from living his life, and I don't want to keep Konstantin from working when he has to.

I just want to be able to see the water in person and not from a window.

The house is close, but it's not nearly close enough. I'll probably be there in thirty minutes if I walk fast enough. And if I'm lucky, no one will even notice I'm missing. Because if I'm really, *really* lucky and no one's watching the cameras, I should be able to get away easily enough.

But sneaking back in?

That's not going to happen.

So I wait.

Once the late morning sun has burned off the fog, there's a small window of opportunity when the guys who have worked since early morning change shifts with the afternoon crew.

I just need to be patient and wait for it.

It isn't my first time watching them. No matter how often they cycle through their routines, they change with the same frequency. Five days on one routine, then four days, then six, then back to five. There's only so many variations of their over-the-top dance, and there's always a pattern.

It might look random on the surface, but it's just a matter of figuring out the numbers. Picking them apart, analyzing them, figuring them out. And from up here, it's easy enough to look at the guards like they're nothing but a number. A puzzle that can be cracked if you give it enough time and dedication.

At exactly three minutes after eleven, the gap I've been waiting for is finally here, and I'm not going to waste a single second.

I pull on a pair of worn-out sneakers, give Spaghetti a kiss, and make a break for it. I hang out by the back door until the guards turn the corner, then break into a run toward the wall around the property.

From the top floor, there's a full view of the drop on the other side of the wall, but it's not so large that I'm worried about hurting myself. It's tall enough that scaling it from the outside would be a challenge, but from the side I'm on?

It'll be a breeze.

I'm a little out of breath by the time I reach it, but I jump up, kicking my feet against the smooth plaster with everything I've got until I'm able to haul myself to the top, cursing internally when I see how long the drop on the other side is.

It looks much taller from here than it does upstairs.

I glance back at the house and spot movement out of the corner of my eye. The next crew is starting their rounds, and if I don't jump now, I'll lose my chance. My stomach flips when I look back at the ground, but I breathe through it, close my eyes, and leap.

A jolt ricochets up my spine as I land, and I pause, taking a breathless moment to evaluate, but nothing hurts.

As I look around, my shoulders fall.

I've never seen the hill from this angle.

The heat has fried the grass to a crisp, and even the trees look like they're standing with a headstrong refusal to die rather than a desire to live. But every brown, fading plant is a sign of life, and somehow seeing them lifts my spirits.

When I stand, my shoulders rest easier than they have in days.

I can do this.

I trace my hand along the wall until I spot the road, and only then do I step away from the relative safety and head further into the trees, giving one last look back at the house before I leave entirely.

Soon, I'll be back home, Konstantin can throw another hissy fit, and I'll have even more evidence to show him I don't actually need him.

There's a voice in the back of my head that whines against the thought, reminding me how nice it felt to fall back, let Konstantin take control, and trust him to deal with whatever happens instead of dealing with everything on my own.

But that voice is wrong, and with enough time, I'll prove it to her.

Because trusting Konstantin is setting myself up for a world of pain. It means being a trophy instead of a real person with my own needs and wants. It means letting him control when I leave, where I go, and what I do until I don't recognize myself anymore.

I follow the street until I reach a bend, and when I turn around again, the house is out of sight.

As much as I wish that it felt like a weight has been lifted from my shoulders, all I can do is stare at my scuffed sneakers as I kick a pebble down the road, wondering what the fuck is wrong with me.

I've never been this reckless before. I'm the one who always has a plan and ten contingencies if things go wrong. Not someone who reacts without thinking because they didn't get their way.

God, is it any wonder Konstantin was such a dick when I told him I was going out? I'd be the same way if I had to put up with me.

It's just stress. I'm still dealing with how totally different my life is from how I pictured it, and I'm feeling suffocated.

Now that I think about it, maybe there isn't anything wrong with me at all. Maybe I'm being well-adjusted, and if I was magically transported back to Chicago, I'd go back to the way things were without any trouble.

I could live my pleasant little life, and I'd learn to ignore the part of me that wants to turn around, march right back into Kostya's office, and demand he apologize and work with me.

He could teach a masterclass on getting on my nerves, but when he lets his guard down? He's so sweet it tilts me off my axis.

When I'm with him, I feel alive, probably for the first time in my life.

I want to blame my mood swings on my period, but I haven't had once since before we got married. I've always been irregular, and between the agent and the shooting, it isn't shocking that I've missed another one.

Still, I make a mental note to find a doctor so I can make sure there's nothing else going on.

Until then, I'll let the sunshine and fresh air work their magic and savor being completely on my own for the first time since I got married.

I haven't had a moment to myself in so long, it's no wonder I've been losing my mind.

It doesn't take nearly as long as it should before I have to stop and catch my breath. I severely underestimated how windy the roads are, and I've had to double back more times than I anticipated while on this little jaunt. What I expected to be a short walk has quickly turned into a journey that's almost enough to make me regret leaving in the first place.

But I'm not going to turn around.

Partly because I'm not ready to face Konstantin's wrath yet, but mostly because if I've already gone this far, I might as well see it through. Besides, the concept of retracing my steps—but this time going uphill—makes me want to find a tree to sit under for some shade and rest until Konstantin finds me on his own.

I pat my pocket, searching for my phone, and come up empty.

Damn it.

Guess I'll have no choice but to walk back when I'm done.

If I'm going to bake in the sun while climbing uphill, I'm going to see the water up close first.

Besides, the view isn't half bad. The houses are pretty, and the further I get, the greener the landscape becomes. I just can't help but wish I had someone to share it all with. Not even to talk to, but just to be with me, enjoying the view.

Especially when I find a gap between the houses and catch a glimpse of the boats floating on the water.

Either I'll have to make sure I remember my phone next time I sneak out so I can take a picture, or I'll have to convince Vasily to come for a long walk when Kostya finally loses the stick wedged in his ass.

Assuming he ever lets me leave the house again. But if he tries to tell me what I can or can't do, I'm just going to sneak into the back of Viktor's car, force him to smuggle me out of the city, and catch the first flight back to Chicago. Then I'll hide behind Alexei until Konstantin learns how to apologize and begs me to come back with him.

It takes ages for me to reach the beach, and when I finally do, I'm almost overwhelmed with conflicting regret and disappointment. Because this isn't a beach. It's nothing but a sidewalk that lines a rocky boat dock.

The water is doing its best to throw a piece of trash onto the rocks, the wind feels gritty, and everything smells so strongly of salt that it's almost oppressing.

This is what I risked pissing off my husband for?

This *sucks*.

I snag the piece of trash and wander down the path until I find a trash can.

At least I can say I tried to do something I wanted, right? I didn't sit around and wait for someone else to make a decision about my life. I saw something I wanted, and I took it.

I watch a couple strolling along the path hand in hand, occasionally stopping to point something out to each other, and it only makes me feel even lonelier.

Maybe it'd be better if Konstantin were here.

I find an old, weathered bench and sit, doing everything I can to shove the thought away. But no matter how hard I try, it lingers, haunting me with the fantasy of holding his hand while watching the water. He'd be unbearable, glaring at everyone and everything, and it'd be perfect.

Whether it's the view or the distance, my temper has cooled significantly.

If I'd kept my head when I talked to him, how different would our conversation have gone? Maybe he would have listened to me. And now, I'll never know. Because I overreacted.

I bend over to claw into the rocks and pebbles until I'm able to dig up a handful of sand, wiggling my fingers until it all falls away, leaving behind a gritty sensation that makes me feel raw both inside and out.

Maybe Konstantin wasn't the only one who handled our conversation poorly.

I brush my hands against my thighs, wiping away the remaining sand.

I really wish I had my phone. I don't know how I'm going to apologize, but I'm pretty sure it would be easier if I could call him. At least then, I wouldn't have to worry about how much it's going to suck walking home.

CHAPTER 28

Konstantin

As thunderous as Viktor's expression is, I'm willing to bet mine is even worse. He wants nothing more than to never see me again, but I won't let him leave until we're closer to finding Dowd.

A lead, a plan, a single fucking *clue* of where to go from here. Because I'm spiraling, my control is paper-thin, and I don't know how I'm going to be able to hold it together when everything else is ruined beyond recognition.

The door crashes against the wall as someone shoves it open, cutting through the tension like a knife. It's too soon for Nadya to be gearing up for another fight, but regardless, I'm struck by a wave of disappointment when I look up and don't see her standing in the doorway.

Instead, I find Tatiana clutching her knitting needles like weapons and wearing an expression I've become all too familiar over the past few weeks.

A mixture of pity, disapproval, and a knowing that spills over me like tar.

I have to fight the instinct to flinch away from that look on the best of days, but today it's mixed with something else. Something conflicted. Cocking a brow, I force myself to meet her eyes without flinching, waiting for whatever it is she has to say.

"Can I help you?" I prompt when she remains silent.

"Did you know how athletic your wife is?"

"What the hell are you talking about?" Nadya is many things, but I wouldn't say *athletic* is one of them.

"Your wife. She left the house about ten minutes ago."

"You interrupted to tell me that Nadya went outside?" I ask, rolling my eyes. As much as I want her to keep someone close whenever she goes out, I don't really expect her to listen to me, especially when she's pissed.

I trust my guards. They'll protect her like their lives depend on it. The odds of anything getting through the many layers of security I have in place without being noticed are slim to none.

At least that's what I tell myself, bouncing my pen against my desk.

"I suppose I misspoke." She sighs. "Your wife left the *property* ten minutes ago. Scaled the wall near the firepit and took off for the road." Tatiana folds her arms over her chest.

"She *what*?" Viktor demands while I stare at the soft yarn looped around the knitting needles. "How the fuck did she do that?"

Tatiana's half-finished project is draped over her shoulder, and for some reason, that's what my brain latches onto as my ears fill with deafening, maddening static.

Half of a blue blanket.

Someone could hurt Nadya.

This could be the opportunity Liam's been waiting for.

Ten minutes could be long enough to lose her forever.

What if saying no to her was the straw the broke that camel's back? What if she ran to the main road, called a cab, and is already well on her way to getting on the first flight back to Chicago?

"The guard in the security room needed a break," Tatiana says with a shake of her head. "He asked me to cover for him, and I got there in time to watch Nadya jump off the wall and stroll toward the hill."

"Why'd you wait this long?" Viktor asks, practically ripping his hair out while the world spins wildly under me.

"It took him that long to get back. But now he is, and now you know."

"You couldn't call? Or send a fucking text?" he demands as he bursts into motion, no doubt ready to round up all his men to track down Nadya.

I can't breathe.

"Language," she chastises. "And you know I hate using phones in the house. It's bad enough you're always staring at yours."

She could have run, or someone could have taken her. But my gut insists that if she went to the trouble of climbing over a wall, then she was acting in the heat of the moment.

My wife wanted to go to the beach. And when I didn't let her, she decided to flip me the proverbial bird and go anyway.

How is it that, even when she's the cause of my stress, think-ing about her is the thing that lets me find my myself again? I should be going out of my mind, my entire body falling apart as the *what-ifs* take over, but instead I'm focused. Planning. Prepared to go out and meet Nadya on her level so she doesn't lash out when I find her.

I pull out my phone and call her, entirely unsurprised when she doesn't answer.

My beautiful, reckless wife is going to be the death of me one of these days, but if she left on foot, she won't get far. She didn't send me straight to voicemail, which means she probably doesn't even have her phone on her to call a cab. And there's a park visible from the top floor.

Viktor shouts commands down the hallway, fully prepared to rip someone apart.

"Zhadt, bratan," I order, pocketing my phone. Tatiana tilts her head curiously while Viktor whips his head around to look at me, his eyes bugging out of his skull. "Call your most trusted men and tell them to meet you here. As soon as they arrive, gather every guard here and have them go to Vlast."

"We need to look for Nadya," he insists. "Not shuffle men around!"

I continue as if he hasn't said a word, "And when I say every-one, I mean *everyone*, Viktor. If they refuse or make excuses, make it clear I'll be dealing with them personally once this is resolved." I nod at Tatiana as I pass her, heading toward the garage.

Behind me, Viktor barks into his phone, following my orders even if he disagrees with them.

His loyalty is why he's my right-hand man.

He'll question me and push back in private, but at the end of the day, Viktor understands that my word is law.

He'll get his answers in time, just like everyone else.

In the meantime, I have more pressing issues to attend to.

No one so much as bats an eye when I tear out of the driveway, only slowing the car when I get to the first turn in the road.

My wife wants space, and she wants to go to the beach. I can't give her both, but I can give her an illusion while she stretches her legs. Even if she thinks she's alone, I'm going to be right behind her, keeping her safe.

My nerves settle within minutes of leaving, my heart returning to a functional rhythm as soon as I lay eyes on Nadya as she kicks at a rock. She doesn't even look up, totally oblivious of to her surroundings. I slow the car to a crawl, keeping close enough that I can be at her side in a moment's notice, but far enough away to let her sink into her distraction.

The curiosity on her face as she takes in the scenery is agonizing in its tenderness.

Would she have learned to fall in love with this neighborhood if I'd let her? Would she be happier if I'd found a way to loosen my hold on the reins? If I'd managed to stop things with Dowd from escalating as far as they have?

Maybe. But I didn't.

I didn't end things, and her unhappiness is the cost. And as heavy as it weighs on me whenever she walks away, I'll pay it as many times as I have to.

I'll pay it every day for the rest of my life, even if it means carving my heart out of my chest with every glare Nadya throws my way. Because the cost of losing her to any of the threats that might be waiting for a moment of weakness would destroy me beyond recognition.

In a different world, maybe I could have been everything she needs, but I can't expect her to want to be with someone as cruel and vicious as I need to be, much less love me.

But she's an oasis in an endless desert. And no matter how hard she fights, I'm not going to let her leave me. Not for an afternoon stroll, and not for a lifetime of freedom.

A seagull soars overhead as I get closer to the water, and Nadya watches it with a smile. The sun embraces her face with an open affection that makes my heart ache. The light itself seems to bend for her, giving her everything it has without the expectation of reciprocation.

If I knew how to be that open with her, would she ever truly want it? Or would it always be undercut by fear?

I'm not sure I want to know.

As she makes her way over the cracked pavement, my attention is stolen by a man wearing a heavy jacket that's out of place in this weather crossing between us. I throw the car into a parking spot, my eyes glued to the bulge at his back as he walks.

But while I'm focused on him, he's busy watching my wife, who remains infuriatingly oblivious to the threat fifty feet away and stalking closer every moment.

I use too much force to slam my car door shut, but this *mudak* has the same spatial awareness as she does. He's oblivious as I approach, eating the distance between us in long strides until I'm pressing my gun against the small of his back.

"If you want any chance of getting out of this alive, I suggest you move quickly and without complaint," I say, keeping my words low enough they'll be lost on the wind if anyone wanders too close. Only a fool would miss the thread of violence in them. Like a smart man, he freezes. "Now, nod and tell me you understand."

Slowly, he does. Every muscle in his neck is knotted so tight it's a wonder he's able to move his head at all.

I'm not gentle as I reach under his jacket and pull out the semi-automatic handgun, quickly shoving it into my pocket before anyone happens to look over and see more than they need to on their afternoon stroll.

Every fiber of my being screams to tear this man limb from limb, but having Nadya out of my sight when she's this exposed is agonizing. Every moment I waste with him, she's left vulnerable. We have no way of knowing if he's the only one gunning for her, and I can't afford to waste time.

Using my gun, I steer him to the back of my car. He twists around the moment I pop the trunk, and even though his adrenaline makes him fast, I'm faster, whipping my gun against this temple. He collapses, his muscles going lax as he loses consciousness.

For the most part, people don't want to know what lurks underneath the pretty veneer they've constructed for themselves, and that makes them willing to ignore what they don't want to see.

If they look over and see something they shouldn't, they can be swayed by a friendly smile and a few reassurances, content to tell themselves they must have imagined it.

Nadya, however, is not most people.

As discreetly as I'm able to in broad daylight, I shove him into the trunk, bind his arms and legs, and shove a gag so far down his throat he'll choke if he tries to scream, watching the back of Nadya's head for any reaction.

She doesn't even notice.

When I finally make my way back to her, my heart is in my throat. She's sitting on a bench, watching the boats with a bland expression. She doesn't react when I join her. No flicker of surprise, no twitch of annoyance, and for some reason, it only makes me feel worse.

"If you're here to yell at me," she eventually says, "I'd like to point out that nothing happened."

It almost did, I don't tell her.

Nadya doesn't need to have this memory ruined. I'll live with the fear of what could have been so she never has to.

"I have enemies, *solnyshka.*" She raises a brow, looking around as if to demonstrate how alone we are. "You don't have to like it, but you do need a bodyguard. If something happens to you…" I trail off while the water lashes against the rocks, slowly but relentlessly wearing them down to nothing but an echo of their whole.

Nadya gives me a skeptical look that makes me want to scream and tell her everything I've ever done. I want her to know exactly what the men wanting to hurt me would do to her if they thought it would repay even an ounce of the grief I've caused them.

I want to rip open my own flesh until she understands the depth of my feelings.

If something were to happen to Nadya, I wouldn't just buckle, I'd shatter. I'd tear the world apart until only ashes remember what stood before. I'd be nothing but an empty shell for the violence I treat like an instinct.

"If you won't accept a guard for your own safety, then do it to save the life of anyone who crosses my path when we get back."

"Has anyone ever told you that you're a little dramatic?"

"If you take Vasily with you," I say, ignoring the way she rolls her eyes, "you'll be saving everyone else a lot of trouble." It's nearly impossible to look at her when I'm caught in my own dread. "If you need me to beg, then just say the word. I'll get on my knees right now."

Whether it's the water, the wind, or the sunlight we're bathed in, Nadya seems settled as she rests her head on my shoulder.

"I need you to stop treating me like a child." She sounds almost as tired of this argument as I am.

Even when we're only a few feet from the water, I can barely smell the salt from it over the fruity sent of her shampoo as I turn my head to press a kiss against her hair. Bracing myself, I flip my hand over against my thigh, sighing shakily when she slides her fingers between mine and squeezing it tightly.

"I know. But there are things going on that you don't know about." She sucks in a sharp breath, but I cut her off. "There are things *I* don't want you to know," I correct. "Not when they'd only cause you worry. I can do that for both of us."

Her thumb strokes over the back of my knuckles, and for a moment, I'm worried her hand will be stained black when she lets go. Every touch risks dirtying her up with the blood and gore that soaks my hands that she'll never be free to be the beacon of light I love.

"All I'm asking is that you humor me, Nadya. Let me protect you."

"Fine," she mutters, leaning against my arm. "But only if you give me your knife."

Despite myself, I smile.

"Which one?"

"The Damascus steel one."

Of course she wants the knife I got for our wedding. I have a veritable arsenal of guns stashed away, and more knives than most would consider sane, but she picked the nicest weapon in my entire collection.

But in exchange for her cooperation? To not be terrified whenever she isn't by my side?

"It's yours."

We sit in silence, ignoring the boats bobbing in the bay until she sighs to herself and stands, keeping my hand in hers while we walk back to the car.

CHAPTER 29

Konstantin

It's more fun to think about the way Nadya's face lit up when I gave her my knife than it is to remember the way all that joy disappeared when Vasily walked into the house with his daughter in tow. Out of the three of them, she was the only one smiling when I left.

But security is going to be light while I'm gone, so they're going to have to find a way to cope until I'm done.

The thug who targeted my wife trips over his own feet when I shove him down the stairs toward the freezer. The sound of metal meeting flesh drowns out his pained grunt as his face slams against the door. He struggles against the grip I have on the back of his neck, but it does nothing as I enter the room and shove him in the middle of it, surrounded by a circle of my men.

"What the fuck is wrong with you people?" I bellow.

I take a slow look around, meeting the eye of everyone waiting for me. They all look back, though some more easily than others. Some most look confused, but a couple shift nervously from foot to foot, their hands either folded in front of them or shoved deep in their pockets.

Every man here was personally vetted. Some have been around so long I was raised alongside them. Others are so old they used to shake their heads at me when I was an obnoxious teenager. A few more are younger, still trying to get their feet under them. More than a couple don't meet my eyes when I shove the creep to his knees.

He ends up seated in the middle of the bloodstain left behind from my last visit.

This room has seen more action than it should have in a short period of time. I can feel every second of it in how hard I'm clenching my jaw.

"While you all were fucking around," I say as I shove a few men to the side so I can look at the wall of instruments, "this motherfucker was trying to ambush my wife." My voice is far calmer than I feel, edged with power that these men should have learned to fear long before now.

I take his gun out of my pocket and dump it heavily on the metal table, trailing my fingers over the various tools until I settle on a metal pipe.

If circumstances were different, I'd ask Vasily to do this. He's always been something of an artist when it comes to getting a point across, and he hasn't had an opportunity to play in a while.

Some people might think it's foolish to use my best torturer as a glorified babysitter, and I know he agrees, but he's the only man I know who will go to whatever lengths it takes to keep Nadya safe. Anyone else might flinch, but not Vasily.

He'd fucking relish in the opportunity.

Next time.

Vasily can take over the wet work, and I'll go back to working relentlessly to keep everything together with the little energy I have left.

But there isn't a universe where I could have asked him to handle this.

Because this? This isn't a task that can be delegated. I need to make my point crystal fucking clear, and that will never happen if someone else is doing the heavy lifting.

"This motherfucker nearly got to Nadya because you were all so incompetent you managed to miss her leaving the property." I fix my eyes on my prisoner, letting my rage and fear consume me as I roll up my shirtsleeves. "And if you managed to miss someone leaving, I wonder how easy it would be for someone to get *in*."

The room is dead silent except for the heavy breathing and muffled curses through the gag.

I turn, looking every single man in the eyes.

They were all trusted enough to make sure my home was safe. I trusted them to make sure no one would come for me in the only place I'm allowed to be vulnerable. I trusted them to look after Nadya.

Maybe I've grown lax.

"You all should be thanking whatever god you believe in." I pull the pipe back before I swing it into the captive's arm as hard as I can, ignoring the resounding crunch of bone that has someone hissing in a sharp breath. "Because if this motherfucker had touched a hair on her head, you'd all be in his place."

I don't know who failed, or how they did it, but someone here does. And after I scour the security footage, so will I.

I want them all to know exactly what's coming to them.

They won't get to hide. They won't push the blame aside. They won't deny their role in this.

They're going to get exactly what they deserve for putting the best part of my life at risk.

With every swing, I show my men what's waiting for them. I'm relentless as I slam the pipe into him again and again, moving with him when he tries to scramble away. All I can picture is every terrible thing he could have done, how he could have broken Nadya.

Her smile is like oxygen, and he would have killed her without a second thought. Gunned her down in broad daylight. Kidnapped her and forced her to beg for mercy he would never give her.

He could have done anything, and no matter what it was, I would have felt it a thousand times over.

There wasn't an ID in his wallet when I searched him, but the accent around his muffled curses is thick enough to tell me what I need to know.

Liam Dowd is more clever than I've given him credit for.

Not only has he evaded me in every way, he's managed to lock in on my only weakness.

Because he could burn down my home, come after any of my men, steal all my clients, and destroy everything I've built, but none of it would have the same impact as a threat against my wife.

She and the child she carries are the only things that matter.

I will not accept my men's failures. I never have, and I never well. The stakes are rising, and perfection is the only acceptable standard.

I'm careful to avoid the blood splatter landing on my clothes as I beat him. As much as I need to draw this out, to make every moment of this as painful as possible, I don't want to upset Nadya any more than I already have.

My arms and shoulders burn when I'm finally satisfied. My chest heaves, and when I toss the pipe aside, his only sign of life are wheezing gasps. Slowly, I take another look around the room, letting my anger bleed into my expression. The men who were working earlier can't meet my eye, sweating nervously.

Good.

"Someone take care of him." I nod at the crumpled heap in the center of the room. "Keep him alive so Vasily can have a conversation with him in the morning." I wipe my mouth with the back of my hand, cringing at the smear of wetness.

Everything reeks of blood, piss, and fear.

"If any of you take the liberty of allowing a fucking *leaf* to fall on my lawn without my permission, you'll face the same fate. Is that understood?"

There are slow mutterings of *yes, Pakhan,* and *yeah, boss.* They stand straighter when I look at them, not wanting to risk setting me off when I'm already on edge.

"See to it that you do."

***

By the time I get home, the sun has set, granting a minor relief from the heat. Viktor's men are simultaneously attentive and wary as I pull through the front gate, not relaxing even when I pull into the garage.

I'll have to kick a little extra cash their way for stepping in at the last minute.

My muscles ache, my head is heavy, and all I want to do is crawl into bed and trace the lines of Nadya's face.

I stop as soon as I enter the living room. Vasily's exactly as I expected—frustrated and half ready to strangle me—but what seizes my heart in my chest is the sight of Nadya sprawled over the couch with Kira draped over her stomach, both sound asleep.

It looks so natural that it knocks the air out of my lungs. She's so damn beautiful like this, like she was made for it.

She's going to be an incredible mother. Fuck, she already has been, and I doubt she even realizes it. God knows Alexei is a little shit, but all things considered, he's turned out alright. I have no doubt it's all due to Nadya's influence.

"Your wife is pissed," Vasily grunts. "And if my daughter starts complaining because she likes Nadya more than me, I won't stop her from trying to take it out on you."

"Don't try to stop her either way." I shrug. "If she wants to hurt me, then let her."

He tilts his head to the side. "She asked when you were coming home. And she wasn't happy when I didn't have an answer."

I grunt in response. If Nadya were pleased with anything I've done lately, I'd be concerned. I like that she fights me.

I want her to be comfortable enough to push back. I want her to view me as an equal, not as the feared Pakhan I am to the rest of the world. I want to be her husband, not a threat. As long as she's angry, I can hold onto hope that eventually, that'll be how she sees me.

Every time she curses my name, it hurts. But one day it won't.

I have to believe that.

Vasily moves to wake his daughter, but before he does, he pauses, giving me a considering look.

"Boss, you mind if I give you some advice?"

Nadya turns her face away from our voices, curling her hand protectively over Kira's back in her sleep. If urging him to leave wouldn't mean waking her, I'd shove him out the door so I can watch her without fear of her reaction. Instead, I find myself nodding.

"She's getting whiplash. Either let her know you care, or tell her it's pointless to hold out any hope."

I cut my eyes to his. He's treading dangerously close to the line, and he knows it.

"She doesn't talk to me about her feelings, but it's clear Nadya likes you more than she lets on. If you insist on keeping her guessing, she's eventually going to give up." He lifts a single shoulder in a half-hearted shrug. "It's what I did to Kira's mom."

There isn't even a hint of bitterness in his tone. He looks older than his twenty-nine years, like he can see the path I'm already set on and knows there's nothing he can do to stop me but has to try anyway.

"It worked out for you."

"Yeah. But you don't look at Nadya the way I looked at Ana. You look at her like you want her to be everything. And if she closes herself off, you'll never get it." He rolls his shoulders, looking uncomfortable. "I know you don't like me, but you're important to Viktor. Your happiness is important to him, so it's important to me."

I don't know what to say to that. I work my jaw as Vasily crouches down to rub Kira's back. She jolts awake, and her movement wakes Nadya almost as quickly. For a few sleepy seconds, she looks around, smiling softly when her eyes land on me.

All too soon, awareness washes over her, twisting her smile into a bitter frown as Vasily lifts his daughter off her. She keeps her arms stretched out, ready to take her back at a moment's notice, and I wonder what would happen if I offered to let Kira stay for the night.

Then I remember there are no beds for her to sleep in.

Besides, what good would it do to keep a child here, anyway? It won't fix the problems that are rising up faster than I can contain them. Nadya still won't trust me. She'll still hate me for everything I've done. It won't change the fact that every time I've made a promise to her, I've failed to deliver.

Nadya will still crave the freedom I can't give her.

She watches as Vasily comforts his daughter, lulling her back to sleep as he holds her. I want to take in every shift of her expression, gather the longing in her eyes as she watches them and bottle it so I can savor it whenever I want.

But I'm so worn out. Physically, emotionally, mentally.

All I can do is brace for a fight as I close the door behind Vasily. Though it feels impossible, I'm going to have to find the strength to let her take her feelings out on me.

She deserves more, but I can give her this.

While I'm exhausted, Nadya's nap appears to have given her all the energy she needs to let me know exactly what she thinks of me. Her eyes blaze with the fire I normally love.

But right now, it feels like a condemnation.

If I ever thought for a moment that having her here would fix me, I was sorely mistaken. Our relationship may be a dream for me, but I'm not so blind that I can't see how she's taking it as a punishment.

But as much as I want to see her happy, I'm not planning on going anywhere. There isn't anything on this earth that could convince me to let her walk away.

There are times when it feels like I'm close to getting her to love me, and those flashes have given me too much hope to give up. I'll redouble my efforts if I have to. I'll give her anything.

"I thought we'd already established I'm not a child. I can stay in the house without a babysitter."

I look her up and down, making sure she feels the weight of my gaze as I fall into familiar habits and cross my arms over my chest.

"You're right, *solnyshka*. You're certainly not a child."

It's the wrong thing to say, but it's so easy to fall into a comfortable persona when I'm scared shitless. It's so effortless to take the full brunt of her anger and hope I can keep her from trying to leave me. That one day her hatred will cross that thin line into something resembling love.

"You're unbelievable, you know that?" Her nostrils flare as she stands so quickly even Spaghetti startles from wherever he was hiding, sprinting out of the room in a flash.

Perhaps he's smarter than I give him credit for.

"And you're irresistible when you're mad at me."

"You have constant security, every inch of the grounds is covered by cameras, and, most importantly, I'm not a fucking moron!" She stalks across the room and jams a finger into my chest, elegance and fury effortlessly twined together.

If Nadya found out how comforting that single point of contact was, she'd snatch it back in a moment. That tiny touch is more grounding than anything has ever been.

"I'm a fucking person, and when you treat me like this, I don't feel like one." To my horror, a tear streaks down her cheek. She pulls away, and when I reach out to comfort her, she glares at me like I'm worth less than the dirt on the bottom of her shoe.

"That's not—"

"You want to be around when it's convenient, and when it isn't, you trot Vasily out. I don't know if you're trying to keep me out of your hair, or if you're concerned I'm going to lash out the instant I'm alone." She runs her hands through her hair, her eyes wild before she stops.

Between one moment and the next, her fire snuffs itself out. Her shoulders slump, and it feels like I've lost something I didn't even know I had.

"You know, my brother told me I'd never be happy with you."

"He did?" I ask. My voice is hollow even to my own ears.

She sits heavily on the couch, not looking at me. "He was right, wasn't he?"

Helplessly, I flounder for words, desperate to think of anything I can do to save this. She nods to herself when I don't answer, apparently taking it as the confirmation she needs.

Her whisper is as loud as a gunshot when she says, "Let me go, Kostya." My stomach drops so fast my head spins. "If you've ever cared about me, then let me go. You can find another wife, but I can't live like a prisoner. I can't keep doing this."

The despair in her voice cuts down my spine, paralyzing me. *She'll never love me.*

If my need for control is enough to break her down, then how will she react when she finds out that she's carrying my child? How will she ever forgive me? How will I ever find light at the end of this bleak fucking existence?

Nothing has ever hurt as much as the realization that I will never know what it's like to be loved by her. She'll never smile just because she's happy to see me, or be willing to hear how my heart beats for her in a way it never has before.

I can tell myself she's overreacting. I can pretend she'll calm down, but the only person I've never been able to lie to is myself.

I'm not a good man. I've never been under any illusions about it, and for once, I wish I was capable of being one. I wish I could give her the world. I wish I could prioritize her happiness and let her go. I wish she didn't have to live with the consequences of being associated with me.

But that's not how it works.

Nadya will be resentful and bitter for the rest of our lives, but I still won't let her go. Not when even her hatred calms me enough to think without feeling like I'm going to pass out.

The most I'll be able to do is pull back a little.

Nadya pulls her knees to her chest, staring straight ahead. Tears flow freely down her cheeks, and each one burns another scar into my irredeemable soul.

She can't leave me.

Resigned, I walk away. Every step presses me further down until it feels like I'm choking on dirt, but there's only one thing that will keep her from trying to run. She needs to know exactly what we stand to lose if something happens to her.

In the few minutes it takes me to go to our room and back, she's managed to dry her tears. Her eyes are red-rimmed and devastated, but she's stopped fighting. Even with herself.

I put the pills on the coffee table, sitting in front of her.

"What're you doing with my birth control?" she asks. Her voice is empty, so detached from the situation that the terror under my skin becomes a living thing. I want to carve it from my flesh and throw it aside, but it would still find its way home.

It always does.

"Nothing. Those are sugar pills." I swallow the acid on the back of my tongue. "You've been taking them since our wedding."

The blood drains from her face.

I don't blink.

I want to memorize every one of her features. Every stray hair. The way her eyelashes hit her cheeks when she blinks.

The way her chin trembles as the weight of my betrayal hits her.

I need to remember this moment when I want to reach for her in the middle of the night and can't find her. I need to soak in the weight of everything I've done. I can't let myself get angry when she does nothing but yell and hate me. I need to remember *why*.

"You've never asked, but I call you *solnyshka* because, when I saw you the first time, it was like seeing the sun after an endless winter. You were curled up on your brother's couch, looking at me like a wild animal, and all I could think was that you felt like finding home. I wanted to know what your lips felt like. I wanted to know what my name would sound like on your tongue.

"The moment I saw you, I wanted to know everything. I was willing to blow up my entire life if it meant I could have you in it. Nothing could ever make me want to give you up. So, no, Nadya. I'm sorry, but I won't be letting you go."

I ache to ease her hands from the tight-knuckled fists she has them in, but I force myself to remain still.

"And I know you're probably thinking up a thousand different ways to get away from me as soon as I blink, but I need you to understand why it can't happen. I understand you hate me"—I choke on my words, and despite my resolve to watch her, I have to look away—"but there's a possibility you're carrying our child. The head of the Irish mob in Boston sent a man to kill you the other day. There was another one this afternoon."

She whimpers, and I hate myself for scaring her. I look down at my hands, clearing my throat, weighing my next words.

She won't want to hear them, but I don't want to risk never getting the chance to tell her. Even if she hates me for it, I want her to know how I feel.

"I love you, Nadya. And I'm sorry for doing that to you, but until I handle the threats, I need to keep you close. If you want to fight me every day for the rest of our lives, then do. I'll follow you until the ends of the earth if I have to, but I won't let you leave me."

She curls up even tighter, wiping her eyes instead of returning my feelings.

Maybe she never will. Maybe she sealed her heart away long before we got married, and any hope I had of having her love were childish at best.

Maybe the only way I'll hear her say *I love you* are when she's talking to our child.

Maybe I'll never hear her say it at all.

I bite my tongue so hard I taste blood.

At least she knows how I feel. I doubt she'll ever give me another opportunity to say it, but at least I tried to tell her how I feel.

It'll have to be enough.

If I thought it would help, I'd carve the useless organ in my chest free and hand it to her so she could inspect every wretched emotion. I'd show her the way it's frozen at the thought of losing her. I'd let her destroy it as long as she'd promise to smile when she's through with me.

"You can have the bedroom," I eventually murmur, wiping my clammy hands against my thighs as I stand so I don't reach for her. "I'll have the beds brought back after I find Dowd, and if you want another room, you're free to choose one. If you need me, I'll be in my office."

I'm not sure anything is strong enough to allow me to claw free of the gaping void opening in my chest. Once I make it to my office, I head straight for the bar cart I leave here for Viktor, grabbing one of his bottles of bourbon and drink deeply, not bothering to grab a glass.

If nothing else, I can drown my sorrows and spend the rest of the night pouring over what little information I have.

For hours, I dig through everything. I look into every lead I can find. I reach out to contacts I haven't spoken to in years, cashing in favors that have long thought to be forgotten.

Nadya might be stuck with me, but the least I can do is try to grant her the freedom she needs to go for a fucking walk without worrying someone's going to kill her.

Chapter 30

Konstantin

It isn't common for me to impose upon Viktor's office at Vlast. As much as I wish he would respect my own home and not intrude unannounced, it's important I give him the same courtesy.

Especially when he's so proud of all the work he's put in and everything he's been able to accomplish here.

In only a few short years, he managed to take it from an abandoned building to one of the premier restaurants in the area. Now, it's the sort of place with a waitlist a mile long and reservations that fill within minutes of being opened.

I should tell him I'm proud of him. Especially since I've taken up so much space and forced him to reschedule so many plans on the fly lately.

Something tells me he'd prefer a check as rent payment for taking over his office, as well as for all the nights he's had to close so I can work in the basement.

It would still be easier than staying home.

Not when I could hear Nadya crying all the way in my office last night.

Each new sob was another fist to my ribs, hitting harder the longer it went on. I'm exhausted from lying awake, trying to find a comfortable position on the couch while her cries echoed through the house.

If I stayed home, I would have broken down and pulled Nadya to my chest until she's so tired of fighting me, she's eventually forced to give in.

Instead, I left as soon as the sun came up and the normal security was back to do their rounds, far sharper than they were the day before. Vasily will come over after he drops Kira off at day care, but he's been instructed to hang out in the camera room unless anything happens.

Everything else I've done might infuriate her, but the least I can do is give her some space while she processes.

"I found someone who says Dowd left the country," Viktor offers from behind the desk, shifting like he isn't sure what to do with me. "Rumor has it he went back to Ireland to say goodbye to a dying family member."

Somehow, I sincerely doubt that.

Despite what his current grudge implies, Dowd isn't a family man. The only reason I can think of why he cares about Ronan's death is because he's decided to take it as a personal insult. But we all know that if Ronan had managed to walk away that night, Liam would have continued to ignore him.

"Is it fair to assume your source is full of shit?"

Viktor shrugs. "He seemed genuine. Doesn't mean he knows what he's talking about, though."

"So, we either send someone to Ireland to look for him, or we keep sitting on our asses and hope he's actually on another continent."

His grim nod is the confirmation I don't want.

I pull out my phone and shoot Ivan a quick text.

If Liam still wants to play pretend, then we can pretend. I'll send my lawyer across an ocean to pass along my condolences for his loss, and we'll either get the confirmation I need, or we can keep looking.

Ivan replies with a thumbs-up, and I toss my phone on Viktor's desk, rolling my neck.

Nadya is going to be livid if I have to keep her in lockdown for a minute longer. I'll need to keep her under lock and key if I don't want to end up chasing her across the country as soon as it's safe.

"You know, once all this shit is handled, I think I might go on a vacation," I say, though *vacation* definitely isn't the right word for what I have in mind.

I'm going to take Nadya as far away from here as I can. Steal her away to Moscow to meet my parents, maybe. Or somewhere warmer. Somewhere with a beach so she learns to associate my presence with being happy.

She might never learn to love me, but maybe I can still convince her to smile around me. And when she does, I'll take her home to visit her brother. She can learn to see that while I may be a monster, I'm not one with her. I'm capable of being more than the monster hiding under her bed.

"Yeah? You finally going to take Nadya on a honeymoon?"

Despite how worn down and tired I am, I can't help but smile at the image.

Nadya, beaming when I take her to a warm, sunny beach. The way she'd light up as she dipped her toes in sand that's softer than the rocks she found yesterday.

Screw my parents. As soon as Dowd is no longer a threat, I'm going to take Nadya somewhere down south so she can do something other than stare longingly out the window, wishing she could enjoy the water. We'll stay for as long as she wants, and even if she doesn't want me there, I'm going to enjoy every minute of it.

"Yeah," I eventually answer. "Something like that."

Honeymoon, babymoon, force-my-wife-to-tolerate-my-presence-moon.

What's the difference?

And if that doesn't work, if she refuses anything to do with me, then what do I do? What if Nadya goes behind my back and summons her brother? What happens if she threatens me with lawyers and custody agreements and divorce?

Despite what I want, will I be able to go through the rest of our lives with her miserable and hating me? Can I really prioritize my own happiness over hers?

No.

Not if she tells me she can't stand it.

Once Liam's handled, divorcing her would prevent anyone else from threatening her. She could take our child, go back to her life, and be perfectly safe under Alexei's care.

I'd burn down the world to keep her by my side, but not if she's going to spend the rest of her days bitter and resentful.

If it's the only way to make her happy, I'll have to force myself to let her go. I'll make due with an occasional report from one of my men. I'll be content with a glance of her from a distance if it's all I can have.

But I'm going to take her somewhere warm first. If I'm going to live the rest of my life cold and alone, I'm going to stockpile memories of Nadya basking in sunshine, humming to herself the way she always does when she's happy before I let her go.

Then I'll go back to being the miserable, empty shell everyone expects me to be. A weapon. A charming smile wrapped around an empty facade with no purpose other than to lead the organization I never wanted in the first place.

Viktor eyes me speculatively, a smile teasing the corners of his mouth.

"She really does make you happy, doesn't she?"

"She does," I admit. Even when she's driving me out of my mind with worry or stomping over the tender feelings that are impossible to ignore when she's around, she makes me happier than I can ever remember being.

Hearing her when she's in her studio, walking in on her when she watching a movie, or even seeing her sitting in the kitchen, poking at the meals Tatiana's insistent on shoving down her throat, is the best part of my day.

When she leaves, everything will go back to being quiet. I'll have no escape from my spiraling thoughts.

Especially since I can't imagine a world where she leaves Spaghetti with me.

I'll have to sell the house when she leaves. If I'm the only one there, there's no point in keeping it. It's probably better if I find somewhere downtown, anyway. If I downsize, the guards can go back to working the streets and making me more money.

It'll be a cold comfort when I have no one to spend it on.

"Good for you, *bratan*. You deserve to be happy," he says with a grin.

How long has it been since I let my guard down enough for my brother to see *me*? How long have I hidden behind the persona I've built for myself that he's started to believe it's real?

There was a time where he could read me like an open book. He knew every thought as soon as I had it, but now he can't even see when I'm drowning on dry land, clinging to desperate plans so I don't break into a million pieces.

But Viktor has always been blinded by loyalty.

When he cares about someone, he sees them through the rose-tinted glasses he hasn't managed to lose, even after everything he's seen and done.

I tilt my head, watching him with a new appreciation and a profound sense of loneliness.

If I had managed to hold onto the childish optimism that comes so easily to him, would it have been easier for me to win over Nadya? Would I have been able to smile at her, make her dinner, spend time with her, and end up with a wife that loved me as much as I love her?

Is that why he's always seemed so much happier? Because he trusts people and doesn't spend hours circling the drain?

I've always done my best to protect him from having to make the hard choices, but is that why he gets to have it all? Is that why he gets to have Vasily and Kira *and* be happy?

For a moment, I'm so jealous that I could destroy him and everything he's ever loved.

But even if I end up having to sign divorce papers and custody agreements and spend the rest of my life wondering what I'm missing out on, it will have to be enough. Nadya will find her own happiness, and Viktor will go through life with everything he needs.

I'll figure out how to cope with it eventually.

"Can I trust you to keep things from falling apart while we're gone?"

Nadya will likely only tolerate me for a week or two before she demands I bring her home, but before I leave, I'll need to set things up so he doesn't need to do much before I come back.

"Of course you can. Take as much time as you two want. I've got your back."

I nod, letting him hold onto his delusions for a while longer.

Chapter 31

Nadya

The two guards who typically joke around and laugh with each other while they make their patrols are stone-faced, their expressions serious whenever they pass by. In fact, all of them look more focused than they normally do.

They're always alert, sure, but they don't always look so tense. Now, they're one stiff wind from snapping in half. Today, everyone keeps looking around warily, on edge every time a tree rustles.

It would be funny if their stress wasn't making me tenser every time I look at them.

But the longer I watch them, the more I start to understand why Konstantin spends so much time in his office.

Technically, it has the worst view in the house. The only thing you can see is the front gate, the dry brush outside the fence, and glimpses of the road through the overgrown trees on the hill. But it has a full view of the driveway.

If anyone turns off the road and approaches the gate, he can see it. Anyone and everything that comes and goes is visible as he sits at his desk.

With someone as anxious and paranoid as he is, I bet Konstantin spent hours checking the sightlines in every room before he bought the house. He probably spent days sitting in each room before he selected which one would be his office.

Despite how pissed I am, I can't help but smile at the image.

Even so, he can't let me leave the property without making it a production. He keeps an eye on everything that happens here, both inside and out, and, worst of all, he switched out my birth control so he could knock me up without telling me.

Who the hell does that?

If Konstantin wanted kids, wouldn't it have been easier to talk to me about it? Even though we've been married less than two months, there's a possibility I would have said yes. And that's what pisses me off most.

Because it's way too soon into our relationship. I still don't even know my way around the city, and what would I do if something happened to Vasya while we were out and I didn't have my phone? I'd be lost. What would happen if something happened to the baby and Vasya was with his daughter and Konstantin wasn't here?

Konstantin wants a baby, but I want to do all the lame touristy things I can't bring myself to ask Vasily to do with me.

I want to visit Lombard Street. And Golden Gate Park. I want to visit Alcatraz.

But if I'm doing that, I want to go with Konstantin, if only because I think it'd be fun to go to a prison with him knowing we can leave whenever we want. And I want to take a picture to send to Dad, because that's the closest he's going to get to seeing me in a prison with him.

And though my brother could make an Olympic-level sport out of avoiding me most of the time, I didn't hate raising him.

At least, if Kostya and I managed to make a baby, I wouldn't be raising myself at the same time.

At least I can admit to myself that I want to be a mother.

The rest of my family has abandoned me in one way or another, but it's something I've always dreamed of. Having a close family that actually cares about each other and won't turn their back when things get scary.

Is that what Konstantin's trying to do? Tie me further to him so I don't leave?

He's an overbearing, controlling ass who worries more than anyone should, but he said he loved me.

I was too overwhelmed to react, but he stripped himself of his pride and made himself vulnerable in a way I'm sure cost him dearly anyway. I've only seen him without his bolster in the middle of the night when he wakes up shaking and near tears from nightmares he doesn't dare share with me.

But he was honest. Real.

I want to get to know *that* man. I like the cocky persona he puts on just fine, but the man who seemed terrified of my reaction? The man that couldn't look me in the eye when he offered to sleep in his office?

That man is the one I know would be an amazing father.

Fiercely protective. Kind. Strong.

For all his faults, I *know* that's the real Konstantin. Not the stubborn dick who refuses to listen to anyone else. Not the smirking jerk who pushes away his emotions the moment they pop up, but the man who holds me at night like he can't stand to have more than an inch between us.

Every time I close my eyes, all I can see is the agony he desperately tried to hide last night.

Deep down, I know that if Konstantin didn't care about me, he wouldn't risk facing my temper as often as he does. He does things because he knows they'll make me smile, he looks after me, and when I speak, he listens. He doesn't brush me aside. He actually cares what I have to say, even if I'm just talking about a movie that's older than the two of us combined.

He's overbearing, controlling, and he worries about me like it's his job, but there's a part of me that likes it, even when it feels suffocating.

Oh, fuck.

Am I in love with my husband?

My heart flutters, a butterfly who's all too happy to confirm that *yes*, I am. I'm so in love with him that I had to physically hold myself back instead of rushing to comfort him when he walked away. I'm so in love that spending a single night without him made me so miserable I couldn't sleep.

I wrap my arms around my stomach as I take another slow look around the office. Was Konstantin alone when he picked this room for his office? Or was Viktor there to give him shit? Did he picture filling this giant house up with children when he bought it?

He could have bought it as a status symbol, but my gut tells me Konstantin wants to build a life here. Why else would he have invested so heavily in making sure everything was secure? He's more than capable of looking after himself, but a family is a different matter entirely.

I blink, focusing my attention on the spreadsheet he left open on his laptop, twirling a pen on the notepad I dug out of a drawer.

Maybe I love my husband.

And maybe I'm pregnant with his child.

You love him, taunts a voice in the back of my head. *And if he wants you pregnant, then odds are he managed it.*

I shove the thought aside, focusing on what I know.

And numbers? I know numbers. They won't change no matter what I do. They just are, and even if I change the inputs, I'm still going to get a hard answer, even if it isn't the one I want.

I squint at another column, checking it against the numbers I've written down.

Whoever last tried to work on Konstantin's accounts apparently thought differently, because very little of their work lines up like it should. They didn't just manipulate the numbers; they engineered them into something unrecognizable.

And if they were trying to hide it, they did a terrible job.

I'm going over the spreadsheet for a third time when the door opens. I sit up straighter, watching as Konstantin walks in with his shoulders slumped. Without looking up, he tosses his jacket onto the couch.

The faint lines around his eyes look even deeper, and the bags under them lead me to believe he didn't sleep last night, either. Seeing him like this is more upsetting than I would have thought. But the way he pauses when he finally notices me, his face shifts between a dozen emotions before he finally settles on a blank mask, makes it hard to breathe.

So I say the first thing that comes to mind, desperate to wave away his hurt like a bad smell.

"Whoever your accountant is, you need a new one."

Kostya searches my face, but I have no idea whether he finds what he's looking for or not. He props his shoulder against the wall, looking like the weight of the world is dragging him down as he blinks.

"Oh?" he asks.

"Your expense sheets have more material missing than the Grand Canyon, and what you *do* have is missing the proper documentation needed to back it up. If this is the sum of your business expenses, then you're begging to be audited."

For what feels like ages, he doesn't say a word. He blinks, looking between me and the security I spent so much of the day watching outside with his hands shoved in his pockets.

"I'll look into it," he murmurs, focusing on the repeating patterns of the men walking along the fence line. It's the second variation of patrols today. Up to the gate, conferring with the men outside, before continuing on, passing the men walking along the neatly trimmed hedges while they watch everything with sharp eyes.

It's almost like a ballet with how carefully choreographed it is. If you watch them long enough, you almost forget how chaotic everything else around them is. The weapons and menacing looks fall away until their movements mimic flowing water.

"If I'm pregnant..." I say through trembling lips. I have to swallow when the words nearly choke me.

God, I could be *pregnant*.

"I don't want you going to jail. Especially not for something this sloppy and easy to fix."

I've lived most of my life with my dad behind bars. My child won't grow up the same way.

Impossibly, Konstantin grows even more still. He doesn't even appear to be breathing before he closes his eyes and takes a deep breath. As painful as it is to see him ready to collapse under all the weight he carries, it's easier to stomach than the smirk he likes to hide behind.

I want his vulnerability. I want him to show me when things are hard. I want to help ease the burden he carries without flinching.

"I'll do my best, then," he says. His jaw flexes as if he's bracing himself, while my heart beats a relentless, aching beat against my ribs.

"I need to be my own person, Kostya."

"I know."

"And if we're starting a family, you're going to have to find a way to accommodate my needs. So do whatever you have to do to make things safe, but do it fast."

For a man who spends so much time hiding himself from the rest of the world, he does a terrible job of hiding the flash of shock on his face.

"You say that like you wouldn't hate having a family with me."

I put the pen down on top of my notes, weighing my next words.

Even though he's holding back, I can't ignore the way he looks at me anymore. Like I'm everything he's ever wanted. Like I have his future in the palm of my hand and he isn't sure if he wants to watch what I do with it or if it would be better to turn away.

"Why did you swap out my birth control?"

"Because I love you," he answers without hesitation. "Because I don't deserve you, but I wanted to keep you anyway. Because I've spent my entire life feeling like I'm standing on a cliff, and you're the only one who's ever been able to pull me back, and you don't even try. Because I wanted you, and I knew you'd always fight me if I didn't force your hand." He shrugs. "Because there isn't a line too far to cross if it means having you in my life, however that happens. Even if you hate me for it, I don't regret it, Nadya. I need you to understand that."

His words should chill me to the bone, but instead they wash over me like a cool wave lapping at my ankles.

Konstantin's a selfish jerk with no respect for boundaries, he doesn't know the definition of the word overbearing, and he'll suffocate me if I let him. But he's also steady, honest, and focused.

And he wants me so much that he was willing to cross every line and do whatever it takes in order to tie me to him.

Out of everyone on the planet, Konstantin Lavrov picked me. He brought me into his life. He brought me into his home. He gave me his last name.

He's better than he gives himself credit for.

"I guess it's a good thing I love you too, then."

He startles as if I just told him war was breaking out on his front lawn.

"What?"

"I know you're old," I say, "but I didn't realize your hearing was going out."

He darts across the room, lifting me out of his chair like I weigh nothing at all. His eyes burn and his hands shake as he sets me on the desk. He pushes my thighs apart, making room for himself as he steps even closer.

It feels like the most natural place in the world for him to be.

"I'm hardly old, *solnyshka*, and my hearing is fine." He presses his forehead against mine, his face so close that all I'd have to do to kiss him is tilt my chin. I can't help but smile. "But say it again anyway. I'll listen this time."

A deadly hope shines in his eyes, pure and devastating.

"I love you," I confess.

Konstantin fists my hair and slams his lips against mine, consuming me in a kiss that steals my breath and wraps around the bruised shards of my heart before piecing them back together, filling me with a warmth that rivals the sun.

His thumb brushes over my cheek so tenderly it aches. And as much as I'd love to explore his softer side, right now it's so far from what I need from him.

I want his usual intensity to chase away the worry that's been lingering all day. I need him to be his usual self. The rug was ripped out from underneath me yesterday, and after the riot of emotions I've been poking through all day, I need his steadiness.

But when I pull back, his eyes settle on mine without the heat and fire. His touch is unbearably gentle, and I can feel his intensity simmering below the surface, waiting to be drawn out. I run my hands over his shirt, wishing I could see his sculpted muscles and ink, but I'll get my chance soon.

He better not make me wait long, though.

"Say it again, Nadya. Tell me you love me."

"Are you going to be one of those unbearable people that needs to be told a thousand times before you believe it?" I ask, smiling despite myself.

Konstantin hums. "If that's what it takes for you to say it again, then yes. I need to hear it every day. Every night. I need to hear you say you love me with every breath."

I scrunch my nose, digging my fingers into the fabric. Konstantin laughs, the sound soft and happy in a way I've never heard him. I want to hear it more often. I want to see the happiness that's lighting up his eyes all the time.

"Earn it," I whisper. He's so close that my lips brush against his. "I'll tell you when you've earned it."

He brushes his thumb over my lower lip and a shiver cascades down my spine.

"It's a good thing I like your fire, Nadya." He bites my lip so hard I hiss. Unbidden, my thighs squeeze around his hips, revealing the way the hint of pain ignites sparks throughout my body. "Especially when you're looking at me like you can't figure out whether you'd rather reach for your pretty little knife or ride my cock until everyone knows exactly who you belong to," he growls.

There he is.

I move my hands to his hair, scraping my nails over the shorter strands at the base of his skull before I grab tight, pulling his mouth back to mine. It feels brand new, but at the same time, it feels like coming home.

Konstantin is everything I didn't want, but maybe he's everything I need.

He shoves aside the items on his desk, not caring where they land, before he pushes me back against the wood. I arch my spine to get closer to him, gasping when he pulls me down until my ass is hanging off the edge. Konstantin kisses along my jaw, and when he drags his teeth over my throat, I sigh.

"Wouldn't the couch be better?" I ask as I slip my fingers over the collar of his shirt.

"After spending the night on that couch, I can assure you the desk is more comfortable." Without waiting for a reply, Konstantin deftly undoes my shorts and lifts my hips, stripping my lower half in one swift movement. "Now, take off your shirt and let me worship you the way I need to."

He stands to his full height as I prop myself up on my elbows. He's practically looming over me, making me feel tiny in comparison. I normally feel tall in a crowd, but Konstantin has a way of making me feel dainty, like he could throw me across the room or bend me in half without any effort at all.

I've never let myself consider how much I like that until he raises a brow, looking me up and down.

"I gave you an order, Nadya. I won't repeat myself."

His tone is almost as dark as his eyes, making my nipples pebble as I shiver. His fingers dig into my thighs, holding them apart while the weight of his gaze feels impossible to bear.

"Now, wife," he orders again.

For once, I don't want to challenge him. The way he commands me should be irritating, but giving him my submission feels too good to push back.

Slowly, I pull off my shirt, teasing him with every new inch of skin until I've gathered the fabric right below my breasts. His hands are glued to my thighs as he clicks his tongue in disappointment.

"I want you to make you come on my tongue, *solnyshka*. But if you're determined to toy with me, I'd just as happily take you over my knee." My cheeks burn as I picture the way his hands would caress me before they'd slam down over-sensitive flesh.

"You like that idea, don't you?" Kostya asks, chuckling under his breath.

I do, I realize.

It's not something I've ever thought to try with anyone else, but with Konstantin? He won't push me too far. He would know how to twine pleasure and pain together until I'm nothing but a sobbing mess.

Biting my lip, I nod.

"Next time," he promises. "When I'm not so desperate to have you, we can try it. For now, I want you bare on my desk so I can devour your wet cunt."

His fingers trail to the place where my thigh and hip meet, spurring me into action faster than anything he says can. My shirt joins the rest of my clothing on the floor as he falls to his knees and consumes my pussy like he needs me to breathe.

I scramble to grab his hair, his shoulders, his shirt, anything that will keep me from spiraling out of control as he licks the length of my slit, sucking my clit with a single-minded focus.

Everything except the way his tongue spins me higher fades away.

All the things we still have left to discuss, all ways he needs to make things right. They mean nothing when he's relentlessly pushing me toward my climax, holding me so tight I wonder if he thinks I'm going to disappear.

The room itself could be on fire around us, and I wouldn't care.

Especially when I know if I were in danger, Kostya would do whatever it took to protect me. But first, he'd remind me that no matter how hard he pushes my buttons, he still knows how to play with my body and make it do whatever he wants.

With agonizing slowness, he stretches me open with two fingers, stroking relentlessly over my G-spot.

"Kostya," I gasp, my neck straining as my body arches. "I'm so fucking close."

I groan as he pulls away, licking his lips with an infuriating smirk I want to slap off his stupid, devastating face.

"Not yet," he says, sitting up to press kisses over my flat stomach. He keeps the same torturous rhythm with his fingers that has my body singing for him, my breath coming in ragged pants. "Not until you're desperate for me. When I finally let you come, I want you so high on your orgasm that when I fuck you, I'm the only thought in that beautiful mind of yours."

I buck my hips, mesmerized by the transparent want in his eyes as he takes in every moan, every twitch of my muscles, like he's starved for more.

I dig my nails into the meat of his shoulder as he returns to working my clit with his tongue, rubbing and nudging his fingers against me until my thighs are shaking and my muscles are clenching so hard it's a wonder he's able to move his hand.

His eyes are glued to mine, sparkling with mirth while he slowly drives me to my limits. When he finally gives in, I don't break. I implode. Every muscle in my body seizes, then melts as I buck against Kostantin's mouth. He doesn't relent, lashing his tongue against me like I'm the best thing he's ever tasted, moaning so hard and loud that I'm already halfway to another orgasm when he finally pulls way.

Deft hands undo his belt as he stands.

I'm practically liquid in his hands as he rubs the head of his cock up and down my slit, looking at me with a question in his eyes. But even if I wanted to, I'm helpless to deny him anything.

He could ask for forever, and I'd hand it to him gladly.

Then again, I don't think I'd be able to walk away no matter what happened. If he tried to let me go, I'd fight as dirty as he has to stay. I'd do whatever it takes to claw my way back into his life and stay there.

I'm not giving him up.

His bare cock slides against my entrance, teasing me. Fuck, I want him to fill me up like that. Even though I might already be pregnant, there's also a chance I might not be. And there's nothing stopping him from filling me until I am.

A thrill shoots through my oversensitive nerves, and it's all I can do to keep myself from outright begging him to fuck me, from making that fantasy a reality.

"Please," I groan. "I need you, Kostya."

His smile as he sinks inside me is the most wonderful thing I've ever seen. "You're mine." His lips brush against mine as he fucks me, consuming the little brain power I had left. "Say it, Nadya. Tell me you're mine."

I don't hesitate.

"I'm yours."

We're so caught up in the safety of this room, of each other, that everything else ceases to exist. My resentment, my hurt feelings. None of it matters in the face of how wholly he loves me.

And I love him enough to let it all go.

We'll grow past it. Whatever comes, we'll deal with it.

As long as we have each other, I don't care.

Chapter 32
Nadya

It's normal to have to pee when you're nervous, right? Or is the opposite? Because I've been sitting here for nearly ten minutes, my stomach twisted up in knots, and I'm no closer to relaxing enough to take the pregnancy test Konstantin handed me before he left for a meeting this morning.

In fact, I've put off taking a test for the past three days because every time I even think about it, my bladder is suddenly bone-dry and I feel like I'm going to pass out.

It hasn't helped that Konstantin has made a show of putting a slew of different pregnancy tests in the bathroom before we go to bed every night. He hasn't outright asked me to take one, but the expectant, hopeful look he gives me when he gets home every night is more telling than he probably wants it to be.

Based on the way he lays a hand over my stomach every night, he sure seems to think I'm pregnant.

I don't know how much longer I'll be able to bear the way his eyes dim in disappointment when he realizes I don't have news for him.

Things between us are easy in a way I never let myself dream of before we got married, but what if pregnancy changes things? Is Kostantin going to triple down on his security and leave me locked inside with Spaghetti until the baby's born? Or will he keep his word and try to do better?

Oh, god, what if I'm *not* pregnant?

There's a hollow ache in my chest as dread fills me.

Why does that feel even more terrifying than the alternative?

I've only known it was a possibility for a matter of days, but the thought that Konstantin's dirty little tricks didn't work makes me feel like I could cry.

I *want* to be pregnant. I want to have his baby and fill this house with the family I always wished I had.

When I finally force myself to pee on the damn stick, I can't tell if my hands are shaking from nerves or excitement. I set it down, wash my hands, and set a timer on my phone. I turn around, staring at the closed door while I wait rather than driving myself mad staring at the little piece of plastic.

I wish Konstantin were here.

If I were holding his hand, maybe waiting for three minutes wouldn't be so daunting. Every second drags, and I end up pulling on a loose thread on the hem of my dress, trying, and failing, to resist the urge to pull it free entirely.

The timer going off nearly makes me jump out of my skin. My knees go weak, and I have to brace my hands on the edge of the counter, my breaths coming out in rapid spurts that only fuel the hesitation and worry souring my gut.

How long can I reasonably stand here and avoid turning around? Ten minutes? Twenty?

I can't avoid checking the results forever.

If I spend the rest of the day locked in the bathroom, eventually someone's going to come looking for me. And as much as I don't want to turn around, I want to explain why I'm hiding in the bathroom to Tatiana or Vasily even less.

But Kostya won't be home for hours, and I'm suddenly desperate to have him here with me when I finally look at the result. I don't want to be alone.

It'll be fine.

Knowing isn't going to change anything. And no matter what the result is, I'll have the rest of the day to figure out how I'm going to tell Konstantin.

All I have to do is pick up a piece of plastic and look down. No problem.

Blowing out a slow breath, I turn around with my eyes glued to the mirror so I don't look at the counter.

I've got this.

Whatever happens when I see the result, I'll figure out how to deal with it, and Konstantin will be right there with me whether it's positive or not.

With my heart in my throat, I look down, blinking several times at the piece of plastic that could either be nothing, or everything.

On the counter, two bold, beautiful blue lines stare back at me.

My hands shake so badly it takes several attempts for me to be able to pick it up. I can hardly dare to believe it. I double-check the instructions to make sure I'm not misreading the results, but it's hard to breathe around the hysterical laughter filling my chest.

I'm not sure if want to laugh or cry.

I'm pregnant.

With Konstantin's baby.

Holy shit, this is actually happening.

I look down at my stomach as it flips, and I can't tell if it's butterflies or the urge to puke from my sudden nerves.

Oh, fuck.

Konstantin's kid is going to be a giant like him, aren't they?

How the hell am I going to fit a baby in me? No matter what I've tried, I've always been skinny. If I haven't gotten hips after eating my weight in pasta, how the hell am I going to fit in a massive baby?

What if they don't fit? What if they end up bursting out of me because I'm not built for them?

Blayd.

I reach for my phone. Maybe Blair will know what to say. Her husband isn't exactly a small man, and she didn't seem freaked out about it when I last talked to her. Maybe because she already has a kid and understands how this all works., but I don't.

And I'm definitely freaking out.

I slink over to the armchair next to the window and wait for Blair to answer my call, doing everything I can to compose myself enough so she doesn't immediately think I'm panicking.

Even if I am.

And even though I need her advice, I can't tell her what's wrong. Konstantin deserves to be the first one I tell, no matter how much I want to blurt out the news to the first person I see.

And the idea of telling him over the phone is even less appealing than waiting for him to get home.

I want to see his face light up when I tell him. I want to kiss him before I change his life.

"I was just thinking about you," Blair says as her face fills the screen. I can't help but grin at her. There are bags under her eyes, and she looks exhausted. For a moment, I regret taking up her time, but I need her right now.

And while Vasya has a kid, something tells me he wouldn't answer if I asked him what his ex's pregnancy was like.

"How're you feeling?" I ask in lieu of spitting out any of the million questions running around my head, burning any sense of peace and quiet they happen to stumble across. "Little Bean treating you well?"

"He's been great," she says, smiling fondly. "Other than deciding he's getting cramped and taking it out on my organs. He's taking to tap dancing whenever I lie down."

I wince sympathetically. "You're due soon through, right?"

"Fortunately."

"You ready to be done?"

"I'm ready for strangers to stop touching my stomach every time I leave the house. I felt like a zoo animal last time I went to the grocery store."

"Let me guess, Andrei wasn't there?"

"If he was, I'd be worrying about bailing him out of jail on top of making sure the nursery is painted in time. He's stuck babysitting Niko until I can't stand to leave the house anymore."

Before I know it, we're both laughing as she regales me with tales of how overprotective Andrei's been, and how curious Niko is over everything that's changed around the house. When she tells me about the day Niko went through his toys and tossed his favorite stuffed dinosaur into the crib so his brother would have something to play with when he gets here, my chest squeezes.

I miss that kid.

Hopefully I can go back and visit them soon. It probably won't happen before her baby's born, but I want to meet him, too.

We talk until we're interrupted by Niko running into the room to monopolize her attention, but I'm smiling as we say our goodbyes. I didn't get to ask her any of my questions, but chatting with her managed to settle some of my unease.

She's going to have a baby, and she's managed not to fall apart. In fact, she seems happy. Tired, but happy.

With a little luck, I might look like her in a few months.

Carrying that thought like a candle in a windstorm, I grab a glass of water and down it to settle the imaginary fluttering in my stomach before I seek out Vasya. It might be approaching a million degrees, but nothing sounds better than sitting outside with a cold glass of water and enjoying the sunshine.

When I finally track him down, he's hanging out in the security room with Tatiana, chatting quietly about her knitting.

I knock on the doorframe, and from the way they both look at me, it's clear I haven't quite managed to erase the panic from my eyes. Thankfully they're both gracious enough not to say anything about it.

"Mind if I steal Vasya? I want to sit outside." He purses his lips, and I roll my eyes. "If I was trying to be a pain in the ass, I'd go outside without you. It's not like I'm asking you to take me galivanting across town." He looks between me and the wall of monitors tracking every inch of the property, both inside and out.

Even though I'm curious exactly how many cameras Konstantin has around the property, I've avoided coming in here to find out. If I think about it too long, I end up feeling exposed.

Some things are better off not knowing.

"Come on. Please?" When he remains unmoved, I change strategies. "I'll let you bring Kira over next time you and Viktor want to go out." My voice isn't quite a whine, but it's close. "I'll even let her play in my studio. We can make you a little trinket dish."

I don't bother pointing out that I can look after myself or threaten to go outside without him, but only because I know it isn't his call to make. And for now, I'd rather keep things peaceful. Besides, once Konstantin hears the good news, I'm going to be lucky if he lets me outside at all, even if I do have a bodyguard glued to my side.

"Fine," he sighs, scrubbing a hand down his face. "But make if for Ana instead. Her birthday's next month." He stands up as the normal guard comes back in to take his spot. "Let me text the guards so they know not to bother you."

Not listening, I practically dart to the back door, waiting impatiently. Slowly, he follows, nodding at Tatiana as she smiles at me, happy to ignore Vasily's scowl.

The sun on my face is so hot it nearly steals my breath, but sitting in the shade keeps it somewhat bearable.

"Where is everyone?" I ask as I look around.

"Boss wanted to give you space. They're still around, but they aren't going to be right on top of you."

My stomach flips, my cheeks burning bright from more than the sun. "He did?" I know he said he'd try, but for some reason, I didn't really believe he would. Not until he's figured out what's going on with the Irish mob, anyway.

I bite my lip to hide my smile, grinning down at my hands as I twist my ring.

As predicted, the ring Konstantin gave me is filthy. There's clay caked around all the little stones, and no matter what I do to try and clean it off, nothing seems to work. I'm going to have to make a habit of going to a jeweler to get it cleaned in the future.

I don't think I'd mind that. Not when the trade-off is Konstantin wearing a ring everywhere he goes, declaring him as mine as much as this ring declares me as his.

Everything is so different from the life I was dreading before we got married, but I've found myself happier here than I was back home. Sure, I went out, I had my job, and I had a friend, but at the end of the day, I'd always come home to an empty apartment and wait for the next time I could insert myself into someone else's life.

But here? There's always someone around. And even if they're only guards who aren't much for conversation, I still have Spaghetti, who's happy to stick to me like glue until I have to hide to get away from him.

The piercing ringing of a phone disturbs the peace around us. I glare at Vasily, but he ignores me to look at his phone, concern lining his features.

"Is something wrong?" I ask, my annoyance crumbling to dust in the face of his obvious distress.

"It's Kira's day care." He looks at me with a storm brewing behind his eyes. "They don't call unless there's something wrong."

"Answer it," I tell him. "I'll wait here for a couple minutes so you can have some privacy."

Vasily doesn't hesitate, nodding as he rushes back inside and answer the phone.

I look away, despite the privacy film blocking my view through the glass. If something's wrong, I'm not going to make it worse by making him feel like he's being watched.

All I can do is give him some room to breathe and hope everything's alright. And if he needs to leave to take care of Kira, I'll go back inside and call Kostya. I'll hang out with Tatiana until either he or Viktor gets here to keep watch.

I close my eyes, listening to the rustle of trees as the warm breeze blows across my face. Maybe it would be better if I go inside once Vasily's done anyway.

It's so hot that I'm already sweating.

There's a rustle in the bushes behind me, and I twist around to make sure Spaghetti didn't slip out to make trouble, but I don't see his green eyes blinking back at me.

Instead, I see dark eyes glaring at me through the eyeholes of a mask.

I freeze for a horrifying second, my body a dead weight and my heart thundering in my chest, but he doesn't stop stalking closer, moving like a predator who knows they already have their prey cornered.

The moment realization hits, I launch myself toward the doors, but I run straight into another body who's managed to sneak up from the other side.

In a panic, I look up, praying it's Vasily, but my stomach hollows out when I find another mask. Before I can scream, he grabs me, forcing a gloved hand over my mouth.

No matter how hard I lash out or struggle, I know I have no way of overpowering him.

But that doesn't keep me from trying.

I sink my teeth into the thick leather of his glove, using all my strength to kick out, to give myself room to scream for Vasily or one of the guards out front, but the instant his other hand wraps around my torso, squeezing around my stomach, I hesitate.

That split second is all the time they need to get a grip on me tight enough that I'll never be able to fight my way free.

My muscles burn, my heart races, and tears flow down my cheeks as I watch my reflection in the windows. Helplessly, I watch as one of the men uncaps a needle and shoves it into my arm.

The last thing I see is the other man lifting a ladder out of the bushes and propping it against the fence before a hood is shoved over my head and everything goes dark.

Chapter 33

Konstantin

Ivan landed in Ireland hours ago and he hasn't been able to find any trace of Dowd. He managed to track down his dying uncle, but Liam is nowhere to be found.

It's not like I was expecting Ivan to root out the man who I suspect isn't even on that side of the ocean, but each passing hour drives me closer to finding out which will break first if they're hit together hard enough: the wall or my skull.

At this point, it's honestly a toss-up.

My lawyer is on another continent, I have men hunting down a rumor that Dowd is somewhere in fucking Modesto, and the longer I go without any real leads, the more if feels like there's a noose around my neck.

I hate being away from Nadya. I'd rather be anywhere in the world with her than stuck chasing down a fucking shadow.

But Liam already went after her.

I try to tell myself that she's surrounded by layers and layers of security as long as she's home. No one is getting onto the property, and for once, I think Nadya is content to wait for me before she tries to leave again.

If Liam wants to hurt me, it would be easier for him to come at me directly, rather than infiltrate the veritable fortress I've engineered around my wife. But doubt screams in the back of my head, a cacophony that's haunted me every moment since I left this morning.

It's louder than normal as I pace the length of Viktor's office, rolling my neck as if it will do anything to help with the stress that's burning through the oxygen in my lungs faster than I can take it in. If I'd stayed home, I would have driven Nadya up a wall with my bullshit.

At least that's what I tell myself.

Really, I just can't risk getting distracted by her. Not now.

When my phone lights up on the desk, I rush to answer, desperate for news that will end this endless waiting game.

I don't care if I have to shut down all streams of income, I'll have every man available searching for this motherfucker. I'll ruin every business relationship. I'll destroy any agreements I have in place if I have to.

Those things can be fixed later.

But Nadya? She won't be willing to wait forever. I'm going to give her the life she deserves, and I don't want to wait.

"Yeah?" I bark as soon as I answer.

"Nadya's gone." Every muscle in my body locks up as the world around me tilts sideways. Vasily is breathless and angry as he says, "We were hanging out on the patio when I got a phone call. I wasn't gone more than two minutes, but when I came back, she was gone."

I'm not sure my heart is beating as all the blood in my body pools at my feet so quickly, I nearly collapse.

Maybe she wanted to go back to the beach, my mind offers unhelpfully. *Maybe she hopped the fence again.*

Except I know better.

Nadya knows it isn't only her life on the line anymore. She wouldn't do anything that could hurt our baby. She wouldn't do this to me.

"Tatiana's checking the cameras, but there's a ladder outside the wall."

No.

I burst into motion, calling for Viktor as I hang up, cutting off whatever Vasily's saying before he can send me into a total tailspin.

Someone took her. And Liam's managed to spin so many tales about his whereabouts that I've scattered most of my men around the state looking for him, instead of being here where I need them.

I don't have time to for everyone to round up, because in a few hours, he could have Nadya across the country. He could put her on a plane, or he could be hiding her right under my nose, and I'd have no way of knowing.

All I do know is that every minute she's away from me, the distance between us could be growing larger and larger until it takes a miracle to find her again.

***

Every single person on the property failed, but no one more than Vasily. And from the way his spine is straight as he stands before me with my gun pressed between his eyes, he feels the weight of it, too.

He's steadfast in ignoring Viktor's protests as he tries to force his way between us.

"You need him, Konstantin," Viktor begs, but his words hardly cut through the fog of my rage. "Save it until after we find Nadya."

I don't even look in his direction, because if I do, I'm going to end up shooting him, too.

"I thought we were clear on exactly what was at stake here, Vasily."

No matter what Viktor says or how hard he pleads for mercy, Vasily is going to die for this. What does it matter if it's now, or after Nadya is home?

"We are, Pakhan," Vasily says. His voice is steady, but there's resignation shining in his eyes.

It's a shame. He was a good solider.

"I trusted you. *Nadya* trusted you." I flex my finger against the trigger guard. "You abandoned her, and that could cost my wife her life." My throat squeezes painfully tight, threatening to strangle me. "It's definitely going to cost yours."

That, finally, makes him close his eyes.

Out of every man in my Bratva, Vasily is one of the few with something to lose. The fact that he's standing in front of me is a testament to how loyal he really is.

A coward would have taken the easy route and run. But he stayed, even knowing he'll never see his daughter again.

As soon as I got home, I ran to the camera room and found him furiously searching the footage, looking as bereft as I've ever seen him. It did nothing to calm my nerves, especially not when I looked down at the motionless body in the corner behind him.

Apparently, Viktor took my demand to get rid of Yuri to mean it was acceptable to reassign him to watching the cameras. I wanted him as far away from my wife as possible, and my brother made him the last line of defense in getting to her.

It didn't take much to connect the broken skin on Vasily's knuckles with Yuri's broken nose, but I'll deal with him later. In the meantime, he can hang out in the wine cellar until I have time to deal with him myself.

Vasily was pissed, but whether it's because he's worried about Nadya or because he knows exactly how painful I'm going to make his death, I can't decide.

No matter the reason, it did nothing to erase the red from my vision when Vasily pulled up the footage that showed two men hanging out over the wall in clear sight of the camera, before they climbed over, drugged my wife, and carried her limp body away like she's nothing.

No one was there to stop them.

Not Vasily.

Not the guards.

In a matter of moments, Nadya went from smiling as she turned her face to the sun, to gone without a trace.

Vasily's throat bobs on a swallow as he opens his eyes. "Kira's day care called. Nadya told me to answer. By the time I turned around, she was gone."

"Is that supposed to make it better?" I press the gun even harder against his head, waiting for him to flinch or blink or react in any way to the fact that he's going to die. He's holding one wrist with the opposite hand in front of him, and he put his own gun on the table as soon as I walked in the room, stepping out of reach of it before I could say a word.

If he thinks his relationship with my brother is going to save him, he has lost the fucking plot.

He's no different from any other man. And I'll use him to send a message as easily as I would with anyone else.

Anger is a relief from the terror riding at my back. For the first time since he called, I can breathe freely.

"Respectfully, boss, I was talking to Viktor. I know no excuse will be good enough, and I won't try to make one. But I wanted him to know."

Viktor pulls on my arm so hard it's painful, but I don't move.

"Focus, Konstantin!" he snaps, still trying to shove himself between us. He might be my brother, but it's an overreach, and we all know it. My eyes flick to him for a single beat, letting him feel the full impact of my fury.

Appearances matter in this life. And even if I typically let Viktor get away with more than I should, he knows better than to blatantly undercut my authority.

Especially when he's next in line for punishment.

He may be family, but right now, he's looking at me like he's never seen me before. He's looking at me with the same fear he used to have when he talked to Dad.

So be it.

If I have to scorch every connection I have, every relationship I've managed to forge in order to get my wife back, then that's what I'll do.

Even if it means losing my brother.

"Deal with him later," he tries again. "You're wasting time."

I hate knowing he's right. I need all the warm bodies I can get. Until Nadya is home, I have no choice but to let Vasily live.

His expression doesn't waver when I flick the safety and re-holster my gun.

"You're going to memorize every frame of footage. Then you're going to search every inch of the property. If you find *anything*, you come straight to me. Fuck knows I can't trust you to handle anything on your own." Vasily's throat bobs as he nods. "And I hope you enjoy the time you have left, because every second of it is borrowed." My chest heaves, my heart beating only out of determination to see Nadya again. "Tell me you understand."

"*Da*, Pakhan."

I turn on my heel, needing to see the spot she was taken from with my own eyes. Vaguely, I remember someone telling me that men had already scoured the area before I got home, and all they managed to find were the used syringe and the ladders that were left behind.

I look around, staring at the indent left on the chair she was sitting on.

This is Nadya's home. She was supposed to be safe here, and again, I failed her.

Dowd hasn't tried to reach out yet. He hasn't asked for a ransom or made any demands. He hasn't said a fucking word, which means he already has what he wants.

Am I going to find Nadya the same way he found Ronan? Chopped up into little pieces and dumped where no one would care to look?

But Nadya doesn't have any tattoos for me to identify.

I may never see any part of her again. Even if I search everywhere from here to Ireland, if Dowd doesn't want me to find her, I don't know if I ever will.

Even as I stand here, I know there's a possibility he could have already killed her. He could be torturing Nadya, and she has no way of knowing if I'm coming or not.

My stomach clenches so hard, I have to brace my hands on my knees.

I'm going to be sick.

I sprint to our bedroom, slamming the door shut behind me before anyone else has a chance to see me break down. The bathroom door bangs against the wall as I throw it open, and I barely make it to the sink before I lose the contents of my stomach, somehow drenched in sweat and freezing cold at the same time.

Get a fucking grip!

Nadya needs me. I can't fall apart. Not when I know down to the fiber of my being that she's out there waiting for me. I won't give up. I can't.

I cup my hands under the stream of water, splashing it over my face. When I reach for a towel, I'm suddenly paralyzed, feeling like I'm going to be sick all over again.

No.

There's no fighting the way my hand shakes as I reach for the little piece of plastic sitting on the counter. I stall, checking the trash to confirm what I already know before I grab it.

Sure enough, there's an empty box for a pregnancy test I brought home resting on top, as unassuming as the test.

For a moment, I'm not sure I want to know the result. On one hand, I want Nadya to be pregnant so much that I'd cut off my right hand to see a positive result. On the other hand, if she's pregnant, that means Liam doesn't just have the woman I love with my whole heart, he has my entire world right at his fingertips.

My stomach lurches, and I have to brace my hand against the counter as I flip over the test.

It's positive.

Nadya's pregnant. And I have no idea where she is.

I toss the piece of plastic at the mirror, slamming my fist down so hard that pain radiates through my whole arm.

Chapter 34

Nadya

There's hair in my face. I rub my head against the hard surface it's resting on, but instead of moving my hair, I only end up rubbing my face against something rough and scratchy. Huffing, I reach to push it away, but pain shoots up my arms from where my hands are bound behind my back.

My heart pounds wildly as I pull against the ties. Whatever I'm tied up with is so tight my hands are numb, and the struggle makes everything painfully raw.

I open my eyes, and all I can see is flashes of light through thick fabric. I try to thrash my head back and forth to free my face, but as soon as I do, my head spins so hard I have to slam my eyes shut again.

Fighting a gag, I draw my knees to my chest, making myself a smaller target while I take stock of my surroundings.

What the fuck happened?

The last thing I remember is hanging out with Vasily, and then nothing.

Slowly, I try to stretch. My muscles are stiff as if I've been in asleep for hours and I haven't moved an inch. Now that I'm paying attention, whatever I'm lying on is painfully hard, the heat so cloying it's soaking into my skin as much as it is the surface beneath me. I can stretch my legs, but pause when I feel how far my dress has ridden up my thighs.

For some reason, that's the thing that solidifies the fact I'm no longer at home.

There's a loud clang of metal on metal that makes me flinch, and I brace myself as I take deep breaths through my nose. The sound is loud but muffled, like it's coming from another room. It echoes off the walls, and flashes of what happened filter back in.

Cruel eyes.

The sharp stab of a needle.

The baby.

Fuck.

Instinctively, I curl up even smaller, doing what little I can to protect them. Every time I open my eyes, it feels like I'm going to puke. My head's killing me and my arms are on fire, but I don't feel any bumps or bruises or signs of anyone hurting me while I was unconscious.

Other than feeling like I'm going to empty the contents of my stomach into the stupid sack over my head, there's no pain in my abdomen.

My baby is fine.

They have to be.

I shift, trying to press myself further into the ground, but when my thigh scrapes over the stone beneath me, I feel like I'm going to faint.

Ever since I was caught alone at the studio, I've made it a point to keep a weapon on my person. They only time I'm ever without one is when I'm sleeping, and that's only because an intruder would have to get through Konstantin if they wanted to get to me, and he'd never let that happen.

But where I expect to find my holster digging into my leg, there's nothing.

Whoever took me, they also took my fucking knife.

When I get my hands on them, I'm going to rip them to shreds. I'm going to make them regret thinking they could come after me and get away with it.

I lie there for who knows how long, straining for any hints of where I am. Sweat beads against my forehead, and every time I turn my head to wipe it away, I'm rewarded with the scrape of fabric. It feels like someone's taken a piece of sandpaper to my face.

At least the nausea eases as time goes on, but I'd give anything for some water to chase away the lingering sense of sickness hanging out in my throat when I finally manage to sit up, keeping my knees tucked against my chest.

It could be either hours or minutes before a door creaks open, the same grating sound that set my nerves on edge as earlier, but this time, far closer.

I brace myself, and I'm rewarded for it when there's a sharp click of expensive leather shoes on the hard floor, each step closer than the last, until they come to a stop right in front of me.

"Do you know where you are, dear?" asks a deep voice with an Irish brogue. He sounds so calm I want to scream.

"As soon as my husband finds me, he's going to fucking kill you," I hiss instead of answering. My voice is surprisingly steady as I turn my face toward his voice.

He sighs heavily. "Language, love. There's no reason to be crude." Faster than I can spit all the hateful words resting on the tip of my tongue, he grabs the bag over my head so hard that my scalp burns where he's grabbed my hair and rips it away.

The stench of dirt and rust is almost overwhelming as I blink against the sudden light. As much as I want to look around, I force myself to keep my eyes glued on the man in front of me. When he leaves—because I have no doubt he's planning on drawing this out—I'll look around. Until then, I'm going to keep my attention on the biggest threat.

"If you wanted manners, you shouldn't have fucking kidnapped me!"

"Oh, don't be bothered by all that unpleasantness. It's not like you'll have to put up with it for long." He crouches down to grab my chin, humming to himself. I jerk my head back, but he digs his fingers in hard enough to leave marks, tilting my head back and forth. "Now, how's your head? I'm afraid my man gave you a bit more than he should have. You weren't supposed to sleep for that long."

He's smiling, but there are too many teeth in his mouth. His deep-set eyes are cold, radiating malintent as he searches my face.

My lip curls back in a snarl, and the only reason I don't spit in his face is because my mouth feels like a desert.

With all the strength I have, I yank my face from his grip.

"Touch me again, and I'll rip your fingers off with my teeth."

His smile sharpens, transforming into a smirk dripping with malice that seems to pour from his very soul. "You're a feisty one, aren't you? I can see why Konstantin likes you."

There's an emptiness behind his eyes that makes me want to cower, but I'm determined to stand my ground as much as I can when I'm tied up and have no weapon or way to defend myself. But underneath the front I'm barely managing to hold together, my heart is thundering so hard it hurts.

"How long was I out?" I ask, even though I'm not sure I really want to know. What the hell did they give me anyway?

He drapes his hands over his knees, looking as casual as he can be, while I swallow past the fear threatening to smother me. His green eyes pierce me like needles, fusing my bones with a fear so cold I crave for the heat of summer to come back and grant me a taste.

"A few hours."

Hours?

That can't be right.

If I had been out for hours, Konstantin would have already tracked me down and made this man regret his own existence.

"What? Did you think Mr. Ink-and-Attitude was going to swoop in and save you?" He winces sympathetically, but there's only amusement glittering in his eyes. "I hate to break it to you, dear, but he's been looking for me for quite a while. And if he hasn't found me yet"—he lifts a single shoulder—"I doubt he'll find you, either."

"He'll want to find me a lot more than he does you. Have you considered that?" If I know anything about my husband, it's that he won't rest until I'm back home, safe in his arms, and probably locked away for the rest of my life.

"And have you considered that I am very, *very* good at what I do, Miss Trenina?"

"It's Lavrovna," I snap without thinking. "My name is Nadya Lavrovna."

Because as much as I'm Konstantin's, he's mine, too. And I'm not going to let this motherfucker dismiss that, even if it would be smarter to play nice.

"It is, isn't it?" He stands, but as he turns, I spot a flash of shiny metal strapped to his ankle. I can't help but lean forward to make sure I'm really seeing it right.

This motherfucker didn't just steal my knife. He's strutting around with it like it's his.

"Are you at least going to cut me loose?" I call out at his back.

My shoulders burn from being restrained this long.

"Not yet. Maybe after you've stopped looking at me like you're planning on slitting my throat." He gestures in my direction, waving his hand up and down. "We'll see how long you can hold up before the real fun starts. Then we can reevaluate, hm?"

Harsh fluorescent light streams through the open doorway before he slams the door shut. A moment later, the clank of a lock being secured is almost enough to make me let lose the sob lurking in my lungs.

Biting my lip, I smother it before I finally look around the room, taking in what looks like an abandoned office. Rocking onto my knees, I slowly shuffle until I'm able to lean against the wall, using it to stand.

The room he's trapped me in is practically empty. Aside from a couple of broken cardboard boxes, there's nothing to hide behind, and nothing I can use to free myself. Even the flooring has been pulled up, exposing the stained, cracked concrete that's sticky beneath my feet. My shoulders scream as I look up, spotting a couple of windows.

They're so high up that even if there was something for me to climb onto, I wouldn't be able to reach them on my own.

Glancing over my shoulder, I curse under my breath. My arms are at the wrong angle for me to see anything, and my hands are so numb that even when I try to make a fist, I'm not sure they're moving at all. Which is a shame.

I'm sure that creep has a camera on me, and I'd love nothing more than to be able to flip him the bird as I circle the room, nudging my foot against the walls like I expect them to crumble to pieces.

If the exposed steel beam in the ceiling is any indication, they just might.

It's going to be agony when I finally get my hands free.

I wipe my forehead against my shoulder to catch the sweat burning over my raw skin and threatening to drip into my eyes.

The last thing I need is to be all teary-eyed because I can't stop sweating, but without fear to keep me level, it feels like a sauna in here.

"If you're planning on taking a hostage, the least you can do is put me in a room that's cooler than the surface of the sun!" I shout, not really caring whether anyone hears me.

From the way the sun is offensively bright as it shines through the windows, I assume it's late afternoon.

With the windows so high up and the door locked behind the bastard who stole my knife, there's no airflow through the room. Only the stale, hot stillness that's pressing down on me from all angles. Now that I can breathe without fabric in the way, I'm able to focus on more.

Mainly on the grime from lying on the filthy floor. But there's nothing I can do to scrape it away.

I need a shower and a change of clothes. I need some water to swallow the dryness in my mouth.

I need my fucking husband.

No matter what that man said, Konstantin is coming for me. He's coming, and before I know it, I'll be back in his arms. I rest my back against the wall furthest from the door, sliding down to the floor all over again.

At least this time I feel slightly less exposed.

If that creep wants me to wait, I'm going to have to save my strength.

I won't let him catch me unaware again.

CHAPTER 35
Konstantin

Time has a habit of working in unexpected ways when you're running out of it. No one has seen my wife in twenty-four hours, but every second has felt like a lifetime. If someone told me it had been twenty-four minutes, I'd believe them. If they said it has been twenty-four years, I'd still believe them.

I can't sleep. I can't eat. I can hardly even *think* without Nadya.

Each moment she's gone has taken another year off my life, but I'd gladly sacrifice them all as long as I knew she was safe. At this point, I'd love it if she sent me a message saying it was all an elaborate ruse and she staged an intricate set up so she could run away and go back to Chicago.

I wouldn't even fight her, because at least I'd know she's *alive*. She would have broken my heart, but she'd be safe.

That's the only thing I care about.

My men are scattered all over the coast, searching everywhere I can think to look, and I've done nothing but pour over the records of every single flight in and out of the area since she disappeared.

And I have nothing to show for it except a massive headache and a growing sense of dread.

Viktor shoves a paper cup in my face, forcing me to either take it from him, or risk him dumping steaming hot coffee in my lap.

"You need to get some rest, *bratan*."

I sniff the coffee before I take a sip. The way it scorches my tongue does as much to wake me up as the actual caffeine will.

I hate coffee. The caffeine always makes me jittery and miserable, but what harm can it do now? My anxiety is already shredding me from the inside out.

"Once Nadya is home, I will," I tell him, pushing the cup away so I can go back to what I was doing before he interrupted. He's made himself scarce, but he's still coordinating the soldiers I have on the ground to search for her. "Have you gotten your boyfriend out of the country, yet?"

"He's refusing to leave," Viktor mutters, hanging his head as he sits on the couch. "He has a fucking kid, Konstantin."

And Nadya is carrying mine.

That didn't stop Liam from taking her, and it won't stop me from teaching the rest of the world how far I'll go to keep her safe. Even if I have to kill someone I damn near thought of as family.

Vasily has been smart enough to keep his distance from me, but I'd have to be blind to see the path he and Viktor were heading toward. If things were different, maybe Kira would have ended up watching my children when she got older. Maybe

Viktor would have been planning his wedding one day instead of trying to keep his partner alive.

"He knew the risks when he turned his back on her."

"And what about Yuri? He's the one who should have kept eyes on her."

"I haven't forgotten him, either," I say, cutting him a look hard enough to make him flinch. "I told you to get rid of him. Vasily isn't the only one who fucked up. You should be grateful I'm giving him the opportunity to say goodbye and get his affairs in order. If he doesn't want to run, then it's the only thing he's managed to do right in this fucking fiasco." I pause, waiting for my brother to meet my eyes, and when he does, he looks at me like I'm a monster.

Well, he can join the fucking club.

"Even if you do manage to talk him into running, I'm still going to track him down and make him pay. Just because he's yours doesn't mean he gets to escape me."

"I'll never forgive you." Viktor swallows, clasping his hands in front of him. "If you hurt Vasily, I'll never let it go."

"I'm going to do more than hurt him," I vow, meaning it with every fiber of my being. "And if anything's happened to Nadya, I will gladly lose you to take it out on him."

For a long moment, neither of us say anything.

"And if she's okay?" he eventually asks. His tone is agonized, and something close to sympathy pangs deep in my chest. "Will it change anything?"

His hope is heavy, crushing me even as I cling to mine like a life raft. But the more time passes without finding Nadya, the more I have to brace for the worst. Even if I wanted to reassure him, dread binds my tongue in a knot I'll never loosen.

If I don't get Nadya back, I'm not sure I'll ever be cognizant enough to know what's happening.

How long can I keep looking for her before everyone decides I've lost it? How long until men start pushing back and demanding we go back to business as usual?

But what use is a fleet of criminals if I can't use them to search for the only one I care about it?

Not the money, or the thrill, or the power.

I only need my wife.

Viktor's expression is bleak as he looks away from me.

"Then deal with Yuri," he offers, though it's clear he's a million miles away as he stands, refusing to look to me. "You want to save Nadya? Fine. I want to save Vasily. So, take my oldest childhood friend as your sacrifice. Interrogate him. Torture him. Kill him if you have to. Find out what he knows while I talk to the only man I've ever loved."

"I don't need your permission."

"You wouldn't ask for it even if you did." He shakes his head, walking out of my office like he's the one heading toward the gallows.

I steel myself as he slams the door, giving him time to walk away before I leave the room. I roll my neck, hoping it will alleviate the pressure in my chest.

Taking deep breaths, I wait until there's a clatter of shouting toward the back of the house. Viktor's pleas are so loud they're impossible to ignore.

If this all goes on much longer, I'm going to have to call Alexei and loop him into what's going on. I laugh without humor.

He has a vested interest in Nadya's safety, too, but he'd happily burn this house down with me inside if he found out I failed to keep her safe like I promised.

When I finally leave my office, I find Spaghetti sitting outside Nadya's studio. He blinks at me dolefully. It makes me feel even worse. "I know," I say, running a hand through my hair. "We'll bring her back."

Unbelieving, he stretches on his back feet, scraping his claws down her door like she's hiding behind it.

I can't stand it.

With my heart almost as heavy as my head, I go straight to the wine cellar. My jaw works when Yuri rolls his head toward me, struggling against his binds. The whites of his eyes are visible when he realizes who's standing on the other side of the glass.

As much as I try to avoid bringing the messier parts of my job home, sometimes it's unavoidable. And I don't have the patience, nor the time, to drag Yuri back and forth between here and Vlast. If needed, the wine cellar works fine for some wet work.

I'll have to put someone on cleaning everything as soon as they can, though. Nadya wouldn't be happy to find blood and gore out in the open when I bring her home.

"How much did he pay you?" I ask as I close the door, ignoring the way Yuri whimpers, scrambling away the best he can in the small space.

"I don't know what you're talking about, boss," Yuri pants. Sweat drips down his brow despite how cool it is in here.

He really should be grateful.

If I wanted him to suffer immediately, I would have left him in the garage. It's nearly a hundred degrees outside. I could have left him somewhere to slowly bake, dripping with sweat until he's desperate for water and panting for cooler temperatures. At least in here the temperature is controlled.

Cool. Humid. Perfect for relaxing on a hot day like today.

And yet, he's sweating like a pig.

"Either you're incompetent beyond imagination, or you're working with Liam Dowd." I crouch in front of him, kicking the toe of his boot. He flinches as if I'd hit him. "The men who took my wife were standing outside the wall as soon as she stepped foot outside. And somehow, they knew the moment she was alone. They checked their phones, and they didn't hesitate."

His nostrils flare as his eyes dart back and forth. Whatever he spots behind me, it causes him to grow so still, it's almost as if he's frozen solid.

"You already understand how thin the ice you're standing on is, right?" He nods rapidly, looking back at me as if he's seen a ghost. "So, tell me, Yuri. Are you blind, or did you decide it was smarter to betray me than it was to do your fucking job?"

Something in his expression shifts, the fear morphing into an angry resignation that makes my blood boil. On instinct, I reach for my ankle, only to realize a moment too late that Nadya has my knife.

Knowing she isn't entirely defenseless settles me enough that I no longer feel like I'm treading water in a hurricane. For all I know, she's being tortured. She could be without food and water. There are still a million things she could be going through, but wherever she is, I know she's giving them as much hell as she'd give me.

Until I get there, she's going to be Dowd's worst nightmare.

"Has anyone ever told you that you're a nutcase?" he snarls. He looks like a wounded animal who's been backed into a corner. His chest heaves in panicked breaths, and even though he's trembling, he's baring his teeth.

I shrug. "Once or twice. But I want you to know that a person in your position has very few options." I tilt my head at him. "The standard survival instincts are flight and fight. Clearly, you think fighting is your smartest move, but you're not slipping those ties. So I'm going to point out your other options."

Reaching out, I tap the side of his head to prove my point. He jerks away like he's bracing for a punch.

"Freeze and fawn. Either shut down and let whatever happens, happen, or trip over yourself to tell me what you know. You may lose your dignity, but, hey"—I grin, leaning close enough to see the way his pupils dilate—"maybe I'll let you see one more sunset. Maybe you can barter for a chance to call your mother. Maybe I'll make your death quick."

Dowd planted a false trail all the way from here to Ireland. The easiest way for him to leave the state would be by plane, but I've studied every flight plan that was filed since she disappeared, both commercial and private, and I haven't found anything that ties back to him.

His men left by car, and they changed vehicles on private roads away from the sight of any traffic cameras. It'd be a hell of a lot of work to keep up that sort of effort for any length of time.

Which means he's still relatively close. He has to be.

But where? I have men keeping an eye out at every airport, every port, every damn tunnel in the state, and still, I have nothing.

"If your wife wasn't such a fucking whore, none of this would have happened!" His voice rings off the glass as the door opens behind me.

"Hm." I lift my chin, looking him dead in the eyes. The weight of his words seems to hit him like a wave, drowning him under a deluge of cold, pitch-black panic.

It's bad enough that this *ublyudok* got to see so much of Nadya that wasn't his to see. The fact he thinks that gives him any right to judge her is yet another nail in his coffin.

"Let me talk to him, Pakhan." I raise a brow, not bothering to turn to look at Vasily. "If he knows anything, I'll get him to talk."

Yuri blanches as the corner of my lip twitches into a vicious smirk.

"Fine. But leave him alive," I order. "You can have your fun as soon as we know where Nadya is."

I lean against the far wall as Vasily moves in, a sadistic grin locked in place as he flips open a pocket-knife. Within minutes, Yuri is begging him to stop between desperate sobs. He can't seem to figure out which part of him hurts most: the hand missing all its fingers, or the eye with the dull knife still embedded deep inside it.

"Where does Dowd have his merchandise shipped to?" I ask casually as Vasily twists the knife with a sickening squelch. "Did anyone mention it?"

It's rapidly becoming clear that Yuri doesn't know as much as I need him to. He was told to send a message when Nadya was alone, sure. But where she was taken?

He's too small a fish to be given that information.

I know Dowd gets most of his weapons from China, and until recently, I've been happy to pretend he pays to have them shipped through either Miami or the East Coast. But as much as I'd like to pretend otherwise, it's far cheaper to have them shipped to California and transported through the country than it is to move them through Europe.

I no longer have the luxury of ignorance. Not if I want Nadya to survive.

"Someone said something about paying border control," he sobs. His words are starting to slur, and when I cut Vasily a look, he steps back. "Someone had to go to San Jose. That's all I know, boss! I swear!"

Realization hits me so hard I'm practically stunned.

Not only has the motherfucker been playing right under my nose, he's been playing in the only port I don't have a finger in. The feds control a port in San Jose, and I've been all too happy to let them have their little lot as long as they left me alone.

And Dowd took advantage of it.

"Do what you need to do," I snap at Vasily before I storm outside, barking orders to every man in the building.

I'm going to get my wife.

Chapter 36

Nadya

"See, you're much more agreeable now."

I jolt awake, flinching when I find the creep right in front of me with a hand resting loosely on my ankle. There's a throbbing in my skull, but that doesn't keep me from pulling away as if I've been burned. He clenches his fingers hard enough that I hiss, refusing to let me free of his grasp.

I stop struggling when the object in his other hand twinkles in the dim light, dangling from the end of his finger.

He smirks when he sees what's drawn my attention. "This is pretty, isn't it?" He spins my wedding ring so carelessly it nearly shoots off his hand. A new wave of sickness rocks me so hard I collapse back against the wall.

How long was he in here while I was asleep? How did he manage to get my ring off without me noticing?

"Don't worry, I'll send it back to him in a few months."

"Konstantin is going to make you see what your still-beating heart looks like before he kills you," I hiss. "But only if I don't do it first."

His answering laugh rattles around in my head, a malicious, evil sound that drives an icepick between my eye. I swallow around my dry tongue, wondering what I need to do for him to give me some water.

"Don't be like that." He smiles sardonically, making me flinch even as he drags me closer. My arms are still bound, and with only one free leg, I can't do much to get away. I kick my other leg in his direction, but he dodges it easily.

I wish I knew how long I've been here. I had to watch as the sun set through the windows, bringing some relief from the heat before it rose again. Now it's once again setting, and the artificial lights outside are bleeding through the windows, showing all the ways I'm falling apart in too much detail to stomach.

For hours, all I've managed to do is shuffle around the room, looking for a cooler spot to rest with little success.

I didn't mean to fall asleep, but at least it was more productive than waiting.

Kostya's coming.

He has to be.

"Now, tell me, Nadya. Does your husband tell you about his work? Do you even know who I am?" I throw all my far and pain behind my glare. "Ah, I guess not."

So quickly I'm barely able to track it, he releases my ankle and shoves his hands underneath my arms. He stands, ignoring me as I cry out when he pulls me up with him.

My shoulders already hurt from being restrained for so long, but forcing them to hold my weight is so painful I wonder if they've finally popped out of their sockets.

I almost hope they have. At least then, the pain would finally be able to settle into numbness like my hands. I scramble to get my legs under me to alleviate some of the pressure.

As soon as my legs are steady, he says, "Personally, I think you should know the name of the man who's going to kill you." My knees almost buckle. "It's a matter of respect."

"You're delusional if you think I'll let you kill me." My voice wavers, and he grins when he hears it.

"You aren't going to *let* me do anything. You don't have to." He drags me from the room like I weigh nothing. If I weren't so dehydrated, the way my joints scream in protest would probably make me puke. "Taking what I want is what makes it fun. And in this case, I want revenge."

He pulls me into a dark hallway, and after a few steps, I manage to find my feet. Still, I can't do much more than desperately try to keep up as he flings me to another man, throwing open another door. The second man tosses me to the floor, and without his support, I collapse, crashing to the ground and landing heavily on my left shoulder.

"Fuck!"

I grunt as white-hot pain consumes my vision. I roll, trying to take pressure off the joint as soon as possible, but at this point, I'm not sure my arms would work even if they were free.

The slow whir of a fan built high into the wall breaks up the desperate sound of my pained panting. Each turn of the blades disturbs the light, giving the room an almost cinematic look. At least it's doing something, because the air is as suffocating as it was when the sun was still high and blinding.

"Didn't we already discuss your language?" He clicks his tongue, lowering himself to a single knee in front of me. "Keep it up, and I'll start thinking you *want* me to hurt you."

"I didn't even do anything to you," I snarl, blinking while his friend flicks a switch, nearly blinding me as harsh, fluorescent lights fill the space. There's nothing to hide behind. Not a single shadow. Not even my own denial. "If you want revenge, then you're doing it wrong."

"True, *you* didn't hurt me." His smile makes my skin crawl as he brushes the hair out of my face, tucking it behind my ear. I turn my head, my teeth clicking around empty air as he pulls away. "But your husband did. He's the one who took my cousin and chopped him up into tiny pieces. And while I didn't care about Ronan, my sister did."

He shakes his head.

"It's worked out, though. I don't have to keep paying the fucker, and I finally have leverage over Lavrov. You know, in all the time I've known him, Konstantin's only soft spot has been a feckin' cat."

"Leave Spaghetti out of this," I say, flicking my eyes to the man who tossed me in here. He nods in our direction and slips out of the room, taking any hope of stepping in to help me with him.

"But now I need to get revenge, and Konstantin conveniently got married. For a man who plays his cards close to his chest, he's awfully transparent when it comes to how he feels about you." He lifts the leg of his slacks enough to allow him access to my knife, pulling it free of the holster on his ankle.

"This is beautiful, isn't it? Was it a gift?" He points it at my throat, pressing the sharp tip to the delicate skin below my chin. I swallow as he reaches behind my head so I can't pull away. "I'll have to leave it with your corpse so he knows it's you, won't I? After all, your husband was so kind as to leave Ronan's tattoo for my sister to find."

He shrugs.

"Can I tell you a secret, Nadya?" My muscles strain as he pulls me close enough that the knife digs even further into my flesh. "This isn't about my cousin. That little shit caused me more problems than he was worth, but your husband lost me an awful lot of money when he ended that spat between Trenin and that other Russian bastard in Chicago."

His words sound like they're a million miles away as blood drips down my throat. He's holding me so tight I'm terrified to even breathe.

"And then the fight with the Italians came to a sudden, uneventful end. I don't know what he did to make it happen, but your *dear* husband cost me more money than you've seen in your life. That he killed Ronan is just a convenient excuse."

My heart pounds wildly in my throat, trapping my breath in my lungs as he finally withdraws.

"But I got distracted, didn't I?" he asks as he puts the knife back in its holster. "The name of the man who's going to kill you is Liam Dowd, dear." I curl up as small as I can, flinching when he steps so close the tips of his shiny shoes nudge against my ribs.

He smiles like the cat who got the cream, and I silently vow not to give him the satisfaction of my fear again.

"Now that introductions are out of the way, we can have some fun."

I need to get out of this in once piece.

I need to protect the baby.

I need Konstantin to find me.

Now.

***

Liam Dowd is a fucking sadist. He laughs every time I cry out or whimper, like this is the most fun he's ever had, drawing out my pain as much as he physically can.

It could have been either moments or days since he started his particular brand of cruelty. I have no way of knowing anymore.

Not when I'm using all the energy I have left to goad him into cutting my arms free. Not when I need to conserve whatever strength I can for the moment he gives me an opportunity to retaliate.

Hate has hardened my heart, letting me comfort myself with images of Liam's guts on the floor around him as he bleeds out. At this rate, I won't even wait for Konstantin to do the heavy lifting.

All I need is a quick break to gather my strength, and I'll do it myself.

Liam used my knife to cut off my dress, but after that, he tossed the blade aside like it was useless. Instead, he's been stabbing at any part of me he can reach with an electric cattle prod, tossing buckets of water on me whenever I don't give him the reaction he wants.

Every time it's a fresh hell, but at least when I lick my lips, they're wet. It's a relief, but I'll be damned if I let him know it.

Eventually, he's going to get bored and lose interest. And when he does, I'm going straight for the knife, and then I'm going after whatever part of him is closest.

I refuse to let a coward who hides behind his tools break me.

But I don't know how much longer I can take this.

"Ah-ah, don't get all dull eyed on me now," Liam says as he puts the now-empty bucket by the door to be refilled, then walks back to me. My skin crawls as he looks me over with empty eyes.

Even though I'm only in my underwear, dripping wet and covered in grime I don't want to think about, his gaze is what makes me feel like I'll never be clean again.

I never thought I'd see the day when I regret not wearing a bra, but the way Liam's eyes clinically look me up and down makes me wish I had.

"Once you lose that spark, things aren't nearly as fun. Then I'll have to step it up so you do what I want, and when I have to do that too often, well..." He sighs. "Then we don't get to have fun anymore. And I was hoping to make this last a while before we got to that point."

"There are better ways to convince women to spend time with you," I grunt. My back is still spasming from the last round, when he kept the cattle prod shoved between my shoulder blades, shocking me until I nearly passed out.

If I can sit up, if I can get to my feet, maybe I can make a break for the door next time his friend comes for the bucket.

He grabs my shoulder, and when I swing my leg in his direction, I connect weakly with his shin. He doesn't even blink.

"I take it back." He shakes his head, brushing his hands on his thighs. "I liked you better when you were quiet. A pretty girl with an attitude is such a waste."

"What do you care? You're going to kill me either way, right?"

"It was the plan," he admits, tilting his head to the side. "And a smart woman would try to change my mind. But you haven't said a word. Is being married to that overgrown bastard really so awful?"

I haven't said a word because I know better than to beg anyone, much less a piece of shit like this. Even if there was a universe where it would get him to stop, I'd never be able to live with my own disgust.

"My husband is a better man than you could ever dream of being."

Liam grabs the cattle prod, and with my heart in my throat, I scramble my legs over the wet concrete, skittering away from him like a fly before a spider. Helplessly, my eyes dart to the corner where he tossed the knife.

He doesn't miss it, a deadly smirk splitting his face.

"And yet, you'd rather die than fight to get back to him." He abandons the tool and stalks over to the knife instead. "I don't understand you."

My stomach rolls, the small amount of water I've been able to consume reigniting my nausea.

"But if facing your own mortality is what finally gives you the will to fight back, then I can accommodate."

Even though I struggle to get away, Liam grabs my hair, holding me in place as she slices through the tape holding my hands together. The agony of blood rushing back in is so sudden and all-consuming that darkness dots the edges of my vision. Before I can blink it away, Liam fists the hair at the base of my skull, shoving the knife I wanted so badly to the base of my throat.

It isn't fair.

I wanted that knife so much I could cry, and once I finally have use of my hands, when it's finally in reach, my arms are dead weights at my sides.

Liam's lip curls in a cruel smile that makes my heart stop.

That look is going to be the last thing I see, isn't it?

I'm never going to get to see my child's face. I'm never going to see the way Konstantin smiles when he kisses me again. I'm never going to have the opportunity to tell Alexei he's going to be an uncle. I'm never going to hear the love in Konstantin's voice when he calls me *solnyshka* again.

After a lifetime of burying my head in the sand and ignoring the Bratva, it's going to be the thing that ends my life.

A tear slips free just as a boom clatters from elsewhere in the building, followed by a muffled shout.

Liam's head whips toward the sound, pulling his focus long enough for me to flex my hands, testing my control of them.

They barely twitch, and I tell myself I'm crying out of frustration, not fear.

This bastard isn't worth tears.

He isn't worth *anything*.

I test my arms, and they move a little better. It isn't much, but I'll take it. I just need a moment. The cattle prod is only a foot away. I need to get my hands on it. If nothing else, I can use it as some small measure of revenge before he slits my throat.

"What now?" Liam groans, dropping me. I go with it, crying out when I land on my already excruciatingly painful shoulder. Now that I'm free and blood is able to work its way back into the joint, I'm pretty sure it's dislocated.

Whatever.

That's a problem to deal with when I get out of here. Not *if*, but *when*. If I do anything less, then I'll never forgive myself.

He made the mistake of giving me an inch, and I'm going to use it to save my life.

There's even more shouting, and if I'm going to take advantage of Liam's distraction, I have to do it now. My hand flops like a dead fish, but I'm able to get it on top of the cattle prod without drawing Liam's attention.

"I swear to all that's holy—"

The next series of shouts and pops are far closer, and I can't bite back a smile. I recognize that furious voice, and I never thought I'd see the day where I could weep with joy hearing a man on the warpath, but Konstantin's fury is the most beautiful thing I've ever heard.

But it also means I don't have any time to waste.

I push away the rush of hope filling my chest and use all my energy to clench my hand into a fist steady enough to pick up the cattle prod before Liam has a chance to turn around.

I pull it close with my finger resting over the button. Taking a breath, I slam it into the back of Liam's knee and turn it on. His knee gives out under him, sending him crashing to the ground.

The knife clatters to the floor.

I'm not sure I've ever smiled harder.

"You little *cunt*," he snarls, his attention split between me and the commotion outside our little room, echoing down the hall and getting closer with each heartbeat.

"You don't get to talk to me like that," I snarl, stabbing the metal points of the prod toward his throat as he lunges for me. At this point, I don't even care if it connects. I want him off-balance and scrambling. I want him wary and desperate, the same way I've been since he stole me from my home.

From my *life*.

And all for what? So he could piss off Konstantin?

I can do that in my fucking sleep.

He put my life at risk for revenge over a man he doesn't give a shit about. And he's going to pay for it.

I'm going to get a round in before my husband gets a chance.

Liam's on top of me in a flash, shoving the prod away like it's nothing. His hands go for my throat, and I throw mine toward his eyes. Only one arm moves the way it should, but I put everything I have into jamming my thumb into the socket while he squeezes tight.

He swears up a storm, rearing back. The door flies open as he lets go.

I cough as he's torn away. The pounding of a fist meeting flesh resounding through the room, barely audible over the ringing in my ears.

"Get." *Smack.* "The." *Smack.* "Fuck." *Smack.* "Off." *Smack.* "My." *Smack.* "Wife."

Chapter 37

Konstantin

I doubt Dowd even knows who's beating his face beyond recognition. His eyes are squeezed shut and blood is pouring from his left eye like a river.

I don't think I'm the one who did that, but I'm too far gone to care.

I can hear Nadya somewhere behind me, coughing as she shifts around, but I can't see anything beyond my own rage. Each man I shot and killed as I went through this fucking warehouse, every obstacle that stood in my way, none of it has managed to mute the roaring in my ears.

My fists are relentless as they connect with Dowd's face until there's a crunch of bone against bone, long after his eyes rolls back and his body goes lax. I can't tell if the blood is coming from him, or from my broken skin on my knuckles. A gentle hand on my shoulder has me snarling. I whirl around, expecting another threat.

Instead, my heart seizes in my chest when my eyes meet Nadya's, terrified and wet with tears as she blinks at me. Her lips are cracked, there are marks around her throat, and burns litter her arms, shoulders, and torso.

Her *bare* torso.

Her thin shoulders tremble with a dry sob.

In an instant, my bloodlust vanishes. All my attention is on her as I undo my shirt, draping it around her and dragging her into my arms.

"I've got you, *solnyshka*," I whisper against her wet hair. "You're alright." She's shaking, and I can't tell if it's from her injuries, or stress, or even relief. It's almost enough for me to go right back to beating Dowd, wanting to keep him alive long enough to feel my fist break through his skull.

But there isn't a force strong enough to pull me away from the way Nadya's hands are clutched against my chest. I'm not sure I'll ever be able to let her go again.

"You came." Her voice is timid in a way I never would have imagined she was capable of. It's enough to break my heart. Those two words are powerful enough to make me bleed out, right here and now.

"Always," I tell her, pulling her even closer. She flinches when my hand brushes over her shoulder, over one of the burn marks I saw when I came in, and I can't hold back the growl building in my chest.

"I'm taking you to the hospital."

"In a minute," she says, pressing her face against my chest. She's shaking like a leaf. For once, I understand where Tatiana's coming from when she's urging Nadya to eat more. She feels so delicate that it's a wonder she isn't breaking from how tightly I'm holding her.

Nadya is the strongest person I've ever met.

Anyone else would have broken before our wedding night. They would have collapsed from everything I put her through.

Nadya hasn't just managed to endure me, she's thrived.

She survived whatever Liam's done, and instead of begging me to take her away, she's looking around the room with bright eyes and a determined expression.

"Give me a minute," she protests as I scoop her into my arms. She struggles to get free as soon as her feet leave the ground.

"No. We're leaving."

"Not until I know if he's still alive."

"If he is, he won't be for long," I snarl, setting her on her down before she's able to get loose and hurts herself even more.

She gives me a glare fiercer than someone in her condition should be able to. With one hand, she clenches the front of my shirt closed, and with the other, she braces herself, using my arm for support. If I didn't think she'd use up whatever strength she has left to fight me, I'd haul her over my shoulder, but I don't know what she's been through.

I don't know how much fight she has left, but I won't be the one to steal it from her.

Especially not when she looks like a stiff breeze could tip her over.

As she finds her footing, I move her hand so I can do up the buttons on my shirt, glancing over my shoulder to see who else followed me in here.

Viktor is standing in the doorway, but he has his back turned, pretending he hasn't seen a damn thing.

Good.

If it didn't look like Nadya's already ruined his vision, I'd cut his eyes from his head and toss them in the ocean for seeing her like this.

"Viktor," I call out, not taking my eyes off Nadya as she searches the room. "Do me a favor and handle this." I nod at Dowd's motionless form. "If he's still alive, I'll deal with him later, and if he's not"—I lift a single shoulder—"then handle it. Properly, this time."

"Not yet," Nadya grits out as Viktor steps forward. "He stole my knife."

Her knife?

She can hardly stand, she's cradling her arm to her chest, and she cares about her *knife*?

This woman is insane. Completely insane.

She's going to run me into an early grave, and I'm going to let her.

As long as she lets me see her brilliant smiles and doesn't try to build a literal wall between us every night, I'll let her do anything.

Even if it means letting her use me for balance while she sways toward her knife. I hold onto her hip so she doesn't fall when she bends over, biting back a sigh when she wipes the blade over my nice dress shirt.

I liked that shirt, but I'll never be able to wear it again without remembering this feeling.

Like I've been tied to a lead weight that's hanging from a cliff, threatening to tear out my spine if I breathe too deeply.

What did Dowd to my wife? She's being strong, but is she going to be okay? Why is she holding her arm like that? Is the baby okay? Why does Nadya have to be so fucking stubborn?

I'm still contemplating the wisdom of picking her up and dragging her out of here kicking and screaming when she leads me over to Dowd and pulls on my arm until we're both crouched in front of him.

I hold her even tighter as she shoots me a grateful look that's so sweet it aches.

That sweetness is gone the moment she presses two fingers against Dowd's throat, checking for a pulse. In fact, she looks downright vicious while she waits, nodding to herself at whatever she finds.

Without a word, she takes her knife and cuts across the back of his knee, slicing through skin, tendons, and muscle with one flick of her wrist. She doesn't hesitate. She doesn't even blink, not even when she pulls her arm back and stabs into the same joint, twisting her blade until it grinds wetly against bone.

Dowd groans, but doesn't stir, and Nadya grins brilliantly at me as she pulls the knife back, flipping it around so I can take the handle.

I've never been more in love with her than I am in this moment.

"I want you to keep him alive," Nadya says as I help her stand, pressing kisses all over her face.

She sounds exhausted, like all her adrenaline has finally burned itself out. I lift her bridal style before I hand the knife to Viktor. She rests her head against my shoulder, breathing deeply.

"I want him to live so he has to deal with that injury. I want him to go through the rest of his life knowing the only reason he gets to wake up every morning is because *I* let him."

My heart trips over itself even further as my gut tells me to deny her.

It'd be so easy. But there isn't anything I would deny her. She could ask for the moon, and I'd find a way to give it to her. It'd lay stars at her feet if she looked at them with longing.

I nod, giving Viktor a look as I carry her from this room.

"If he lives, he might try to get revenge," I say as I navigate around the old warehouse that's adjacent to the port the feds like to use when no one's paying attention.

They may have turned a blind eye to Dowd as he conducted business here, but it's only a matter of time before they get curious about all the noise I made as I searched for Nadya.

"And if he dies, he won't have to remember my face every time his leg is in agonizing pain." She smothers a yawn against my throat. "I'll take my chances."

"Rest," I tell her. "You're safe now." Wordlessly, I lift my chin in Viktor's direction, but I know he hears the order loud and clear.

Dowd gets to live. Assuming someone comes for him, he'll make it out of here. He'll possibly be blind, and he'll definitely never be able to walk without pain, but he won't die today.

Nadya falls silent, and by the time I settle her into my car, she's fast asleep.

***

Nadya fought the doctor when they tried to give her pain medication before they reset her dislocated shoulder. She tried to push back against the IV she desperately needed. She barely wanted them to touch her at all.

I have no such qualms.

I made her take the IV, and when I paid the nurse to look the other way, I gladly gave Nadya the sedatives they'd been coaxing her to accept so the doctors could do what they needed.

There will be hell to pay once she wakes up, and I'm looking forward to it. But for now, I'll hold her hand while she sleeps, waiting impatiently for her to wake up.

After she was knocked out and the doctors were able to examine her, they said she was dehydrated, exhausted, and that her arm needed to be in a sling for a while until her shoulder heals. Other than that, she's going to be fine.

Despite how earnestly they said it, or how often they repeated it, I can't bring myself to believe it.

I doubt I will until she's able to tell me herself.

Because whatever Nadya is—loud, stubborn, quick to anger and slow to forgive—she isn't a liar. She'll tell me how she feels even if it hurts. And once she's had some time to wake up and settle in, she can tell me about the baby herself.

Pretending I didn't know anything while she protested against taking any drugs, pretending I couldn't see the panicked look in her eyes while she whispered questions to the doctors and nurses, was fucking torture.

I stroke my thumb over her hand, stunned speechless as I watch her chest rise and fall with even breaths.

At one point during her exam, she kicked me out, threatening to walk out of the hospital if I didn't give her the room, so I have no way of knowing if the baby is alright or not. While she seemed mildly calmer when she let me back in, her eyes were red-rimmed like she'd been crying.

If anything's happened to our child, I'll have to walk back my promise to let Dowd live.

I'll hunt down him and every member of his family and make sure they all suffer. I'll hit him so hard his grandparent's *ghosts* will regret allowing him to be born.

"Don't do that again," I whisper against the back of her hand, keeping it pressed against my lips. "Don't scare me like that. I won't be able to handle it a second time."

Not when just sitting here is so painful it could still very well end me. Christ, I must have aged a decade in the past day and a half.

Once she tells Alexei about this, it'll only get worse. He tried calling her an hour after she was taken. And when Nadya didn't answer, he switched to texts.

I wonder which he'll do first: fly across the country to lay eyes on her himself, or call me to ask if there's something wrong with Nadya. If he does show up, I'll chase him away so she can rest.

Despite the drugs keeping her under, she looks like she'd collapse if she woke up.

Right on cue, my phone buzzes in my pocket.

Without checking the caller ID, I answer, "Nadya's fine."

"Then why isn't she calling me back?" Alexei asks, sounding almost as worn out as I feel.

The smart move would be to make a joke and divert his attention. But I'm too damn tired to lie. If that means I have to put up with him coming out here to scream and rage and try to demand Nadya come home with him, then that's what I'll do.

His position is still too tenuous to challenge me, and I won't let him take her from me.

"Because she's in the hospital," I say as I close my eyes. "And I'll say it again in case you missed it the first time, your sister is fine."

I wait for the explosion. The threats, the shouting, the hissed words. Instead, I'm met with an icy silence.

"Why the *fuck* is my sister in the hospital, Lavrov?" he eventually demands, his tone cold enough that I wonder if the heatwave has finally broken. I take in every burn on Nadya's arms. Every scrape on her face. The clunky brace on her arm.

As badly as I want to see her doe eyes blinking at me when she wakes, I want her to rest for as long as the drugs will allow even more.

She's going to be in pain when she wakes up, and that's my fault.

Sure, Dowd was the one who carried out the act, but if it wasn't for me, she wouldn't have been put in this position to begin with. Whether it's because of our marriage or because of my inability to handle both Yuri and Dowd the way I needed to, this is my fault.

"Because one of my enemies found a flaw in my security and kidnapped her. But I handled it, she's been checked out by doctors, and she's *fine*."

"What?" he snarls, cursing so loudly I have to pull the phone from my ear, watching the screen dispassionately until he finally calms down. "When did this happen?" Alexei asks when I put the phone to my ear again.

"About thirty-six hours ago," I answer honestly, weighing my next words very carefully. If I bite my tongue, I can probably spare myself a few hours before I have to deal with him trying to punch me in the face.

But I'd rather deal with him before Nadya's awake to witness it. Even if it means having to put up with her brother before I'm ready.

"Before you start screaming again, I've already sent my jet to Chicago. If you hurry, you can be here in five hours."

I hang up as he inhales, gearing up for another reminder of how much he'd like to see his sister become a widow, and press send on the flight information I've had loaded up since Nadya kicked me out of the room.

As little as I want to deal with him, it's better if he gets here sooner rather than later. That way he can list all my failures while Nadya's still sleeping.

I watch her eyes shift under her eyelids and press another kiss to her hand, stroking my hand over hers as I settle in to keep watch.

***

It feels like no time has passed before Alexei rushes into the room, but seeing Nadya seems to take the wind from his sails.

Instead, he flops heavily into the other chair, watching his sister like he's never been more terrified in his life.

"Who was it?" he asks, his eyes darting around like he isn't sure where to look: Nadya's face, the heart monitor, or at my hand still clamped around hers. "The man who did this. Who was it?"

"Liam Dowd."

He jolts.

"I could have your head for this," he eventually says, slumping forward with his hands clasped together.

"You could try." I shrug. "We both know you can't afford it. Even though you're done exchanging pot shots with the Italians, you don't have the footing to stage the kind of army you'd need to take me on."

There's a long beat of silence as I let go of her hand to brush back a strand of hair that's fallen over her forehead, fluttering with every breath she takes.

It feels like she's been asleep for ages. How much of it is the drugs, and how much is from shock? I'm too much of a coward to ask the doctors when they come in to check on her, but they don't look concerned. They keep making note after note on their clipboards before scurrying away as quickly as possible.

But Nadya always wakes up like she's being dragged out of a coma. Even if it's just from a nap on the couch, she fights consciousness with every fiber of her being, and if she wasn't promised coffee behind Tatiana's back, I'm not sure she'd leave our bed at all most days.

"I was curious why they suddenly initiated peace talks," Alexei says, shaking his head. "So, that was your doing?"

I hum, neither confirming nor denying.

"If she tells me she wants to leave, I'm taking her with me, Konstantin. You know that, right?"

"Again, you could try." I refuse to take my eyes off Nadya as I tell him, "I'm not letting her go. I fucked up, but you're not the one I need to apologize to. So if it's all the same, I'd rather you speak your piece and leave so she can rest. I can come and get you from the waiting room when she's awake and ready for visitors."

He stands, running a hand through his hair as he paces the length of the room.

For a moment, he looks so much like Nadya when she's mad at me that it's almost endearing.

"If this is your lingering guilt over agreeing to let her marry me, then drop it," I say. "I don't have the energy for it. Besides, we both know she would have married me whether you agreed or not."

"You think I don't know that?" He whirls around to face me but stops as he watches Nadya's nose twitch in her sleep. "The only reason I agreed is because she threatened to do it anyway! I would have rather sent her to another continent then let her marry you. And look what fucking happened to her, Lavrov. She's here because of *you*."

His words have no impact as Nadya frowns, turning her head away from Alexei, groaning as if she's being awoken by the devil himself.

"Don't move, *solnyshka*," I murmur, pressing a hand against her cheek when she tries to lift her arm to cover her eyes and ends up groaning in pain.

Alexei lurches forward, like her distress is somehow my fault and he's willing to kill me for it.

At this point, I wouldn't be surprised if that's exactly what he's thinking.

"You need to rest," I tell her.

"And as soon as you're cleared to go home, we're going on the first plane back to Chicago," Alexei mutters darkly.

"Give it ten minutes, Trenin."

That finally convinces Nadya to crack open an eye, confusion coloring her features as she looks between the two of us. When she registers Alexei, she lights up, all her pain pushed aside as she tries to reach for him.

I don't mind.

How can I when her happiness is so mesmerizing? I'd dare any man to feel even an ounce of resentment when Nadya looks as happy as she does in this moment. Even though all I want to do is pull her against my chest and never let her go, I help her sit up so she can hug her brother, smiling at the way she grabs him by the breast pocket of his jacket and pulling hard enough that I hear the seam tear.

"What're you doing here?" she asks. She holds him like he's made of glass, and he clutches her like he's terrified she's going to disappear. He's careful not to put any pressure on her shoulder, but he's holding her so tight she ends up hissing in pain anyway.

"I'm taking you home."

"Why?" She sounds so confused, and I can't help but let out a breathless laugh, one that gets a little easier when Alexei's expression hardens.

"Because I'm not leaving you with this fucking *mudak* again," he snarls, studiously ignoring the way Nadya reaches for my hand, running her thumb over my wedding band.

"Wait, do you mean you're taking me back to Illinois?" She yawns, despite the smile on her face. "Because thanks for the offer, but last time I checked, you weren't in charge of jack shit. And you definitely don't control my life."

"I'm in charge of a lot, actually," he mumbles, but neither of us pay him any attention. I'm only focused on Nadya and the way she scowls at her bare ring finger.

There wasn't time to scour the warehouse for her ring. I don't know if Dowd dumped it somewhere, or if he still has it.

I'm not exactly eager to hunt him down and ask, either.

As far as I'm concerned, the next time Dowd crosses my path, he's a dead man.

No matter how much my wife would like me to say otherwise.

"I'll get you another one," I murmur against the side of her head. "Pick any ring you want, and it's yours."

"What if I want the most expensive one I can find?"

"Done."

Her eyes light up with mischief, and I smile at her barely contained grin. Carefully, I move to sit next to her on the tiny bed, maneuvering so my back is against the pillows and she has no choice but to lean into me.

"And what if I want something tiny? No diamonds, no flash. Just a plain, simple band."

"Then you can have that, too. I'll buy you a fancy car to make up for it." She rests her head against my chest, humming to herself. "Another studio, too. Maybe even a second house. Or would you prefer an island?"

"That'd be a terrible investment." She shakes her head as her eyes fall shut. "You're ridiculous."

"And you're stuck with me. Which I tried to tell your brother, but he chose not to listen."

"Careful." She smiles, already ready to fall asleep again. "You have to be gentle with him. When he gets stressed, he responds better when you speak softly. Like with a child. Or an injured animal."

"Don't refer to me as an animal again," Alexei grunts, glaring at the two of us. "Especially not when you're cuddling with this bastard."

"Then stop assuming you know what's best for me," Nadya says, smothering another yawn. "This is my home. And you pretending otherwise is giving me a headache."

Even though she can't see it, he flips her off.

CHAPTER 38

Nadya

I've never been so happy to see my brother walk away in my entire life.

Even though I've missed him like a phantom limb, his hovering is driving me up a wall. I can't handle his worried looks. Or the way he glares at Konstantin every time he thinks I'm not looking. Or the mumbling under his breath about how I'm high on pain meds and don't know what I'm saying.

Compared to Kostya's quiet, steady presence, Alexei has been overwhelming, stoking a fire under my skin every time he even looks at me. And when you add in the doctors and nurses intent on checking on me every ten minutes, I'm ready to scream.

I must not be hiding my annoyance as well as I think I am. Within a half hour of waking again, Konstantin is quick to command everyone to find somewhere else to be. When Alexei pushes back, my husband physically drags him out of the room before he locks the door behind him.

It feels like I can breathe again when Kostya turns back to me, finally alone and free to let loose the feelings that have been eating him alive since I opened my eyes for the first time.

He might be able to hide it from all the medical professionals who have rushed through the door, and Alexei might be oblivious to everything that isn't bright, shiny, and personal, but Konstantin can't hide from me.

Not when his shoulders keep bunching up by his ears no matter how many times he forces them to relax. Not when his jaw is so sharp and his hands are buried in his pockets whenever I look at him.

The beeping of the heart rate monitor fills the space I don't have words to fill. Because as anxious as he is, I'm even worse. I have so many things I want to tell him, and I don't even know where to start.

"Are you feeling alright?" he asks. His voice is as tentative as I've ever heard it.

I'm sure he talked to the doctors while I was knocked out and heard everything they had to say, but he's still looking at me like he won't believe it until the words come from me. And even though the doctors assured me they wouldn't tell him about the results of the pregnancy test they had me take, or the ultrasound I pushed for, he's looking at me with longing, his eyes darting down to my stomach before flicking back to mine.

He probably has X-ray vision and can see the little blob floating around in my womb. Formless, tiny, and perfect, despite everything.

There wasn't much to look at, and I didn't want to hear the heartbeat without Kostya, but the doctor could see it.

He said it was strong.

I was so terrified they were going to give me something that would hurt the baby. I don't know what strings my husband pulled to knock me out so they could medicate me, and I'm not sure I want to.

But I feel a lot better than I did when he brought me here.

"I've been better," I confess. "Did you kill Vasily?"

His face is dark as he glowers at nothing in particular. "Not yet."

"Good." I nod. "You're not going to kill him, either," I say, looking at him seriously. "And if you do, I'll be getting on a plane with Alexei and you'll never hear from me again." His glare is thunderous, but I'm not going to back down. "He was worried about Kira. And frankly, so was I."

If I didn't hate seeing him like this, it would almost be comical how quickly his shoulders tense.

"Is she okay?" I ask softly.

Scowling, he nods, pulling his phone out and showing me a text thread from Viktor.

Pain in the Ass

Not that you asked but there was a woman at the daycare asking about Kira and no one knew who she was

He didn't see Nadya because he was calling Ana to go get her

I get that your pissed but don't do this. To either of us

Three short texts that were sent more than twelve hours ago, and Konstantin hasn't bothered to reply to.

Fuck, he has to be freaking out. As quick as I can, I type out a new text to reassure him, but Konstantin plucks the phone from my hands before I can hit send.

"Hey!"

"She's fine. Ana picked her up without issue, and she's working from home to keep an eye on her until school starts."

I flutter my lashes and smile as sweetly as I can when I probably look like death warmed over. "I will kill you and let Spaghetti eat your remains if you touch a single hair on that man's head, Kostya."

I don't care if he wants to make a point, or how betrayed he feels by Vasily's perceived shortcomings.

My child's father isn't going to take that girl's dad from her.

"That's preferable to you fleeing with your brother." He shrugs. "You'd look gorgeous with my blood on your hands."

Konstantin searches my face, but he must realize how serious I am. Eventually, his shoulder slump on a heavy sigh. "Fine."

He drags a hand over his face. I've never seen him look so ragged and run down. How long has it been since he slept? His eyes have lost their usual spark, and his hair looks like he's offered it to local birds as a nesting material.

None of it makes me any more inclined to take him at face value.

"Fine?"

"As long as you tell me," he says. He smiles, but it doesn't reach his eyes. "Put me out of my misery, and I won't do anything to harm Vasily." I swear my heart skips a beat as he drops his hand to my stomach. "Just tell me, Nadya. *Please.*"

"Did the doctors tell you?" I whisper.

"No. I wanted to hear it from you. Anything they told me would have been tainted by the way they looked at me." He smiles, his expression equal parts hopeful and resigned. "When they look at me, they only see the blood on my hands, *solynshka.* You don't. You care for me, and when you look at me, I feel it. So, please, Nadya. Tell me." His throat bobs on a thick swallow.

As he closes his eyes, it hits me that Konstantin doesn't know if the baby is alright. The doctors didn't tell him.

It's clear he knows that I'm pregnant, but he doesn't know if there's still a baby to hope for.

He saw where I was taken. He has the evidence of what was done to me. And even if we haven't talked about it, I'm sure he's managed to figure out what happened.

Is this going to be another one of the nightmares that wake him in the middle of the night?

If it is, I'll have to hold him closer on those nights. I'll have to remind him that I'm safe and that he saved me. I won't let him endure another one of those nightmares on his own, hiding from himself as much as he is me.

"Please," Konstantin begs, sounding agonized.

With the hand not trapped in the stupid sling, I point toward the little table next to the hospital bed.

With more caution than I've ever seen him use, Kostya opens the drawer and pulls out the ultrasound photo I asked the doctor to print off while I did my best to avoid crying in front of a room full of strangers.

I did a poor job of it, too. Especially when she pointed at the screen and said *that's your baby.*

Konstantin braces a hand on the table, staring at the formless shape with wonder.

For a man so capable of callous indifference to nearly everything around him, who's worked so hard to bury all his feelings, the awe on Konstantin's face is clear for all to see as he takes in the blurry image.

The same tears I worked so hard to hide when I first saw it threaten to make a reappearance.

Why did no one ever tell me how beautiful it is to watch a hard man melt as he realizes he's going to be a father?

"The baby is fine," I say, watching the way his shoulders tremble. "It's still really early, and things could change, but—"

"But they're okay."

Like it's made of spun glass, he puts down the picture before taking my face in his hands. He presses his lips against mine, as if he isn't sure if this is all a dream. My heart soars in my chest, threatening to break free and fly far away from here as I wrap my good arm around him, playing with the short hairs at the base of his skull.

"I love you," he breathes against my lips. "I love you, and if you think I'm going to let you leave with your brother, then I can't wait to show you how wrong you are. Even if you kill me, I'll haunt you until the world destroys itself and you join me in death."

I can't contain my laughter. Every muscle in my body protests, but I can't help it. Because if anyone could find a way to make it happen, it would be Konstantin.

"I'm not joking, Nadya."

"I know."

"You're having my baby."

"Yeah." Konstantin's eyes are warm as he rests his forehead against mine and smiles to himself. A swarm of butterflies tickle my ribs, and even if I wanted to, I wouldn't be able to hold them back. "I just hope they aren't as moody as you."

He snorts. "*I'm* moody? You ran away because I didn't let you go out."

"You look at your cat like he's coming for your throat whenever he walks in the room." He rolls his eyes. "And you looked like you were contemplating every method of hurting a man that you know when Alexei asked me if I was sure I didn't want to go with him. I'm not the moody one."

"Sure, *solnyshka*." The way he brushes his thumb over my cheek is so delicate that I can't help but lean into it. "If that's what you want to tell yourself. Though, if that cat goes anywhere near our child, I'm going to toss him back on the streets where I found him."

"If you do, I'll toss you in the bay." His shoulders shake on a quiet chuckle even though we both know I'm not joking. "And I already told you that I don't want to be a single mother. I don't know how much help Viktor would be, you know?"

"For the record, my brother isn't getting any closer to our child than the cat is."

"Don't be dramatic. He hangs out with Kira all the time, and she's fine."

"I'm not willing to take that risk."

The safety I feel in his arms settles something inside my chest. And even if the version of me who existed before we got married would be screaming in my face to run, I don't want to be her anymore. I just want to love Kostya and trust him to give me a safe space to land.

Konstantin doesn't need me to be anything. He doesn't ask me to be strong when I want to fall apart. He meets me where I am.

Sometimes that means waiting, and sometimes that means working behind the scenes, but he never demands more than I'm ready to give him.

"How did you know I was pregnant?" I ask.

"You left the test on the bathroom counter." His eyes are soft as he looks me up and down, needing to reassure himself that I'm still in one piece. "And before you ask, the sedatives I gave you were safe."

I sigh, but I can't find it in me to be mad at him. So I lie back against the pillows, tracing my pointer finger over the designs inked on the back of his hand. My nail catches on his wedding ring.

"I want a tattoo," I decide out loud.

"Yeah?"

I nod, swallowing a lump. "I want a band on my finger. Something that can't be taken from me again."

"Then we'll get matching ones."

"Do you even have room for another?" I snort.

Konstantin nods and slides his ring down his finger enough to show off a single inch of untouched skin. The sight is as startling as it is incredible. "Enough room for you to leave a mark." Without thinking, I force the ring back onto his finger.

"After the baby's born, let's get tattoos."

"It's a date."

CHAPTER 39

Nadya

Spaghetti's meows are loud as Konstantin opens the door, sprinting toward us with all the fury he can summon. He doesn't stop until he's at my feet, stretching to claw at my thigh until I pick him up. Only then does he dissolve into a puddle of purrs, headbutting my chin as I scratch his ears as much as I can.

He's never been happier to see me, and frankly, I feel the same way.

But maybe Tatiana's right, and he really could do with less treats in his life. I don't even realize how much I'm struggling to keep my grip on him until Konstantin swoops in and lifts him from my arms.

Those happy purrs morph into an angry yowl and a flurry of hissing as he struggles to free himself. His glare flits between Konstantin and my sling like he can't decide which has caused him more offense.

"Get out of here, you tiny psycho," Konstantin mutters as he puts him down, shooing him away as if Spaghetti has ever bothered to listen to his suggestions before.

"Pot, meet kettle," I mumble under my breath, but his eyes narrow in warning anyway. I try to hurry past, but if I thought I had a chance of getting away, I was just as delusional. Konstantin lifts me with ease, careful not to jostle my shoulder as he carries me toward our bedroom.

"Don't antagonize me, wife."

"I'm not," I protest. "I'm just—"

"I don't want an excuse. I want to get you out of these terrible clothes."

I look down at the scrubs the hospital gave me, and as much as I want to argue with him, they're stiff and uncomfortable, and I can't wait to throw them away.

"Then I want to lie you out on the bed and worship you until I forget why I'm so furious with every man I employ."

Konstantin's eyes are smoldering as he looks at me, his gaze scorching my face. I wish I could will away the blush, but the heat runs deeper than my skin. His expression has my blood running hot, crying out to touch him. To have him touch me. To let him consume me however he wants.

"What if that isn't what I want?" I ask, unable to tear my eyes away from the way his lips twitch into that maddening smirk. "What if I want to look at something other than your face for a while?"

"Conveniently, you don't have to look at me while I fuck you. You can look at the ceiling, or the wall. Or, if you insist, I can blindfold you. But rest assured"—he strokes the sliver of skin exposed from where my top has ridden up before he lays me on the bed, standing between my spread thighs—"by the time the sun goes down, you're going to be screaming my name while you come apart for me."

"*Oh.*"

"And if that isn't enough incentive, consider that while I'm with you, I'm not outside making sure heads roll." Kostya hums. "But if you'd rather I spill someone's blood..."

It's hard to think when he's steadily pushing up the hem of my shirt, each move calculated and unhurried. His threats have no impact. Not when I'm busy gaping at him. Not when I can feel wetness building between my thighs despite the fact we're both fully dressed.

There has to be a day where I'm able to look at him without getting caught up in him, right? One day I'll be able to look at him without squirming. But every time he does something new, whether it's revealing a new layer of himself, a new facet, it reveals another piece of the puzzle that makes him so incredible.

His eyes are dark as he smirks, his tongue tracing his lower lip.

"Close your mouth, wife, or I'll find something to fill it with." My jaw closes with a click. "Now, do you want the blindfold, or not?"

"I've never..."

Something sparks in the depths of his expression, dark and pleased.

"You've never been blindfolded?"

No. Every man I was with before Kostya was as boring and vanilla as they could be, but I have no interest in mentioning other men when he's staring at me with blatant hunger as he unbuttons his shirt.

I shake my head.

"Before we met, you were never fucked properly, were you?" He shakes his head, as if answering his own question. "You never knew what it was like to have someone filling you up until it was hard to breathe. You never screamed someone's name while they filled you with their cum. I bet I'm the only one who knows what it feels like to have your pussy clench like a fucking fist around their cock, aren't I?"

When I don't answer, Konstantin smirks before he slips the knot on his tie free, folding it in his hand.

"Do you trust me, Nadya?"

He has no right to ask me questions as he shrugs off his shirt, when his bare chest could drive even the strongest woman to distraction. My eyes trail down his taut abs, following the trail of hair that disappears beneath his waistband.

Konstantin stills as he looks at me, and it takes me longer than it should to realize he's waiting for an answer.

My thoughts are scattered and my nerves are buzzing with anticipation, but he won't move forward until I tell him to.

It's as easy as breathing when I answer, "I do."

He's gentle as he leans forward to brush my hair back. His lips are so close they brush against my ear as he whispers, "Then close your eyes."

I do, and my skin erupts in chills as he places his tie across them, knotting the ends at the back of my head. He's careful, making sure not to trap my hair in the knot before he pulls it slightly, checking the fit.

Even though they're covered, I don't open my eyes. There's something freeing in disconnecting and trusting Konstantin to protect me and control my pleasure. I sink into the darkness, embracing whatever comes next.

"If it's too tight, or you want it off, then tell me, okay?"

"Okay," I say. The breathiness of my own voice catches me off guard, as does the way I shiver as Kostya runs his hands over my body.

My arms, my legs, my neck. He never seems to touch me in the same place twice, darting from one spot to the next without rhyme or reason. Without the ability to see him, to anticipate his next touch, every other sensation is heightened.

The brush of fabric underneath me as I arch into him, the whisper of his movements—all of it is overwhelming in the best way.

So when I feel the cold embrace of the flat of a knife pressing between my collarbones, I can't help but gasp. My instincts scream at me to flinch away, but my heartbeat remains steady, throbbing in time with the arousal building low in my stomach.

"Beautiful," Kostantin murmurs before the knife shifts, pulling against the collar of my top. It puts up as much resistance as I have, splitting down the center like it's made of tissue paper.

"Look at you." Konstantin's voice is husky as he presses his lips against my throat, tapping the knife against my thigh like a warning. "I could do anything I want to you, and you wouldn't say a word, would you, *solnyshka*?" He doesn't wait before shifting to cut through the sleeve on my injured shoulder, tossing the fabric aside.

I shiver, but his heat chases away the chill.

My clit is throbbing between my thighs, and if I could, I'd plant my arms down and arch my hips against his. This gentle teasing is driving me wild, but I want to feel his hands on my hips. I want him to tear these stupid pants away so there's nothing separating us.

"So impatient." He clicks his tongue like he can read my mind as he trails kisses down my stomach. "Relax. You'll get what you want. Well..." He hums. "Eventually. I'm getting what I want, first."

His fingers rake over my ribs and down to my hips before he traces the waistband of the drawstring pants.

"And what is it you want?"

"I already told you." He pulls the waist away from my stomach, and before I know it, the pants are nothing but rags, facing the same fate as the top. "And I'm not going to repeat himself."

Blindly, I reach out for him, digging my fingers into the meat of his shoulder as he sinks to his knees between my thighs, tracing the tip of the blade over my thigh. Not deep enough to draw blood, but enough to have me sucking in a breath.

"Though, I must admit, the view down here is inspiring."

Konstantin groans, pressing a kiss against the line he drew with the knife before he slides something blunt up the length of my slit, teasing my clit with the lightest pressure imaginable. I buck my hips into it.

"Fuck me, Kostya."

"No. Not until I watch you come on your knife."

Every single one of my muscles jolt with the realization. "My knife?"

"Mm-hmm. You're perfect like this." There's movement under my hands, and then his other hand is on my thigh. He grips the muscle tight, and when it shifts, I can feel how wet his hand is. "Soaking the handle. Spread out for me." He bites my thigh sharply as he circles my clit with the handle of the knife. "Wearing my blood like the prettiest present."

"You're bleeding?" I snap, sitting up as much as I can. "Konstantin, don't—"

I shift my hand to his hair, but he stops me, moving it back to the side of his neck. "You don't get to make demands of me, Nadya. Not after how terrified I was." His voice is rough, choked with more emotion than I've ever heard from him. "Try to force my hand again, and I'll tie you to the bed for the rest of the day. Is that what you want?"

His breath cools against my skin, but my flesh burns as he runs his tongue over the same spot a moment later.

Fuck.

It drives me even higher, my back arching toward the knife. I have a half thought that I should be embarrassed by how wet I am, but shame would have to fight past the arousal clouding every breath, and it wouldn't stand a chance.

The only sensations I have room for is whatever Konstantin wants. And he wants me to *feel*.

Not shame, or embarrassment, or worry.

Only pleasure.

And even if he had to take away my sight to make it happen, I want him to take control. I want the buzzing under my skin to go quiet under his command.

He's relentless as he works my clit with the smooth handle, rubbing slow circles that have me biting my lip. The last thing I need to do is cry out his name and reveal how much I'm enjoying this.

"I didn't think so." He chuckles before he slips his hand from my thigh. A split second later, he pulls the knife away, taking over with his tongue.

When he sucks my clit between his teeth and nudges the handle of the knife against my entrance, he's no longer teasing. He eats my pussy as if he's starved, thrusting the handle inside me. I fall back against the bed, clinging to his neck so I don't shatter into a million pieces.

Burning hot ecstasy consumes me, sparks firing behind my eyelids as Konstantin brings me to an earth-shattering orgasm. "Kostya!" I whimper. My thighs shake, clenching so hard on either side of his head that I have to be hurting him.

He doesn't budge, lapping at me like it's all he wants and everything he needs.

I'm still lost in the pleasure, distantly registering the thud of a knife meeting wood, when Konstantin pulls away, grabs me by my hips, and pulls me closer until my ass is hanging off the edge of the bed.

"So good, Nadya. You're so pretty when you come for me."

I wrap my legs around his waist, blinking heavily when the blindfold is ripped away. I have only a moment to take in the sight of his blood on my thighs, my hips, smeared over his cock like he couldn't help himself while he drove me mad with want, before he kisses me like I'm the only thing tethering him to this earth.

Even his tongue tastes of blood as Konstantin licks against the seem of my lips, overwhelming every part of me.

When he pulls away, I catch a glimpse of the cut on his hand as he caresses my hip.

He sinks into me in a single thrust, his hard cock filling me so totally it's impossible to focus on anything.

Just him.

Just *us*.

His arms are tight around my waist, clenching his fingers so tight I know I'll be able to admire the bruises for days. And, fuck, I need that. I need him to leave marks so when I look at myself in the mirror, the burns and scrapes will pale in comparison.

I need the reminder that I'm still his, despite anyone's attempts to take me from him.

I bury my face in his neck, each breath coming out as a punctuated moan as Konstantin fucks me hard and fast.

"Perfect, Nadya," he grunts, tracing his lips over my shoulder before he nips at the skin irritated by my sling. "Squeezing my cock like you're made for me." His voice is so soft and affectionate, so unlike him, that it melts me.

He shifts his hips, giving me more room to move with him, bucking my hips as he hits my G-spot with every thrust.

"You can take a little more. Give me another one," Konstantin urges. "Use me, Nadya. Use me like you need me."

I twist my hand through his hair, letting my body tell him everything I'm feeling. I tell him how much I missed him with my hips. I whisper how much I love him with every brush of my lips against his throat. With every breath, I beg him to hold me tight and never let me go.

I don't want to picture a world where I don't have him with me. Not ever again. Not now that I know how incredible it is to have someone who wants me like he does.

I'm Konstantin's.

Mind, body, and fucking soul.

My muscles flutter around him as the slick slide of his chest against mine drives me to the edge. "I love you," I whisper, watching the storms that brew in his eyes part, burning themselves out to make room for the pure bliss that rushes in. "I love you so much, Kostya."

"I love you too, Nadya."

My orgasm cleanses me like the sea.

CHAPTER 40

Konstantin

I'm not sure how, but I've managed to become the least popular person in my own home. Tatiana has reshuffled her hierarchy, and it's taking more effort than I'm willing to admit to contain my resentment for it.

She took Alexei under her wing the moment he showed up a few hours after we left the hospital, treating him as warmly as she ever has me or Viktor. She's practically ignored me since I brought Nadya home, and she's taken to keeping Vasily close whenever he's here.

Now, she and Nadya are piled on the couch between Viktor and Alexei with Spaghetti sprawled across the back as they all watch a movie. The only one keeping their distance, other than me, is Vasily, who's leaning against a wall, remaining as still as possible.

It does nothing to stop me from seeing him.

Nadya's been home for a week, and I haven't been able to compose myself long enough to say a single word to the man. Since he isn't avoiding me like the plague, he either thinks his life is safe, or is waiting to see how far my goodwill is going to take him.

I can't decide if it's an indication of integrity or stupidity that he hasn't packed up Kira and gone somewhere far, far away from here.

Though if he had, he either would have either broken Viktor's heart, or taken him with him. Either way, he still would have had to face me eventually.

The little shit may be the biggest source of stress in my life on any given day, but I won't let my brother walk away from me. Even if he wants to.

I've lain awake most nights watching Nadya sleep, picturing my hand wrapped around Vasily's throat when the fear becomes more than I can stand. No matter how many times I remember the promise I made her, it doesn't do anything to keep my hand from flexing at my side. I take another sip of water, focusing my gaze on the back of Nadya's head as she laughs, reaching back to scratch Spaghetti's head.

He gives me a smug look, like he knows I'd kill to be in his place.

I should chuck him back into the same bush I found him in.

My temper only burns hotter when Vasily visibly steels himself and approaches me with his hands in his pockets. My glower does little to warn him away. His constant exposure to Viktor must have helped him build up a resistance to the Lavrov glare that buckles everyone else we encounter.

It's a shame. A healthy dose of fear goes a long way toward keeping a man alive.

"May I have a word, Pakhan?"

My gut reaction is to dismiss him outright, but the last thing I need is to cause a scene in front of all the people my wife cares for.

I nod toward the stairs. Vasily doesn't need to be told to go to my office. He simply dips his chin and goes.

I remain where I am, closing my eyes and taking a deep breath. As soon as I open them, I catch Nadya and Viktor's heads whirl back toward the television. Those two are about as subtle as a brick to the face, but I appreciate the way Nadya clings to Viktor's arm, keeping him right where he is.

If he insists on inserting himself into this conversation, it's only going to make it worse for everyone. His talents for getting under my skin are nothing to dismiss, and I'm not confident enough in my ability to keep my temper in line when he's trying to piss me off to avoid painting the walls a lovely shade of red.

The sensation of eyes on my back as I climb the stairs is heavier than it should be.

Vasily looks no more relaxed when I walk in than he's been since I pressed a gun to his head. He still looks like he's preparing for an execution, and I can't say I blame him for it.

I settle in my chair, rolling my neck while he shifts from foot to foot.

"Say what you came to say. There are things I'd much rather be doing than holding your hand while your tail's tucked between your legs."

There's a moment of hesitation before he tears his eyes away from mine and blurts, "What do you need for me to make this right, boss?"

Your head on a pike, I don't tell him, if only because I don't want to risk Nadya overhearing.

Instead, I bite my tongue and let him stew in the silence. Now that I have the opportunity to look at him, it's clear the burden of his guilt has taken its toll. His eyes are sunken, his cheeks sallow, like he hasn't slept for days.

"Do you want me to pay with my blood? For me to leave the state? The country?" He rubs a hand over his jaw, looking lost as he looks around the room. "I know I fucked up. I don't deserve forgiveness, and I'm not going to insult either of us by asking for it. I hate that Nadya had to pay for my fuckup. That shit's going to wear on me until the day I die."

"But?" I prompt after he trails off. Because there's always a *but.* Everyone makes excuses, blurts out some justification that means what happened isn't really their fault.

There's no such thing as accountability when you're waiting for a knife to the back.

Vasily wasn't the one who took Nadya, but he is the one who failed her. If he'd stayed by her side like he was supposed to, Dowd's thugs wouldn't have been able to get their hands on her while she was vulnerable. She wouldn't have her arm in a sling. She wouldn't have woken up in the middle of the night last night gasping for air.

But she did. Because he left her, and there's no excuse that will erase how deeply that betrayal cuts.

"But Kira wants to know if she can see Nadya again because she had fun with her when I brought her here," he eventually says. "And she wants to know if I'm going to be there to take her to her first day of school. She wants to know if I'll be there to walk home with her afterward. And I'm running out of ways to tell her I don't know how long how long my boss is planning on dragging this out.

"I want to know if I'll live long enough to take my daughter to day care again. I want to know if it's worth the hassle of picking up the ring I bought for Viktor."

He finally sits, sighing heavily.

"You're the boss. You're the only one who knows what your plans are, and I'm not going to ask you to change them. But I'd appreciate it as a personal favor—if not to me, then to Viktor—if you'd let me know what to expect, because not knowing is killing me."

His expression is blank as he looks out the window, but his eyes are anguished.

"I mean, Kira lost her first tooth last night, and I couldn't figure out if I was sad to see her growing up, or miserable because I don't know if I'll be around long enough to watch her lose another."

I lean forward, resting my elbows on my desk. His hands are clasped so tight, his knuckles are bleeding white.

For a long moment, Vasily is silent, and I wait, sorting through everything he said.

"You bought my brother a ring?" I eventually ask.

Vasily huffs out a brittle laugh, sounding resigned.

"Yeah. I was planning on asking him on our anniversary next month." His shoulders slump for a moment before he takes a deep breath and dons a familiar mask. In one breath, he transforms from a devastated father and boyfriend back into the emotionless soldier I expect him to be.

Fuck.

"But I don't want to make this any harder on him than it already is. If I'm not going to be around long enough to use it, I'm not going to pick up a ring so he can find it after I'm gone. He doesn't need to deal with the *what-ifs*."

No. I guess he doesn't.

"And Kira lost a tooth?"

I'm surprised that wasn't the first thing out of Viktor's mouth when he walked through the door. He loves that girl like she's his own.

Maybe he didn't mention it because he hasn't looked me in the eye since he left me and Nadya at the hospital.

Vasily nods. "Yeah. She was so excited she talked us into letting her stay up late to write a letter to the tooth fairy."

I bet she did.

While Vasily's a robot most of the time, Kira's the complete opposite. She must have gotten her outgoing, happy nature from Ana, because fuck knows Vasily would have raised her to keep to herself and reign in her emotions if he'd done it alone.

"I trusted you to keep my wife safe, Vasily. *Nadya* trusted you."

"I know."

"What the fuck happened, man?"

He shrugs. "Day care called. A woman walked inside and told them she was Kira's aunt. Wanted to take her home."

"Is Kira okay?"

"Yeah. I don't hand her off to idiots every day, so they called me, and Ana was able to pick her up without any issues." He doesn't look me in the eye as he says, "My guess is Dowd did some digging after the shooting, and after he found out I have a kid…" He sighs, shaking his head.

Dowd found out Nadya's bodyguard has a kid, and he found a weakness to exploit. Something that would pull him away from her in an instant, and one Nadya would never keep him from.

If I had a time machine, I would go back and sedate Nadya before we left the warehouse. Then Dowd would be nothing but another stain rotting on the floor.

Before everything happened, I would have said Vasily was one of the few people I trusted. Not only with my life, but with my brother's. If someone asked me whether I would accept him as a brother-in-law, it would have been an easy yes.

He's as decent as a man in our world can get.

Smart, loyal, protective.

And even after he fucked up, it's hard for me to erase that image of him. Those traits make him a good solider, but they make him an even better father. Can I really blame him for making sure his daughter was safe?

Because even after he got that call, he stayed. He didn't run off to take care of Kira himself or hide to save his own ass. He made sure someone was looking after his daughter, and then he stayed to search for Nadya.

For fuck's sake, he was the one who got the information I needed out of Yuri.

And now he's working himself into the ground with worry that I'll kill him for not being the man I respected.

I don't know if I'll ever be able to forgive him, but I sure as fuck need to try.

"You know, Nadya made me promise I wouldn't kill you." His eyes cut to mine. "But so we're clear, that doesn't mean I'm ever going to trust you again. I wouldn't trust you to watch Spaghetti at this point."

"Yeah. I get that."

The despair behind his eyes fades enough for him to look more like the man I know, even if his shoulders still look ready to collapse under the weight of his reluctant relief.

I'm not sure if I can trust myself at this point. But the difference between Vasily and everyone else is that I can't touch a hair on his head without losing my family. I don't trust him, but Nadya does. Viktor does. Tatiana does.

I'm so caught up in Nadya and my own worry that I can't even trust my own judgment right now, but I trust them. And until I sort through the mess that is my head, I'll have to rely on that.

"Choose a team of men. People you trust."

"What?"

"I'm taking Nadya down south in the morning. She wants a beach day, so I'm giving her one. Clearly, my judgment's off. So pick a crew you trust to act as security tomorrow."

He blinks at me with his brows drawn together. "Alright, boss. If you say so."

"Stop looking at me like I'm losing my mind," I order. Vasily sits up straighter, drawing his shoulders back. "And cheer the fuck up. You're getting a promotion. Viktor has too much on his plate to deal with all the security, and you're more than competent enough for the role. So pick your jaw off the floor and figure it out, because we're leaving at sunrise."

The corner of his lip twitches, some of the weight from his shoulders slipping away.

I'm not the kind of man to apologize, and neither is he. But if he's going to join this family, I'm not going to put up with him walking on eggshells every day. This is a step toward getting back to where we used to be, and I can only hope Vasily takes the opportunity and runs with it.

***

The water is beautiful today, and Nadya is kind enough to pretend she doesn't see the guards along the entire perimeter of the beach I've blocked off for her as she bends over to pick up another seashell, proudly adding it to the small pile she's tasked me with carrying for her.

Even though it's hard to give her the attention she deserves when she's out in public like this, all the bribes I had to pay off to get the officials to look the other way so I could close the beach are worth it to see her pleased smile.

It's a good thing she managed to sleep through the hours-long drive it took to get her to a real beach, because she's practically bouncing with energy now.

The wind whips around us, tossing her hair in all directions as she kicks at the waves crashing around her shins.

"Happiness looks good on you, *solnyshka*," I say when she plops another shell in my hand.

It always has, but there's something about her looking relaxed and carefree that feels like a physical blow to my chest. This is how she should look all the time.

Am I going to have to move to southern California?

That'd be inconvenient. But for Nadya, it would be worth it.

"Good thing you make me happy," she says, cheeks getting pinker the higher the sun rises. She steps close enough for me to capture her chin in my free hand so I can tilt her head to see whether she's blushing or getting a sunburn.

She only appears to be getting warm, but I make note to urge her to sit in the shade soon, just in case.

"I make you happy?"

In answer, she wraps her free arm around my torso and rests her head against my chest.

"Thank you for bringing me here."

Her words are quiet, almost lost to the wind and the water gently lapping against the wet sand. I rub my thumb over the soft skin of her shoulder, running it under the strap of the sundress she insisted on wearing. I'm not even sure if she brought a swimsuit in the pile of things she haphazardly threw in the trunk before we left.

"Even though you insisted on bringing half an army."

Despite her words, she's still smiling.

"I would have brought a whole army, but something tells me you would have complained it was over the top."

"I don't have to say something for it to be true, you know."

I snort as I press my lips against the top of her head. "Whatever you say, wife."

"Come on, you know you're being ridiculous, right? Because I need to hear you say that you know it."

"I don't want to feed into your delusion."

"Delusion?" She pulls back from me like she's been burned, and her outrage is absolutely stunning. And if that's the only reaction I'm able to get out of her, then it will make her gentle moments, her sweetness, that much better.

Besides, for as happy as she is to wield her anger like a weapon, I'm not afraid of her. For all her threats and bluster, she still melts like a kitten when I pull her back, pressing her head over my heart.

Even if she did change her mind and decide to follow through on all her threats to kill me, it would be a privilege to die by her hand.

Whatever my wife wants, I will find a way to give it to her. Even if it's my corpse at her feet.

But that doesn't mean I won't have fun getting a rise out of her in the meantime.

"Yes, Nadya. Delusion. I'm only looking out for you." Before she's able to work herself into a frenzy, I tilt her chin up so I can press my thumb against her pouty lips. "I'm going to protect my family. What's the worst I can do? Drive you a little crazier?"

"Up a fucking wall, Kostya," she murmurs, kissing the pad of my thumb.

The corner of her lips twitches up a moment before she buries her face in my shirt, keeping her pleased expression locked up tight. I'll let her, only because I know exactly how to draw it out of her in small, measured doses.

If it's the reward I get for a lifetime of nightmares, blood, and violence, then it's all been worth it.

Epilogue 1
NADYA

"Kostya!" I call out, dropping my phone to the floor in my hurry to sprint from my studio. Clay smears against anything I touch, spreading over the wall as I turn the corner and decorating the banister as I sprint up the stairs.

I'll apologize to Tatiana and help clean it up later, once I'm no longer smiling so hard my face hurts.

"Konstantin!" I call again.

The door to his office crashes against the wall moments before he meets me in the hall, looking panicked.

"What's wrong?" He runs his hands over my face and down my arms like he's checking for blood, staring at my smile like I've finally lost my mind. "Is it the baby?" His eyes drop to my stomach even though it's still too early for him to see anything.

"Yes!" Konstantin blanches, and I rush add, "Not our baby! Blair's baby. She's having her baby." He gives me a look but doesn't put me down.

Which is probably a good thing. I'm so excited I'd be bouncing on my feet if I had the chance, and this is the first time I haven't felt sick all day. Something tells me bouncing up and down would kick off another round of kneeling in front of the toilet.

I wish I hadn't left my phone in my studio. I want to show him the picture she sent me, the one where Blair's exhausted and smiling weakly, but clearly sitting in a hospital bed. God, I'm so excited to meet this kid. Is he going to shy and sweet, like his mom? Or is going to be a broody asshole, like his dad?

Niko must be so excited. I can't wait to see what he's like when he meets his little brother. He has such a good family around him, and I'm so thrilled that I'm going to be part of their life, and—

Reality hits me all at once, deflating my bubble of delight until my shoulders slump.

If I'm involved in either of their lives, it's going to be a limited role. I don't even know when I'm going to get a chance to meet this kid. Is it going to be weeks from now? Months? A year?

Konstantin has managed to relax lately, but I doubt it's enough for him to let me go back to Chicago. I bite my tongue, refusing to voice my request.

I don't want to deal with the disappointment of him telling me I can't go. I'll have to make a point of dropping subtle hints and needle him for a while until he eventually relents.

"What just went through your head?" Konstantin asks, tilting my head back so I have no choice but to look at him. I force my face to relax, but he only narrows his eyes. "Don't do that."

"Do what?"

"Act like you aren't upset when you are. You stopped smiling. What's wrong?"

I chew on my lip. "I'd like to be there for this, you know? And I wish I knew when I was going to see her again, that's all."

A muscle in his jaw ticks as he grinds his teeth, clearly biting back his gut reaction. "You want to go to Chicago? We only just managed to get rid of your brother." He manages to sound both put out and amused.

Honestly, I think he liked getting to know Alexei more than he let on. I spent most of the time he was here sleeping, but when I did emerge from our room, I caught Konstantin and Alexei hanging out more often than not.

There wasn't even *that* much shouting.

Granted, Alexei was only here for ten days. But still.

But when he left, they gave each other that look that guys tend to do, ignoring me while I rolled my eyes at them.

"Yeah, a month ago," I point out. "But I want to meet Blair's son. And in a few months it won't be nearly as easy to travel across the country."

"Because you're pregnant." Konstantin smiles proudly, his shoulders relaxing like they do whenever I bring up anything to do with my pregnancy. Whether it's complaining about morning sickness, or whining about how tender my breasts are, or complaining that my clay smells weird.

Every time it's brought up, he looks so pleased with himself. I can't decide whether it's endearing, or if I should smack him for it before he gets any ideas about making this a frequent occurrence.

"Yes, Kostya," I say, rolling my eyes. "Because I'm pregnant."

There's a reluctance to the way he puts me down on my feet, his hands warm as they slide over my back, trailing to the back of my neck with a tender caress.

"Do you realize what a massive pain it's going to be to re-arrange things so I can take you halfway across the country, *solnyshka*?"

"A huge one," I agree, winding my arms around his neck. "You'll have to ask Viktor to hold down the fort here, probably reschedule a few meetings, make travel arrangements…" I trail off as I shrug. "Oh, wait. You're terrible at managing financial risks and you own a private jet. So you'll only have to do the first two."

As much as I enjoy teasing him about his jet, traveling commercially with Konstantin would be a nightmare. Not only because I'd hate to watch him contort himself to fit comfortably on a plane, but because he still looks like he's going to pass out every time I leave the house.

Being locked in a metal tube with a hundred strangers after going through a public airport where he wouldn't be able to bring his weapons or guards would probably be enough to give him a panic attack.

I have no interest in making this any harder for him than it has to be.

Konstantin runs a hand down his face, looking exhausted. "Can't you wait a few weeks?"

"I *can*. But I don't want to."

"And you're going to pout until I say yes, aren't you?"

"Maybe," I say, blinking at him from under my lashes.

"Fine," he sighs, pressing his forehead to mine. "Go pack a bag while I make some phone calls. Once things are settled, we can go."

I grin triumphantly, standing on my toes to press a kiss to his cheek.

"Thank you, Konstantin." His eyes are soft as I pull away, my heart light in my chest as I practically skip toward our bedroom.

***

For some reason, I thought it would be easy for Konstantin to set things up with Viktor so we could leave. I don't know why I thought it would only take him a couple phone calls, but it's almost a full day later before I'm finally darting through the hospital with Konstantin hot on my heels.

It probably didn't help that I kept poking my head into his office every ten minutes, asking again and again if he was ready to go yet. But can he really blame me?

I waited for him for so long that I ended up falling asleep on the couch, using the weekend bag I'd packed as a pillow. I nearly throttled him when I realized Konstantin hadn't just tucked me into bed, but also joined me for the night.

Hearing that his pilot had been out of town and wouldn't be able to get back until morning helped. Hearing that he was paying the man a handsome bonus for the trouble helped even more.

Instead of being upset, I chose to let Konstantin hold me as I fell back asleep, giving me the most peaceful night's sleep I've had all month.

Besides, we still got to the airport before his pilot did.

But after a turbulent four-hour flight, I'm not feeling nearly as generous. My stomach lurches unpleasantly, and no matter how many times I tell myself I'm just anxious to see my best friend and make sure she's alright, it won't go away. Sure, Andrei texted me a couple of hours before we landed to tell me that the baby was here and that they were both healthy and happy, but I'll believe it when I see them for myself.

But despite my excitement guiding me, I have no clue where I'm supposed to go. Or what to do.

Should I have brought a gift? Does Blair even want to see me right now? Or would it have been better if I waited until they went home? Should I get flowers from the gift shop?

I don't even know what room she's in.

As soon as I've talked myself into turning around and heading to Alexei's until Blair asks me to visit, Konstantin approaches someone in scrubs and asks them to point us in the direction of the maternity ward.

For as freaked out as I am, Kostya looks cool and collected as he takes my hand in his. He looks like nothing could ruffle him, even though I know he's on high alert.

"Thank you," I say, smiling at him. Not only is he without the typical security that makes him comfortable when he's out with me, but we're somewhere he couldn't vet before we showed up. He doesn't know how many people are in this hospital any more than he knew what the traffic was going to be like before we left the airport.

But the only signs of his discomfort are the way his eyes dart around whenever we're standing still, and how closely he keeps me tucked against his side as we follow the directions the nurse gave. I rest my head against his shoulder as he glares at our reflection in the elevator doors.

"I love you." I turn my head to press a kiss to his arm as the doors open and we step out into a bright hallway.

"I love you too," he says.

"And when we get a chance to be alone, I'll be sure to show you how much I appreciate this."

He doesn't say anything, but one corner of his lips twitches as we follow the signs leading toward the maternity ward. I let him keep me close until we're standing outside Blair's door while I try to work up the nerve to knock, feeling stupid that I'm worried about seeing her again.

It's only been a few months, but what if things aren't as easy with as they used to be? What if distance has set us back to that initial *friendly strangers* stage of friendship that always sucks the life out of the room?

Our friendship is still easy when we talk on the phone, but the *what-ifs* keep my feet rooted to the ground, doubt swirling like smoke. Konstantin stands next to me the entire time, acting like a silent sentinel as he allows me to take all the time I need.

With a deep breath, I knock, opening the door enough to poke my head inside.

Blair looks up from the tiny bundle in her arms, her whole face breaking into a smile that melts away the last of my hesitation. She reaches for me as I approach, pulling me into a hug that melts all my worries away.

How on earth could I have thought things would change? She's *Blair*. She's only the best friend I've ever had, and even if it's been months since we last saw each other, nothing could change that.

I hug her as gently as I can, and it feels exactly like it did at my wedding.

"I didn't know you were coming," she says with a smile.

"Of course I'd come. I wanted to meet this little guy." I glance down at the baby in her arms. Dark hair peeks out from under the hospital-issued hat, and my heart melts as he yawns, his little face scrunching up.

"He's beautiful, Blair."

"Isn't he?" Blair's expression is soft as she strokes the back of her finger over his cheek. The sheer amount of love radiating from her is as awe-inspiring as it is humbling. I blink hard, not wanting to spoil the moment by crying over nothing.

"Would you like to hold him?" she asks as I vaguely register Andrei moving behind us. He strategically positions himself between us and Konstantin, but I can't find it in me to care.

"I'd love to."

Carefully, she lays him in my arms, and I'm almost shocked by how tiny he is. He doesn't wake, only frowning at the movement before he settles again.

He has Blair's nose.

"Lavrov," Andrei all but growls when my husband shuffles closer, reaching out to brush his hand over mine on the back of the baby's head.

I don't have to turn around to hear the smirk in Konstantin's voice as he says, "Nice to see you again, Andrei. It's been a while."

"What's his name?" I ask before he can weaponize his charm to get under Andrei's skin. Blair looks too blissed out to notice the pissing match our husbands are trying to start, but if I have any say in it, they're going to have to calm down. Quickly.

"Ilya," she says.

Like she said the magic word, Andrei returns to her side, smiling at her so reverently feels like I'm intruding. "Ilya Andreevich Voronov." He says it so softly it might as well be a prayer. "And he's absolutely perfect."

Konstantin's gaze burns against the side of my face, but when I look at him, he's smiling, watching me like he can't wait to be in Andrei's shoes.

Neither can I.

***

The way Alexei's face falls when we show up at his front door feels like coming home in a way I hadn't expected. How he manages to look both thrilled to see me and dismayed to realize I'm not alone is a wonder, but I should know better than to underestimate my brother.

"Surprise," Kostya says with a shit-eating grin.

Alexei pulls me into a hug, but his glare is so fierce over my shoulder that I'm a little surprised Konstantin doesn't wither underneath it. But, fuck, even though it hasn't been long since we last saw each other, it feels good to hug him again.

And this time, I don't even have to worry about the arm brace getting in the way.

"What the fuck are you doing here?" he asks, holding my shoulders like he doesn't quite believe I'm really here. He urges me through the doorway, but remains standing where he is, refusing to let Konstantin into his condo.

"Is this how you typically greet family?" Konstantin *tsks*. "Not very welcoming."

Alexei flips him off, not even sparing him a glance before he tries to shut the door in my husband's face.

As soon as I'm past the door, I'm greeted by loud, pulsing music and the sound of Emiliya shuffling around in the kitchen. My stomach growls at the smell.

I was too excited about seeing Blair to eat anything before we left, and I'm paying for it now. But Emiliya is an excellent cook, and I'm willing to bet she won't mind sharing.

"We came to meet the baby," I explain, shoving my foot in front of the door before Alexei can slam it shut. "And then I figured that since we're in town, we might as well stay with my baby brother." The excitement on his face fades as Konstantin walks in, and it makes me smile almost as much as seeing his grumpy ass.

"I haven't sold your apartment. You could have stayed there," Alexei protests.

"I could have. But I sold the furniture before the wedding, and unfortunately, I'm a fan of having a bed to sleep in." I shrug. "But lucky for me, you have a perfectly good guest room."

Alexei folds his arms over his chest, his nostrils flaring as Konstantin shoulders his way past him, venturing further into his condo to poke over his decor. "If it changes your mind, I've fucked my fiancée in that bed."

"Gross." I make a face. "I don't need to hear about your— Wait. Did you say *fiancée*?"

"If it makes you feel better, I can tell you how I knocked up your sister," Konstantin says nonchalantly, tilting his head as he looks at a painting on the wall.

"Kostya!"

"You *what*?" Alexei hisses, launching himself toward Konstantin like a man on a mission. Rolling my eyes, I follow the smells until I find Emiliya, leaving them to exchange snarky remarks and hushed, furious threats.

She grins at me as she turns away from the stove.

"Did I hear him say he knocked you up?"

"You agreed to marry that little shit?" I ask instead of answering. My cheeks burn, but I refuse to acknowledge it. Out of all the ways he could have announced our news, Kostantin had to pick *that*?

He's so lucky I love him.

"You know you're hot, right? Alexei sucks. You can do so much better."

"Maybe. But he can be sweet when he wants to be. And he's rich enough to buy me this." Her grin softens as she looks over my shoulder toward the spot where Alexei's stopped hissing curses, holding up her hand so I can see the giant rock on her finger. "Besides, I kinda like him."

"I'd hope it's more than like," he grumbles, crossing the room to press a kiss against Emiliya's cheek.

"I mean, you'll do for now." She shrugs, ignoring the way he scowls.

Heat burns along my spine as Konstantin wraps his arm around my waist. "Is there anything we can do to help?" he asks.

"Get a better sense of timing," Alexei mutters, moving to the other side of the island. "Nadya, tell me he's lying. Tell me you didn't let this *mudak* touch you with a ten-foot pole."

"Well…" I hedge with a cringe. "I mean, I have blood tests and an ultrasound that say I did, but"—I shrug while Alexei covers his mouth with his hand, looking horrified—"you can pretend it's a virgin birth if you really want to."

Emiliya laughs, pulling me into a hug as Alexei rolls his head back with a groan.

Konstantin's pride rolls off him in waves, and when I look back at him, everything seems to settle into place.

Being here with him is the opposite of what I pictured when we got married, but now that I know what it's like to be the focus of his love, to be so fully cared for that I can't picture being without him, I wouldn't have it any other way.

Epilogue 2

Konstantin

After the doctors and nurses spent what felt like hours buzzing around us, the three of us are finally alone. And I've never been more terrified in my life.

How can I not be when our son is so impossibly small in Nadya's arms? He's fast asleep on her chest, and I've never more awed or intimidated. Until I watched him curl into Nadya's touch with an instinctive trust that would melt the coldest hearts, I didn't even know I *could* be intimidated.

Especially not by someone who weighs just over nine pounds.

Nadya sighs happily, brushing her finger over his cheek. Reluctantly, I tear my eyes away from the spot where her hand is curled protectively over his back. Despite having just given birth, she's never looked more beautiful than she does with her drowsy smile and a quiet pride that lights her up from within.

I ignore the way my hand shakes as I brush away the hair stuck to her forehead.

She managed hours of labor with a grace that amazes me, and somehow she still has the energy to wipe away the tears

I've been blinking back since the moment his loud, brilliant cry burst from his chest.

I'd never heard a more beautiful sound.

He can't even hold up his own head, but he has more power over me than anyone ever has. I'd lay down my life for him without hesitation, throw away my entire empire if it made him happy.

"He looks like you," Nadya says, her voice barely above a whisper.

"It's just his hair."

I clear my throat, hoping to ease the raw, vulnerable note in my voice.

"Yeah," she agrees with a smirk. "And his chin. And the way he's scowling." She lifts one of his clenched fists. "Look, he even holds his hands like you."

I'd roll my eyes if she weren't right.

But the way he tucked his hands under his chin the moment he was in Nadya's arms? The way his mouth is hanging open as he sleeps?

That's all her.

"He's beautiful, *solnyshka*. He gets that from you."

She hums, apparently content to put aside her desire to argue as I press my lips against her temple.

"He looks like a Kirill, doesn't he?" I can't help but ask.

She nods as he yawns in his sleep, rubbing his cheek against her chest.

"We got lucky. Can you imagine what Tatiana would have done if we'd changed it?"

I don't need to imagine.

Tatiana would have taken it as a personal offense, bribed Viktor to hack the hospital records to change his name back to Kirill, and refused to call him anything else for the rest of her life. After she went to the effort of making an embroidered sign with his name on it for Nadya's baby shower, I can't say I'd blame her.

My hand flexes at my side, torn between reaching for Kirill and keeping my distance.

The moment he was born, doctors and nurses were fussing over him. They wiped his face clean and checked him over for minutes that felt like hours before they finally let Nadya hold him.

While they were buzzing around the room, I was able to tell myself that she needed to hold him, that they needed to bond, and I could wait to hold him until she was ready.

But now we're all alone, and he's so fragile.

I've struggled to sleep nearly every night since I found out she was pregnant. The all-consuming anticipation of finally being able to hold my child kept me on the edge of consciousness until exhaustion finally took over. But now that Kirill is finally here, I'm terrified I'm only going to hurt him.

Instead, I drop my hand to the back of Nadya's, trusting her to keep him safe.

"Good thing we don't have to find out," I force out around the emotions threatening to choke me.

With more strength than I would have expected from someone in her state, Nadya flips her hand over to trap mine, holding tight when I try to jerk away. The simple wedding band she's wearing until we're able to get matching tattoos glints in the light as she forces my hand to move so my fingers brush against Kirill's.

He's so warm that it shocks me almost as much as the realization of how soft his skin is.

Is that normal? Does he have a fever? The doctors said he was healthy, but maybe we should have them check again.

But I can't bring myself to leave them for even a moment.

Someone else could hurt him.

Hell, we wouldn't even have to wait for someone else. All I'd have to do is hold him the wrong way, or squeeze tighter than I should, and his tender skin would bruise and his tiny bones would snap.

What would happen if my grip slipped? What if I'm no different than my father, and I'm only setting him up for a lifetime of misery and pain?

I can't break him the way my dad broke me.

I'd never be able to forgive myself.

"Kostya?" Nadya asks as I slip my hand free of hers. "I want to see you holding him." I don't realize how hard my chest is heaving with each breath until she clears her throat, her eyes both gentle and knowing.

I step backward, but Nadya only holds my hand tighter, refusing to let me walk away.

"I've wanted to know what you look like with our baby in your arms since I found out I was pregnant." I cling to her smile, grounding myself in the intensity of her gaze. "I really want to see you hold your son for the first time. Preferably soon, because I also really want to take a nap."

Kirill coos as she shifts his weight, twisting our hands so mine is draped over his back. I brace myself, waiting for him to cry or show some sign of discomfort.

Instead, he yawns.

Between one breath and the next, my heart cracks in two. The love I carry for both of them spills out into all the dark, empty spaces that have kept me company throughout my life until there's no part of my soul that's left untouched.

"I want to," I admit, hating the way the words reek of vulnerability. "I just—"

"I'm scared, too." Her tired eyes find mine, and all my tangled, messy emotions are reflected in them. The terror, the love, the overwhelming happiness.

We've both spent hours reading books on parenting, even attending classes so we could be prepared, but now that we're faced with the reality of the helpless baby in her arms? We have no clue what the hell we're doing.

"I'm scared." She lifts one shoulder in a half-hearted shrug. "I'm overwhelmed, I'm tired, and I have no clue what we're supposed to do. But I do know that whatever it is, we'll figure it out. We have each other, and we're not going to let him deal with the shit our parents put us through."

Unbidden, a laugh bubbles in my chest. It doesn't sound nearly as panicked as I feel.

Maybe she has a point.

If I did anything that might hurt Kirill, she'd stop me before I could. And I can't imagine treating him the way my father treated me and Viktor.

He deserves so much more than what we had. He deserves a family that will always be there to support and love him. And I refuse to let anyone allow him to believe otherwise.

Even me. Even if that means being terrified.

I only want him to know happiness and comfort. I want him to know what it's like to be loved unconditionally.

I want to give him the world.

"Are you sure you want to swear in front of him so early?" I ask as I swallow.

"He'll hear worse eventually," she points out with a soft smile before stifling a yawn. "If he doesn't hear it from us, Viktor will be the one teaching him how to swear. Do you want to risk that happening?"

"Fuck no."

Nadya laughs, resting her head against the pillow.

"I've been picturing a baby in your arms for months, Kostya. Let me see if reality lives up to the fantasy," she says, blinking slowly.

If I wait much longer, she'll fall asleep before she gets the chance, and I can't deny Nadya anything. Especially not when the affection in her eyes buries the last of my fear behind a wall of determination.

Carefully, I take Kirill in my arms. He's so light it knocks the air from my lungs, but all the tension in my shoulders is gone as soon as he's settled.

"Hi, Kirill," I whisper, my throat squeezing tight. He turns his head to bury his face against my chest, and I'm not sure if the choked sound I hear comes from me or Nadya. "I love you."

Nadya sniffs, and when I look at her she's wiping her cheeks.

"Stupid hormones," she laments, covering her face while I smile at her. "You can't look like that when you hold him. It isn't fair." Despite her tears, she looks so happy that the only thing I can do is kiss her.

"You're incredible," I murmur, pressing my forehead against hers. She melts against me, looking between Kirill and I like she can't get enough of us. "He's perfect. You both are."

"I love you," she says around a watery smile as she wipes the wetness from her cheeks, then from mine.

"I love you too, *solnyshka*."

My heart has never been as full as it is when I have my family in my arms and a future I can't wait to share with them.

Want more?

For a glimpse at Nadya and Konstantin and what they're like as parents, check out the bonus epilogue at: https://dl.bookfun nel.com/1trp723hgm

Acknowledgements

Much like Konstantin, I hated being in his head. In a lot of ways, writing this book was one of the most isolating experiences I've had in a long time. More than once, I contemplated putting it down, walking away, and pretending this book never happened.

But I didn't, and that's only because I had so much help along the way.

First of all, thanks always to my incredible editor Yvette! The way you clocked Konstantin and Nadya the instant they were mentioned in the same paragraph in the second book brought me so much joy, and I'm so glad I was able to share these two with you! I couldn't have done this without your support and ability to wrangle commas and run-on sentences that love to hide in my blind spots, and your comments help me add a new layer of depth to these books that I didn't know was even possible.

Working with you has been one of the best parts of writing this series, and I can't thank you enough for all of your hard work. You're fantastic.

To Dad, thank you. I don't want to know where I'd be if I hadn't had your support. Though I do know that I probably would have thrown this book in the trash and given up on ever writing anything ever again.

And to you, the reader. Thank you so much for taking the time to read this series. Whether it was just this book, or just a few pages, or every single word, it means the world to me that you would welcome my stories into your lives.

And, while we're on the topic of book series, man, that conversation between Konstantin and Carlo was a little weird, right?

Anyway, on a totally unrelated note, the Heavenly Anodyne series is coming later this year! We'll meet some new faces, and maybe we'll get to catch up on some characters we've only met in passing before, too.

About the author

E rin Robinson writes dark romance for readers who like complicated men and the women who make them fall to their knees.

When she isn't writing, she can be found digging around in her garden, herding her ridiculous cat, or curled up with a book in hand. She hopes that in time, she'll be able to pursue writing full time.

For updates on future releases, including sneak peeks, sign up for her newsletter on her website, authorerinrobinson.com.

Also by Erin Robinson

Splintered Empire

Plaintive Vow

Sacred Bond

Impenitent Ties

Heavenly Anodyne

Reticent Sinner (Coming late 2026)